I0688121

Hugh E. M. Stutfield

The Brethren of Mount Atlas

Being the First Part of an African Theosophical Story

Hugh E. M. Stutfield

The Brethren of Mount Atlas
Being the First Part of an African Theosophical Story

ISBN/EAN: 9783744757508

Printed in Europe, USA, Canada, Australia, Japan

Cover: Foto ©Andreas Hilbeck / pixelio.de

More available books at **www.hansebooks.com**

THE BRETHREN

OF

MOUNT ATLAS

BEING THE FIRST PART OF

AN AFRICAN THEOSOPHICAL STORY

BY

HUGH E. M. STUTFIELD, F.R.G.S.

AUTHOR OF

"EL MAGHREB: 1200 MILES' RIDE THROUGH MAROCCO"

"A Lady-Witch there lived on Atlas Mountain"
SHELLEY'S *Witch of Atlas*

LONDON

LONGMANS, GREEN, & CO.

AND NEW YORK: 15 EAST 16th STREET

1891

(*All rights reserved*)

CONTENTS.

CONTENTS.

THE
BRETHREN OF MOUNT ATLAS.

CHAPTER I.

CONCERNING DIVERS OCCULT MATTERS.

"HERE'S a spring, so let's stop and have lunch and count the bag. Twenty-three and a half brace of grouse, nine hares, and a couple of snipe, I make it."

The scene was a moor in Inverness-shire, the speaker a fair-haired young man about twenty-five years of age, his audience two fellow grouse-shooters. It was piping hot, and the proposal seemed to find favour with the other two sportsmen, as they promptly threw themselves at full length on the heather and called loudly for drinks.

"Gerald walks us off our legs all the morning, but I notice he's always the first to call a halt for lunch," remarked one of them, a man some fifteen years the senior of the first speaker.

"Yes; and I notice you are remarkably prompt in responding to the call," retorted Gerald; "and you always begin by saying you're not a bit hungry, and then play the best knife and fork of any of us."

The business of unpacking the luncheon-basket and spreading out its contents put an end to further banter, and conversation flagged until the viands were disposed of and pipes had been filled for a few minutes' quiet smoke.

"Do you know," said Gerald, the young man who spoke first, "that, fond as I am of shooting over these hills, I often feel a longing to go further afield for wilder and bigger game. I had a few days' chamois-hunting in Switzerland last year, and I must say that this bird-slaughter has seemed to me rather tame sport ever since."

"What a discontented chap you are, to be sure," said the second speaker; "tired of grousing already before the evening of the Twelfth!"

"On the contrary," returned Gerald, "I'm not tired of it at all. There's nothing I enjoy more; but that doesn't prevent my wanting to travel a bit. I've never been out of Europe yet. Will you fellows join me in a trip to South Africa? I should like to go up into the Kalahari Desert and get some lions. Or stay, let's all go to Cashmere. We should get some first-class shooting, and we might pass over into the unexplored parts of Thibet. The trip would suit Urquhart, as an occultist, down to the ground, as we should be sure to come across some of his friends the Mahatmas (that's the right word, isn't it?), trotting round in their astral bodies, and we might even reach the abode of the Thibetan Brothers themselves. What do you say to it, David?"

The individual addressed as David made no reply, but kept puffing away mechanically at his pipe, with his eyes fixed on the ground, as though absorbed in thought.

"Why don't you answer?" continued the younger

man. " Don't you approve of the idea, or have you something better of your own to suggest ? "

" Well, perhaps I have, and perhaps I have not," was the enigmatical reply. " I may say that earlier in the year I had some idea of making a long journey this coming winter, but not to Thibet or Cashmere, where, by the way, one can only go in the summer. But I vote that we postpone further discussion of the subject till this evening. It's half-past two already, and time we were on the move again."

" Dear me, David, you are very mysterious to-day," said Gerald. " I shall look forward to the adjourned debate on this important topic with much interest. Meanwhile, let's be off. I want to make the bag up to fifty brace this afternoon."

So saying, he shouldered his gun, and, his companions following suit, the trio spread out in a line over the moor, and were soon blazing away merrily. Never does time pass more quickly than when one is enjoying good sport, and the afternoon wore on until the sun sank in golden glory to the rim of the purple hills which bounded the western landscape. Then as the light failed, and Nature became wrapped in the soft shades of twilight, they turned their footsteps homewards. The hour and the fatigues of the day were not conducive to conversation, and the three sportsmen strode on in silence till they reached the shooting-lodge of Inverfechan, which lay half hidden by a clump of pines in a wooded glen.

But it is time the reader was introduced to his new company. In the first place, to begin at the wrong end—by which I mean, in inverse order of importance —I, James Browne (don't forget the *e*, please), stock-jobber of Capel Court, and the writer of this history, make my bow to the company, and beg to be excused the delicate task of describing myself.

"Well, but we must at least hear what sort of looking man he is, you know."

Then, Madam, if it so please you, to the best of my belief I am not very much to look at. Not that I mean to emulate the excessive modesty of some autobiographical heroes of fiction, and describe myself as a sort of baboon, combining in my own person the ugliness and the muscular power of that anthropoid. But if not exactly a Caliban, neither am I an Adonis. I am slightly above the middle height, not particularly fair nor yet excessively dark. My age—well, I don't think that is quite a fair question, but it is within a decade of forty. My hair *used* to be black. I am a bachelor. My talents, like my means, are moderate ; my disposition and temper even. My ideas, like my profession, are of the commonplace order. In fact, as the intelligent reader will have already discerned, there runs through me and my surroundings a current of mediocrity, unrelieved either by genius or even by its cheap modern substitute, eccentricity. Therefore, having said enough to satisfy all legitimate curiosity on the subject of myself, we will pass on to other and more interesting matters.

Gerald Somervell, on the contrary, is distinctly a striking figure. Tall, broad-shouldered, athletic-look-ing, with his fair hair, clear blue eyes and ruddy complexion, his face full of frankness and beaming with good humour, he looks the very beau-ideal of a young Englishman. Not that he is altogether English, either ; and the humour which plays about

the corners of his mouth and sparkles in his eyes
bespeaks, together with his name, the Irish blood
which runs in his veins. He would be decidedly
handsome (personally, I think he is) were it not that
his features are very strongly marked and somewhat
irregular. Rumour has it that the prominence of one
organ in particular secured him the appellation of
"Nosey" among his schoolfellows. Like most young
Englishmen of our own day, he could hardly be
described as intellectual; but he is richly endowed
with that shrewd common sense which in all practical
affairs of life is a more valuable quality.

Last, but not least, of our trio of grouse-shooters
comes Urquhart—David Urquhart—who is in many
respects the counterpart of Somervell, yet his dearest
friend. Urquhart has just turned forty; but he looks
older, partly owing to a certain gravity—I had almost
said austerity—of demeanour, and partly because of
the grey threads which here and there streak his
thick brown hair. His is distinctly a striking face.
Massively formed brows overshadow deep-set grey
eyes full of intellectuality. The forehead is broad
and moderately lofty. The square jaw and sharply
cut lips tell of resolution. Altogether the whole
appearance of the man indicating, as it does, will-
power and intellectual force, commands the respect
and interest of the beholder.

Though he has many friends, Urquhart could
hardly be called a popular man. He is too reserved
for that. Some people call him cynical, but his
cynicism is, at any rate, not of the kind which, having
an eye only for the bad side of human nature, is
wanting in sympathy with human weakness. It is

rather that of a lofty nature disappointed at not finding the world better than it is, and failing in some degree to recognize the fact that average humanity is actuated by lower motives than those with which it had been credited. His friends have always written Urquhart down a confirmed bachelor. If asked why he did not marry, he would always turn the question in some way or another. It was whispered that he had odd ideas on the subject of matrimony—ideas of a soul-union, in which passion should have no part and love on the physical plane would be non-existent, with some complementary being, or guardian-inspiring angel, destined to form part of his nature.

> " Somewhere beneath the sun—
>   These quivering heart-strings prove it—
> Somewhere there must be one
>   Made for this heart to move it."

Be that as it may, certain it is that he had never yet succeeded in coming across the person whose being should blend, and whose heart-strings should beat in unison, with his own ; and at the time of which I am now speaking people thought it was likely to be a long while before he found himself " suited."

Urquhart had no profession. His means were sufficient to enable him to devote himself to a life of learned leisure, varied by travel and athletic sports. He was a many-sided man ; a man with numerous and diverse tastes and interests, who made it his business to extract as much interest out of life as possible, and, to do him justice, he succeeded admirably in his efforts. He was the keenest of sportsmen, a bold rider, and a first-class shot. In his younger days he used to be a fair cricketer, and, like a good Scotchman, he was devoted to golf. Mountaineering was his favourite pastime, however, and his name was well-known in Alpine circles as that of a daring and successful climber. None the less was he essentially a man of books. Student and sportsman, and withal a shrewd, hard-headed man of the world, in him the practical and contemplative faculties were curiously blended. His imaginative temperament gave a metaphysical turn to his studies, for metaphysics, particularly of the Oriental type, were his chief delight. From metaphysics to mysticism is not a far cry, and during a visit to India he had come in contact with the devotees of the Occult Fraternity of Thibet, and had even been enrolled as a member of the Theosophical Society. Yet was he no vulgar "spookist"— of the type, I mean, of those who simply hanker after "manifestations" or marvellous phenomena. His occultism was rather the search after abstractions, and the striving to get on a higher plane of spiritual life. Moreover, though he disapproved of "manifestations" as tending to trickery, he had none the less a firm belief in certain forces of nature with which mankind in its present stage of development is unacquainted, and also in the existence of persons possessing a command over those forces.

It was only to be expected that Urquhart should have to bear much chaff from unbelieving friends on account of his theosophical proclivities. Gerald in particular was never tired of rallying him on the subject.

"How on earth," he would say, "a sensible chap like David can believe in all that fantastic fiddle-faddle about Mahatmas and astral bodies, and the rest of it, passes my comprehension."

Urquhart, however, was not the man to be deterred from his purpose by any amount of chaff, and he continued to devote his very considerable energies to the investigation of psychical problems and the hidden laws of Nature.

My readers may recollect the genesis and growth of that strange metaphysical medley of Hindoo and Hebrew mysticism, Platonic and Pythagorean transcendentalism, and modern spiritualism—variously labelled as Theosophy, Occultism, or Esoteric Buddhism—whose apostles in the West claim to have received their inspiration direct from the fountain head, pretty much as Mohammed received his Suras from the angel Gabriel, or as Joe Smith the Mormon was prompted by the angel of the Lord. The earlier students of Theosophy, like the early Christians, were seekers after a sign, and some strange signs were given them. The wonders worked by Madame Blavatsky were accepted by her faithful followers as a proof of her mission. She did not encourage "manifestations," for, like her Thibetan instructors, she had "an unconquerable aversion to showing off," but none the less did the "manifestations" persist in asserting themselves. Tables and chairs waltzed round the room in aggravating style, luminous balls of fire played about the furniture, cigarette cases came to hand of their own accord, and on one occasion a large spoon which was required for the performance flew out of the opposite wall into Madame's lap. All this and much more—such as occult bells in the air, the astral call of the distant Mahatma, the finding of cups and saucers under trees—are they not written with artless simplicity in the book of the chronicles of Mr. Sinnett? An irreverent world, however—the "laughing jackasses," as he aptly styles them, of sceptical criticism — snorted and jeered at these phenomena. Unkind people said the cups and saucers were buried beforehand, and that the "astral call-bell" was in reality concealed in Madame's bustle. Hence subsequent occult publications have dealt more with the philosophical aspect of the subject, leaving aside the question of the miraculous powers of the Brethren till a more favourable opportunity occurs for their vindication. Such an opportunity has now arrived, and I trust that this volume will be accepted as a complete, if tardy, proof of the accuracy of Mr. Sinnett and his brothers and sisters in the field of hermetic research.

In the days of which I am now writing I was not an occultist myself. For instance, I never used to believe even in the existence of the occult Adepts. Now, however, that I have myself had two or three tame Mahatmas on hand for a considerable time (a privilege few other men have enjoyed), I know what wonderful people they are, and I can add my testimony to that of the other authors who have written on the subject. It is asserted,[1] for example, that the Adept can make himself "visible and invisible at will, fly through the air, walk on water as other people would on dry land, . . . dry up the sea, grasp the sun and moon, hide the earth with the tip of his finger, shake to their foundations earth and heaven." Most people would refuse to credit such statements. I, on the

[1] " The Mystery of the Ages," by the Countess of Caithness, p. 55.

other hand, know very well that these are only a few of the minor feats of the Adepts, and nothing to what they could do if they really tried.

It will be seen, therefore, by those who persevere to the end of this volume, that circumstances over which I had no control have made of me an occultist of the first water. I have emerged from the slough of ignorance in which the practical work-a-day world is at present immersed. The City man that in the darkness sat of the Eldorado Railway Share Market has seen a great light ; and, illumined by the rays flashed upon me from the Hidden Wisdom, I can afford, along with my brother occultists, to look down with sublime pity on those who yet grovel in purblind ignorance of the higher teaching. True, that with my study of the Great Arcanum I combine the trade of a stock-jobber ; that to my struggle to attain the ideal and the absolute I add the pursuit of the nimble ninepence ; and that my literature is a judicious blend of Esoteric Buddhism and Eldorado Railway traffic returns. Yet can mundane pursuit never wholly engross a soul once imbued with the infinite mysteries of the unknowable, and the lessons I learned in the course of my intimacy with the Adepts remain with me as a precious heirloom, beside which the things of this phenomenal world are but as dross.

At the same time, I must confess that my participation in the priceless wisdom distilled from the lips of the initiates is a grave responsibility which weighs heavily upon me. I feel that the world is not yet fitted to share in the dazzling revelations of which I have been the unworthy recipient—revelations which, if published in their entirety, would take the

shine out of "The Secret Doctrine" and "Isis Unveiled," and make Mr. Sinnett's disclosures appear
the smallest of small potatoes. Some modicum, however, of the secret knowledge I have, after due delibera-
tion, decided to make known to the world. It may
be said that I am profaning the mysteries of the
Great Arcanum ; that I am casting the precious
pearls of esoteric lore to be trampled under the
swine-hoofs of Western sceptics. I am, moreover,
aware that, as has recently been pointed out,[1] to
impart to the profane multitude secrets of such vast
importance, involving cognizance of occult agencies
of tremendous power, is highly dangerous and like
giving a child a lighted candle in a powder magazine.
I fully accept the responsibility for my action in the
matter. Nay, more, I admit that if the world is blown
up, or if any other cosmical cataclysm occurs in consequence of the publication of this book, the fault
will be mine. As, however, in that case I shall not
be here to be called to account, perhaps that does not
matter much. But this much I will say in my own
defence, that I was not the first to offend in this
matter of letting the occult cat out of the theosophical
bag. Had not Madame Blavatsky, Mr. Sinnett, Mr.
Laurence Oliphant, and their various disciples,
flooded the world with such scraps of the Hidden
Wisdom as they possess—"scraps," I say, compared
with the full measure of spiritual enlightenment which
has been vouchsafed to me—wild horses could not
have torn the dread secret from my bosom. As it is,
they were the first to begin, and on their heads be it
if evil ensues.

[1] "The Secret Doctrine," by Madame Blavatsky.

But enough of this for the present. It is time I got on with my story. I have only to add that this book, like many other works of travel, is written to "supply a long-felt want," viz. the want of the narrator to publish his experiences and adventures to the world.

CHAPTER II.

THE STORY OF ALI THE PERSIAN.

" Now, David," said Gerald as we were enjoying our
pipes in the smoking-room after dinner, "we want to
hear what you have got to say on the matter of
our expedition to foreign parts. You looked so
mysterious this morning when I mentioned it, that I
am sure you must have some proposition to make.
Out with it now ; we are all ears."

"Don't be impatient, my dear boy," replied
Urquhart, puffing away in a leisurely manner at
his pipe, "and above all beware of jumping too
hastily to conclusions. How do you know I have
any suggestion to make? The idea emanated
entirely from you. I have no objection to your going
to Cashmere, if you like ; only please don't ask me
to accompany you."

"What, not even for the chance of seeing your
friends the Thibetan Brothers? I am dying to see
those remarkable people myself."

"Not even for the chance of seeing my friends
the Thibetan Brothers, as you call them, though,
as a matter of fact, I never had the privilege of

their acquaintance ; and I can assure you that they are not so prodigal of their society as to lavish it on any wandering sportsman who may happen to be in the neighbourhood of their retreats."

" Well, then, I must try and get Browne to come."

" Thanks," said I, " I fear my arduous duties in the City would hardly permit of my being away for so long a time. Besides, I fancy the shooting in Cashmere is getting rather played out. So many people go there nowadays."

Gerald seemed rather mortified at not meeting with more encouragement in his sporting plans, so, putting his legs up on a chair, he took refuge in silence and an extra stiff glass of whiskey toddy.

" Why don't you organize a shooting party for the wilds of Central Africa ? " I suggested. " It would be a far more novel and interesting trip than Cashmere, and you would come across fifty times more game. Only, if you are so anxious to see the occult brethren, I don't suppose there are any Mahatmas in that part of the world."

" How do you know that ? " interposed Urquhart somewhat sharply, laying down his pipe and looking at me.

" I don't pretend to know anything about it. I only said I supposed there were none."

" Hullo, David ! " cried Gerald, observing his friend's unusually animated manner. " What's up now ? I'm sure you've got some deep game on with your mysterious airs and reticence."

But Urquhart had returned to his impassive demeanour and his pipe, at which he kept puffing away in a deliberate fashion which somewhat irritated

Gerald, whose curiosity was aroused by the air of mystery which Urquhart, partly to tease him, had assumed.

"I am not at all averse to going to Central Africa," said Gerald, "only it would be a much bigger affair than the trip to Cashmere, and would want a lot more time and money. Besides, if neither of you fellows will go with me, it's no use thinking any more about it, as I wouldn't dream of starting on an expedition of that sort with men I did not know thoroughly well."

"I never said that I wouldn't go to Africa," rejoined Urquhart; "I am not aware that you ever asked me to accompany you there. Look here," he continued after a pause, "now that we are on the subject of African travel, and as our friend Gerald seems so curious about it, I don't mind unburdening my mind to you of a project which has long been in my thoughts, and, if either or both you will assist me in carrying it out, I shall be very well pleased.

"Last winter, as you know, I was travelling with three friends in the interior of Marocco. We did not get as far up country as I had hoped, and I was disappointed in my main desire to penetrate into the heart of the Atlas mountains. Still we had an excellent time, had lots of pig-sticking, shot innumerable snipe and partridges and bustards, and saw many strange things. But to me neither the sport nor the sight-seeing, much as I enjoyed both, compared in point of interest with a certain discovery which I accidentally made. I say 'discovery' because, although I have not yet had an opportunity of verifying the information I received, I am satisfied in my own mind of its substantial accuracy, and am prepared to act on it without further inquiry. The thing came about in this way.

"After wandering about for several months, our party had settled down for a few days in the city of Marocco, which, as you know, is the southern capital of the Moorish empire. Desirous of seeing all the sights of the place, even the most unpleasant, we were making the round of the city prisons. Those dark and horrible dens, reeking with every sort of abomination, were crowded with miserable beings in every stage of disease and emaciation. In one I remember seeing a raving lunatic chained by the neck with a steel collar to a pillar in the midst of his fellow-prisoners. His struggles to get free were something awful to witness, and the place resounded with his shrieks. Beside him, in the filth which lay thick upon the floor, lay an unhappy wretch, with a cannon-ball tied to his ankles, and heavy manacles on both hands. As with difficulty, owing to the stench, we put our heads through the aperture where the prisoners receive their scanty pittance of bread, the whole crowd rose and begged for food and succour, but beyond thrusting in a few loaves, which were greedily devoured, we could do nothing.

"Filled with horror at the sight of such cruel suffering, I cast about me to see if I could not do something towards securing the liberty of some of the prisoners. An opportunity was not long in presenting itself. The cases which appeared to me the saddest were those of certain unhappy debtors, who were the victims of that abominable system of foreign protection, which eats like a canker into the heart of the Moorish political system. I had heard much of the iniquities perpetrated by Jews and Moors, especially the former, who, having secured 'patents' of foreign nationality, used them for the purpose of extorting money out of the natives, and now I saw with my own eyes the victims of their machinations. From trustworthy sources of information I learned that some of the dungeons were filled with people against whom claims for imaginary debts had been preferred. Unwilling or unable to pay, powerless to obtain redress against men who sheltered themselves beneath the ægis of a foreign flag, they had been clapped in the debtors' prisons. It was in one of these prisons that I happened to come across the man to whom I owe the discovery of which I spoke just now.

"Having bought a good supply of bread, I had taken it to one of the foulest and most crowded of the dungeons. As the first loaf was pushed through the aperture, the mob of prisoners came crowding round, jabbering and gesticulating like lunatics, and fighting for their share of the food. Behind this mass of squalid and despairing humanity, but taking no part in the struggle for the bread, I noticed one prisoner of a type superior to the rest. He was a man entering upon the evening of life, with a long iron-grey beard, and there was a look of despair and suffering, both physical and mental, on his face, which was pitiful to behold. His features were distinctly Oriental, but cast in a more refined and intellectual mould than those of the barbarous natives of Marocco. When I first observed him he was squatting on the floor ; but presently he rose slowly and painfully to his feet, and I could see that there were fetters round both his legs which, from their size and weight, were eating into the flesh. Struck with the appearance of the man, and full of pity for his miserable plight, I endeavoured to induce him to come and speak to me. The gaoler, seeing what I wanted, and hoping to get backsheesh out of the Nazarene, laid lustily about him with his cowhide whip, and the famished crew of prisoners soon fell back, jabbering and howling, from the opening, leaving a passage clear for the man I wanted. With a pitiable air of weariness and dejection, and hanging his head in shamefaced fashion, he dragged himself to the aperture. He seemed unwilling to speak at first, but at length, convinced that he was dealing with a friend, and that his words would not be used against him, he proceeded to unfold a tale of cruelty and wrong which, unfortunately, is only an instance of what is going on every day throughout that beautiful but most unhappy country.

"He said that his name was Ali Abd el Ressool— Ali the Slave of the Prophet, or, more correctly, the Apostle. He was a Persian by birth, but had resided for the last ten years in Marocco. During the greater part of that time he had been engaged in trade as a wool and hide merchant in one of the coast towns, and had managed in that way to amass a tolerable competence. Having the misfortune to become embroiled in a quarrel with a rich Jew who enjoyed American 'protection,' the latter cast about him for the means of obtaining his revenge. Nor was opportunity long in presenting itself to the Jew's vindictiveness. An American merchant residing in the same town was returning one evening from a shooting expedition when he was set upon by a band of robbers, who, after brutally ill-using him, stripped him of his effects, and left him dying by the roadside. It happened that the outrage took place close to the house which Ali occupied on the outskirts of the town ; and the Jew, seizing his occasion, denounced Ali as the real author and instigator of the crime. Colour was further lent to the charge by the fact, which Ali could not deny, that at the time of the murder he was in the merchant's debt for a considerable sum. Hoping to kill two birds with one stone, and seeing his way to do a little business on his own account, the Jew, besides accusing Ali of murder and robbery, preferred against him a false claim for several thousand dollars, which he said Ali owed him in connection with some commercial transactions in the interior.

"Shortly afterwards the unhappy Ali, who little suspected the plot that was hatching against him, was arrested on the double charge of murder and debt, despoiled of all his possessions, and, after being brutally flogged, was marched off in chains with a gang of criminals to the city of Marocco. Here he was cast into prison, and had remained for more than a year in durance vile until I appeared on the scene.

"To make a long story short, by dint of urgent representations at the Moorish Court and a substantial bribe to the Grand Vizier, we managed to secure the unfortunate Ali's release. I can never forget the poor fellow's surprise and joy on receiving the news that he was a free man. He seemed literally overwhelmed by the shock, and it was not until we had brought the gaoler in to knock the fetters from his feet that he could realize the extent of his good fortune. With tears and protestations of gratitude, and oft-repeated promises to repay at the first opportunity the money we had expended on his behalf, he staggered out of the prison door into the light of day. Being too weak and ill to walk, he was placed on a mule and conveyed to our lodgings in the town, where, after a few days' rest and careful treatment, he recovered sufficiently to accompany us on our journey to the sea-coast."

"A very interesting story indeed," remarked Gerald during a short interval, in the course of which Urquhart helped himself to some light refreshment in the shape of a whiskey-and-soda ; "but what has it to do with your discovery and our projected trip to Central Africa?"

"Don't be in a hurry," rejoined Urquhart. "You are always so impatient. I am coming to all that presently. Well, after the turn I had been able to do him, it was only natural that Ali and I should become pretty firm friends. Among other things he told me his history previous to his arrival in Marocco, and a very interesting story it was. He appears to have left his native country, Persia, at an early age, and to have entered the employ of a wool merchant who was starting upon a trading tour through Turkestan and Afghanistan. Near the borders of the two countries their caravan was attacked by robbers, his master the merchant slain, and himself taken prisoner and sold into slavery. His captors, who were hillmen of the Hindoo Koosh, conveyed

him several days' march to their village in a remote
valley among the mountains. Here he was kept a
close prisoner for several weeks, till at length, having
by his docility and industry won the confidence of
his new masters, he was allowed more liberty, and
finally employed by them as a shepherd.

" While engaged in this capacity, he was climbing
the hillside one day in search of a lamb which had
strayed from the flock, when he came upon a tiny hut
built upon the banks of a brook which flowed through
a rocky glen. The hut proved to be the abode of
a hermit whose holiness and supernatural powers
were the frequent theme of conversation among the
simple peasantry of the district. This hermit was
in reality a mystic, who had retired to these mountain
fastnesses in order, by a life of austerity and solitary
contemplation, to attain to that lofty state of spiritual
exaltation so hard to achieve amid the turmoil and
bustle of the civilized world. He was a member of
one of the occult fraternities which are scattered
over all that part of Asia—not a Mahatma, or Adept,
but a devotee and student, of advanced grade, of the
esoteric sciences. To be brief, Ali entered into conversation with the hermit, and this was the beginning
of a more intimate and lasting acquaintance. During
an intercourse which extended over several months,
the mystic discerned in the youthful Persian the
germs of a spiritual nature far transcending those of
the barbarous tribesmen with whom he lived, and he
began gradually to plant in his new pupil's mind the
seeds of hermetic knowledge. For this purpose Ali
was compelled to absent himself a good deal from his
other duties, but the awe and veneration in which the

hermit was held obviated any difficulties which might otherwise have arisen on that account. As a Persian, Ali had naturally been reared in the Shiite branch of the Mohammedan creed, but the more liberal opinions entertained by the sectaries of that Church enabled him to prosecute his studies without doing violence to his conscience as an orthodox follower of the Prophet. Under the hermit's guidance he passed rapidly through those earlier stages of occult development which the novice in mysticism must surmount before he even attains the subordinate rank of *chela*."

For the benefit of those of my readers who are not " esoteric," I will here explain that a chela is an occult neophyte. Chelaship is the lowest grade in the occult hierarchy, if I may so express it, yet its attainment is so difficult, the necessary training so severe, and success so precarious and uncertain, that many people give up the attempt in despair. For instance, if you abjure soap and nourishing food, wear a hair shirt, and sit on the point of a nail for twenty or thirty years, you may perhaps become a chela. On the other hand, you may not. Whether the game is worth the candle must be left to individual taste and judgment to decide.

" I will not weary you," continued Urquhart, " with the details of Ali's progress, as recounted by him to me, in the study and practice of occult science. Suffice it to say that, through the influence of the hermit, he ultimately regained his liberty and made his way down into India, where he continued with ardour the studies he had commenced under the tuition of the mystic of the Hindoo Koosh. And now I approach that part of my story which is more immediately pertinent to the subject we were discussing a few minutes ago. Ali had taken up his abode in Calcutta. In that town, through the good offices of a theosophical Baboo, he secured the privilege of the acquaintance of a certain Arhat, or Adept, of great eminence, from whom he learned many of the deeper truths of the Secret Doctrine. This Arhat was a member of the occult Brotherhood of Thibet, and he had studied esoteric science at the celebrated lamasery of Sakia Djong, alluded to by Mr. Sinnett[1] as the Thibetan residence of Gong Sso Rimbo Chay, the spiritual chief of the heretical sect of Dugpas, or Red Caps. From Sakia Djong the Arhat made frequent journeys in his astral body (in which, as you know, the higher Adepts can flit about the world at will), and in the course of one of these journeys he found himself in the middle of Africa—— "

"Oh, I say, come now!" murmured Gerald in a sleepy tone. "I've a pretty good digestion, as you are aware, but I can't quite swallow all that. When are you coming to the point?"

"Don't interrupt," said Urquhart. "I know I am rather long-winded, but I am getting near the end of my story. Besides, please remember that it was you who insisted on dragging it all out of me. To resume. The Arhat, in conjunction with two or three brother Adepts, had conceived the idea of planting, in the most remote and unexplored regions of Africa, an occult community which should rival, or even outshine, the famous Brotherhood of Thibet, and the project once conceived was promptly put into execution. As you are doubtless aware, the

---

[1] "Esoteric Buddhism," p. 191.

Mahatmas seek the most isolated spots on the world's surface for their abodes, where all contact with impure Western magnetism is rendered impossible. As far as I can learn, the place selected by our Arhat for his experiment was already tenanted by a small band of mystics, and he proposed to engraft thereon a colony of Initiates versed in the higher mysteries of occult enlightenment.

"In the course of their long acquaintance and intercourse the Arhat conceived a feeling of genuine affection for his new chela, in whose rapidly expanding spiritual understanding he saw reflected the accumulated stores of his own ripe wisdom, and regarded him as his most promising pupil. This affection was amply reciprocated by Ali, who added thereto a sentiment of reverential awe for his *gooroo*, or teacher. Hence it came about that on the Arhat's return to Africa (this time in his full *rupa*, or material body), he took Ali with him, though the latter did not accompany his master on his journey into the far interior. At the same time the Persian was entrusted with the secret of the locality of the African Brotherhood's retreat, and he has had full permission to confide the same to me. Nevertheless, if I now impart it to you it must be under a promise of the strictest secrecy, at any rate for the present. Do you understand?"

"We swear it," I solemnly replied for myself and Gerald, whose head was nodding over the side of his arm-chair and emitting strange guttural sounds at intervals.

"Well, the spot chosen as the earthly home of this mysterious colony is a lofty and solitary mountain, rising among the sands in the middle of the Sahara, which has never been visited or even seen by European explorers. During my travels in Marocco I heard stories among the natives of a mighty peak far in the interior, called the 'Djebel Tselj' (the Mountain of Snow), or simply, 'Djebel Kebeer' (the Great Mountain), which was popularly supposed to be tenanted by Marabouts, or holy men, gifted with supernatural powers. I had, however, regarded all these rumours as inventions of the natives until I learned from Ali the above-mentioned facts."

"Do you really think it possible," I asked, "that such a mountain could exist without modern geographers being aware of it?"

"I certainly think it quite possible," replied Urquhart, "as the peak in question lies far to the east of the ordinary caravan routes to Timbuctoo and the Soudan. Besides, the desert which has to be crossed before you reach it is of immense extent and very difficult to traverse, the wells being few in number, and the water in them scanty and brackish.

"Let me tell you, further, that, however much our modern geographers may be at fault in not having discovered this mountain, it is plain to my mind that it was known to the ancients. Herodotus, to begin with, locates Mount Atlas and the Atlanteans in the Sahara far to the south of Marocco, and he describes the mountain as being 'taper and circular.' Who was responsible for the information I know not, but if you read your Pliny you will find that his description of Atlas, fabled to be the supporter of the world, tallies in almost every respect with that given to me by Ali of the Djebel Kebeer. They both speak of it as a single solitary mountain in the African Desert, surrounded on all sides by sandy wastes. Now, it is absurd to suppose that when Pliny and Herodotus allude to an isolated peak [1] rearing its majestic head out of an expanse of surrounding desert, they can have meant the Atlas Mountains near the city of Marocco. In the first place, the latter form a chain of great length and of singular uniformity as regards height. The range does not contain a single peak of conspicuous eminence throughout its extent. Secondly, they do not rise out of the sand, as there is no desert within a hundred miles of their base, and their sides are not rugged but gently sloping. You must remember, too, that 'Atlas' is a widely used term. It is applied to the Algerian highlands, to the Beni Hassan range near Tetuan, as well as to the main chain of Marocco. To my mind it is patent that the Mount Atlas of the ancients is the Djebel Kebeer, or Great Mountain, of which I heard rumours in Marocco, and that it has no more connection with the Atlas range near Marocco city than Ben Nevis has with Kinchinjunga. Anyhow, be that as it may, and laugh as you will at my credulity, I believe in the accuracy of the stories I have heard, and, what is more, I mean to go and test their truth myself and to explore Mount Atlas. The question is, will you fellows come with me?"

Gerald, who had just woke up and had heard Urquhart's concluding sentence, expressed himself as willing to go anywhere his friend liked, "if only for the fun of the thing," though at that moment he

---

[1] "E mediis hunc (Atlantem) arenis attolli prodiderunt."—Pliny, De Rerum Nat., Book v., ch. I.

had but the vaguest notion of what Urquhart had been talking about. "Of course," he said to me afterwards, "it's all humbug about this mountain and its mysterious inhabitants ; but still, as old David seems bent on going, I shall go with him. Only, as I am not particularly keen about the Atlantean Brethren myself, I hope we shall get a bit of shooting on the way."

There was something rather touching about Gerald's devotion to his friend and the readiness with which he fell in with his views. I verily believe that if Urquhart had suggested a trip to the moon Gerald would have ordered a flying-machine on his own account in order to keep him company. For my own part, I could not acquiesce so readily in taking part in an expedition which I knew would require an absence from England of more than a year—I mean on the most favourable supposition that we did not leave our bones to bleach on the sands of the Sahara. I therefore declined to give a definite answer until I had had time to think the matter over carefully.

I heard little further on the subject for some months after I had left Inverfechan and returned to London, and I had begun to think that Urquhart had abandoned his project. One day, however, early in the following January, I chanced to run up against him in Piccadilly, and he told me that he and Somervell had almost made up their minds to leave England for Africa in the course of the next month.

"Come and dine with me at the club," he said ; "Gerald's coming, and I want to talk to you about that matter we were discussing last summer at Inverfechan. It is pretty well settled that Gerald and I start in a month's time for Marocco city. Old Ali is living there now, and he has promised to take us to Mount Atlas. What we want to know is, whether you will come with us. You've had lots of time to think the matter over, and to come to a decision one way or the other."

Well, to make a long story short, at that dinner we discussed the matter fully, and, under the influence of Urquhart's good cheer, and the pressure put upon me by him and Somervell, I consented to join them on their madcap enterprise.

"Come along, Jim," cried Gerald, in his cheerily persuasive way; "life is short, and you've no ties at home beyond your Eldorado Railway shares. What's the use of making money if you can't enjoy yourself?"

So it was arranged that I should go with them. An Englishman's ideas of enjoyment are different from those of most other people, but I doubt whether if we had known what the next year had in store for us all, we should have set forth in this light-hearted fashion ; and Gerald might have talked less glibly about "enjoying" himself. It is well, perhaps, for human nature that it does not know all that the future has in store for it. Our present troubles are enough, in all conscience, and we should be thankful that we have not to add to them the anticipation of evil to come.

CHAPTER III.

"*FESTINARE in medias res*" is a golden rule of composition, and I fear that I have been an unconscionable time about beginning my story. However, it is a fault that I share with many other tellers of tales. How many a good and otherwise interesting book is marred by the unutterable tediousness of its opening chapters! In our case the *mediæ res* would be somewhere in the middle of the Sahara, which, you will agree with me, would be from Piccadilly too big and sudden a jump.

. Behold us, therefore, encamped, on this morning of the 15th of May, in a *duar*, or Arab tent village, on the road to Marakesh, the city of Marocco. We started from the seaport town of Mazagan, and have already been four days on the march. We ought to be almost at Marakesh by now, but having come out to enjoy ourselves we are taking things easy. The sun has just risen, and the dew diamonds yet sparkle on the tender grass-blades, and the air is keen and fresh. Our Moorish servants are just striking the tents and loading the mules, chattering, squabbling, gesticulating, as they always do whenever they have any work on hand. What a noise and fuss they make! That tall Moor looks as if he is just going to cut his fellow-servant's throat, but as a matter of fact he is only asking him to give a hand with that big box. Wasn't it Longfellow who wrote those pretty lines—

> " And shall fold their tents like the Arabs,
>   And as silently steal away " ?

Whoever it was, he can never have had much to do with Arabs, as no member of that lively race was ever known to behave as there described. When folded, the tent has still to be put on the back of the pack-animal, and he is sure to require much whacking and objurgation. Then it is even betting that one of the mules will start kicking. To stop him an extra hundredweight of cargo is put on his back, and a Moor jumps on the top to keep his heels down. The mule resents this, and sends the whole bag of tricks flying, and probably finishes by landing the Moor a nasty one as he lies on the ground. All this engenders a vast amount of heat and profanity, so that it will be seen that the poet's picture of the breaking up of an Eastern encampment is entirely a creation of fancy, and has no foundation in fact.

While these preliminaries are being concluded we mount our horses and enjoy a scamper over the plain. Oh, the sense of exhilaration at being once more in the wilds amid a primitive people; far from the busy town with its petty cares and still pettier pleasures, its Mammon-seeking and tuft-hunting, its muffin-fights and money-grubbing; the desert before you, and the broad blue African sky above! Look at

Urquhart galloping away on his handsome black barb; isn't he just enjoying himself! And Gerald, too, on his natty little chestnut, which I had an eye on for myself, by the way, before he bought him. For real, genuine pleasure give me foreign travel in out-of-the-way places, where everything is new and interesting—rich food for eye and brain for those who can take in what they see.

"Fools wander, wise men travel," and though some there be who, as Sterne says, may travel from Dan to Beersheba, and find it all barren, yet to the man of understanding a journey through this quaint land is an education in itself. It seems to quicken one's perceptions, and to open up a whole vista of new thoughts and ideas. It is to take a plunge two thousand years back in the history of the world; to be reborn in Old Testament days; to see our ancestors, as it were, living before us in the flesh. The country, too, is looking its best just now. The prayers of the natives have been answered, and a grateful rain has succeeded to a long and disastrous drought. Inanimate Nature is radiant, but the scarcity of animal life is somewhat depressing. A few grey vultures of solemn aspect sit by the roadside, seemingly taking deep thought concerning their mid-day meal, and wondering where on earth they will get it. Some miserable draggled peewits there are, too, who have strayed further south than is their wont.

> "In the spring the wanton lapwing gets himself another crest,"

according to the poet. That is just what these birds don't do, and they certainly look anything but wanton.   I love plovers' eggs, so Gerald and I go out hunting for them, but without success.   If this were England the birds would be feverishly occupied in laying beautiful eggs at fourpence apiece, but there is no market for such things out here, so I suppose they don't think it worth while.

The third day we crossed a range of hills of moderate height, and had our first view of the gleaming snows of the giant Atlas range, and Marocco city, with its groves of palm trees, its minarets and spires, lying, as it were, at our feet.   Below us a mighty plain stretched away for hundreds of miles in one unbroken level, bounded on the south by the Atlas. A magnificent and, as far as my experience goes, a unique panorama.   Our caravan descends the barren, treeless mountain side by an execrable path, and defiles across the plain.   We pass the night in a tiny duar, the sheikh whereof looks askance at the dogs of *kafirs*, or unbelievers, who ask for his hospitality, and at first he seems disinclined to take us in.   Greed of gain, however, triumphs, as it generally does, over sectarian animosity; and, as there are said to be bands of marauding Arabs of the Rhammena tribe infesting the district, the tents are pitched in the middle of the village, instead of outside, as we should have preferred.   We turn in early, but sleep is made impossible owing to the odours and the noises—the bleating of sheep and lowing of cattle, and the melody of wakeful jackasses, themselves disturbed by the watch-dogs baying at imaginary foes.

The afternoon of the next day sees us approaching the crumbling walls, with their square towers and bogus battlements, which encircle the southern capital. What are those grisly objects nailed to that whitewashed bit of wall, with the dark spots below them?

"Good heavens!" cried Urquhart, "look at those heads on the wall over there."

Heads they were—human ones too—and no mistake about it ; two rows of at least a dozen each, and the blood dripping down had congealed in black stains on the plaster. " Sidna, our Lord the Sultan (may Allah prolong his life)," the Moors inform us, had been engaged in the congenial occupation of " eating up " a refractory tribe who showed a disposition to keep the tribute they owed his Majesty in their own pockets, and these ghastly relicts of humanity had a short time before stood on the shoulders of the leaders of the revolt. Shocking as such sights must be to every humane person, it is strange how soon in the East one becomes acclimatized to horrors of every kind. Things which in Europe would cause a shudder to run through you out here attract little more than passing notice.

We had letters of introduction to the Bascha of the city, and were graciously received by that functionary. With many complimentary tropes and figures of speech, he assured us how welcome we were, and of the tremendous regard he had for us. All the same, in his heart of hearts didn't he just wish us at the bottom of the sea ! They lay the butter on a little too thick for our English tastes; but then, we are such a very plain-spoken people. The Bascha at the time of our visit was a mulatto with more black than white blood in his veins. He had started life as a slave, and had earned a living by cleaning out the

refuse from Moors' houses and by other menial
employments, till by a turn of fortune's wheel he had
managed to ingratiate himself in the Sultan's eyes
and had been raised to his present position. His
ambition was, however, not yet sated, and he now
aspired to the Grand Viziership, which office it was
said he had an excellent chance of obtaining. His
qualifications for the post were undeniable, as he was
a fanatical, pig-headed, and entirely bigoted despot.

A pretty specimen of fortune's favouritism truly!
Yet such it seems to me is life, not only in the
East, but pretty much all the world over. Power
and place, success of every description, often fall to
the lot of the least worthy, and Dame Fortune awards
her prizes without regard to the merits of the
recipient. The unintelligent "accident of an accident"
is born to wealth and good things, while men of
talent struggle on unheeded and unrewarded. The
more one thinks about it the more one is impressed
by the part which sheer luck plays in all affairs of
life. For my own part, I believe the Mohammedan
theory of predestination is only a doctrinal method
of expressing this fact. Some one has wittily
observed that life in general is a " speculation for the
rise." Ἀιεν ἀριστεύειν is our motto, in the sense that
we are most of us trying to better ourselves. And
the factors of success are the same in this speculation
as in all others. Judgment, nerve, intelligence,
knowledge, and other qualities, go for something, but
luck is in every case the main arbiter of our destinies.
Take the case of the professions. Genius, I admit,
will probably force its way to the front, but for the
ordinary run of fairly instructed humanity (and the

bulk of us are now educated up to an even, if tolerably high, standard of mediocrity) luck, and trivial, or even contemptible, qualities usually determine the issue. An engaging smile and a talent for tittle-tattle may do more for a medical man than the profoundest knowledge of the healing art. As a barrister friend of mine once remarked, "the disheartening thing about the Bar is, not so much the number of good men who fail to get on, as the unutterable duffers who do." And so it is in nearly every walk of life. You may think, gentle reader, that it is some cynic soured by misfortune who addresses you in this fashion, but it is not so. The world has treated me not unkindly, and I find it very pleasant on the whole. Fortune has reserved her heaviest blows for other, and perhaps worthier, shoulders than mine. Though not rich, I have sufficient for my wants, good health, friends who are more than kind ; and what can reasonable mortal wish for more in this vale of tears ? Yet it does seem to me that to the man who has brains to think, eyes to see, and a heart to feel, the mass of hopeless and undeserved suffering in the world, and the still more undeserved good fortune, cannot but suggest saddening reflections. In another sphere of existence, let us hope, the balance will be struck and each man's account made even. Meanwhile we must be content to do our best, to work and wait, and leave to Providence the issue.

But to resume. The practical result of our interview with the Bascha was the placing at our disposal a very tolerable house with a good-sized garden. As soon as we had settled down comfortably in our new quarters we set out on what had been the main object of our journey hither, to find Ali Abd el Ressool. Urquhart had been in correspondence with the Persian on the subject of our expedition for some time prior to our departure from England, so that our arrival did not take him altogether by surprise. After diligent search, we found the old man in a small house down one of the tortuous alleys which pass for streets in Moorish towns. Passing through the narrow door, we found ourselves in a tesselated court surrounded with a portico, and having a tiny fountain playing in the centre. Our arrival was made known to the master of the house by a buxom Jewish maid-of-all-work, and in a few minutes there appeared a tall well-built man with an iron-grey beard, who proved to be Ali. I spoke of him just now as an old man, but from his looks he should be little more than fifty. He wore the ordinary dress of the country— *jellabia*, or burnoos, yellow leathern slippers, fez, and turban; but a glance at his intelligent face, with its chiselled features and transparent olive complexion, told you he was not of Moorish extraction. He received Urquhart with transports, but his method of greeting Gerald and myself, though not uncourteous, was, to say the least of it, peculiar. He commenced by shaking hands, making a semi-circular sweep with his arm pretty much in the idiotic style now in vogue among fashionable ladies (why is it that one always has to do or to wear something idiotic in order to be in the fashion ?) which suggests a dislocated shoulder or malformation of the elbow joint. Only, instead of grasping my hand by the palm, as any ordinary mortal would, he seized my thumb, and, waggling it violently for some seconds, inquired in tolerable

English if my brains were in good order, and trusted that I was feeling tolerably sane. Being new to this latter form of salutation, I at first felt inclined to resent it, not knowing that it is a common Persian form of speech. Old Ali's conversation was, indeed, generally a curiosity, being an odd mixture of Persian and Maroquin figures of speech, interlarded now and again with fragments of colloquial English. Urquhart and he soon fell to talking together, so Gerald and I left them and mounted to the flat roof of the house (a most improper proceeding out here, as it gives you a view of your neighbour's harems) and had a look round. It was getting on towards seven o'clock, and the fiery orb of the sun was just burying itself in the distant plain, suffusing the sky with a flood of red, green, and gold light. Then, as the tide of crimson glory ebbed in the western heavens, a rosy flush overspread the Atlas snows. The great red mosque tower of the Kutubia glowed like some mighty obelisk of flame as the solemn *magreb*, the evening *mueddin*, or call to prayer, pealed forth from the belfry. A truly impressive scene. We gazed on it awhile in silence, neither of us caring to talk, and then as the evening shades sprang rapidly up the leaden eastern sky we went down into the house. There we found the other two still engaged in conversation, and making plans for our expedition into the interior. Urquhart had little difficulty in persuading Ali to accompany us. Indeed, I believe the old man would have been ready to go anywhere or to do anything that his benefactor asked him, such were the depths of his gratitude and affection. He said he had been debating the matter in his mind for some time past, and went so far as to assert that he had received communications from two of his occult masters who were now in Mount Atlas, namely, those very eminent Thibetan Mahatmas, Messrs. Singmya Songo and Kikkuppa Row, who had expressed themselves as being much in favour of his making the journey. In fact, he believed those gentlemen had been actually present in their *lingas shariras*, or astral bodies, in the city of Marocco during the past week, but they had whisked themselves in the twinkling of an eye over the summits of the Atlas range before he could even get a sight of them. I should mention here that the first named of these Mahatmas, Mr. Singmya Songo, was none other than the Arhat alluded to by Urquhart as having been Ali's *gooroo*, or instructor in esoteric science, in India.

The details of our journey and the outline of the route we were to take were mainly left to Ali. Concerning the latter, he continued to profess to have received information from occult sources, but Gerald and I were naturally sceptical on the point, and thought that if he knew anything about it (which we rather doubted) he had learned it from the natives. On our asking him if he thought we should ever arrive at Mount Atlas, "Inshallah," he replied with a shrug, "please God. Shkoon araf, who knows? May your footsteps be fortunate and may your end be happy. Who can forecast the lot of man or say what a day may bring forth? Behold! our comings and our goings are written in the book of Fate. The issue is with Allah, and on His will all things depend, for there is no power or strength except in God."

The reader may imagine that neither of us believed

in the existence of Mount Atlas or its mystic inhabitants, though Urquhart's faith in both remained unshaken. We recognized the fact that we were starting on a dangerous expedition involving great toil and danger, and if any one had asked us what induced us to go it would have been difficult to give a satisfactory answer. Primarily, Gerald went because Urquhart was bent on going, and I went—well, because both of them were going. Add to this an inborn love of adventure, and vague ideas of big game shooting in the heart of the Dark Continent, and you have the sum total of the motives that influenced us. At the same time, on calmly thinking the matter over, after the lighthearted consent I had given in Urquhart's club, I could not help having grave misgivings as to the result. I knew that we should have to cross the Atlas range by passes eleven or twelve thousand feet high, whereon civilized men had never yet set foot, through tribes of wild and dangerous Schlohs; that in the oasis of the Draa and in Southern Marocco we should encounter a population among the most bloodthirsty and fanatical in Africa; and that the journey across the Great Desert, if we ever reached its borders alive, by a way far removed from the ordinary caravan routes to the interior, would be environed by the greatest peril. And all this to gratify a fantastic idea of Urquhart's, which probably had not the slightest basis in fact. However, in for a penny in for a pound; I had put my hand to the plough and must not now draw back.

It was ten o'clock before we left Ali's house and began to thread our way back to our own quarters. How strange and weird are our surroundings! Beneath

the sable canopy of night the great city sleeps—
sleeps, too, with a stillness that strikes with wonder us
Europeans accustomed to the never-ceasing hum and
roar of London streets. We have brought a lantern
with us, and it is well that we have done so. The
moon is not yet risen, and the faint starlight scarcely
penetrates these narrow alleys where the eaves of the
tumble-down houses almost meet overhead, leaving
only a thin line of steel-blue sky visible between. We
grope our way slowly along, stumbling over the cobble-
stones and refuse heaps that choke the streets ; down
main thoroughfares which sometimes attain the
majestic width of ten or twelve feet ; through quaint
gateways and wynds where three men could scarcely
walk abreast, till at length we find ourselves in the
great square of the city. Here it is barely three
minutes' walk to our house, so we pause awhile to
await the rising of the moon. It is growing less dark
every moment, and she cannot delay us long. And
now the stars begin to flicker feebly in the augmenting
light, and the snowy counterpane of Atlas gleams
with a ghostly brilliancy, as, trailing behind her a
gauzy robe of silvery vapour, the pale goddess climbs
the heavens.

How different from the scene a few hours ago!
In the daytime all is heat and dust and bustle, while
dirt, misery, and decay are everywhere painfully
apparent. Now not a living thing is to be seen.
Merchants and stall-keepers are snoring in their beds ;
the beggars, the halt, the lame, and the blind, have
betaken themselves Heaven knows where, and their
places are filled by long phantom-like shadows. Not
a sound is to be heard save the breeze whispering

through the feathery palm-tops. The pale witchery of night casts a mysterious glamour over everything, causing these tumbledown buildings of tabbia to appear like ruined castles. Even yon Alpine heights, whose snows at noontime seem to shine so strangely in the blaze of the African sun, now appear quite natural and appropriate in the cold shimmer of the moonbeams. It is a scene to dream of and to linger over; and as we silently watch the light fleecy clouds drifting lazily, like opalescent snowflakes along the glistening sides of the mountains, our thoughts are transported by its weird beauty to other worlds, and fancy runs riot even in the prosaic brain of Gerald Somervell.

Suddenly our reveries are disturbed by the shrill tones of a *rhectah* (pipe) and its inevitable accompaniment, the tom-tom. What midnight orgie thus breaks so rudely on our ears? Only a few rioters keeping late carouse after the wedding of a relation. They do not keep it up for long, but the spell is broken, and as we wend our way homewards all is once more calm and still as in a city of the dead.

CHAPTER IV.

ACROSS THE ATLAS MOUNTAINS.

CIRCUMSTANCES compelled us to make a long stay in Marakesh, the last fortnight of which was spent in the purchasing of tents and animals, the hiring of servants, and in otherwise preparing for our departure. Urquhart's thorough knowledge of Arabic was of great use to us at this time. For myself, I already possessed a smattering of the language, and after a few months' practice could talk it pretty fluently, while Gerald showed a surprising facility in picking it up.

Our destination was kept a profound secret even from the servants. Had they known where we were going they would never have entered our employ, and Ali assured us that if the matter came to the ears of the Moorish authorities they would dispatch a troop of cavalry after us and bring us back before even we reached the foot of the mountains. The Sultan of Marocco has a rooted aversion to strangers travelling about his " happy dominions " otherwise than along certain beaten tracks. Accordingly, as soon as our preparations were completed, we sallied forth by the

Bab el Debagh, or eastern gate of the city, and took the road which leads through the beautiful palm forests, as if *en route* for the coast. We passed the night in the village of Tamilelt, not far from the foot of the Atlas, and leaving it early next morning, we struck off in a south-easterly direction straight towards the mountains. And now our difficulties began. Our servants on learning whither we were bound began to mutiny, raising a tremendous hubbub and crying out that we should all be murdered. For awhile threats, bribes, and entreaties were alike of no avail, so that in the end we had to discharge the greater number of them. Fortunately we managed to retain one of the best, a muleteer named Almarakshi, a big strapping mulatto, who did a power of work and was very willing. Our cook also consented to remain with us, a worthy but very corpulent native of Marakesh, and a master of his art. Needless to say that his name was Mohammed. To distinguish him from his numerous namesakes we called him "Staferallah Mohammed" (Allah-forgive-me Mohammed), because of his frequent use of that expression. Moorish speech is always interlarded with pious ejaculations, such as "Bismillah," "Hamdoollah," etc., pitchforked in without any relevance or connection to the subject-matter of the conversation, like our English "you know" and "don't you know;" and "Staferallah" was Mohammed's favourite phrase.

Two or three of the smartest of the muleteers were also induced by offers of increased pay not to desert. With these, and such additional hands as we hoped to be able to pick up on the way, we thought we should get on pretty well. As we expected to have a lot of mountain work, we had sold our horses in the Soko, or, as the Scotch would say, " by public roup," in the city of Marocco, and had procured some fine big mules in their stead. Personally I detest mules, but they have this advantage, that, as the Moors say, they have no disease but what a stick will cure. None the less, they are most unpleasant beasts to ride. They have no shoulder to speak of, and their action is as irritating as their tempers are uncertain.

We took up our quarters the next night in a Schloh village amid the foot-hills of the main chain. The inhabitants regarded us with great curiosity, but made no signs of open hostility. All this part of Marocco is inhabited by wild and semi-independent tribes of Schlohs, who form one of the largest branches of the great Berber race. Driven from the plains by the early Arab invaders, they withdrew to these mountain fastnesses, where even now the troops of their nominal ruler, the Sultan, dare not follow them. Ali happened to be acquainted with the head man of the village, and through his good offices we secured the services of a native who for a moderate sum volunteered to guide us over the mountains. I cannot give you this individual's name, for the simple reason that, like so many of these jaw-breaking Arabic words, it is simply untranscribable. Suffice it to say that it commenced with a hiccough, the middle was an expectoration, and the termination a sneeze. He was a truculent-looking ruffian, sallow and lantern-jawed, with high cheek-bones like most of his race; and his generally sinister aspect was further heightened by a most tremendous squint.

He wore a dark jellabia, tricked out with parti-coloured fringes, yellow top boots, and a pair of voluminous breeches of dirty red cloth. On his head was a greasy *tarboosh*, or fez cap, from under which descended oily, black, curly elf-locks. An armament of antique weapons completed his equipment—portentous pistols that would not go off, and would blow your hand off if they did ; a curved scimitar in a pink leathern sheath, ghastly-looking Sus knives stuck in his belt and slung by red cords over his shoulder. He was for ever boasting of his prowess in battle, having once, I believe, lain in ambush and shot an enemy in the back and then chopped the head and hands off the dead body. He also prided himself on his horsemanship, giving himself out as a sort of centaur, though Mohammed, who took a great dislike to him, had a different tale to tell. He assured us that his chief equestrian feat was performed on a certain memorable occasion in Marakesh, when, having been detected in some act of petty theft, he was mounted on an ass with his face to its tail, and, holding that appendage of the animal in his hand, was whacked through the streets for three hours by the citizens. Besides his other weapons he carried a matchlock of portentous length, so that Gerald, who was getting on very fast with his Arabic, nicknamed him "Beni M'cohhella," which, being interpreted, signifies the "Son of a Gun," and this appellation stuck to him to the day of his death.

Talking of nicknames, the Arabs are past masters in the art of inventing them, and they were not long in spotting our individual peculiarities and labelling us accordingly. It was not likely that Gerald's proboscis would escape their observant eyes, and he was promptly dubbed "Aboo Nokhra," or "The Father of the Nose." Urquhart, whose whiskers in their untrained luxuriance had almost attained the dignity of those appendages once known as "Piccadilly Weepers," went by the name of "The Father of Whiskers." My physiognomy not having any features worthy of a nickname I was styled plain Tajjer, or merchant, the title usually given in the interior to Christians who do not bear any official rank.

Our bivouac was amid the most enchanting scenery. Before us a broad and fertile valley stretched away seemingly up into the heart of the mountains. A small stream, its banks clothed in with oleanders in full bloom, flowed down through meadows of a brilliant green such as is never to be found in the plains. About the hillsides occasional houses and villages lay embosomed in groves of olive, fig, and orange trees, and tiny corn-fields dotted about made a singular patchwork of gold and green landscape.

Our progress at first, after leaving the village, was easy and tolerably rapid. Higher up, the valley narrowed to a gorge, with precipitous sides fringed with forests of lentisk and evergreen oak. The mountains on either hand grew steeper and loftier, and the road—well, there wasn't much road. The Son of a Gun led the way on foot, chattering of his deeds of valour and the foes he had slain, hopping over the boulders and other obstacles in the path with marvellous agility. Urquhart came next, with Ali close at his heels on a big brindled *bghull*, or he-mule (pray do not try and pronounce this word, fair reader, or you will dislocate your pretty jaw), with stripes like a hyæna. Then followed Gerald and myself and the pack-mules and the Moors of our train. For the first two days we had met with nothing but civility from the natives, who, while they naturally regarded our advent with much wonder, abstained from all hostile action ; but further on we heard rumours of marauding tribes inhabiting the southern slopes of the Atlas, who lay in ambush for and plundered passing caravans. In particular, a certain tribe, rejoicing in the name of the Beniboogoozgoo, seemed to be notorious for their cruelty and ferocity, and they were now, we were informed, on the war-path. Some merchants from the Draa oasis, journey-ing northwards, had been waylaid and murdered by these ruffians not many days previously.

The danger not being near or immediate, Beni M'cohhela assumed a lofty air of protection towards all the rest of the party, assuring us that we had no need to fear as long as he was with us. To poor old Ali especially, who was visibly getting very nervous and uncomfortable, he was beyond measure patronizing, taking him under his wing in a manner that was excessively galling to that sensitive old gentleman.

"Verily, O Ali," he cried, "there is no need for fear. Blessings on your beard, you old ass, am I not with you ? Oollah ! by Allah, ere now this right arm hath put a score of stout warriors to flight ; and if those sons of unmentionable mothers, the Beniboo-goozgoo (may their fathers' graves be eternally defiled), dare to attack the Oolad Ingleez (sons of the English), woe betide them."

"Loor kebar ! God is great," rejoined the Persian ; "what dirt is this we are eating ? My trust is in

Allah ; but I should indeed be afraid if we had to rely on you and your rusty old blunderbuss for protection. Do you laugh at our beards ? "

" Ya lateef ! Merciful Allah," exclaimed the Son of a Gun, executing a sort of war-dance, and spinning his gun round and catching it after the fashion of the jugglers at Moorish fairs. " Ya lateef ! Do you question my valour ? Have I not eaten of the lion's heart ? " [1]

" Staferallah ! if he only fights as well as he talks, we can all lay down our arms and look on," remarked Mohammed in his most sarcastic tones ; and he went on to suggest that our guide had probably eaten less of the lion's heart than of the *ras ed dubbah*,[2] or hyæna's brain, and that, however much he might be the Son of a Gun, he was, at any rate, the father of all asses. There was no love lost between these two, and they were perpetually squabbling in this fashion. " Of a verity, O Father of Whiskers," said Mohammed to Urquhart, " there will be no peace in the *goffla* (caravan) so long as this *kilb ibn kilb* (dog and son of a dog) remains with us. Lai sti shimlek, may God scatter your relations," he continued, apostrophizing Beni M'cohhela ; " the wind has got into your brain, you jackanapes. Inshallah ! Please Allah, I will yet live to defile your grave, or my name is not Mohammed."

The Son of a Gun was too much pumped with his antics and chatter, and the increasing steepness of

---

[1] According to Moorish belief a person who has eaten of the heart of a lion, becomes endowed with great bravery in battle.

[2] To say that a person has tasted the hyæna's brain is equivalent to calling him a fool, the hyæna being considered the stupidest of beasts.

the road, to make a suitable reply to the sallies of
our cook, so he relapsed into silence. For awhile
nothing broke the stillness of the mountain air except
the roar of the torrent, the " click-click " of our mules'
hoofs against the stones, and the occasional, " Arrah,
arrah ny mek " ("Go on ; go along to your mother "),
of a muleteer to his lagging beast. Our route led up
the left or western side of the stream, which foamed
and brawled on its impetuous course several hundred
feet below. The path in places lay along the edge of
an almost sheer cliff, and of course our mules, in
their usual pig-headed fashion, insisted on walking as
close to the brink as possible. It is never any sort of
use remonstrating with the brutes. You must try
and fancy yourself far safer with one foot dangling
over the abyss, and remember that the maxim,
" Medio tutissimus ibis," was not meant to apply to
jackasses.

I shall not attempt to describe in detail our journey
over this magnificent chain of mountains, though I
could say a good deal about it. We journeyed by
easy stages for two or three days, resting one Sunday
in a small grass-plot by the edge of the stream. The
track grew worse as we advanced higher up the
valley. In places it had been swept entirely away by
avalanches, and it was necessary for us to cut it
afresh out of steep slopes of slippery shale. Deep
rifts and gorges, too, cleft by rushing torrents, with
fantastically shaped rocks about their sides, continually impeded our progress. The valley grew
narrower and narrower, and the mountains on either
side higher and more rugged, till at last we were
forced to quit the line of the stream, and climbed up

a small zig-zag path to the right. In a few hours we reached a sort of plateau, which, like a Swiss Alp, lay along the summit of the lower precipitous face of the mountain. My aneroid here gave the height as 9500 feet. We followed this plateau for a considerable distance. The slope was very moderate, and the going altogether much better. At this elevation patches of snow began to show themselves, and the white slope, which stretched above us in billowy undulations to the summit of the range, caused me some misgivings as to our being able to get the beasts over.

However, as so often happens in worldly affairs, our difficulties were greater in the prospect than in the reality, and a laborious trudge of a few hours at length brought us to the summit of the pass. A glorious view here burst upon us. Northwards the city of Marocco lay, as it were, at our feet, though in reality many miles distant, its red towers and spires and battlements being plainly visible. Westwards the great plain stretched away to where, in the far distance, we fancied we could discern the blue Atlantic. Several miniature rivers, including the Wad Tensift and the Wad N'fys, glinted like silvery threads in the sunlight. Near us were no Alpine cliffs or jagged peaks, only huge, white, rounded mountain masses, about whose sides fleecy clouds floated like pieces of cotton wool. On the southern slopes the mists were gathered more thickly. Now and again, as they dispersed, glimpses were afforded us of the fertile valley of the Sus, down which the river flowed in serpentine windings. Beyond the valley, to the south-east, the blue outlines of the Anti-

Atlas peaks were plainly visible whenever the curtain of vapour parted asunder, and far to the south the desert floated in a yellow haze.

We did not stay long on the summit, as, although the sun was shining brightly, a keen wind blowing from the east made the Moors' teeth chatter and their bodies shiver with cold. Not far below the top of the pass we met some ragged-looking natives, toiling painfully up the steep incline. After burning our grandparents *sotto voce* in orthodox fashion, and expressing a pious hope that all *N'sara*, or Nazarenes, might frizzle in Jehannum, they bestowed a *salaam alikum*, or "peace be with you," on the Son of a Gun, and informed us that they had travelled all the way from Tafilet on foot, and were now bound for Marocco City. They pointed us out our route, concerning which the Son of a Gun evidently had not the foggiest notion, and gave us some useful information concerning the movements of the Beniboogoozgoo. They said we might expect to encounter that truculent tribe at some place not far from the foot of the mountains. They had themselves been apprehensive of an attack, and attributed their escape solely to their poverty-stricken appearance. A caravan like our own, however, which consisted partly of Christians, could hardly hope for similar good fortune, as in our case the motive of plunder would be supplemented by that of religious fanaticism.

After bestowing some small backsheesh on our new friends, which they pocketed without any outward sign of gratitude, whatever their innermost feelings may have been, we resumed our downward journey. There was little that was remarkable in the way of scenery ; but we noticed a decided change for the warmer in the temperature, and the vegetation climbed at least a thousand feet higher up the mountain side. We selected an open spot for our encampment that evening in order to be more secure against surprises, and we had a watch set all night. The Son of a Gun redoubled his maledictions against those sons of Sheitan, the Beniboogoozgoo, whose fathers he hoped to burn, and for whose reception he was persuaded the fires of Jehannum were already kindled ; but his boastings of his personal prowess had grown much fainter of late. On the march next day he resigned his position in the van on the plea of a sore foot, and located himself in the centre of the caravan alongside of Mohammed. We had not gone far when shrill voices raised in anger told us that fresh ructions had broken out between the two.

"Lai harak abook, may God burn your father !" screamed Mohammed, in a passion, and a volley of other imprecations followed.

It appeared that the Son of a Gun was carrying his matchlock on his shoulder and the muzzle had caught our cook a pretty hard knock on the head, which gave him an opportunity of picking a quarrel with his enemy. But the approach of danger had made Beni M'cohhela humble and submissive.

"Aywa, rajjel" ("Well, man "), he rejoined in that curious, sing-song, deprecatory tone affected by the Moors, "do not be angry. Bismillah ! in the name of Allah, it was but an accident."

"Staferallah ! I'll 'accident' you, you greasy son of Jehannum ! Don't you dare to come near me, or I'll pull your beard ! May your sister have an old jackass for a sweetheart, and may the dogs defile your father's grave!"

This last affront was more than the Son of a Gun could endure. He did not mind personal insults; he could even put up with imputations on the moral character of his living female relations, but the tombs of his ancestors were sacred. Abandoning his submissive attitude, he broke out in wrath—

"Lai sti shimlek; ma andish book! May God scatter your relations, you man without a father!" he cried. "Where was your mother married, you tun-bellied old father of a cooking-pot? Don't speak to me like that, or I'll put a bullet through you;" and he raised his matchlock threateningly.

"Holy Prophet! but I'll punch your head, you ill-conditioned dog's son!" howled Mohammed, making a dive for his antagonist, whom he grabbed by his long greasy love-locks, tearing them out by handfuls. The pair rolled over on the ground, and it was with difficulty that they could be separated.

We gave them both, especially Mohammed, a good rating for their unseemly behaviour at a crisis when it was beyond all things necessary that we should present a united front to our expected foes.

CHAPTER V.

THE ROBBER ATTACK.

As we neared the foothills, which here, as on the northern side, extended for some distance from the base of the main chain, the road entered a narrow defile, through which a stream, fed by the melting of the mountain snows, flowed down into the Sus valley. It was necessary to keep a sharp look-out here, as the locality was favourable for an ambush. We three Englishmen carried double-barrelled Express rifles, and, with our revolvers in our belts, we felt we ought to be a match for any reasonable number of the Beniboogoozgoo. Our servants all carried swords, and some of them were armed in addition with matchlocks and Moorish pistols. Gerald offered Ali one of our spare revolvers; but the poor old fellow, who was trembling all over like an aspen leaf, would not take it.

"May I be your sacrifice, O Father of the Nose!" he cried. "Allow me to explain, for the good of your service, that I am a man of peace, not of war. Staferallah! may God forgive me, but fear hath already gat hold of my loins. My knees are loosened;

my liver is become water; my bowels are much moved; and my heart is as wax. Wherefore, by your favour, if an enemy should attack us (which may Allah in His mercy avert), I will extinguish the fires of audacity with the waters of prudence, and conceal my person beneath the veil of obscurity;" by which figure of speech I imagine he intended to convey that he would hide in a ditch till the fight was over.

"In that case," rejoined the heartless Gerald, "I shall feel constrained to prick the flanks of timidity with the goad of coercion; or, to vary the metaphor slightly, to plant the boot of contumely upon the rump of pusillanimity. Come, take the pistol, you old funk."

"God be gracious to my brother!" cried the Persian in great distress; "ashes are fallen upon my head, and I devour much grief. My trust is in Allah, but I fear lest our faces be made black in the sight of our enemies" (poor old Ali's was white enough in all conscience), "and we be covered with a mantle of shame."

"It's not a bit of good, Gerald," said Urquhart; "he would never hit anything if he had the pistol, unless it was a mule or one of ourselves."

Thus admonished, Gerald left our faint-hearted retainer to his own devices. It was just past midday, and the sun was beating fiercely down on our heads. Not a breath stirred. We carefully scanned the ground in our neighbourhood, but could see no sign of the enemy. The hillsides were rocky and covered with thick bush, and anything like effective scouting was out of the question. We were approaching a spot where a high rock rose almost perpendicularly from the bed of the stream, and the road narrowed to a sort of ledge cut out of the face of the precipice, where mules with burdens could not pass. Accordingly, the caravan was halted, the animals were unloaded, and the luggage carried past the obstacle on the backs of the Moors. We had all got safely by, and the last muleteer with his beast had regained the path which here turned sharply to the right. A halt was again called and the process of reloading the mules commenced. Suddenly a white puff of smoke issued from behind a rock thirty yards on our right; there was a report, followed by the scream of a bullet and a dull thud. One of the finest of the mules, which carried our sleeping tent, staggered and rolled over the precipice with his burden. In a moment all was dire confusion. The Moors screamed and jabbered and swore. The muleteers in the rear whacked their beasts to make them go on, while those in front backed into those behind. Two or three of the more vicious mules started kicking, and everything in a few moments got hopelessly mixed. The first discharge was followed by six or eight dropping shots, which, however, did little damage. Simultaneously there swarmed out of the bush a band of Berbers, tall, lithe, active-looking fellows, with comparatively light hair and complexions. They wore short dark-coloured *jellabias* and red gun-covers twisted as turbans round their heads, and long plaited scalplocks falling down over their shoulders. At the second discharge the Son of a Gun, calling out, "Allah! Allah! the Beniboogoozgoo are upon us!" flung aside his matchlock and fled precipitately up the path. Mohammed, who had drawn his sword, made a furious cut at him as he passed ; but, making a bad shot, he only chopped off a mule's tail, and the Son of a Gun continued his way unhurt. Not for long, however. As he neared the precipitous rock the tall form of a Beniboogoozgoo warrior rose from behind a stone and covered him with his matchlock. The unhappy man, seeing his retreat cut off, turned, screaming with terror, and endeavoured to rejoin the caravan. But it was too late. A well-directed shot sent a bullet crashing through his spine, and with a cry of agony he fell prone to the earth.

Meanwhile Urquhart, Gerald, and myself had plunged into the bush, and, taking advantage of the cover offered by a small watercourse, whose sides were overgrown with ferns and flowering shrubs, we advanced to the attack. We were not long in picking off three or four of the Beniboogoozgoo, who, fancying that they had met with an easy prey, were rushing to the loot of the caravan. An ill-aimed volley in reply emptied the matchlocks of the remainder of our assailants ; so, laying aside our rifles, we rushed upon them with revolver in hand. Our foes evidently did not understand what six-shooters were ; but, drawing their swords, they prepared to make short work of the presumptuous and, as they thought, unarmed infidels. Their boldness, however, gave way to panic when a hailstorm of bullets rained upon them, dropping five or six of their number in less than half as many minutes. The survivors took to their heels and bolted into the bush. Gerald, who had emptied his revolver, snatched a sword from the hand of one of the dead robbers and started in pursuit of a big, strapping Beniboogoozgoo, who, from his bearing and commanding presence, seemed to be the leader of the gang.

Urquhart and myself returned to the mules. A pitched battle was being waged around them with sabre and knife between several of the enemy and our servants. The latter were outnumbered in the proportion of at least three to two; but they were, nevertheless, defending themselves valiantly. In the midst of the *mêlée* I could see the portly form of Mohammed hacking and hewing away with a vengeance, but, as far as we could see, doing surprisingly little execution for such a large expenditure of labour and breath. In fact, the hitting was altogether too wild, and the scrimmage too confused, for much serious damage to be done. A few shots from our revolvers made matters more even, and the attacking force, seeing reinforcements arriving on the scene of action, scampered off like rabbits into the thicket. Two or three of our Moors had received more or less severe sword-cuts, but none of them were of a particularly serious nature. Almarakshi, who, by the way, had shown great pluck throughout, had sustained the worst injuries, and he required a good deal of bandaging in the evening.

This over, and the enemy being now routed at all points, Urquhart and I went back into the bush in search of Gerald. I felt anxious lest his impetuosity should lead him into a trap, and he should be overpowered by numbers. Hearing a clatter of falling stones above us, we looked up in the direction whence the sound come, and saw the Berber bounding up the hillside like a deer, with Gerald pressing hotly in his rear. Gerald was a good stayer, and had won his college mile race at Cambridge; but the native, lithe and active as a cat, was having the best of him in the race, till he suddenly found his upward progress barred by a band of perpendicular rock which ran for a considerable distance along the mountain-side. Here he paused a moment, uncertain whether to turn to the right or left, and Gerald lessened the gap between them by several yards.

Seeing little hope of escape in flight, the African turned to bay, and, springing from his vantage ground on his pursuer, aimed a furious stroke at Gerald's head. The latter seemed to be taken by surprise, but raised his sword to parry the blow. Whether it was that Gerald was pumped by his long run, or merely that the force of the blow broke down his guard, I cannot say, but we were horrified to see his pith helmet fly from his head, and from the way he staggered it was plain he was wounded. Happily, he managed to recover himself sufficiently before his antagonist could repeat the blow, and, hitting out wildly, he wounded the Berber on the shoulder. With a howl of pain and rage, the latter sprang upon him like a wild beast; but Gerald evaded his onset, and, getting on even terms with his assailant, the two went at it hammer and tongs, blow following blow with astonishing rapidity.

Meanwhile Urquhart and myself were straining every nerve to get to Gerald's assistance; but the fight was over before we came up. Blood was flowing freely from both combatants. Gerald had received an ugly gash on the left side of his head, from which a red stream trickled down his cheeks. The Berber, too, was evidently weakened by his wound, and began to show signs of tiring. Gerald saw his advantage, and, pressing hotly on the enemy, delivered a succession of blows, which were but feebly returned. One final stroke ended the fight, and the Berber, letting his weapon drop from his nerveless hand, fell flat on the earth, with his head cleft almost in two.

"Well done, old chap!" cried Urquhart, coming up just as it was all over; "that last knock was a splendid one. Hullo! hold up, though," he exclaimed, as Gerald, turning ashy pale, reeled and would have fallen had we not supported him.

We carried him down to the caravan and tried to bring him back to consciousness by rubbing his temples and dashing water in his face. Some time elapsed, however, before our efforts were successful, and we began to grow alarmed lest he should be more seriously injured than we had supposed. I think it must have been nearly a quarter of an hour before a faint flush returned to his cheeks and his eyes opened and he tried to sit up.

"Where am I? what has happened?" were his first questions.

"Never mind, old fellow," said Urquhart, "lie still. You've had a nasty knock, but you will soon be all right. By the way," he continued, turning to me, "what has become of old Ali? I hope he hasn't got knocked on the head. We can't get along without him."

At this moment we heard loud cries of "Allah! Allah!" and other exclamations of woe accompanied by appeals for help. Looking in the direction of the sounds I saw the turbaned form of Mohammed descending the hillside, and a little lower down a white figure lying huddled up under a big stone. This last proved to be Ali, who in the extremity of his fear imagined Mohammed to be one of the Beniboogoozgoo who had discovered his hiding-place and was coming to kill him. Thinking he might have been wounded, I left Gerald in charge of Urquhart and went down to see what was the matter. It appeared that Ali, following the example of the Son of a Gun, had taken to his heels at the first appearance of the enemy, but, more fortunate than that luckless son of Araby, he had managed to gain the friendly shelter of a rock. From this coign of vantage he had witnessed the fight between Gerald and the Beniboogoozgoo, though a hillock had prevented his seeing the rout of the main body of the enemy.

"La bas, Hamdoollah! Hamdoollah la bas! Praise be to Allah, you have escaped injury. Allah is the only conqueror ; but the Father of the Nose is a very lion in the fight. How he vanquished that big son of Sheitan, the chief of the Beniboogoozgoo ! With my eyes I saw it."

"Well, you wouldn't be likely to have seen it with your ears, eh, stupid ! " I remarked.

"Oollah ! his bowels are immovable ; he has eaten of the lion's heart. As he pursued the enemy up the hill curiosity overcame timidity, and, stretching my head above the stone, with these eyes I beheld his prowess. But tell me, for the love of Allah, where is the Son of a Gun ? "

"Dead," I replied ; "he fled at the first shock of battle, and met with the fate which Allah in His justice sooner or later metes out to all cowards," I added severely.

"Holy Prophet!" he exclaimed, in no whit abashed; "dead? then is his soul even now in Jehannum."

This last reflection seemed to afford him unspeakable comfort, so that, having assured us that his brains were dried up (with astonishment), and having once more minutely described the state of his heart and liver and other internal organs, as he always did when under the influence of strong emotion, he was induced to get up and accompany us back to the caravan.

CHAPTER VI.

THROUGH THE SUS VALLEY.

THE events of the day rendered a halt of a week absolutely necessary. After searching about some time for a suitable spot we pitched the camp in a grassy glen watered by a limpid stream. Gerald was not in a fit state to travel, and several of the Moors had wounds which required care and rest. Urquhart was a very fair amateur surgeon, and for a while he was fully occupied in plastering and bandaging the sufferers, who under his treatment made rapid progress towards recovery.

The evening of the day of the fight was spent in burying the slain. We interred the unfortunate Son of a Gun at sundown in orthodox Mohammedan fashion. The corpse was placed in the grave in a sitting posture; the face turned towards Mecca, ready to spring up at the sound of the last trumpet. The Moors combed and plaited the oily scalplocks by which, according to Moorish belief, Azrael, the Angel of Death, would haul him up into paradise; and they chanted in unison the plaintive Moorish funeral dirge as they filled in the grave.

Urquhart and I spent a couple of days wandering over the mountains in search of *aoudad,* or wild mountain sheep, of which we were told a few were to be found in the more inaccessible places. Our first day was a blank ; but returning in the evening, we descried with the telescope a ram and his mate browsing on the patches of grass which grew at the foot of the precipices, and we arranged to go after them the following morning. Starting some hours before daybreak, we cautiously approached the place where the game had last been seen, and, hiding ourselves behind the rocks, we awaited the dawn. Gradually the silver moonbeams waned, and the stars paled before the conquering light of day. The eastern sky became of a pale saffron hue, flecked with streaks of pink ; while the west still retained the steely blue of night. As the light grew stronger and the golden sunbeams tipped the loftier peaks, and fell at length on the distant summits of Anti-Atlas, we took out our telescopes and carefully scanned the mountain-side. We had not long to look. Standing on a pinnacle of rock in sharp relief against the sky, with his forefeet gathered close together under him, was a splendid aoudad. There he stood, his massive horns curving gracefully backwards, and a white fringe of hair lining his throat and chest—a most dignified object—sniffing the morning breeze, and taking a look round before he began his breakfast. It was no use trying to stalk him while he remained up there ; we should have to wait until he came down. Presently, having thoroughly satisfied himself that the coast was clear, he made a couple of tremendous bounds forward, and, landing easily at the foot of the rock, he commenced to browse quietly.

Now is our time. Having first ascertained the direction of the wind, we make a long détour higher up the mountain, so as to approach him from above. Some long slopes of shale and detritus render our progress very slow, as we must as far as possible avoid making any noise. A scramble down some nasty rocks brings us to a low band of cliff, below which we hope to find our game. Creeping quietly to the edge, we look over. Yes, he is still there, and not fifteen yards apart is his consort, whom we have not seen this morning, both of them browsing without suspicion of danger.

Urquhart, being by far the better marksman, generously gives me the first shot. The animals are not more than a hundred yards off; but my hand is shaking like a leaf, and I feel sure that I shall miss. Those who know what "stag-fever" is will be able to sympathize with the feelings of a comparative tyro on the occasion of his first shot at big game.

Bang! The aoudad does not move, but stands still in the same spot. I must have missed him. Urquhart, however, who has more experience, knows better. He sees the beast straddle his legs apart—a ture sign that he is hit. Meanwhile the female makes off at full speed up the rocks. When about two hundred yards distant, she stops to look round for one moment after her mate. Urquhart, seizing his opportunity, lets drive a splendid shot, which takes effect behind the shoulder, and she tumbles headlong down a precipice nearly a hundred feet in height.

F

I then fired the second barrel of my Express at the ram, and missed him clean ; but it made no difference, as, sinking slowly to the ground, he rolled over on his side dead. They were a splendid pair, and it was with difficulty that we managed to carry the ram down to the encampment, leaving the female for the Moors to fetch the next day.

The following afternoon we continued our journey towards the Wad Sus. Our wounded had all made great progress, though Gerald complained occasionally of a severe pain in his head. As we got lower down, the country became more thickly, or perhaps I should say somewhat less sparsely, populated. The river Sus flowed through the broad smiling valley of the same name, enclosed on either side by lofty mountain ranges. Narrow lanes between high banks led us among gardens of acacia, fig, peach, and pomegranate trees, and the rose and honeysuckle bloomed in the hedges. The Sus was in flood, owing to the melting of the snows on the Atlas ; but we managed to cross without mishap, and made our way to a village close to the southern bank.

The inhabitants were naturally much surprised to see Christians ; but they were very friendly, and the sheikh of the village was almost demonstrative in his greeting.

"Salaam alikum, peace be with you. Mahhaba bik, you are welcome, O father of England," said he to Urquhart, touching the latter's hands and kissing his finger-tips, according to the graceful fashion of the Moors. He then assured us that we were his brothers, and that all that he possessed was ours. Arab hospitality is proverbial, and we very soon mooted the question of provisions. A long consultation followed among the villagers, resulting in the son of the sheikh being sent off by his father. In a few minutes he returned, bringing with him a very elderly-looking, long-bearded he-goat, who was introduced with all the ceremony his great age and dignity demanded. His appearance elicited a universal grunt of approbation from our retainers, who saw in him the prospect of savoury meat at our expense. Exclamations of "Oollah!" "Barikallah!" etc., were raised, mingled with the customary asseverations of the unity and greatness of Allah and the apostolic mission of Mohammed, though what on earth these things had to do with the bringing in of an old billy-goat I don't know. And then they all fell to praising the goat.

"Mashallah! isn't he a beauty?" said one.

"By the beard of the Prophet," cried another, "it makes my mouth water to look at him! Thanks be to Allah for His numerous mercies."

"Loor kebar, God is great! He will indeed make an excellent stew," remarked the third.

It was evident that our entertainers thought it a good opportunity to dispose of some of their stock on favourable terms; but we represented to our host that we could not on any account consent to rob him of such a venerable adjunct to his premises, especially as it would be impossible to do justice to him during our short stay.

"Allah kreem, God is bountiful," said our host. "If you do not like him, in the name of the blessed Moulai Idrees, have we not others? Ah-h Mohammed!" and he called his son, who promptly obeyed the paternal summons, and whispered a few words in his ear.

The boy again went out with the goat, and returned shortly with a small kid, the son or more remote descendant, we presumed, of the reverend animal we had just seen. A bargain was struck, and, simply exclaiming "Bismillah!" a Moor cut the poor little creature's throat, and we supped heartily off "bifteks" of kid, and very good they were.

Bidding adieu next morning to our courteous host, we continued our journey in a southerly direction. It is not my intention to describe the daily details of this part of our journey. Suffice it to say that after leaving the fertile, cultivated plains of the Sus valley, we entered a mountainous region of surpassing sterility and desolation. Here and there an occasional oasis, formed by the few and scanty streams which flowed down from the hills, broke the monotony of the scenery. We were now in the heart of the Anti-Atlas mountains, which we had hitherto supposed to be a chain running parallel to the main Atlas range, whereas, as a matter of fact, they constitute a hilly district of wide area. Now and again we passed over flat plains covered with a species of thorny scrub, and then once more found ourselves among the mountains. This part of the country appeared to be almost entirely uninhabited, and for days we never passed a soul upon the road, or saw a single human dwelling.

One evening, however, while sitting in the tents, we were surprised by the arrival of a visitor. He was a strange-looking creature, very ragged and unkempt, and his personal luggage consisted of a large leathern wallet which he carried on his back. He told us that he was a *hakim*, or physician, on his way to the Draa oasis, and he begged to be allowed to avail himself of the company and protection of our *goffla*, or caravan. Accordingly we had the pleasure of the fellow's society for the next two weeks, and he proved to be not unentertaining. In reality, he was an itinerant pedlar, a *weld el terek*, or son of the road, as the Moors phrased it. He was, withal, a terrible rogue, a quack and charlatan who lived on his wits. He knew no more about medicine than my mule, but traded on the superstition and ignorance of the people, to whom he dispensed charms and amulets, charging them extortionate fees for his services. He had not been long with us before he tried to palm off some of the contents of his wallet on our servants. To Almarakshi, who suffered from indigestion, he sold pills which, if all he said was true, must have outrivalled Beecham's. To others of the Moors who came to be doctored, he gave talismans of various sorts—charms to ward off the evil eye, hyæna's brains, and white powders, which he said were pounded dead men's bones, and which, if administered to an enemy, would bring him evil fortune. He also had for sale owls' eyes, frogs' hearts, lizards' tails, and verses of the Koran on bits of paper to be worn round the neck. His speciality, however, was some pieces of rag, which he swore were fragments of the nether garments of the Prophet. These he retailed at the rate of two *mitkal* (about three shillings) apiece, saying that they were a sure preventive against dysentery. The result of it all was that Almarakshi came to us with a wry face one morning, and said that that son of a burnt father, the hakim, had poisoned him. Personally, I did not believe that the pills contained any ingredient more injurious than camel-dung, which, indeed, formed the basis of most of the rascal's *materia medica ;* but he was, nevertheless, summoned before us, and warned not to play any more of his tricks on us.

" Have a care, have a care, Mr. Hakim," said Ali severely. " Eat your abominations yourself, or by the hairs of the Prophet's beard, and by your death, you shall finish your journey alone and with sore feet."

This dark threat of the bastinado, which of course we had not the least idea of carrying out, had its effect upon the hakim, and he did not try to palm off upon us any more of his wares. During the remainder of the time he journeyed with us he became exceedingly communicative and gave us an account of his past experiences, which were somewhat amusing. He was strongly of opinion that life was a game of see-saw, and he certainly seemed to have had a full measure of its ups and downs. Sometimes, he said, he was well off; but prosperity made him careless, and he generally ended by being detected in some piece of roguery which resulted in his being flogged and his ill-gotten gains being taken from him. However, he never grew discouraged. His latest speculation had been in what he was pleased to call tobacco, a taste for which he had been endeavouring to instil among the natives of North Marocco.

" Let's see some of your best smoking mixture," said Gerald, and the rogue pulled out of his wallet a vile compound, smelling abominably. It was a fine blend of camel-dung, dried leaves, and straw, and he doled out this concoction to the natives at the rate of three mitkal the pound.

"Allah !" he said, "I should have made a fine thing out of it had not the kaid (may the dogs defile his grave) found me out one day and, after giving me one hundred stripes, burned my whole stock."

A few days afterwards he told us he was about to leave us. We asked him where he was going, and he replied, "May your kindness never be less. May Allah prolong your life, and may your end be happy. Whither I go, or what I shall do, I know not. Iftshallah ! God will show. One thing only I know, that as long as there are fools in the world and I have a moderate supply of camel-dung, I shall never want for a livelihood. There is but one God, and Mohammed is His Prophet."

With these words the hakim took his leave.

CHAPTER VII.

THE LION HUNT.

LYING awake that evening in my camp-bed, I was meditating on these parting remarks of the hakim and his strange career. "As long as there are fools in the world!" Verily, O hakim, thou needest have no fear on the score of the supply diminishing. And then, as I deplored the dark ignorance and superstition which made him find these poor Moors so easy a prey, I fell to debating in my own mind whether, after all, we civilized inhabitants of northern climes are very much wiser. Have we not, too, our sleek charlatans with their social, religious, or æsthetic crazes; our seemingly cracked-brained, but in reality calculating eccentrics, and do not they prey upon society even as the hakim preyed upon the Moors? Do not our spiritualists and magic-mongers trade upon the credulity of civilized mankind (and I take it that the superstitions of the West differ from those of the East in kind rather than degree) in precisely the same way as our hakim friend traded upon the ignorance of the Arabs? Impudence it is, impudence, that wins the day all the world over, whether it be in a London drawing-room or in the wilds of Africa, and the man who has un-limited faith in himself and in the boundless gulli-bility of his fellow-men may achieve great things, whatever or wherever may be his sphere of action.

The place where the hakim left us was at the commencement of an oasis near the outskirts of the Anti-Atlas. Crossing a range of barren rugged mountains by a pass called Onkh el Jimmel, or Camel's Neck, we came in sight of the oasis, which was formed by a streamlet that issued from a narrow cleft in the mountains. Small groves of palm-trees were dotted about here and there, presenting a most inviting appearance after the sterile regions we had passed through. The sides of the mountains, too, became less barren, being clothed in places with dense scrub, the bushes of which attained in places a height of several feet. The meadows were inter-sected by numerous water-conduits, and tiny patches of cultivation were scattered about among collections of mud huts, which could hardly be dignified with the title of villages.

Our servants were fagged with the continuous long marches, and some of the pack-animals were begin-ning to develop sore backs, so we arranged to rest a few days in the oasis before continuing our journey southwards. Moreover, Gerald, whose wound had not yet completely healed, felt a return of the pains in his head, doubtless the result of over-exertion following upon a considerable loss of blood. Another induce-ment to remain lay in the fact that game was reported to abound in the neighbourhood. The natives assured us that there were *halloof bezzuf* (any number of wild boar), and that the surrounding hills were infested with lions, who were the terror of the villagers and committed great depredations on their flocks. They had lately been so bold in their attacks that the cattle at night had to be enclosed in a pound, surrounded by a ditch and rampart surmounted by a formidable *cheveux de frise* of thornbushes, but the lions had actually leaped inside and killed some of the animals in the enclosure. Moreover, the boars destroyed their crops, and the Moors could do little or nothing to stop their inroads. Accordingly, a few days after our arrival we arranged a great hunt, to the delight of the natives, who, besides being the keenest of sportsmen, were only too pleased to have an opportunity of taking vengeance on their four-footed foes.

"May God preserve you, Nazarenes," said an old white-haired sheikh. "We are well-nigh ruined by the inroads of the swine, and our hearts are faint with terror by reason of the lions."

Urquhart told Ali to make inquiries as to the best way of going to work. "Ala rasi, on my head be it," said he, "to perform your bidding;" and he set forth to interview some of the Arabs in the neighbourhood. On his return in the evening he told us that he had made the acquaintance of the sheikh of a neighbouring village, one Hadj Mohammed Abd el Kader, a gentleman, he assured us, of immovable bowels, an eater of the lion's heart, and possessing great experience in the chase. Ali advised us to entrust this man with the principal arrangements for the hunt, which was to take place the next day but one.

The following evening we left the oasis, and made

our way up a narrow gorge to a small collection of
mud huts, which was said to be the village of Hadj
Mohammed. That worthy was at his prayers when
we arrived, but was not long in putting in an appearance. After the customary greetings, and his usual
inquiries after the state of the sheikh's brain, and
trusting that the latter was feeling as sane as could
be expected, considering the unseasonable weather,
etc., etc., Ali introduced us. The sheikh received us
with great cordiality, touching our hands and placing
his own on his heart to show the depth of his good
will towards us. He exclaimed that we were not only
his brothers, but also his father and mother and all
the rest of his relations, including, no doubt, as Gerald
afterwards remarked, his grandmothers, aunts, and
female cousins to the third degree. He told us that
he had selected a spot for the hunt some three or
four miles further up the valley, and he suggested
that we should camp out there for the evening so as
to make an early start the following morning.

The next evening, accordingly, our tent was pitched
in a curious cup-like hollow—a sort of Devil's Punch-
bowl—surrounded by low hills. These hills were
covered with dense scrub, and were the chosen haunts
of the boars and lions, whence they issued to make their
nocturnal raids on the crops and flocks of the Moors.
As the evening wore on several natives who were to
act as our beaters on the morrow, put in an appearance. A wild-looking lot they were, many of them
having singularly fair complexions, which are not an
uncommon feature among the mountain tribes of
Marocco. A roaring fire was lit, the flames whereof
blazed and crackled merrily, sending forth showers of

sparks, which leaped high into the darkness. Overhead the smoke hung like a grey pall, on which the firelight shed lurid red reflections. The Moors squatted round and warmed their stomachs at the blaze, looking like so many bundles of old clothes. The talk was chiefly of wild beasts and hunting, as was only to be expected, and some splendid yarns were soon in circulation. Legend was particularly rife concerning the size and ferocity of a certain man-eating lion who had devoured several of the natives and was the terror of the entire neighbourhood.

"Allah kreem!" said an old Moor, who was nursing his long gun on his knee, "God is merciful! it was scarce two moons ago when I was returning home late one evening, that I saw the *s'ba* (lion). May I never see the houris of Paradise if he was not as big as an ox, and his eyes glowed like coals of fire. My heart was in my throat, my liver descended, and my knees were loosened with fear; but God was merciful, and withheld the beast from attacking me. How wonderful is Allah!"

"Ya lateef, God have pity!" cried a youth on whose chin the beard of manhood was just beginning to sprout, determined not to be outdone; "why, I saw the lion myself only last night."

This assertion being received with grunts expressive of incredulity, the youth proceeded to tell of a conversation he had heard the previous evening between the lion in question and an enormous boar. The Moors, I should mention, like the peasantry in some of the more out-of-the-way parts of Europe, credit all animals with powers of speech and understanding, and maintain imaginary conversations with them at great length. "Mashallah!" cried the youth, "it is true every word of it. Ala rasi, on my head be it if I lie." He then proceeded to deliver his narrative with much volubility and emphatic gestures. He was lying out, he said, by night beside a pool in the forest on the look out for the game which came thither to drink. Soon after midnight a huge boar appeared, followed at a short interval by the man-eating lion. He was sure it was the man-eater because his skin was mangy and the hair had come off in patches on his back.

"Salaam alikum, peace be with you," said the lion politely.

"And with you peace," returned the boar. And then they fell to talking together just as might two human beings.

The youth could not catch all the rest of the conversation, as the animals were some distance off, but he distinctly heard the lion say that some pigs of Christians had arrived in the country and that, by the camel of Mohammed, he meant to burn their fathers—*anglicé*, "do for them"—and scatter their relations at the earliest opportunity. The Father of Tusks approved the sentiments of the tawny-maned sheikh of the forest, but he took exception to the phrase "pigs of Christians." Not by any means because it was an insult to the Christians, but because he (the boar) objected to being named in such company. He was as good a Moslem, or a better, than the lion, and would prove it to him in battle if the latter wished. "La ilaha il Allah, there is but one God," concluded the boar defiantly, glaring at the lion and whetting his tusks significantly.

The lion, terrified by the ferocious aspect of the boar, whose ivories gleamed in the moonlight, and whose bristles stood on end with rage, apologetically said that he meant no offence when speaking of "pigs." He was alluding to the effeminate inmate of the domestic sty, not to the free, powerful, and noble creature he saw before him. The boar was pacified, and commenced grubbing up the ground, and the Arab, being too frightened to fire, crept away to his home.

"Holy Prophet!" said the old Arab who had spoken first, and who was by no means pleased at having his tale capped by another and more astounding yarn,—"Holy Prophet! did you ever hear such a liar? In the name of Moulai Idrees, what dogs' sons are we that we should each eat such dirt, and eat it at the hands of a boy, too?"

The youth sprang up with his hand on his dagger, and would have made a hole in the old gentleman's skin, had not his companions restrained him. "By my beard"—the oath could hardly be considered a binding one, for he swore by what did not exist— "by my beard, but I will finish you off, you son of a burnt father. Lai sti shimlek, may God scatter your relations!"

An end was put to the fracas by the sheikh rising and announcing his intention of retiring to rest.

"Good evening to you, Nazarenes," he said. "May your slumbers be light. Take your rest now. Ghadda, inshallah, to-morrow, please Allah, we will prevail against the Father of Tusks and defile the graves of the marauding lions."

Not feeling inclined to turn in immediately, Gerald

and I lit our pipes and strolled out a short distance
into the forest. The night was fine and warm, so,
seating ourselves on the top of a boulder of rock, we
puffed away in silence. It was a strangely weird
scene. One side of the hollow wherein we were
encamped was in deep shadow; on the other, the
moonbeams glinted from the white rocks with a
peculiarly ghostly effect, and the stars flickered like
fire-flies in the steel-blue firmament. Below us the
flashes of light from the dying embers of the camp
fire fell fitfully on the wild forms of the recumbent
Moors. Now and again an owl would raise its
melancholy cry, as if presaging woe; and the hyæna's
laugh and the hideously human cry of the jackal
jarred discordantly on our ears. Save for these
sounds and the shivering of the breeze in the thicket
all was still and silent as the grave.

We must have sat on the rock nearly half an hour,
until at length, our pipes being out, we prepared to
go in.

"Hist! What is that?" whispered Gerald, clutch-
ing my arm and pointing towards a small gully
enveloped in shadow, which descended to our camping-ground.

Straining my eyes in the direction indicated, I
fancied I could discern the form of some large animal
creeping stealthily through the bushes, but before I
could form any conception as to what it was, a most
awful roar like a thunder-clap, followed by a succession
of piercing shrieks, broke the stillness of the night.
A huge lion, doubtless the man-eater spoken of by
the Moors, had sprung out of the bushes upon a man
who was lying curled up a little outside the circle

round the fire, and, with his victim in his jaws, made off up the hill. In the camp all was shouting and confusion. A few random shots were fired in the direction where the lion had last been seen, and some of the bolder spirits started in pursuit. Snatching up our rifles, Gerald and I joined in the chase, though our hopes of saving the man's life were but small. We were forcing our way with difficulty through the thicket, little more than a hundred yards from the tents, when I stumbled over something soft. Looking down, I saw that it was the body of the Moor, which the lion, alarmed by the number of pursuers, had been compelled to drop. Striking a match, I recognized the features of the youth who had regaled us with the story of the boar and the lion. He little thought, poor fellow, when he told us the tale, that he was destined to make the man-eater's acquaintance in so speedy and tragic a manner. He was quite dead, having received terrible injuries. The back of his head was smashed completely in, evidently by a blow from the brute's paws, and his left shoulder was bitten nearly through.

" Allah kreem, God be merciful to us! " said the old Arab with whom he had the quarrel. " Azrael hath indeed taken him from us. He will never tell any more stories. Ah welli, woe is me! may his soul rest in peace! 'twas the will of Allah."

On our return to the tents with the body the fire was rekindled and we set a watch of three Moors. The latter were all terrified out of their lives, being convinced that the lion was a *djin*, or evil spirit, if he was not the Sheitan himself, and I don't think any of them slept very much more that night.

Nothing further, however, occurred to alarm us, and the following morning saw us afoot, eager to avenge the death of the Moor. At the start we had perhaps fifty beaters, but as the day wore on men kept dropping in by twos and threes till there must have been nearly a hundred of them. Every man who had a *selokee* (greyhound) or a gun brought them with him. The selokees were not exactly the sort of animals one would see at a coursing meeting in England. In fact, though they called them greyhounds, I should imagine the breed was as ambiguous as that of the dog described by the station-master as having been "got by a porter out of a third-class carriage." The first beat was in that part of the forest where boars principally abounded. The guns, to the number of nearly twenty, were posted in line half-way up the hillside. Some of them climbed up into the branches of stunted olive trees; others perched themselves on rocks anywhere their fancy took them, and all kept their long matchlocks ready primed. Seeing the irregularity of the line, and knowing the recklessness of the natives in their use of firearms, I did not feel at all comfortable, and secretly hoped that the Father of Tusks would not break cover in my direction. The sequel proved my fears to be not unfounded.

When everything was ready the line of beaters advanced. The sheikh led off with the customary adjuration, "Lain el Sheitan, may God curse the devil!" and spat on the ground as he said it. The other Moors followed his example. Whenever any game was started shouts of "How! How!" "Deeb, How! How!" when a jackal was seen; "Thaleb,

How! How!" when a fox broke cover,[1] with much jabbering and pantomime. At last louder howls of "Halloof, How! How!" accompanied by the braying of horns and the yapping of innumerable curs told us that a boar was on foot. And then they all started swearing with one accord. Heavens, how those Arabs do swear! None of your commonplace monosyllabic oaths, but long-winded, elaborate maledictions which would cover half a page of writing. The boar's father and grandfather were burnt. All sorts of unpleasant scandals in his family history were raked up. His mother and sister, it appeared, each had an old jackass for a sweetheart; his great-grandfather, who was the miserable offspring of an incestuous union between two other pigs higher up the family tree, was now being consumed to a cinder in Jehannum. The various improprieties of all the other pigs and piglings were set forth at length, and the graves of the whole lot were indiscriminately defiled.

The sturdiest tusker could not weather such a storm of imprecations, so I was not surprised to see a grand old boar, a regular "forty-incher," as they say in India, with gleaming tusks and bristles grizzled with age, break cover. A pack of sclokees yapped and yelped at his heels as he came charging along like a thousand of bricks up the hill. As he neared the line of ambushed sportsmen he was received with a volley

---

[1] This view-holloa of the Moors has suggested a derivation for a phrase whose origin is enveloped in much obscurity. Is it not just possible that "Tally Ho" may be an Anglicized version of "Thaleb How?" In any case, if the similarity be but a coincidence, it must be admitted that it is a very curious one.

accompanied by more shouts and curses. Bullets screamed through the air in all directions, and one of the native hunters shouted out that the *harami* (accursed beast) had "devoured much lead."

"Nay," replied an old white-haired hunter, "your words are wind. I know you boar of old. He is a djin. Many times have I fired at him (and ye know my aim never misses), and the bullets have fallen harmless from his side. May Allah curse the devil!"

The result seemed to lend colour to the old fellow's theory, for, with a defiant whisk of his tail, piggy bounded up the hill and cantered into the thicket apparently untouched. The firing, however, had not been altogether without effect, for, hearing a prolonged howl of woe, I turned round in time to see the gun next but one on my right leap up into the air on one leg, and subside violently in a sitting posture to the ground. Running up, I inquired what was the matter.

"Walo! walo! la bas; nothing, nothing; it is all right," said my next neighbour. He had only put a slug through the calf of the unfortunate man's leg, and that is a mere trifle in these parts. If he had shot a favourite dog it would have been a very different matter. "Mektoob Allah, 'twas written by Allah. Who can resist the decrees of Fate?" he remarked sententiously.

His victim was in no wise comforted by these pious reflections, but set to work to curse him with a will. "Ah welli, welli, woe is me!" he wailed piteously; and once more the air grew blue and thick with Arab profanity levelled at the head of the clumsy marksman. With much inconsistency he called him a man without a father, expressing in the same breath the wish that the said father might grill in the lower regions. He insulted his female kinsfolk, and asked for his mother's marriage certificate ; and he announced his intention, as soon as the wound in his leg was healed, of performing a pilgrimage for the express purpose of defiling his grandfather's grave.

The object of all this bad language listened with great calmness, made some sagacious and highly original observations upon the unalterable laws of destiny, and commenced reloading his gun, shovelling in the powder by handfuls and ramming the lead vigorously home.

The wounded man having been removed and his hurts attended to, the hunt was proceeded with. At midday a halt was called, and the Moors set to work to call off the dogs. Some of the latter had been killed by the boar, others had received rips, and the grief of their owners testified to the affection with which the Moors regard their four-footed friends. We found that seven boars, besides smaller game, such as foxes and jackals, had been bagged. The beaters had worked hard and showed themselves well up to their work.

"Smart, intelligent fellows, these hunters," remarked Urquhart to me as we shouldered our rifles and followed the beaters. " I have often noticed in un-civilized countries that the best hunters are the most intelligent men in general matters, while with us I fear the reverse is the case. How is it that in England hunting—perhaps the finest of all sports—tends to make gruel of people's brains? Your in-veterate fox-hunter can so seldom be got to take a rational interest in anything beyond his horses and hounds."

"Perhaps," I replied, "it is because with these people hunting is business as well as pleasure. Anyhow, what you say about our country Nimrods at home is perfectly true."

The more serious business of the day, the lion hunt, had been reserved for the afternoon. Under the guidance of the sheikh, we crossed a low range of hills, from whose summit we had an extensive view of the rugged mountain country we had passed through. Peak beyond peak reared its head towards the north, and over all could be seen the looming white mass of the main Atlas chain. The scenery was not in itself strictly beautiful, yet the mellow light of the African autumn shed a peculiar glamour over everything, and, veiling the landscape in a soft delicate haze, robbed it of its sterner features. A tramp of half an hour brought us to the hill where the man-eater had last been seen on the previous night; and with a gravity befitting the occasion the sheikh commenced his dispositions for the hunt. Complete silence was enforced, and the Moors, repressing for once their propensity to chatter, conversed only in whispers. Indeed, dread of the man-eater had so damped their ardour that I had some doubts as to their beating the covert properly. However, when once they had begun, their sporting instincts got the better of their fears, and they stuck manfully to the work.

At Urquhart's request some of the Moors armed with guns were induced to join the ranks of the beaters, instead of endangering our lives and their own by posting themselves near us. At the top of the hill above our camping-ground was a plateau nearly half a mile in width. In the centre of this plateau there was a slight depression covered with a dense jungle of thorny bushes. A low band of precipitous rocks ran along the further side of the depression, which would effectually prevent any game from making its escape in that direction. Six or eight of the best native marksmen were posted in a line opposite these rocks, while Gerald, Urquhart, and myself took up our position facing the beaters.

The hunt commenced with prayer to Allah and the usual imprecations upon the lions, and then the beaters, keeping close together and in good line, entered the bush. As they neared the dense thicket the dogs suddenly started barking furiously, and then there was a hullabaloo, similar to, but louder than, that caused by the finding of the boar. Cries of " S'ba ! S'ba !" (the lion ! the lion !), mingled with curses both loud and deep, rent the air and put us all on the alert. For awhile nothing could be seen, but presently I caught sight of a very old lion, his coat grey and mangy with age, making off slowly in the direction of the line of native sportsmen. They, perceiving he was not likely to prove a very formidable foe, stood their ground and fired at him. Some of the shots, strange to say, took effect, and, with a feeble growl, the wretched beast rolled over dead. The delight of the natives was unbounded. They yelled with triumph and heaped insults on their prostrate enemy. Emboldened by this success, the beaters summoned up courage to enter the thicket. They had not proceeded far when a most tremendous roar, which seemed to come from the centre of the jungle, sent them flying pell-mell back. Louder and louder grew the roars, and it became evident there were at least two lions, probably the man-eater and his mate. The dogs showed more pluck than their masters, who contented themselves with standing outside and throwing stones and mud into the bush.

Meanwhile the selokees kept barking loudly and and viciously, the Moors redoubled their yells, and what with the roaring of the lions, there was an indescribable hubbub. At length, finding her quarters getting too hot for her, the lioness made a bolt of it, but, catching sight of the hunters, she quickly went back into the thicket. The dogs, however, pressing close upon her, she burst once more out of the bush and charged down on the line of beaters, who broke and scattered in all directions, and so made her escape.

The place where I was stationed was about eighteen yards' distance from the thicket, the intervening space being covered with a sparse growth of underwood. Round knobs of rock here and there protruded their bald crowns from out the hairy growth of scrub and brushwood. I was looking at one of these knobs, when I suddenly espied an enormous lion crouching, with his head turned towards me and his body partially hidden by the rock. The distance was not much over fifty yards, so, though I am by no means a good shot, I let drive at him with the right barrel of my Express. I heard a savage growl, and when the smoke cleared away there was the lion in the same position on the rock, his shaggy head between his paws. " I've done for him," thought I; " he is disabled, and I'll finish him off with the left barrel." Suddenly, just as I was drawing a bead on him, he sprang up with a terrific roar, and bounded towards me, making a curious grumbling noise something like the barking of a dog. I took a snap shot at him, and then he disappeared from my sight in some thick underwood. One moment I fancied I could see the bushes shaking about twenty yards off, as though some large beast was moving through them, but I could distinguish nothing. About a minute passed in this way. I was peering in the direction where I thought I had last seen the lion, when a roar, which seemed to issue from the bowels of the earth, split the drum of my ear. I was conscious of a large body darkening the air as it flew towards me ; a tremendous blow descended like a thunder-bolt on my left shoulder, and the next moment I was lying on my back on the ground in the grip of the man-eater.

For awhile—I know not how long, but it was probably only a few moments—the shock deprived me of consciousness. When I came round my senses were numbed, and I could not realize the awful nature of the situation in which I was placed. The brute was standing over me, making that fearful noise which visitors to the "Zoo" may hear any day at feeding time. In the bush the shouts and cries of the Arabs who had seen me fall sounded confused and indistinct in my ear. The lion's paw was resting heavily on my chest, his eyes glared at me like two live coals, and his filthy breath came full in my face. The teeth of a man-eater are always decayed and rotten, owing to his diet of human flesh, which disagrees with him and also makes his skin mangy. An age seemed to pass as I lay in the brute's grip, but Urquhart told me afterwards that the whole thing was over in little more than a minute. Of course I thought it was all up with me. Every moment I expected that my head would be in his mouth, and that with one crunch of those mighty jaws an end would be put to my existence. Yet I do not remember feeling any particular sensation of fear, no doubt owing to the fact of my being in a state of partial stupor. Yet in a way my faculties seemed awake, and, indeed, abnormally active. A thousand things passed in rapid review through my brain. Innumerable scenes of my early youth, long-forgotten trivial incidents, came before me, just as drowning men are said to recall at the point of death all the events of their past life.

Happily, the beast did not use his fangs upon me. The instinct which causes all creatures of the cat tribe to toy with their victims before destroying them no doubt saved my life, as it gave my companions time to come to my rescue. Presently there was heard the crack of a rifle. Urquhart had fired. There was a dull thud as the Express bullet crashed into the man-eater's side, expanding within and tearing his vitals to pieces. With a hideous noise, half growl, half snarl, the beast fell right on me, ripping my thigh badly with his hind paws in his death-agony. Gerald and Urquhart came running up and pulled me out from under the carcase ; then the natural reaction set in, and I swooned away once more.

*   *   *   *   *

These stars are not put in for the sake of effect, but in order to help me to convey to my readers my sensations as I went off. Ten thousand constellations danced before my eyes. The firmament waltzed round me, the sun became as blood, and everything seemed turned topsy-turvy.

When I regained consciousness Urquhart and Gerald were bending over me, dashing water in my face. I tried to move, but a terrible pain in my shoulder caused me to cry out, and I was forced to lie still. I thought my shoulder was dislocated, but on examination it proved to be only terribly bruised, while the claws of the man-eater had inflicted some ugly scratches on my thighs. Otherwise I had got off pretty well. The Moors skilfully improvised a sort of litter out of a couple of poles and some branches, on which I was carried down to the tent, and on the following morning they took me down to our main camp in the oasis.

The lion proved to be a very large one, but the skin was in such bad condition that it was not worth preserving. One of my shots, probably the first, had struck him in the lower part of the belly, inflicting a slight wound, which only served to infuriate him. There was great rejoicing among the Moors when the result of our hunt became known. Bonfires were lit, and there was much blowing of horns and rheetahs, and beating of tom-toms, and feasting and merry-making. True, we had only killed two lions, but we were assured that this was all that was needed, as the others would be scared out of the country and would not venture to return for a long time. My injuries necessitated our prolonging our stay in the oasis, and two or three days elapsed before I could get about at all. My shoulder was very stiff and painful for a long time, while the wounds in my thigh would not heal readily and from time to time gave me trouble long afterwards.

CHAPTER VIII.

A MOORISH DINNER-PARTY.

IN gratitude for our delivering them from the man-eating pest, the sheikh of our village entertained us at a great feast on the evening of the fourth day after the hunt. Soon after sundown a deputation of Moors arrived at our tents, bearing dishes with tall bee-hive shaped wicker covers, and a variety of delicacies were set down before us. The first course consisted of the inevitable *kuskussoo*, the national dish of Marocco, a mess of flour, *smin* (rancid butter) and shredded meat. Next followed sundry highly flavoured stews reeking of oil and garlic, chickens, and a kind of moist cake like half-baked muffins. The repast was washed down with weak green tea as sweet as syrup, and strongly flavoured with mint and verbena. Altogether, as may be imagined, the meal was a rather trying one, and I was not sorry when the sheikh, who had come in to see how we were enjoying ourselves, took his leave and gave us a chance of sending the stuff away.

As soon as our appetites were appeased (and we found that a little of such viands went a long way) the dishes and their wicker covers were removed, and the servants' dinner was brought in. We were anxious to see what a Moorish dinner-party was like, and certainly we came in for a very comic entertainment. Through the door of their tent we could see Ali, Mohammed, Almarakshi, and the sheikh seated in a circle round a veritable mountain of kuskussoo which was steaming away like a volcano in their midst.

"Barikallah! Praised be Allah!" exclaimed Ali. "A sweet savour of kuskussoo assaileth my nostrils, and my senses are gratified at the prospect of repletion."

"Staferallah!" chimed in Mohammed with his favourite ejaculation. "The sight of yonder dishes is grateful to mine eyes as the sound of bubbling fountains to the ears of thirsty travellers ; for, verily, hunger gnaweth like a wolf at my entrails, and in the pit of my stomach a great gulf is fixed, and needs must it be replenished."

A sheep had been killed for the occasion, and roast mutton *ad libitum* was served up along with the kuskussoo. The bread having been broken in orthodox fashion, and the " Bismillah " pronounced, they all fell to. The Moors eat with their hands, everybody thrusting his fingers into the steaming pile and gobbling away like mad so as not to come short. For some time the whole party was too busily engaged in stuffing to talk, the silence only being broken by occasional eructations, which are considered quite good form at meals in Marocco so long as they are followed by some pious exclamation, such as "Hamdoollah!" "Bismillah!" or "Staferallah!"

I never saw such guzzling, but they showed no signs of stopping, till each man had swallowed enough to satisfy five hungry Christians, when Mohammed, who seemed to play the best knife and fork (metaphorically speaking) of the party, leaned back with a deep sigh of satisfaction and commenced sucking his fingers. This operation concluded, he tore a big piece of fat meat from the joint and stuffed it into the sheikh's mouth, a compliment quite *à la mode Marocaine*, which was seemingly much appreciated by the latter. Our cook then commenced a little speech lauding the generosity of his entertainer, but he had not proceeded far before he was seized with a violent attack of hiccoughs, which considerably marred the effect of his after-dinner oratory.

"Holy Prophet! friend Ali," he said, turning towards the Persian, "but this is indeed an excellent repast. Our worthy host here (hiccough)—may Allah prolong his life—hath feasted us right royally. Mashallah! (hiccough) Ya lateef! What a pity! I was about to say (hiccough) Bismillah!—that (three hiccoughs)—Staferallah!" and he stopped for want of breath.

"Hamdoollah! God be praised," gravely returned the sheikh, taking a handful of kuskussoo and shovelling it into Mohammed's mouth, well nigh choking him and causing more strange noises and invocations to Allah and the Prophet, and finally sending him off into a fit of coughing, which lasted until he was black in the face.

The unfortunate Mohammed not being sufficiently recovered to continue his speech, Ali presently took up his parable and finished it for him.

"By my soul, Hadj Mohammed, and by your death," he said, helping himself to a juicy morsel of mutton, "of a verity, this is a most toothsome sheep. I trow our father Mohammed (the peace and blessing of Allah be upon him and his descendants!) never tasted a better. Verily, our footsteps have been fortunate; our ways have been set in pleasant places. The sun of contentment and prosperity hath shone upon our faces. The cravings of appetite have been sated with the bread of plenteousness, and the oil of gratitude shall anoint the head of generosity. The blessing of Allah and His holy Prophet be upon your beard, O sheikh."

This oration was received with violent eructations all round, expressive of their approbation of the speaker's sentiments, accompanied by more exclamations of "Mashallah!" "Hamdoollah!" and other pious, but utterly irrelevant, expressions. Then the hubble-bubble was lit, and after they had sat and smoked for awhile the party broke up and we all went to bed.

Next morning Mohammed came up to us and complained of a severe stomach-ache. He assured us that his digestion had never been right since he had made the acquaintance of the Son of a Gun, and he was convinced that he had been bewitched by that squinting offspring of the powers of darkness. One would have thought that a man who had disposed of a cubit foot or so of kuskussoo and half a leg of mutton, had fairly earned an attack of indigestion, but human nature is never willing to allow its gastric disorders to be the result of its own excesses. Mr. Pickwick said it was all the salmon. Mohammed, who carried his animosity beyond the grave, laid the blame on the evil eye of the Son of a Gun. He was, further, particularly indignant because the dried leg of a toad, which he had purchased from the hakim to be worn next the pit of his stomach as a sure preventive against indigestion, had completely failed of its purpose.

Gerald promised to prepare him a charm which would work far more quickly than his toad's leg, and produced from his pocket a couple of Seltzer powders. Putting the contents of the papers in a glass, he poured in the water, and, as the mixture bubbled and fizzed, Mohammed took to his heels, exclaiming that the Sheitan was in the cup, and it was with much difficulty that he was persuaded to drink it off.

"May Allah preserve us from wicked spirits and from the influence of the evil eye," he exclaimed, as he tossed off the potion and nearly choked himself.

The next morning he appeared a trifle paler than usual.

"Well, my old great-grandfather of a brass-handled stewpan," cried Gerald (in allusion to an article of Mohammed's *batterie de cuisine*), slapping him on the back, "how goes it this morning? Are not the charms of the kaffirs in truth more efficacious than those of the Moors?"

"La bas, Hamdoollah! Well, praise be to Allah, I am very well, all things considered. But "— here he placed his hand on his portly front, as he winced visibly and big drops of perspiration stood out on his forehead—"of a verity, O Father of the Nose, the medicines of the Nazarenes be potent."

As soon as my wounds were sufficiently healed we prepared to resume our journey. Our servants, especially Mohammed, were by no means pleased to leave the comfortable quarters and good living they had been enjoying in the oasis, and, truth to tell, it was not without regret that we ourselves bade adieu to the simple, kindly peasant folk, among whom we had passed so many pleasant days. With all their faults, I cannot help loving the Arabs. There is something wonderfully taking about their quaint ways and keen sense of humour, their earnestness, and wonderful patience under misfortune, and I really believe that though the whole tribe of them were always burning our fathers and consigning us Christians to everlasting perdition, they were all very sorry to see us depart. Their hatred of the Nazarene is not natural to them, but is simply the result of their religious training. They have been taught to look upon us as people whose throats are to be cut in this world, and who are to be grilled eternally in the next, and, to do them justice, many of them endeavour to carry out their part of the programme to the letter. After awhile, when you get to know them better, and have penetrated this outer crust of barbarous fanaticism, you come upon the true, kindly nature beneath. You then discover that, far from being demons actuated by a spirit of hideous malevolence towards those who have the misfortune to disagree with their religious convictions, they are ordinary human beings endowed with a full share of the milk of human kindness.

Truly, it is a curious thing to think what fiends to all outward appearance the spirit of religious intolerance makes of men otherwise the most amiable and inoffensive.

Take the case of our worthy friend the sheikh of this village, a person whom we all like and esteem. Mingled with his prayers for his own welfare and deliverance from the wrath to come, are imprecations on the heads of all unbelievers, and the expression of his hope for their speedy destruction and eternal torment. Yet I would not do him the injustice to suppose that it would afford him the slightest satisfaction—nay, I am sure his good heart would be much distressed—if he knew that we were suffering the horrible things he invoked upon us. But, after all, are the members of our own faith much less merciless in this respect than the followers of the Prophet? Do not we on certain solemn occasions consign to everlasting anguish all who think differently from ourselves on certain matters concerning which we profess to have exclusive knowledge? Paterfamilias solemnly mumbles his Athanasian Creed, then takes his stroll at Church Parade in the Park, and eats a hearty lunch in the serene consciousness of having done his duty as a man and a Christian in consigning three-fourths of the entire human race to perdition; and the matter doesn't distress him in the slightest.

But I am being drawn into a religious discussion, and that will never do. The one fact I wish to bring out is that the sheikh, in spite of his fanaticism, was as Gerald phrased it, "a thundering good chap," and we were all sorry to leave him. He had expressed great admiration for Urquhart's mule, and before we left he said he would be glad to buy it. Finding, however, that the owner was unwilling to part with

the beast, he forbore from pressing him. " Suboork-
allah ! may God bless it," he politely remarked, and
with many expressions of good-will, invoking (in most
unorthodox fashion, by the way) the blessings of
Allah on our heads, he bade us God-speed upon our
journey.

CHAPTER IX.

THE FAIR AT SOK EL ARBA.

AFTER leaving the oasis, we soon got beyond the mountains. The increasing scarcity of vegetation, and the wide tracts of sand which had to be crossed, showed that we were getting nearer the desert, though as yet we were far from the Sahara proper. Wells, too, were becoming less frequent, and the water of worse quality, so it was with a feeling of relief that, after several days' travelling in a south-easterly direction, we caught sight of a few palm-trees in the distance which we knew betokened the presence of an oasis. Our pleasure was still greater when we found that we had arrived at the valley of the Wad Draa, the largest and most important river in this part of Africa. For some days our course would be along its banks, and all natural obstacles to our progress would cease for a time. The valley was far less fertile than that of the Wad Sus, but it was nevertheless fairly well populated. Negroes appeared to form a large proportion of the natives, and we heard the Berber tongue more frequently spoken than Arabic. The river flowed in a tortuous course between high mud-banks clothed here and there with tamarisk and oleanders. The cultivable ground on either side was not of great extent, and often the road took us outside its borders and on to the barren, treeless waste of the desert. On these occasions it was always refreshing to get back to the palm-groves and the comparatively fertile slopes of the Draa valley. The country, as a glance at any map will show, was studded with numerous *zaouias*, or sanctuaries. These zaouias are generally the burial places of Marabouts, or holy men, whose *kubbe* (white, dome-shaped tombs) are a frequent and conspicuous feature of the landscape, both here and in north Marocco. Villages, small clusters of *tabbia*, or mud-built huts, spring up round these sanctuaries. The zaouia is generally presided over, and owned by a *shereef*, or descendant of the Prophet, who makes a good thing out of the offerings of pilgrims at the shrine of the departed saint.

We were passing one of these Marabouts' alcoves, or *kubbe* (the word "alcove" is simply *al kubba*) one day, when we saw a miserable half-starved looking creature cowering inside. A few yards from the entrance three truculent-looking natives sat keeping guard. We asked Ali what was up, and he said that the man had killed a relation of one of the three watchers, and, fleeing from their vengeance, he had gone upon the *bust*.

"'Been upon the bust,' has he?" cried Gerald. "Well, just tell him not to do it again. It's evident dissipation don't agree with him. Just see how pale and thin he looks."

Ali hastened to explain that "bust" was Persian

for sanctuary, and that the unhappy criminal had taken refuge in the zaouia, the sanctity of which he knew his pursuers would not dare to violate. There was nothing, however, to prevent them sitting down and starving the poor wretch out; and this was just what they were doing. After some haggling we managed to purchase the intended victim's liberty by payment of a few dollars' blood-money, though I for one would not answer for his life as soon as our backs were turned, in spite of the oaths and promises made to us that not a hair of his head should be injured.

We stayed a few days in a place called Sok el Arba, or Place of the Wednesday Market, the sheikh of which was good enough to extend to us his friendship and protection. He told us that the zaouia was a rendezvous for the *hadjis*, or pilgrims, on their journey from the shrine of the Prophet at Mecca, and that a great yearly fair was about to be held, which would be attended by a vast concourse of people. Merchants had been daily arriving with caravans from the south, trains of pilgrims eager to pray at the shrine of a very high-class saint, one Moulai Hamed Abd El Kader Gil Ali Ben Absalam, whose bones reposed in a large kubba in the vicinity. Already the place was full of tents, with their owners' camels and horses picketed around, and cattle and goats and sheep innumerable. Every one was on the move, preparing for the great festival, which would last over the three following days. Troops of mounted men were practising the *lab el baroud*, or powder-play on horseback, conspicuous in their mad charges being the shereefs in their soulhams of sea-green, the colour reserved for those who can boast that the blood of the Prophet runs in their veins. A perpetual piping and tom-tomming was kept up, which, combined with the rattle of musketry and the shrill "lu, lu, lu," of the women encouraging their lords, made a tremendous din.

On the morrow all the Moorish world and his wife were early astir, and by the time we arrived on the scene the dusty plain was covered by a buzzing multitude, whose attention was concentrated upon the various entertainments which had been provided for their amusement. It was a curious, and, I must say, a marvellously picturesque scene. From a distance we looked down on what seemed like a sea of turbans, and fezzes, and shaven scalps. All was bustle and confusion. The sun beat fiercely down upon the shadeless expanse, and a choking dust enveloped everything. Knots of Moors were squatted on the ground, listening open-mouthed to the story-tellers, who, with much pantomime and vigorous gesticulation, regaled them with Æsopian fables. Others were gathered round the snake-charmers, clowns, tumblers, fortune-tellers, single-stick players, and jugglers, who, after performing their marvellous feats, "sent round the hat" just as their *confrères* would do in England. What a motley crew, to be sure! Rich and poor, robes and rags, the starved and the overfed. And what a jabber of contending jargons! What a mixture of types and colours and costumes! from the white-faced Moorish merchant, clad in his eight yards or more of cloth, to the big Bambara nigger, whose raiment is a loin-cloth, a few flies, and a never-ceasing grin. Nor is the ubiquitous Jew absent. He wears a dark jellabia, and his cap is black (the colour of Jehannum) and he is compelled to walk slipperless, having the cringing, dejected air natural to a despised and persecuted race.

Above us, on that bank up yonder, are the muffled women, in their white, flowing haiks, each squealing away at the top of her voice, as her husband performs some more than usually startling feat in the dance, or nearly blows his neighbour's head off as he discharges his matchlock in the air. Beggars—all sores and rags, blind, lame, deformed—are all over the place, hoarsely demanding backsheesh in the name of Allah and Moulai Idrees. Itinerant hawkers perambulate the mob, just as they would at a fair in England, only, instead of oranges and gingerbeer, they sell syrups, cakes, and lollypops in the name of Moulai Idrees. This saint, who, as I have said, is a very great gun out in these parts, seems to have a finger in every pie. Yon nigger water-carrier, ringing his bell as he pours the filthy liquid he has just collected from the nearest puddle through the brass nozzle of his goatskin bag, claims the patronage of the holy man, and charges an extra mozuna per cup on that account.

"El ma, el ma! Water, pure water, from the holy Ain el Beida (white spring), dug by our father Moulai Idrees. Balak! balak! make room, make room! Ya Mohammed! Ya Moulai Idrees! Come and drink, come and drink. In the name of Allah and His holy Prophet, who'll have a cooler, who'll have a cooler?"

Yes! change the costumes; put a steam-organ or hurdy-gurdy in place of those musicians with their rheetahs and tom-toms, and alter one or two minor details, and you might almost fancy yourself at some country fair in the Midlands, or amongst our English bedouins on Epsom Downs. The same idea evidently strikes Gerald, who enters thoroughly into the fun of the fair, and he suggests that we should start Aunt Sally, or, in lack of cocoa-nuts, play leap-frog.

"La ilaha ill' Allah! Three shies a penny! Ya lateef. What a pity we have no cocoa-nuts. Bismillah! tuck in your twopenny," he cried, "making a back" for Urquhart, who was over him like a shot, I following. The natives were highly diverted, thinking some new species of mountebank had arrived from the land of the Roum (Europeans).

"Oollah!" exclaimed a young athletic-looking Moor, gazing admiringly at Urquhart, "but he jumps like a gazelle."

Ali, far from sharing in the delight of the Moors, viewed these proceedings with grave concern, and expostulated with Urquhart on his undignified conduct.

"By the soul of your great-grandfather, and by your beard," he said, "do not, I pray you, eat dirt before the eyes of this people, or Allah only knows what mischief may befall you, and I shall be powerless to avert it. The robe of dignity is as steel armour against the shafts of insult, but they who clothe themselves in a garment of shame must be prepared to chew the cud of mortification. There is but one God, and Mohammed is the Prophet of God."

"Mohammed be blowed!" cried the irrepressible Gerald. "Here's the only real sporting Prophet. Allah akbar! two to one, bar one! May your shadows never be less! What price outsiders?" And he mounted on a stone, pencil and note-book in hand, like any genuine "bookie," amid a throng of

gaping and astonished natives, who imagined him to
be a kaffir story-teller about to start upon a new and
original yarn.

Almarakshi, who shared Ali's opinion of our conduct, wagged his head gravely and said to our cook
that he feared the Father of the Nose was "hhamak"
(*scottice*, "had a bee in his bonnet"). This presumption
on Almarakshi's part called forth a stern rebuke from
Mohammed, who asked him, in the name of Moulai
Idrees, what dog he could name as his father that he
should presume to criticize his betters, remarking
further that, "Hamdoollah! blessed be Allah!" if it
pleased the tajjers to play the giddy goat, it was no
business of his (Almarakshi's) to interfere.

Yielding to Ali's expostulations, we desisted from
larking, to the evident disappointment of the natives,
who were in hopes of witnessing some novel performance, and continued our way through the crowd,
which seemed to grow denser every moment. Presently a troop of gaily attired horsemen come
prancing and caracoling through the mob, and
following them is a shereef in turban and sea-green
soulham, mounted on a tall dromedary. His satel-
lites, crying "Balak! Balak!" clear a passage for
him among the people, who meekly withdraw before
the holy man. Every step reveals something new
and picturesque. Lines of pious pilgrims are filing
wearily up a slight eminence to the tomb of the saint,
leading the sacrificial heifer by a cord. Troops of
gaudily-clad warriors perform military quadrilles
amid shouts and the din of musketry. A portly
merchant from some far-off town rides by on his
sleek mule, and a peasant on his humble ass drives

his sheep and goats to the soko. Just look, too, at that maniac yonder, naked to the waist, his long matted hair streaming in the wind, jibbering away to himself as he brandishes a rusty old spear with gaudy rags and bits of ribbon tied on the head. The people of course reverence him as a saint, saying that he has been visited of Heaven, and that his reason is in the keeping of Allah. If he hits you over the head with his spear, or spits in your face, you will have to look as though you liked it and render thanks to Allah that the holy man has condescended to notice you.

"Look here, old man," said Gerald to Ali, "it's evidently considered a high distinction out here to be a drivelling idiot, so don't you go insulting people by asking after their sanity, or making polite speeches about their brains being in good order ; or you'll get into hot water. They'll take it as a deadly insult, they will. You must say, 'Good morning to you, sir ; I trust you are feeling tolerably cracked to-day.' 'Peace be with you,' he will reply. 'I had a slight return of my lucid intervals yesterday, but the attack has since left me, and I am now thoroughly insane, thanks be to Allah !' Hullo ! what's all this noise about ?"

As he spoke, a great shout was raised of "Aissaouie ! Aissaouie !" and a rush was made by the crowd to an open space on the right. We allowed ourselves to be carried along with the stream, and, descending a sandy lane enclosed on either side by hedges of cactus and aloe, we saw what looked like a mob of lunatics in convulsions slowly approaching us. These were the Aissaouie, the followers of the sect of Aissa, a species of howling dervishes who are held in great repute throughout Barbary. There were nearly a hundred of them altogether, men and women, half-naked, save that a few were clad in panther-skins, of which they were tremendously proud. On they came in circles of two lines each, performing a sort of hideous double shuffle to the music of pipes and tom-toms and the clash of cymbals, which mingled with the shouts and howls of the mob and the shrill cries of the women. In their midst devotees carried great embroidered banners of green and gold. Not daring to approach too near, we planted ourselves on a hillock hard by, whence we had a full view of the Bacchantic orgies.

It was a strange and revolting spectacle on which we gazed. Methinks I can see those horrible faces now—some wearing an expression of agony, others simply with the vacant grin of idiocy—faces as of men possessed with a thousand devils, such as are only to be seen in a madhouse or a night-mare. In delirious transports, with convulsive gulps and groans and howls, the fanatics called upon Allah for aid, tossing their heads and shaking their long black elf-locks, rocking their bodies to and fro in contortions as they kept up the hideous dance. Some grovelled about on the ground, pretending to be goats and pigs and other animals; others cut and bit and scratched themselves till the blood flowed out upon them. In the midst of them all, a huge black negress clad in a long white chemise, who had been jumping about with frantic vehemence, fell to the ground in a fit, foaming at the mouth, and swallowing mud and stones, and performing the most revolting antics. Near her a tall emaciated Moor, a sort of walking skeleton in rags, held a piece of red-hot charcoal between a pair of tongs, which he applied to his left arm, keeping it there for fully a minute. He uttered no cry, and the quivering muscles, which seemed distended almost to breaking point as the steam arose from the frizzling flesh, were the only indications that he suffered pain, while, with eyes half starting from their sockets, he grinned idiotically, as though he were enjoying it.

Then an aged fanatic with long, flowing, white beard, who, from the superior quality of his contortions and the howls which accompanied them, seemed to be the *mokaddem*, or high priest, of the band, called in a loud voice for the "father of wool." Immediately half a dozen sturdy natives appeared, dragging along between them a sheep and a goat. The wretched creatures struggled and bleated piteously, as though conscious of the fate that awaited them, for, with a simultaneous howl, the pack of dervishes rushed, like tigers lusting for blood, upon their prey. Some seized the head, others the legs, of their victims, and pulled and pulled till they literally tore the animals asunder, and then there was a general scramble for the pieces. Tossing them in the air and smearing themselves with blood, the fanatics swallowed bits of the raw flesh, shrieking out "Allah! Allah!" at the top of their voices. At last, seemingly drunk with blood, and exhausted with their superhuman exertions, some of them staggered and fell to the ground, where they lay in a state of stupor.

Meanwhile the crowd were hugely delighted. Every one gave praise and thanks to Allah for vouchsafing to them so excellent a festival ; and they seemed to think that being present at such a loathsome spectacle was a cause for deep gratitude. For ourselves, we had had more than enough of it, so, as the afternoon was now wearing on, and the red ball of the sun was sinking in the desert to the west, we elbowed our way through the crowd and made our way back to the tents, leaving the turbaned throng of the faithful still hard at work at their festivities.

CHAPTER X.

THE SHEIKH ABD EL KREEM.

WE did not stay in Sok el Arba beyond the fifth day,
being anxious to make our way as soon as we con-
veniently could to the zaouia of one Sheikh Seedy
Mohammed Selim Alarby Barghash Abd el Kreem,
who, we were told, was the independent chieftain of
a conglomeration of Arab tribes on the borders of the
Great Desert. It was of the utmost importance for
us to obtain the good will of this potentate, as, otherwise, we should hardly be able to continue our journey
into the interior. We had heard most alarming
reports concerning his tyranny, rapacity, and fiendish
cruelty, and the brutal way in which he oppressed his
unfortunate subjects. Ali was provided with a letter
of introduction to the sheikh from a Moorish merchant
residing in Marakesh, who had once befriended Abd
el Kreem while the latter was staying in that city
some years before. The sheikh's territory would be
the last inhabited country that we should pass
through before we commenced our journey across the
Sahara, and we reckoned on being able to purchase
from him camels, desert horses, and other necessary

equipment.   Should he prove hostile to our enterprise, or, indeed, if he simply refused to give us his co-operation and aid, it would be almost impossible for us even to make the attempt to reach Mount Atlas.

The following are a few notes I find in my diary of a not very interesting part of our journey.

September 15*th.*—Up at dawn.   Got quickly through the business of breakfast and packing, and off before seven, as it is getting too hot to travel in the middle of the day, and we must cover as much ground as possible in the cool.   The country presents no new features.   We pass through alternate stretches of desert and oasis, sometimes keeping along the river-bank, sometimes leaving it far on our left.

16*th*, 17*th, and* 18*th.*—Crossed the river on the 16th, and travelled along the left bank for some hours, recrossing it the next day.   The population is growing scantier, and we see very few zaouias. Food, too, is getting short.   We have tasted little or no meat since leaving Sok el Arba, and live chiefly on cakes of flour and dates.

19*th.*—Had a long march to-day, as we are cutting off a big bend which the river makes to the east, and there are fifty or sixty miles of desert to be crossed before we strike it again.   Camped by a muddy little pool of tepid water called the Ain el Wad el Bared, or Spring of the Cold River.   There is no river, and the water is anything but cold ; but that is a mere trifle—these Arabs have such splendid imaginations.

On the 20th we rejoined the Wad Draa close to where it makes its final turn to the west.   From this point it flows straight away to the Atlantic—at least it does so when it has enough water.   In the dry

season its stream is swallowed up in the thirsty sands
of the desert long before it arrives at the ocean. We
were now within an easy day's march of Zaouia Seedy
Idrees, the dwelling-place of the Sheikh Abd el
Kreem, but instead of proceeding there at once we
struck off on a journey of half a day in a westerly
direction, to visit the great lake of Ed Debaia. This
lake becomes completely dry at certain seasons, and
the natives grow fine crops of corn on its bed. It is
only filled with water when the melting of the Atlas
snows brings the Draa down in flood. On the
occasion of our visit it was in an intermediate state, a
sort of shallow swamp formed of alternate patches of
dry ground and reedy lagoons. These lagoons were
covered with flocks of innumerable wild fowl. As we
approached they rose and circled round our heads,
forming thin, wavy lines like some huge aerial serpent.
Troops of herons and flamingoes lined the banks, like
regiments of grey and red-coated soldiers. We did
not camp near the marsh for fear of malaria, but
from our tents at nightfall we could distinctly hear
the booming of the wild swans, the squeaking of the
boomenkoosh, or " father of the pick," as the Moors in
their absurd fashion call the snipe, and the hoarse
murmur of cranes winging their way to the south.

We had a short day's shooting in the marsh—
simply for the pot, as we could not afford to waste our
ammunition on mere amusement—and bagged several
duck and widgeon. They tasted most delicious after
the tough mutton, goat, and camel that had died a
natural death, which had formed our staple fare till
the last few days. The next morning we made an
early start, intending to dispense with our usual

noontide siesta and to travel all day so as to arrive before nightfall at the Zaouia Seedy Idrees. The heat and the roughness of the road, however, frustrated our endeavours, and we were compelled to pass a most uncomfortable night encamped in a stony waste, without water for ourselves or herbage for our animals.

Before noon next day a few stunted palms came into view, and soon we saw the mud walls and battlements, with square towers of the same material at the angles and salient points, and two or three mosque towers, of a Moorish town. This was the *kasbah*, or fortress, of Seedy Idrees, the zaouia itself being a short distance away.

Outside the gate of the kasbah we came on a knot of Moors, in the midst of whom was seated a big, burly mulatto of indescribably forbidding aspect. This, Ali told us, was the Sheikh Abd el Kreem. He was a man somewhat under the middle height, enormously broad-chested and corpulent withal, with a short thick neck like a bull's, set on between a pair of high square shoulders. His face was deeply pitted with smallpox, and wore an expression of ferocity, gluttony, and brute voluptuousness. He had a leer like a satyr, while a big scar over his left eye heightened the general sinister effect. On one of the Moors drawing his attention to us he rose and glared at us for about a minute. Being anxious to create a favourable impression on this truculent potentate, we had smartened ourselves up a bit for the occasion. We had donned our best riding-breeches, and, for the first time since leaving England, had indulged in the luxury of a shave. But our hopes of winning

the sheikh's good-will by the charm of our appearance were rudely dashed to the ground.

"Lain el Sheitan ! curses be upon the Sheitan !" he
roared out with a voice like a bull of Bashan, at the same
time spitting on the ground in a most offensive fashion.
" Who are these, with bald, white chins like those of
old and mangy camels, and tightly fitting garments
about their legs ? In the name of Allah, let them
be provided with raiment that their limbs may be
suitably covered and that they put not the faces of
our women to shame. And then let their heads
be taken off, as a warning to all strangers who
may be tempted to commit a similar indecency.
There is but one God, and Mohammed is the Prophet
of God."

Urquhart, undismayed by his ferocious bluster,
boldly approached and spoke as follows.

" Peace be with you, O Sheikh. We are three
strangers from the *Belad el Roum* (land of the
Europeans), journeying in search of a far-off country,
and we crave your protection and hospitality."

" That is no reason why ye should not cover your
legs with proper raiment," retorted the sheikh, returning to the charge. " And what dog's son is this ? "
he continued, as Ali, trembling all over, came timidly
up behind Urquhart with the letter of introduction in
his hand. " May his father's grave be eternally
defiled ! "

Ali replied in a low tone, and with head bent
down submissively, " May your Highness's favour
never diminish, and may the condescension of your
Highness continue to shine upon his servant " (nice
sort of condescension, thought I, to call a man a dog

and defile his father's grave). "Behold, I am less than dirt, but we are travellers from a distant country and crave leave to bask for a few days in the sunshine of your Highness's presence. These gentlemen" (pointing to us) "have journeyed thus far to repose in the shadow of your protection. Good men are they, and true, men of ripe understanding, whose hands have gathered of the fruits of the tree of knowledge. Your servant is further charged by the Tajjer Abd er Rahman Sliman Embarck to deliver a letter into the hands of your Highness, and, having endeavoured faithfully to discharge his duty in the matter, your servant now begs your Highness to deign to accept the same."

"A letter!" exclaimed the sheikh. "By the beard of the Prophet, we do not often get letters in these parts. Show it me; in the name of the blessed Moulai Idrees, let me see it."

I could well imagine that the postman's knock sounded but rarely on the portals of the Zaouia Seedy Idrees, and that the arrival of a messenger charged with a missive from a distant country was regarded as an event of some importance. The sheikh, whose interest was now thoroughly aroused, took the precious document from Ali's hands, pressed it first to his lips and then to his forehead, and broke the seal. But an unlooked-for difficulty here arose. How were the contents to be deciphered? The sheikh himself was guiltless of the art of reading, and his retainers likewise. A consultation was held, and there was much knitting of eyebrows and wagging of heads, and staferallahing and hamdoollahing, till suddenly one of the Moors was struck with a bright idea.

"Barikallah! blessed be Allah!" said he; "I have it. Send for the Thaleb Mohammed."

Thaleb Mohammed, a middle-aged man wearing an expression of fatuous solemnity, as became one credited with colossal erudition, soon arrived. I believe his reputation rested on the fact of his being able to read, or, more probably, to repeat by heart under pretence of reading, a few verses of the Koran. He took up the letter with an air of portentous wisdom, and, murmuring a prayer to Allah to clear his brain and enlighten his understanding, he set about the formidable task of spelling out its contents. He turned the document every way, upside down, sideways, wagged his head, and finally, muttering something of which I could not catch the sense, he gave it up as a bad job.

Briefly remarking that he was a jackass, and in all probability the father of the greater number of jackasses now existent, the sheikh ordered the unfortunate thaleb to receive a hundred blows on the soles of his feet, in order, as he said, to give him better understanding. In the end, the letter was handed to Ali to read, and the pains of Jehannum were invoked on his head if he did not do it correctly.

"May I never see the blessed houris of Paradise," humbly ejaculated the Persian, "if I alter one single word, or attempt in any way (which would, indeed, be a foolish thing) to deceive the wisdom of your Highness."

The letter commenced as follows:—"In the name of Allah, the All-Powerful, the Compassionate. The blessing of Allah be upon His holy Prophet Mohammed, and upon all who walk in the right way.

"From the Tajjer Abd er Rahman Sliman Embarek to the Sheikh Seedy Mohammed Barghash Abd el Kreem, greeting. The peace of Allah and Seedna Mohammed be upon our friends."

The letter went on to say, after more oriental rigmarole, that three Nazarenes, and a certain Ali Abd el Ressool from the land of Iran, all friends of the writer, were setting forth upon a journey to the navel of the desert, and that the said four friends hoped, by the blessing of Allah and the aid of Moulai Idrees, to pass through the happy dominions under the benevolent sway of the Sheikh Abd el Kreem. The tajjer, therefore, begged the sheikh, for the love of Allah, and because of the friendship which subsisted between them, to be gracious to the Nazarenes and to afford them every assistance in his power. The peace.

The sheikh's manner softened on hearing this letter read, and an expression almost approaching amiability crossed his ill-favoured countenance.

"Mahhaba bik, you are welcome," said he ; "the friends of my friends are friends of mine. On my head be it to perform the wishes of the Tajjer Abd er Rhaman in this matter."

As he spoke he seized Urquhart's hand and pressed his own to his heart and then on the top of his head. This last gesture signified that he took all our faults and trespasses on his own hand, which was very obliging of him, as, unless rumour and his looks greatly belied him, he had quite enough of his own to carry.

"But why don't they cover their legs ? " said he, turning to Ali, and again harping on the old theme.

"May it please your Highness," said Ali, "in the

Belad el Roum it is not the custom for the people to wear the jellabia."

"Holy Prophet! do the Christian dogs, then, go about naked?"

"Allah forbid!" returned the Persian; "but the Oolad Ingleez (sons of the English) are a race of accomplished horsemen, and the steeds of that country are so fiery and untamed that no man may bestride them unless he has tight-fitting raiment on his legs."

The sheikh replied, in effect, that he would rather be kicked off his horse than make an ass of himself by going about in such ridiculous and unbecoming attire. "But after all," he philosophically added, "what does it matter what the swine-eating infidels do? In any case, they and their fathers will burn eternally in Jehannum."

The sheikh evidently considered that this clinched the matter and that further argument was useless, so, gathering up his garments and raising his portly person to its full height, and throwing his haik jauntily over his left shoulder, he waddled majestically towards the gate of the kasbah.

Abd el Kreem, as we learned afterwards, was vastly proud of his personal appearance. His ambition was to be considered "the glass of fashion and the mould of form," the "Kreem de la Kreem," to quote Gerald's vile pun, of the manhood of Seedy Idrees; and he was always surrounded by a band of sycophants who pandered to his vanity. These were never tired of applying to him the epithet of "moon-faced," which was appropriate only in so far that his countenance possessed, not only the rotundity, but also the eruptive surface peculiar to that orb. Being of the lineage of the Prophet, he wore the green robe of the shereefs, and was reverenced by all the Moors as a saint. It was only natural that they should pay this honour to a person possessing so peculiarly iniquitous a character as the sheikh, since, next to idiocy, that is the best passport to canonization in Marocco. Seekers after a sign of his mission were referred to a large wart on his nose as proof positive of his being one chosen by Allah ; and no sceptic was found so hardened as not to be convinced by this irrefragable evidence. He was the Marabout of the neighbouring zaouia, which dignity, and the emoluments attaching thereto, he had inherited from a long line of ancestors. Needless to say that he made a good thing out of it. His blessing was a marketable commodity, the price varying according to the means of the person blessed. Pieces of cloth from his old jellabias,. and even the parings of his nails and the trimmings of his beard fetched money as talismans against the evil eye and other misfortunes. Strings of beads, which had been worn round his sanctified neck, were in great request as rosaries, but perhaps the sale of relics and charms formed the most profitable part of his business. "A questionable kind of saint," the reader will say ; yet I am not sure that the Christian calendar could not furnish parallels with scarcely more enviable records.

By permission of Abd el Kreem, we lived in our tents outside the walls, thereby avoiding the discomforts of Moorish houses and the evil odours of the town. Thanks chiefly to Abd er Rhaman's letter, and to Ali's skill in deciphering it, we were treated with every consideration. Plenteous *mona*, or gifts of

provisions, were provided for ourselves and our
servants, and a guard of warriors armed with matchlocks was told off for our protection. Nevertheless,
we were anxious not to waste more time in the
place than was absolutely necessary. Our chief aim
was to obtain, if possible, some reliable information
as to the existence and whereabouts of the Djebel
Kebeer. Legend was rife, as Urquhart had told us
in the smoking-room of Inverfechan, concerning it
and the race of holy Marabutin who dwelt at its
base, and the wonders the latter worked. Not a soul,
however, seemed to possess any definite knowledge
on the subject. It was further rumoured that gold in
abundance was to be found along the banks of a
river which, taking its rise somewhere in the mountain, flowed thence out into the desert; but no man
had ever seen this river. A band of adventurous
Moors, it was said, attracted by the prospect of
finding gold, had set out many moons ago across the
desert; but they had never been heard of since, and
it was supposed that they had all perished on the
way. The existence of the Djebel Kebeer, we
observed, was universally believed in; but no one
seemed to have the haziest notion of its locality,
further than that it lay somewhere to the south in
the Sahara, and many days' journey distant from the
Zaouia Seedy Idrees.

In addition to this difficulty of getting any reliable
information, a new and unexpected obstacle to our
departure arose in the shape of a sudden whim of the
sheikh's. Our fear had been lest we should find his
hostility a bar to our enterprise, and, knowing the
suspicion and dislike with which the natives as a

rule regard foreign travellers, we little imagined that any trouble could arise from his taking too great a fancy to us. Yet this was what actually happened. He was by no means pleased to see us at first, and, as the reader will remember, expressed his sentiments concerning us in no measured terms. In his case, however, as in many others, intercourse broke down the barrier which barbarism and bigotry interposes between men of different race and creed. As he saw more of us his aversion gradually lessened, and, to our surprise and not unqualified delight, finally turned into a positive liking. He seemed to take a particular fancy to Gerald, and lost no opportunity of making himself agreeable to him. The upshot of it all was that when we expressed a desire to start on our journey and mooted the question of camels and other equipment, he positively refused to let us go. So obstinate did he show himself on the point, that we judged it wise to let the matter rest for awhile.

Meanwhile, our stay was made as pleasant for us as possible, and everything was done to show the esteem in which the sheikh held us. We were actually honoured one day by an invitation from Mrs. Abd el Kreem, who, enamoured either of Urquhart's whiskers or, more probably, Gerald's fair hair and winning smile, requested us to take afternoon tea, or, as the French would say, to "fivocloquer," with her at four o'clock. It was impossible to refuse, so, donning our smartest attire, and putting our best leg forward, we presented ourselves at the appointed hour at the door of the sheikh's mansion. He received us graciously in person, and, invoking the peace of Allah on our heads, assured us that, once having passed his threshold and eaten of his bread, we were his father, mother, brother, and all the rest of his relations, and that everything he possessed was ours.

So saying, he led the way across the tesselated court and under the portico, leaving in his train a strong odour of garlic, which, in a holy man who was supposed to daily hold converse with angels and other spiritual beings, was highly improper.[1]

Passing through a narrow door, we found ourselves in a cosy inner apartment spread over with rich Rabat rugs, and surrounded by a low divan. At one end of this divan there reclined a portly middle-aged dame, with a hook-nose and a swarthy complexion and large black eyes of singular brightness, who was presented to us as the sheikh's head wife. I was somewhat surprised at our being introduced in this fashion to the interior of a Mussulman's household ; but, as a matter of fact, the country Moors are far less particular about secluding their women than those of the towns. Anyhow, Mrs. Abd el Kreem seemed delighted to see us, paying particular attention, I observed, to Gerald. Indeed, Urquhart and myself were at first not a little astonished at the way in which both she and her spouse combined to do him honour, but after tea the secret of their attentions came out. A matrimonial scheme was on foot between them, of which poor Gerald was the intended victim. Tea was served in the usual Moorish fashion with cakes and sweetmeats, and, when we had swallowed the three cups prescribed by native eti-

---

[1] The saints of the East are expected to follow the example of their master Mohammed, and to abstain from onions and garlic for fear of giving offence to good spirits who hold communion with them.

quette, the sheikh introduced in a characteristically
blunt fashion the subject nearest to his heart.

"Behold, O Nazarenes," said he, addressing us
collectively, but meaning his remarks for Gerald's
ear, "I have a daughter, a virgin, named Fatma, who
is passing fair. Her face is like the moon. Her
mouth is as a ring; she hath wide hips, and she is
of goodly proportions. Already doth she weigh
170 lbs., and, with moderate stuffing,[1] she will scale
very much more. In short," said he, turning to
Gerald, "she is just the sort of damsel a good-looking
young tajjer like thee ought to marry. Take her, O
Father of the Nose; she is thine; and with her my
blessing and a goodly dower of land and camels
and cattle shall be her portion. Ala rasi, on my head
be it."

At this moment the door opened and, doubtless
by preconcerted arrangement, the young lady entered.
And a very fine girl she was for her age. She was
tall, immensely fat, and almost as dark as her father;
and, as she walked, or rather wobbled, across the
room, we had full opportunity of admiring her
magnificent proportions, which the sheikh had in
no wise exaggerated. Arriving at the divan, she
flopped down beside her mother, the exertion causing
her fat cheeks to quiver like blubber; and then she
opened on poor Gerald with the whole battery of her
ample fascinations. Her mouth, which Gerald said
resembled, for all the world, a slit cut in a haggis,

---

[1] Orientals, as is well known, value their women pretty much according to their size and weight. Hence Moorish girls, as soon as they
are engaged, enter upon a process of cramming in order to increase
their bulk. An Eastern Paris would adjudge the apple not "to the
fairest," but to the fattest.

was fixed in an engaging grin, and her big goggle eyes, round which the kohl was thickly plastered, melted in what was meant to be a soft, languishing gaze.

"There!" exclaimed the sheikh, "is she not a beauty? Dost thou not long to taste the sweetness of those coral lips? By my beard, in the days of my hot youth such a face would have made my heart aflame with passion, but ye Roum are a cold-blooded race. What sayest thou, my young tajjer? Wilt thou have her?"

Gerald, though somewhat taken aback by the unexpected turn affairs had taken, was equal to the occasion.

"Tell the sheikh," said he to Urquhart, preferring to make his excuses through the medium of an interpreter, "that the beauty of his daughter hath made roast meat of my heart. Verily, she is a pearl among women." ("Much more like a big oyster," he murmured *sotto voce*.) "Her eyes are like two stars, and gladly would I wed her were I free to do so, but, alas! my heart is fixed on a fair maid of my own country" ("Good heavens, what a cram!" muttered Urquhart), "and Allah forbid that I should break my plighted troth."

The sheikh's face clouded over at this reply. He was not accustomed to be thwarted in his plans, and, having set his heart upon getting Gerald for his son-in-law, he renewed his persuasions and entreaties, till at length, finding his importunity of no avail against Gerald's obstinate refusal to embrace the opportunity —or the lady—he assumed a more peremptory tone. This nettled Gerald considerably, and, being at a loss for a satisfactory reply, he muttered something to himself about Abd el Kreem being "an old Juggins."

The observation did not escape the quick ears of the sheikh, who at once divined from Gerald's somewhat sulky expression, that some opprobrious epithet was being levelled at him. Jumping up from his seat, he plucked his beard in a passion and screamed out—

"What is this I hear? Lai sti shimlek. What filth is this we are eating? By the camel of the holy Prophet, and by the ram he sacrificed at the first Ramadan, if I am Juggins, you are the great-grandfather of all the Jugginses. Oollah! may fifty curs defile the grave of Juggins's grandmother. Whose dog am I, that swine-eating sons of Sheitan should laugh at my beard? May Juggins burn in Jehannum!"

The ladies were much moved at this ebullition of the shereefian wrath, and Mademoiselle Fatma burst into a fit of hysterical tears, which aggravated rather than soothed her parent's bad temper. Urquhart, however, hastened to explain that Juggins, so far from being an insult, was often used as a term of endearment and respect amongst the sons of the English, and the sheikh's anger subsided as quickly as it had been roused.

"La bas, la bas, it is well. Our ears are gratified; our wrath is appeased. Only, I would not have it be supposed that the fingers of contumely were plucking at the beard of dignity."

This unpleasant little episode being satisfactorily ended, we soon after rose to take our leave, and returned to the tents, where we told Ali what had happened. He was much amused, and said he had heard that the sheikh had long been trying to get his daughter off his hands, but owing to her unprepossessing appearance and abominable temper, he had so far been unsuccessful. About a year ago she had been engaged to a young merchant from the Draa oasis, but after a fortnight's courtship he had broken off the match, vowing he would rather wed one of the houris of Jehannum than this female Sheitan. During a slight quarrel they had she had scratched his face and bit him to such good purpose that he bore the marks about his person for many a day after. In this case the *amantium iræ* did not prove to be the *redintegratio amoris*, and the intended bridegroom was happily spared from affording ˙a practical answer to the all-important question, " Is marriage a failure ? "

CHAPTER XI.

THE EXECUTIONS.

IN consequence of Gerald's obduracy a slight coolness subsisted between us and the sheikh for the next few days, though the lovely Fatma ceased not to languish and ogle upon Gerald whenever an opportunity offered, and he began to find her attentions somewhat embarrassing.

"What with the sheep's eyes of the charming Fatma," he remarked, "and the importunities of her fat pa, life isn't half good enough for me here, and I vote we make tracks as soon as possible."

This, however, was easier said than done, for, though we did everything we could to bring matters to a climax and to induce the sheikh to consent to our departure, he, like another African potentate of earlier date, "would not let Israel go." He had got over his fit of ill-temper ; the presence of Christians in his "happy dominions" was a novelty and a distraction for him, and he did not despair of overcoming Gerald's aversion to becoming his son-in-law. Accordingly, we had no alternative but to grin and bear it, and wait till some opportunity should arrive of making our escape.

Meanwhile, our too amiable host, anxious to afford us every diversion in his power, told us that a great festival was about to take place, when a number of criminals and rebels who had taken up arms against him would be led out to execution, or to suffer such other penalties for their crimes as were meted out to them by the kadi. We assured him that such a spectacle would afford us no gratification ; that, on the contrary, it would be most repugnant to our feelings, and we begged him at any rate to postpone the day until after we had taken our departure. The wretch seemed astonished that we did not look forward to the entertainment with the same gusto as himself, and said that justice, as he was pleased to call it, must take its course, and that the date of the executions could not be altered. We had heard horrible tales of his cruelty and the barbarous tortures he inflicted on his unfortunate subjects, but the fiendish pleasure which the anticipations of their sufferings seemed to afford him was inexpressibly shocking to us.

However, when the morning of the appointed day broke, we repaired, along with a crowd of natives, to the scene of the "festival." We looked forward to the entertainment with anything but pleasurable feelings, but, under the peculiar circumstances in which we were placed, the success of our expedition being largely dependent on the sheikh's good will, it would have been highly impolitic to absent ourselves. I fear, too, that a spirit of morbid curiosity likewise prompted us in some measure. The place of execution was on the outskirts of the town, and when we arrived a large concourse of people had already gathered together on the spot. In their midst a square space about two hundred yards wide was kept clear by the soldiers, the spectators being congregated round in rows of four and five deep. On one side of the open space was a marquee, open at the sides ; beneath we could see the portly forms of the sheikh's wife and the colossal Fatma seated on a carpet. Presently, the sheikh himself, clad in his green robes, came riding up on a handsome white barb, surrounded by a numerous escort all mounted on gorgeously caparisoned steeds. Obedient to the cruel spur, they curvetted and caracoled, standing on their hind-legs and performing the various other antics and feats of noble horsemanship with which the Moorish rider delights to witch the world. As the sheikh approached every knee was bent and every head bowed in that vast throng, and a roar as from ten thousand throats rent the air, "Allah protect Sidna."

Seeing us standing in the crowd, the sheikh sent one of his retainers to invite us to join him in the tent. We entered, and after the customary salutations had been exchanged he bade us be seated on the carpet beside him.

"Ye are come, Nazarenes," said he, "to witness an act of exemplary vengeance upon those who have offended against the laws of Allah, as expounded by His holy Prophet, and also upon the rebellers against the shereefian authority constituted by Allah and represented in our person. Let the dogs be brought forth to their doom ! " he roared ; and his face assumed the satanic expression which we had observed upon it once or twice before.

In obedience to his command, the kadi, a tall Moor wearing a blue soulham and enormous turban strode, forth and took up his position about fifty yards in front of the tent. He was followed by the executioner, a gigantic negro, who bore the implement of his office —a long broad-bladed double-edged sword. Then came the melancholy procession of the condemned criminals. They were in two gangs, the members of each gang being fastened together by massive chains round their ankles, and their hands were heavily manacled. They marched slowly forward, dragging their irons painfully after them, some looking pale and dejected, others with an air of proud and defiant resolution. The foremost gang, about fifteen in number, consisted of the leaders of the revolt, and they were condemned to be beheaded. The remainder, to the number of nine, had been convicted of theft, or robbery with violence, and their punishment was to be that ordained by Mohammedan law in such cases —namely, to lose one hand or foot.

At a signal from the kadi, two Moors undid the fastenings of the chains and led the first of the condemned men forward. An ashy paleness overspread his features, but he showed no other sign of fear. " La ilaha ill' Allah, there is but one God," he cried in a loud clear voice, as he knelt down and bared his neck to the executioner's sword. The black approached and took aim ; there was a sweep and a flash of light, and the head rolled upon the ground.

" Mezian ! excellent ! " exclaimed the sheikh, rubbing his hands in great glee. " By my beard, 'twas a brave stroke. Now for the others. Barikallah ! praised be Allah ! we have still fourteen left."

At this Urquhart could hardly contain himself with rage, and it was with difficulty that Gerald and I prevailed on him to keep quiet. The remainder of the condemned men followed in succession, till the whole fifteen had been decapitated, and the sands ran red with the blood of the slain. The victims were of all ages, some being white-haired old men, others in the prime of manhood, and two or three mere striplings. Most of them met their doom with stoical fortitude, but there were some who shrieked aloud in the extremity of their terror, and had to be dragged to the place of execution. The heads were gathered in a heap and carried off, preparatory to their being salted and nailed up on the wall of the kasbah, as a warning to all who should venture to defy the sheikh's authority.

A brief interval followed, during which preparations were made for the completion of the bloody drama. Sand was sprinkled over the dark red stains, and three Moors presently came up bearing a large cauldron full of some hot steaming liquid. This was the boiling pitch, in which the stumps of the severed limbs were to be plunged to stop the bleeding. The manacles were knocked off the hands of two of the second gang, and they were led forward to the executioner. The crime with which they were charged was highway robbery upon a travelling merchant, but we were afterwards told that they had been falsely accused by a Moor who had a quarrel with them. Our nerves were already highly strung after all that we had witnessed, and we felt that we could scarcely bear to watch the infliction of this torture. Gerald begged Urquhart to intercede with the sheikh for the prisoners, and he did so, but his pleading was of no avail.

"By the beard of the Prophet, and by all the saints," said he, "the sentences must be carried out, or no man's life or property will be safe."

The first of the two prisoners was now laid upon the ground, and the executioner with one blow severed his right foot above the ankle. Two Moors carried him to the cauldron and thrust the bleeding limb into the seething pitch, when, with a howl of rage and agony, the unhappy wretch struggled out of the grasp of his tormentors, and, after a vain attempt to stand upright upon his remaining foot, fell senseless to the ground. A thrill of horror ran round the multitude, and in the confusion the second of the prisoners, a tall handsome young Moor with a most engaging expression of countenance, eluding his guards, darted forward to the tent and prostrated himself at the feet of the sheikh.

"Mercy! O Sheikh Abd el Kreem, slave of the Compassionate,"[1] he cried; "have mercy, even as Allah is merciful, and the blessing of Mohammed and the holy saints be upon you. By Allah, I swear it, I am guiltless of the crime laid to my charge."

But the sheikh was in no way moved by this touching appeal. "Ho! there, guards," he shouted, "remove this dog from the tent, and let his right hand as well as his foot be cut off for his presumption in daring to intrude into our presence. By my beard! but ye shall smart for this carelessness, ye sons of burnt fathers."

The warders, fearful of the consequence of their negligence in letting their prisoner escape, came running up with the intention of binding him hand

---

[1] Abd el Kreem signifies "Slave of the Compassionate."

and foot, when Urquhart, who throughout this harrowing scene had with difficulty smothered his indignation, unable to contain himself any longer, sprang up and interposed himself between them and their victim.

"Hearken, O Sheikh, to my words," he exclaimed, "and do not deny your guests this slight boon they crave of you. Spare the youth, and let him go free. Surely, blood enough and to spare has been shed this day, and already your people are sick of the slaughter. Let not the sun go down upon the blood of more victims, but let the hand of the executioner be stayed."

For a moment the sheikh remained silent, and Gerald and myself, seeing him waver in his resolution, seconded Urquhart's appeal for mercy with all the eloquence at our command. The sheikh's brow clouded, and he seemed anything but pleased at our interposition. At length, however, he yielded, and answered as follows :—

"Behold, the men have sinned and deserve to suffer the just penalty of their crimes. However, our ears are open to the intercession of our guests. The beams of the sun of clemency shall shine upon those who rest in the shadow of guilt, and the sword of retribution shall be sheathed in the scabbard of forgiveness. Yea, verily, *al oojak*, because of your countenance, O Father of Whiskers, and because of the countenance of my brother, the Father of the Nose, they shall be spared. Let their chains be struck off, and let them all go free ; and let proclamation to that effect be made unto the people. There is but one God, and Mohammed is the Prophet of God."

Accordingly, a herald in due course made proclamation to the multitude that it had pleased his Shereefian Highness, in the exercise of his infinite wisdom and mercy, to extend a free pardon to the malefactors who for their heinous crimes deserved to suffer the full penalty of the law. Whereupon the crowd once more sent up a great shout of "May Allah prolong the life of Sidna!" and then, the performance being over for the day, they gradually dispersed every man to his own home.

That evening, as we were sitting outside the tents smoking our pipes after dinner and talking over the events of the day, we were surprised by the apparition of a tall Moor. We could not discern the features, as he kept his face half hidden in the folds of his haik. The gates of the town being locked soon after sundown, it was a most unusual thing to see anybody out at such an hour, so, after the usual interchange of greetings, we asked him what he wanted.

Throwing back his haik he placed himself in the full light of the moon, and we at once recognized the young Moor whom our intercession had saved from the executioner's sword.

"The blessing of Allah and His holy saints be upon you, Nazarenes," said he. "May your footsteps be prosperous, and may your end be peace. Ye have done a good and a noble deed this day, O sons of the English, and Allah will reward you. For myself, I rest in the shadow of your condescension, and the waters of gratitude overflow my soul. Ye have saved my life, and behold! it is now yours to make what use of it ye will. My name is Absalam Gil Ali Embarck. I am poor and alone in the world. My father and mother are dead, and yon fiend of Jehannum " (meaning the sheikh) "hath confiscated all my substance. Yet is my trust in Allah, into whose hands I commend myself, and He will surely requite my enemies for their wickedness." Here the young Moor paused, and a dark look of concentrated hate and anger crossed his handsome face, and his brows were knitted as he thought of his wrongs. "Rumour hath it, Nazarenes," he continued, "that ye purpose to essay to visit the distant mountain where the holy Marabutin dwell; yet would I fain believe the tale to be false, and that ye have no mind for such an enterprise; for lo! the peak thereof, cloud-capped and snow-covered, and environed by leagues of desert sand, no man hath ever trod upon—no, nor yet ever will tread, for it is very high, and the djins who minister to the Marabutin encompass it round about, and prevent the uninitiated from approaching."

"You seem to know a great deal about this mountain, my good friend," said Urquhart, fixing his eyes on the Moor. "What if after all they speak truth when they say we purpose going there?"

"Then surely, Nazarenes, ye know not what it is ye are attempting, and it were well ye gave up the idea. Without the aid of the blessed Marabutin (to whom are revealed all secrets both of heaven and earth), no man may hope to cross the intervening desert, for the way is long and the wells are scarce and hard to find. The simoom will parch you with his fiery breath, before whom the life of man is withered up like the grass of the field. Many there be who, drawn on by lust of gold, have set forth on that terrible journey, and behold! their bones are bleaching in the desert wilds, and not a man of them hath returned alive to tell the tale. Wherefore, Nazarenes, be warned in time and rush not upon certain death."

"We thank you for your warning," said Urquhart ; "but nevertheless our minds are made up. We mean to take the risk, and to start as soon as possible. The only thing which delays us is that we hope to come across some one with a knowledge of the desert who may act as our guide."

"There is but one I wot of who knows aught of the way," answered the Moor ; "but to guide you to the Djebel Kebeer is beyond even his power. Listen, Nazarenes," he went on after a pause, "and I will open my heart unto you. The man of whom I spoke just now stands before you. Three years ago I joined a caravan belonging to a merchant of Tafilet on a journey across the Great Desert to Timbuctoo. We arrived at that city without mishap, and, having disposed of our merchandise and loaded our camels with the produce of the Soudan, we started upon our journey homewards. I will not weary you by re-counting all that befell us ; suffice it to say that on the fifteenth day after leaving Timbuctoo we discovered, to our horror, that we had strayed from the right track, and were hopelessly lost in the Great Desert. For some days we wandered about trying to find our way, but our efforts were of no avail. Our scanty stock of water was exhausted, death was staring us in the face, and we had resigned our souls to Allah, when, just as we were in the extremity of our despair, we were found and rescued by a body of men who proved to be Arabs of the oasis of the

Djebel Kebeer engaged on a distant expedition. These men conveyed us two days' journey to the foot of the mountain, where we were hospitably received by the Marabutin, and fed and lodged for the space of about two moons. At the end of this time my master, the merchant, being anxious to return home, prevailed upon the Marabout whose hospitality we had been enjoying to supply us with guides. This he did, and by their aid we were enabled to accomplish the remainder of our journey across the desert in safety. I remember little concerning this journey, except that it took us fully ten or twelve days to reach this place, during which time we suffered torments of thirst and many men and animals died of the hot wind. Also, that at midday as we journeyed the sun was behind us and slightly over the left shoulder."

"Why, then," cried Urquhart, "you are the very man we have been looking for. Can we not prevail upon you to repeat the journey once more, and in our company? Name the sum you require for your services, and if it be anything in reason it shall be yours upon our return to civilization."

Embarek made no reply, but bowed his head as though lost in thought. At length he spoke.

"Ye have heard, Nazarenes, what I have said concerning the perils ye are about to encounter, and how none have yet surmounted them, or survived to tell of what befell them on the way. But ye Roum are a daring race. Death hath no terrors for you. Ye are the fathers of knowledge and power, and ye devour distances and conquer obstacles which other men would shun to encounter. Once more, and for the last time, I say, have a care, lest haply in this thing ye essay too much and perish in the attempt."

"Useless words," said Urquhart; "our minds are fixed as adamant."

"So be it. I will try no more to dissuade you. A fool wasteth his words upon vain disputations, but the wise man knoweth to retain his tongue. And now for my answer. Behold! ye have saved me from a fate worse than death, yet hath life but little left to attract me. I will not stay here to expose myself to the persecution of my enemies, who directly your backs are turned will wreak their vengeance upon me. Rather a thousand times will I go forth with you into the wilderness, and share with you whatever fate it may please Allah to have in store for you. Behold! death comes to us all sooner or later, and it comes but once. Wherefore, Nazarenes, from this time henceforth command me as your servant to do your bidding. For the rest, the pay, I leave it in your hands to do what seemeth best to you. I have spoken. And now the night is far spent, and I would crave to be allowed to rest in the shadow of your protection, for the gates of the city are closed, and no man may enter therein."

Bidding him good night, we turned in, not to sleep, but to discuss the new turn which our affairs had taken. Urquhart and Gerald were all for taking on Embarek as our guide, and for making a start as soon as the sheikh's leave could be obtained and the necessary preparations made. For myself, I had never taken a sanguine view of the prospects of our expedition, and after all that we had heard from Embarek it may be imagined that the outlook did

not strike me as particularly promising. However,
I readily fell in with the wishes of the others; so,
being all three in accord upon the matter, we sought
our respective camp-beds, and, rolling ourselves up in
the blankets, we were soon sleeping the sleep of the
just.

CHAPTER XII.

WE were up betimes next morning, being resolved to bring matters to a head one way or another, and to depart from Seedy Idrees, either with Abd el Kreem's leave or without it. Accordingly, Urquhart and Gerald went off after breakfast to interview the sheikh, and, if possible, to secure his consent to our departure, leaving me to superintend certain matters which required looking after in camp. In their absence I had a talk with Embarck as to the equipment necessary for our march into the desert, and particularly as to what animals we ought to get. He advised us to sell all our mules and to buy camels, and also, if we liked, desert horses to ride. The latter, he assured me, were fully equal to camels in endurance and the power of going without water.

Soon after noon Gerald and Urquhart returned looking very much pleased with themselves, from which I conjectured that the result of their interview had been satisfactory. And so it proved. At first, they said, the sheikh was obstinate, and refused to listen to them.

"Wherefore would ye go, Nazarenes," he had cried, "to seek death in the wilderness? Have ye aught to complain of in my treatment of you here? Allah knoweth, all that I possess is yours. If ye require at my hands aught else than ye now have, ask, and, if it be in my power, I will give it to you, whether it be land or cattle or slaves. If your hearts go out in desire unto the women of my tribe, choose ye wives from out of their number, and settle down amongst my people ; and, by the beard of the Prophet, all men shall honour you, and ye shall be second in authority only to myself."

In reply, Urquhart said that, so far from having anything to complain of in his treatment of us, our hearts were overflowing with gratitude for his kindness. Nevertheless, we had travelled from afar for a certain purpose, and could not relinquish that purpose now. On our return from the Djebel Kebeer, which he hoped would be at no distant date, we would, if it still pleased the sheikh to receive us, make a longer stay.

In the end Abd el Kreem gave way, consoling himself with the reflection that it was the will of Allah, against which it was no use contending. It was arranged that we should remain one more week, and then that no obstacle should be placed in the way of our departure.

The week was spent in buying animals and hiring drivers. Besides our camels we purchased three desert horses—lean, weedy animals, with rough coats of a pale bay colour. They presented a most miserable appearance, but after a week's trial we began to learn their value.

On the eighth day after Urquhart's interview with the sheikh, all being now ready, we set forth. Abd el Kreem himself and the greater part of his family came to bid us God-speed on our journey. The fair Fatma was there, with no eye for any one but Gerald, and something like a tear stood in her big goggle eyes as he mounted his horse and bade her a long, and, as it turned out, a last adieu.

" Farewell, Nazarenes," cried the sheikh. " My heart will be heavy until ye come back and I see your faces once more. Even now I know not wherefore ye will go, but the ways of fate are inscrutable. Meanwhile, let the desire of home be a spur to hasten your return, and may Allah attend your footsteps in the wilderness, and the blessing of His holy Prophet be upon you as ye travel through waste places. Fare ye well."

Reciprocating the sheikh's good wishes, and hoping that the very considerable shadow cast by his portly person might not diminish in our absence, we gave the word to start, and our caravan got under weigh.

" A pretty set of madmen we are!" thought I, as I took a last look at the battlements of the kasbah, which, after we had been two hours on the march, were just disappearing behind the crest of a range of sandhills. And, truly, there was something delightfully sketchy about the whole of our proceedings. None of us had any exact idea where we were going. We were plunging into the trackless wastes of the Sahara in the hope that after a fortnight or so of travelling we might hit upon the Djebel Kebeer ; if we did not, which seemed to me a far more probable contingency, die of hunger and thirst on the way.

Our course lay south-south-east, because Embarek had a vague idea that Mount Atlas lay somewhere to the left of the midday sun, and also because some of the older inhabitants of Seedy Idrees had told us that that was the direction taken by the other caravans who had set forth on the same fool's errand as ourselves.

I shall condense as far as possible my account of our march across the Sahara, partly because this history is already growing too long, and also because the every-day incidents of desert travel have been so often before narrated by other and more graphic pens than mine. One day's tramp succeeded another for nearly a week with unvarying monotony. To describe the details of one would be to describe them all—the start in the delicious cool of the early morning hours, the halt in the scorching noontide glare, the evening march, and the pitching of the camp as the heavy dews of night begin to fall. There are people who have found a charm and an interest of its own in desert scenery and travel, but I must confess that I am not one of them. True, there is a certain indescribable weirdness in the never-ending stretches of barren, desolate plain ; the monotonous undulations of wind-drifted sand ; in the vast solitude and the deathlike silence, scarce broken by the velvet tread of the spongy-footed camel. Even the habitual chatter of the Arabs is hushed, for talking induces thirst, and our water-bottles are none too capacious, and fresh supplies of the precious liquid are precarious in the extreme. To my mind the whole thing would be terribly wearisome and uninteresting were it not for the excitement of ever-present peril, and the strange fascination which lands untrodden by the foot of civilized man must always possess for the explorer. And then the sun, whose beams in England, like angels' visits, we long for and welcome when we see them—out here one gets to hate them as one's worst enemy, while his remorseless rays beat down upon you from out of the cloudless vault of blue.

For several days we tramped along on our monotonous journey across the wilderness, camping by night wherever water could by any possibility be procured. Of vegetation there was almost none, save that here and there a few scarecrows of shrubs grew about the beds of dried-up torrents. In these places water could generally be obtained by digging, but it was scanty and of very bad quality. On the miserable herbage which grew about the banks of these watercourses our animals had to eke out the slender supplies of grain we had brought with us for their consumption, and the camels soon began to grow thin. Many people have an idea that a camel will live upon anything, and that if you provide him with a moderate diet of empty soda-water bottles and biscuit-tins he will thrive and be thankful. The fact is quite the reverse. He likes good food and plenty of it, and he is, moreover, quite incapable of hard work for long if he does not get it. I am afraid I fail to appreciate the merits of the Ship of the Desert. He is most aggravatingly slow in his paces, excessively ugly, and incurably vicious. The Arabs say that a camel harbours revenge for exactly a year, and one of our newly hired drivers, with the inventive genius of his species, told us a curious yarn illustrative of this

L

theory. He said that once, while in charge of a camel in Northern Marocco, he had occasion to give the animal a severe beating. Happening to return to the same village a year later, he was walking through the soko, or market-place, where a number of animals were tethered, and was passing close to a camel, when the brute suddenly turned on him and seized him by the seat of his breeches, inflicting considerable damage on his raiment and also what lay beneath it. He fortunately managed to escape from the camel's clutches without serious injury, and, looking at him, he recognized him as the identical animal which he had beaten a year before. Further, on thinking the matter over, he remembered that it was upon the very same day the previous year that he had administered the beating. Strangest thing of all, when he saw the camel the next morning he was as amiable as possible and wanted to fraternize with his quondam persecutor, thereby proving beyond possibility of doubt that the creature's memory lasted exactly one year and no more.

"Mashallah!" exclaimed Mohammed at the end of the tale, "but the jimmel is indeed a sagacious beast."

We three Englishmen were all of opinion that the camel-driver was a credit to a race whose splendid mendacity has always gained my warmest admiration. I believe the natives of Marocco to be nearly, if not quite, the finest liars in the world. Was there not a cynical man of law who divided the race of liars into three classes, thus—"liars, d——d liars, and scientific witnesses"? Yet I cannot help thinking that the finest efforts of the most hardened "expert" in the witness-box would pale before the triumphs of imagination of even a moderately truthful Moor.

But this is digressing. On the seventh day Embarek told us that we should encamp in a real oasis, and our expectations were raised accordingly. We had not seen a bit of green or a drop of running water since leaving Seedy Idrees, for our way was through a land which, in its utter desolation, seemed to be cursed of Heaven. Yet the reader must not suppose that the desert here was that of the popular imagination—a level plain of sand destitute of vegetation. On the contrary, the surface of the ground was diversified by hills and valleys ; the soil was hard and barren, but sparsely covered in places with stunted herbage, and it would only have required a few showers of rain to render it tolerably productive. In one place we passed through a gloomy ravine with precipitous cliffs on either side. Boulders of limestone, which had fallen from the heights above, lay tumbled about in wild confusion, giving the camels, who are always at their worst on stony ground, a great deal of trouble. Down the sides of the hills torrents, which had long since ceased to run, had cleft deep rifts and gorges. Stripped of every atom of verdure and vegetation, Nature, all flayed and scarified, displayed herself in naked sterility, unrelieved by a single softening feature. We called this defile the " Valley of the Shadow of Death."

True to his promise, on the evening of the seventh day after our departure from Seedy Idrees, Embarek brought us to the "oasis." Heavens! how we were disillusioned. Our visions of cool rills and fountains, bubbling forth amid verdant meads and shady palm-groves, were rudely dispelled in face of the sordid reality. In a hollow, surrounded by bare rocks, was a small puddle of dirty water ; the verdant meadows of our too lively imaginations were represented by a few stalks of rank camel-grass and some miserable artemisia shrubs, which maintained a dire struggle for existence against the niggardliness of Nature.

However, this was the last water we should find for at least four days, so it behoved us to make the most of it. Before us lay league upon league of the yellow sands of the Sahara—the true desert of the popular fancy, as Mr. Carl Haag has familiarized us with it, only lacking the conventional accompaniment of palm tree and Arab sheikh. We rested one day by the well, and the next morning I rose early, just as the first faint saffron streaks of dawn appeared in the east, and gazed forth with gloomy forebodings across the dreary waste. Far as the eye could reach it stretched away to the utmost horizon, and fancy multiplied the distance till it almost reached infinity. Could we reasonably hope to reach alive whatever shore might lie beyond that ocean of sand ? The odds seemed to me to be decidedly against it.

We carefully tested our water-skins before setting forth, for upon their soundness our lives would for the next few days depend. We also watered the camels to their full capacity, as their stomachs would contain our reserve supply in the event of the skins giving out. Then, filling our gourds and bottles and every available receptacle we could get together with the muddy, but all too precious, liquid, we set our faces southwards, and were soon in the heart of the inhospitable waste. This was desert with a vengeance, and my heart beat quicker as I thought what the next few days might have in store for us. We moved slowly on in single file. The straggling goffla looked from a distance like some huge snake dragging itself lazily along. It was Embarek's opinion that eight or nine days must elapse before we could hope to reach the Djebel Kebeer—always supposing that we were steering our course in the proper direction, which, having regard to the exceeding vagueness of his ideas on the subject, seemed to me, to say the least of it, doubtful in the extreme. He also said that, to the best of his recollection, there were not more than two wells on the way, situated two or three days' journey apart. He could not remember that there was any particular landmark indicating the position of the first of these wells, but the second had a couple of palm trees growing beside it, which he thought, with the aid of our telescopes, we should have a fair chance of discovering.

A cheerful prospect truly! We were in search of a mountain, which, granting that it actually existed —and I was by no means satisfied even of this—lay *somewhere* to the south-east in the Great Desert; it might be ten days' journey off, it might be fifteen, it might be more. Then, our chance of stumbling upon those two wells seemed to be quite as remote as our prospects of finding Mount Atlas. Taking everything into consideration, I thought the betting was about ten to one that we should all be dead and done for before the end of the week, and I could not help expressing myself in this sense to Urquhart. He, however, was full of hope and as sanguine as ever.

"Oh," he cried, "we shall get along somehow.

Embarck has a pretty fair idea of the direction to take, and our compasses will keep us from getting far out of the track."

Urquhart's somewhat vague optimism was not particularly reassuring, even when backed by Gerald's unfailing faith in his friend, which rose superior to every trial. However, as I said before, there was nothing to be done but to go on and hope for the best. A comical incident occurred just at this time to divert my thoughts, and, as this part of our journey contained few things of that nature, I may as well chronicle it. It was Mohammed's duty to clean and otherwise take care of our saddles, and, to do him justice, he did the work admirably. Unfortunately, he now learned for the first time, probably from Ali, that the saddles were made of pig-skin. The knowledge that he had been handling every morning and evening the hide of the unclean beast was a terrible shock to so strict a Mohammedan as our cook, and his disgust grew to positive horror when he made the further discovery that the brush wherewith he scrubbed the leather was formed of the bristles of the same animal.

"Staferallah!" he exclaimed in accents of woe, "may God forgive me! ashes have fallen on my head, and I am indeed brought low! What pollution is this that I have been daily devouring? To think that every morning and evening I have been in contact with the harami, the accursed thing, and knew it not! O Ali, you son of a burnt father, why did you not tell me sooner? Ah welli, woe is me! How shall I ever cleanse myself from such abomination? May Allah have mercy upon all such as sin unawares, and upon those who unwittingly transgress His laws."

" We are in the hands of Allah, and to His keeping we return," piously observed Ali, though I failed to see the exact bearing of the remark. " May your trespasses be forgiven you, and may your end be peace."

By way of commencing his expiation, poor Mohammed prayed that evening twice as long as usual, and performed several times over *el timoom*, or the washing with sand prescribed by the Koran whenever water is not procurable. A picturesque figure he was as he stood silhouetted against the lurid sunset glow, which, as the great red disc sank into the sandy waste, filled the sky like the light from some vast hidden conflagration. Spreading his jellabia on the ground to serve as a prayer-carpet, he repeated over and over again the *magreb*, or sunset prayer. Now bowing down upon his knees he touched the earth with his forehead ; then raising himself upright, with hands now uplifted, now pressed to his side, he testified to the unity and greatness of Allah. Next, with more bowing and salaaming, sitting awhile on his heels, with knees touching the ground and hands on his thighs, he went through the whole of the rest of the formula prescribed by the Moorish sect of Malek, of whose rites he was a scrupulous observer.

This was the last we heard of the matter, for Mohammed's fears of religious contamination soon yielded to graver apprehensions as to his personal safety and that of the caravan. We covered a good stretch of ground that morning until the fierce heat of the sun compelled us to make our midday halt. A shimmering mist rose from the face of the desert, and some fine effects of mirage appeared. Wide lakes, studded with wooded islets, stretched away to imaginary banks which seemed to slope down in forest-clad declivities to the water's edge. Even though I knew only too well the impossibility of such things in this thirsty land, it was with difficulty that I could bring myself to disbelieve the evidence of my senses, so perfect was the illusion. At another time visions of aerial castles, cloud-ramparts crowned with lofty battlements and towers, presented themselves to our bewildered gaze. Phantasmagoric camels, guided by the spectres of Titanic Moors, stalked with giant strides across the heavens, the ghostlike reflections of our own caravan. A sight calculated to impress the most unemotional observer with wonder and awe. Upon ourselves, situated as we were, our nerves strung to the highest pitch, it had a powerful effect. The superstitious natives believe these apparitions to be the djins of the desert hovering round their intended victims, and they regard them as portents of impending disaster.

October 15.—It looks as though the forebodings of the Moors were likely to be soon realized. Our stock of water is all but exhausted, and as yet there is no sign of the well. We halt for six hours at midday, enduring agonies of thirst and prickly heat. This sort of thing cannot last much longer. It must soon end one way or another, and I think I know which way is the most likely.

16*th.*—Thank God, we are saved for the present! Just as we had given up all hope, Almarakshi's sharp eyes caught sight of a white paddy-bird, the first living creature we had seen since leaving Seedy Idrees. The Moors are wild with joy. They say there must be water near, or such a bird could not exist. We whip out our telescopes and watch his flight, which follows a straight line for a considerable distance. Carefully taking our bearings, we turn our horses' heads in the same direction, and at the end of a couple of hours' march we are rewarded by the sight of a few stunted bushes and scrappy patches of camel grass, which betoken the presence of water. The well is similar to that in the last oasis, and the water, if possible, muddier and more tepid. Heaven knows, however, we do not stop to criticize its quality, but drain our cups as though it were veritable nectar.

18*th.*—Off again, after one day's halt by the well. The heat grows fiercer and fiercer as we get further south and deeper into the heart of the Great Desert. The ground to-day is stonier and less sandy, with rocks cropping out here and there, and the earth burns like red-hot iron. .

An hour before noon on this day we sought the scanty shade cast by some large boulders of rock, and lay grilling there for four or five hours. While scooping myself a hole in some tiny hillocks of sand which had formed at the base of the rocks, so as to make myself as comfortable as possible, I came upon something hard. At first I took it to be a round stone, but on removing it, to my surprise and horror, I found that it was a human skull. Presently Urquhart found more bones, some of them undoubtedly human. This set us all searching, and after scratching away a short time we came upon a number of skeletons, all lying huddled together and covered only by a few inches of drifted sand. Other bones, which were not human seemed to be without exception those of camels.

"Good heavens!" exclaimed Urquhart: "we seem to be in a perfect Golgotha. Who on earth can these have been?"

"Ya lateef! O merciful God!" cried Embarek: "'tis the goffla which set forth some years ago from Seedy Idrees and perished in the wilderness. May their souls rest in peace, and may Allah in His mercy save us from a like fate."

Yes; there could be little doubt about the matter. These sandy hillocks were the graves of our hapless predecessors in the mad attempt to cross the desert. Perishing of thirst, or else more likely overwhelmed by the simoon, they had dragged themselves to the base of the rock we lay under, but only to die there engulfed by the sandy billow driven by the desert wind.

And we—we whom mocking Fate had sent here to snatch a few hours' repose in their last resting-place—were we about to leave our bones to bleach in some similar spot ; or, strangest of coincidences, here under the very rock where they had died? For now a strange languor and despondency, such as we had not known before, came over us, so that we felt disinclined to stir even from our present gruesome surroundings. Our spirits, which had been raised by the fortunate discovery of the first well, sank lower than ever, and the future painted itself in the darkest colours to our heat-oppressed fancies. All the pluck seemed taken out of us. We were at a loss to account for this feeling of depression, until at length we became aware of a distinct change in the state of the atmosphere. Ordinarily the air of the desert, in spite of the great heat, possesses strangely invigorating properties, and in the early morning hours it is deliciously cool and bracing. To-day, however, as the afternoon wore on, a distressing sultriness set in, and we struggled in vain against the feeling of lassitude which it induced. To Embarek, and those others of our servants who had had experience in desert travel, this was a familiar symptom, but they made no effort to overcome it, and it was easy to see from their faces that their minds were filled with gloomy forebodings.

CHAPTER XIII.

THE SIMOOM.

ALL that afternoon of the 18th we lay amid the mortal remains of the band of adventurers from Seedy Idrees.

Every moment the air grew closer and more unwholesome. The sky, too, from out of whose stainless blue the sun was wont to pour down upon us his merciless rays, now became filled with thick clouds which, as the hour of sunset approached, assumed strange and magnificent shapes. Purple masses of vapour, turreted like the bastions of some vast aerial fortress; huge brazen pyramids; vast mountain ranges—nebular Alps, massive and solid looking, their jagged crests rimmed with fire—formed a grand aerial panorama.

Towards six o'clock the sun set. Girt with a blood-red canopy of lurid cloud, he strode royally down to the western horizon; and as his fiery orb disappeared, the desert caught the crimson glare till the vast expanse of sand glowed like a lake of flame. The brief African twilight followed, and the life of day ebbed rapidly away until complete darkness overspread the earth.

We roused ourselves sufficiently to take a scanty evening meal, but the burning thirst, which our limited stock of water forbade us to satisfy, made us forget our hunger, and we ate but little. At present it was too dark for us to think of travelling, as the camels would probably lame themselves, in which case it would be all up with us. An hour after midnight, however, the clouds partially dispersed, and a few faint, shimmering moonbeams afforded us sufficient light to make a start. We took our bearings carefully with the compasses, and ordered the camels to be loaded. The night air, instead of being cool and dewy as usual, was distressingly muggy, which made travelling much more laborious than usual. The hours of darkness passed slowly by, and a few faint streaks of light heralded the advent of day, and then the sun rose, shining in a sickly fashion through a yellow haze, with shafts of pallid light radiating from his disc like the spokes of a wheel. It was evident that a storm of some kind was brewing, and we cherished the fond hope that it might end in rain.

At half-past seven we halted for breakfast, and also to give the camels a feed of corn, of which they stood in sore need ; and from that spot we never stirred for two whole days. As the morning wore on new and unaccountable effects of mirage appeared. Fresh spectres of terrific aspect presented themselves to our gaze, apparition following apparition with startling rapidity and variation, and filling our minds with undefined apprehensions. Nor was this all. Far away on our right, across the tawny billows of the wilderness, we saw for the first time gigantic columns of sand scudding along on the horizon, their tall, slender shafts waving gracefully as they advanced, and expanding on high into wide flat tops like gigantic mushrooms. Now and again they were dissipated by the wind, and, bursting aloft, blurred the azure of the sky with a yellow haze. Immediately in front of us a murky mass of violet-coloured nimbus had gathered, which now seemed to be bearing straight down upon us.

The Moors were the first to see these alarming phenomena, the sure precursors of the hot wind of the desert, and something like a panic broke out among them.

"Allah be merciful to us!" cried Embarek in accents of terror. "'Tis the simoom. Already I can feel his fiery breath upon my cheek, and I smell the sand-cloud as it advances on us from afar."

"Embarek speaks sooth," chimed in Ali, who always took a cheerful view of things. "If it strikes us before we reach the well it is all over with us, and Azrael will take us, even as he hath taken those who rest beneath the shadow of yonder rock. May the holy Prophet and his saints be near us, and aid us in the hour of need."

For a while these gruesome portents, pregnant with death and disaster, threatened us from a distance, till suddenly they disappeared. Not for long, however. Fresh clusters of sand-pillars formed on every side, and the violet-coloured cloud appeared once more upon our left. Nearer and nearer came the yellow, undulating columns, now with a stately gliding motion, now sweeping swiftly by on the murky pinions of the whirlwind ; now circling slowly round, coiling, twisting, eddying, in strange curves and sinuosities. Anon, to our heated imaginations they seemed to take shape and form, as of djins of the desert ; ghostly arms beckoned and waved with menacing gestures. Anon, the thin shaft of some tall pillar would be parted in twain, and the flat top, poised in mid air, hung silent and motionless over our heads, as though Azrael, Death's angel, were hovering near, ready to enwrap us in his sable plumes.

At the first sign of this new danger we made the best preparations we could to meet it. The camels were made to kneel down and tethered in a circle, with ourselves in the centre, ready to lie on our faces in the sand the moment the hot blast should strike us. The heat was suffocating, and already fine particles of sand getting into our mouths and nostrils caused an almost insupportable irritation. And now the violet cloud came nearer, increasing in size and volume, until it became apparent that our fate could not be much longer delayed. A parching wind, the herald of worse horrors to come, parched our cheeks as the simoom, charioted upon the suffocating cloud, bore down upon us. Through the whirling mists of dust the red disc of the sun shed a lurid light upon the scene, causing the sand-storm to glare like the smoke from some infernal furnace. At last the tempest broke upon us with all its fury. In a moment the sun, whose brazen globe had hitherto loomed threateningly through the vapour, was blotted out completely, and all was darkness—darkness unspeakable—darkness which choked and could be felt.

Embarek uttered a muffled cry of warning, but it was not needed, for with one accord we had thrown ourselves flat on our stomachs, giving ourselves up for lost. For myself, I thrust my face under my camel's belly in the endeavour to escape from the suffocating blast; but it was of little avail. The scorching wind howled and moaned above; the fine sand penetrated everywhere, filtrating through our clothes, and choking up the pores of our skins and making breathing almost an impossibility.

Oh, the agony of those long hours of torment! Above the wailing of the storm I could hear the muffled shrieks of half-stifled men, mingled with the moaning of the camels, and I remember that in the midst of it all the thought struck me, "What will become of us if the camels die?" It would be all up with us then with a vengeance.

Profiting by a slight lull in the storm, I ventured to raise my head. My eyes encountered a strange spectacle. All the men and the beasts were covered several inches deep with a fine dust, which left only their heads showing. On every side the pillars of sand were whirling and eddying about in mad frolic, lit up by the sickly glare of the sun. Then once more the hot blast burst on us, and I was forced to shelter myself as well as I could from its fury. A tormenting thirst now asserted itself, and I expected every moment to be my last. I fetched my breath with painful gulps and gasps, and the fine, choking sand seemed to have got down into and filled my very lungs. I had not conceived that Death could present himself to suffering humanity in such fearful guise. How I cursed myself for my folly in consenting to come to this inhospitable region, only to die thus miserably! To make matters worse, in the middle of the storm the camel next to mine broke loose and passed like some huge four-footed phantom into the gloom, leaving his driver exposed to the full force of the blast. Presently the wretched man, whose sufferings throughout had wrung my heart, turned over on his side with a dreadful groan and expired. A few hours later, when the storm had abated for a while, I saw that the body had swollen to an unnatural size, and putrefaction set in almost directly, as usually happens with those who die of the poisonous desert wind. This added to the unutterable horror of our situation. To remove the body was utterly impossible so long as the simoom blew, for rising to one's feet would have meant instant death.

All that day and night we lay in the same spot, twelve wretched, cowering mortals, suffering unspeakable torments, and silently beseeching the God of Heaven to spare our lives, or, if we were fated to die, at least quickly to put us out of our misery. I do not mean to say that the simoom was blowing all this time, else not a man or beast of us would have been left alive. But the sky never sufficiently cleared to allow us to rise or resume our journey, and every now and again in the night hours the hot breeze and the falling sand told us that the force of the blast was not yet entirely expended. Daylight came at length, but it brought us little relief. The heavens had the same terrible hue of burnished brass, alternating with pale yellow, and the moving pillars of sand still waltzed madly round, though at a greater distance. Thank God, however, that horrible simoom cloud was no longer to be seen, which gave us some hope that we had experienced the worst.

Towards nine o'clock the sand ceased to fall, and we could rise and breathe freely. The sun came out, and, the sand-cloud gradually dispersing, the heavens became clear. My first impulse was to see how Urquhart and Gerald were faring. The former had spoken once or twice during the night, but Gerald had given no sign of life since the previous evening. We found him in a state of semi-unconsciousness, but the pure morning air soon brought him round. We were like three moving sand-pillars ourselves when we stood upright, and we had great difficulty in shaking the dust out of our clothes. On going round the goffla we found that two of the camels and another of their drivers had died from the effects of the simoom. Strange to say, these Arabs, children of the desert as they are, seem less capable of enduring thirst and the other hardships of travel in the wilderness than their brethren from northern climes who are less accustomed to heat. Our horses, tough little beasts that they were, seemed to have suffered least of the whole party, and were surprisingly well, considering what they had gone through.

Our first care was to examine the water-skins, for we all felt that we must drink, and that soon, or die. Fortunately, we found them all intact, but their contents had half evaporated since they had last been opened. To eke out our scanty stock Embarek skilfully transferred the water from the stomachs of the two dead camels into our skins, and a small ration was served out to horses and men. We calculated that with the utmost economy we could not make our small supply last over the next day, so if we did not find the second well by that time, we should only have lived through the horrors of the simoom to die another death of lingering torture. In any case, it was useless to remain longer where we were, so, though the sun was now pouring down his fiercest rays upon us, we determined to make a start. In spite of the heat, however, the air was decidedly fresher since the sand-storm, and if only we could get water we felt that all would be right. That "if," however, I thought ought to be writ in capital letters.

We felt too ill and weak to bury the two dead Moors, but, placing the bodies side by side, we left the work of interment to the sands and winds of the desert. I remember remarking to Urquhart, by way of making things as cheerful as possible, that the simoom would soon have other sexton's work to perform. He did not seem to relish my grim humour, and answered rather snappishly that things were quite bad enough already, without making them out worse than they were. We were also compelled to leave behind some of our heavier *impedimenta*, including one of the tents, as the number of our camels was now reduced by three, and those that survived were nearly worn-out. We had not gone far before we came across the one which had broken loose during the sand-storm. He was in a very bad way, and, after a short consultation, Embarek decided to cut his throat, and the water in his stomach was soon in one of our empty skins. We travelled all that afternoon and far into the night before we halted, without seeing a sign of the well, though Embarek was confident that it could not be far away. But I am tired of detailing the miseries of this horrible journey, and would fain pass them over as quickly as possible. For the sake of brevity, therefore, I shall revert for the present to my diary.

22nd.—No sign of water. The end cannot be far off. We are pretty well at the last gasp, and suffering agonies of thirst. Gerald is especially bad. He is delirious at times, and raves incoherently about forests and meadows and bubbling fountains. I feel myself as if I had a brain-fever coming on. When will it all end? It would have saved trouble, and been far simpler, had we all been suffocated in the simoom instead of lingering on like this. However, to-morrow will probably be the last of it.

23rd.—Killed another camel this morning, partly because he was worn-out and refused to rise, but chiefly in order to get the water from his stomach. We are all worse, if possible, than yesterday. We were just on the point of calling a final halt and giving ourselves up for lost, when Urquhart, after carefully scanning the whole horizon through his telescope, espies the wavy plumes of two tall palm trees. They are far away on our left and, if anything, rather behind us. Embarek is overjoyed at the sight, saying that it is the well, and that we have been steering our course a little too far to the west. I don't feel very sanguine about it myself. We turn the animals' heads in the direction indicated, but the trees are many miles off, and the animals are too utterly exhausted to cover the distance. Accordingly we are obliged to halt another night. Shall we ever live to see to-morrow's sun?

24th.—Managed to get the animals to start, and continued our way towards the trees. We are all utterly exhausted, man and beast, and can scarce drag one foot after the other. The horses, who have borne up most pluckily so far, are now dead beat, and we are forced to dismount and lead them. Suddenly, after an hour and a half's march, the animals one after another throw up their noses in the air, as though scenting something, and quicken their paces. The Moors are half frantic with excitement and joy.

"El hamdu l'Illah," says Ali slowly and with emphasis; "let us render praises to Allah and His *Nebi* (prophet). The camels sniff the water from afar. Allah Kreem, God hath been bountiful to us! It is the well, and we are saved."

Ali is right. Our lives are spared for the present.

CHAPTER XIV.

MOUNT ATLAS AT LAST.

IT had been a near thing, for another day without water would certainly have finished us. However, "all's well that ends at a well," as Gerald remarks—from which melancholy effort at humour I infer that he is feeling better—and our troubles are over for awhile. This "oasis" is a more respectable one than the last. There is some very tolerable grass growing in it, which enables us to economize our barley, and so to make a longer halt than otherwise we should have done. Moreover, the day after we arrived, I flushed a big covey of *hajjil el sahhara*,[1] (desert partridges, or sand-grouse). They only flew a short distance and were perfectly tame, evidently not being accustomed to the sight of man, so by "browning" the covey several times in most unsportsmanlike fashion we managed to bag no less than five brace. It may well be imagined that they were a most welcome addition to our scantily stocked larder. These sand-grouse were the only living creatures we

[1] The word "Sahara" is habitually mispronounced, the second syllable being short.

had seen for the last ten days, with the exception of the solitary paddy-bird who had so providentially guided us to the well on the 16th. Embarek infers from our coming across these birds that we cannot be very far from some inhabited country, and he is surprised that we have not yet sighted Mount Atlas, which, to the best of his recollection, is not more than about three days' journey from the well. A slight haze, however, which pervades the lower atmosphere throughout the day would easily account for this.

The rest of our voyaging in the desert is soon told. The second day after leaving the oasis we came across another small well by accident, the existence of which Embarek had not known, and encamped beside it for the night. We noticed that evening that the ground to the south-east rose in a gradual slope as far as we could see, and the sky in that direction was filled with a bank of heavy cloud. We regarded this cloud with some alarm, fearing that it might be the precursor of another simoom, but Embarek laughed at our fears, saying that it did not bear the slightest resemblance to the simoom-cloud, which was smaller and of a different colour.

"Yon cloud is formed by cold, not by heat," he added, nodding his head significantly.

"And, pray, what are we to understand by that?" I inquired.

"I mean," said he, "that somewhere behind yon curtain of vapour the Djebel Tselj is concealed, and that in two or three days at the latest we shall be breaking bread with the blessed Marabutin."

This seemed to be too good news to be true, but the bare idea of our being near the end of this horrible journey, and of seeing Ali's Mahatma friends in the flesh, was enough to send us to bed in a far happier frame of mind. I slept soundly on till about seven o'clock next morning, when I was awoke by Gerald's voice calling outside the tent in loud and excited tones—

"Hi! Jim, David, get up, quick, and come out. Mount Atlas! Mount Atlas!"

Hastily throwing a blanket over my shoulders, I ran out to see what was up, and the sight that met my gaze almost took my breath away, and made me rub my eyes to see if I was really awake, or still dreaming. The grey, rounded masses of cloud still hung thick about the horizon to the south-east, but above them rose, as though suspended in mid-air between heaven and earth, with nought but mist for its foundation, a dazzling snow-white peak, piercing with its colossal spike the stainless azure of the early morning sky. I can well remember my first near view of the Alps—it was from the window of a hotel in Interlaken—and the impression which the majesty of the Jungfrau made upon me. But there, one's mind had been gradually attuned to the splendours of snowy summits and mountain masses by distant views and by travelling among the lower outlying ranges. Here, the effect was far more sudden and overpowering. For days and weeks we had been tramping over the dead level of the sandy sea, which still stretched away without a break on every side far as the eye could reach. And now this glorious vision had risen suddenly from the vast plain, as though conjured up in a single night by some wizard's hand. Was that really snow we saw, or was the mirage mocking us once more with its airy nothingnesses? Would this glittering peak pass into the limbo wherein had disappeared the lakes and mountains, and the "baseless fabrics" of the cloud-castles and towers, which we had seen in the Sahara?

No; there could be no mistake about it this time. Even Gerald, who on previous occasions had been a consistent backer of the deceitful mirage, is now ready to lay any odds on the reality of Mount Atlas. Heavens! what a glorious sight! and how our hearts bounded at the prospect! Mr. Stanley has vindicated the geographical accuracy of Herodotus as regards the pigmies, Ruwenzori, and the true sources of the Nile, and now we were about to perform a similar service for the shade of the grand old geographer and for Pliny. What an exquisite "arrangement" in gold and silver and turquoise is formed by the Sahara's yellow waves and that snowy peak cleaving the vault of blue. As the sun rose higher the clouds at the base began to disperse; a few light fragments of fleecy mist parted from the main mass, and floated slowly up the flanks of the mountain till they melted away into space. And now the lower slopes began to appear. The leaden vapours parted asunder, like curtains drawn aside by some invisible hand, and, through the openings in the wreathing mists, dark precipices of seemingly enormous height frowned forth, and lower peaks, the buttresses and supports of the central massif, came into view. We calculated that the mountain could not be more than thirty miles off, if so much, and, judging from the amount of snow we saw, it must be at least as high as Mont Blanc.

It was curious to see the different effect this spectacle had upon the various members of our caravan. As for us three Englishmen, we neither moved or spoke for some minutes. A Frenchman or an Italian would probably have cut capers or shed tears of joy, but in such supreme moments an Englishman restrains himself. Yet what varied thoughts and memories, what strange, conflicting emotions came crowding tumultuously in upon our minds! Our hearts were full to overflowing, yet words seemed to fail us. Not so the Moors. They laughed and shouted aloud in their glee, and Embarek and Almarakshi sang out a veritable pœan of triumph. As for Ali, he embraced Mohammed with effusion, and shed copious tears of gratitude and joy on that worthy's fat neck. The dream of the Persian's life was about to be realized. He would soon meet face to face his old *gvorvo*, or instructor in the occult mysteries, that revered being whose inspired words and teaching had once been the lodestar of his life, but from whom fate had sundered him for so many years. Urquhart, too, his friend and benefactor, would now achieve the object for which he had dared and suffered so much, and, this attained, the old man could die happy.

From our camp by the well the mountain mass, of which the snow-peak formed the culminating point, appeared to rise from a sort of elevated plateau, from which the ground sloped gradually down into the desert. Closer inspection, however, at the end of five hours' march from the well, showed us that what we thought was the edge of a plateau was in reality a low range of rocky hills running nearly due east and west. Over these hills it would be necessary for us to pass before we could reach the foot of the Djebel Kebeer. We camped for the evening near the foot of these hills, so as, if possible, to arrive at our destination before midday on the morrow. We could see no sign of human dwellings, and, considering the proximity to the snow, the hills seemed singularly destitute of vegetation. A few scanty patches of artemisia were visible here and there, but the soil was almost as sterile and unproductive as in the middle of the desert. No doubt the water flowing down from Mount Atlas found its outlet somewhere to the south. Nor could we discern anything in the shape of a road or path leading down into the desert, from which I inferred that the natives of these parts (if any such really existed) did not trouble this side of the hills much, and no wonder.

We rose early next morning, and, mounting our horses, we rode for some distance along the hills looking for some pass which our tired and heavily laden beasts could get over. About two miles from the camp we found a narrow gorge, with what looked like an old disused road leading up to the top of the range. The track did not look particularly favourable for camels, but we nevertheless determined to try it, and after a troublesome climb, which badly lamed two of them, we got to the top of the pass, and our curiosity as to what lay on the other side was gratified.

The vast snow-fields of the Djebel Kebeer had led us to hope for something better than the meagre oases of the desert, or even of the Draa valley, but we were fairly amazed at the splendidly fertile and cuchanting prospect which opened out beneath us. Between the hills on which we stood and the central mountain mass was a lovely smiling valley formed by a stream which flowed down from the upper snow region. To our right, a spur of the Djebel Kebeer descended to the range of hills on which we stood, and formed the head of the glen. Lower down, the valley broadened out to a width of apparently about two miles, and the stream, following the line of the base of the mountain, made a sharp bend to the south and flowed down in serpentine windings through meadows of a most exquisite green, alternating with patches of cultivation. On the left bank hills of moderate height divided the valley from the desert. On the right, or western, bank the lower slopes of the Djebel Kebeer were clothed with forests of holm-oak, cork, olive, and other trees, and groves of orange and lemon. Above the trees a line of lofty cliff ran parallel to the stream, surmounted in its turn by upland pastures, whereon, by the aid of our glasses, we could descry herds of innumerable cattle feeding. Yet higher up the mountain-side a glacier forced its way down far below the snow-line between two opposing walls of rock, and from out its hanging-wall of blue ice a stream leaped down in a succession of cataracts to the river below. Dotted about the lower landscape were numerous hamlets and white houses and cottages, and some distance down the valley we could see a small town of flat-roofed houses built after the ordinary eastern fashion. In this town, Embarek told us, resided most of the Marabutin ; so, without more delay, we determined to direct our footsteps thither.

At the bottom of the hill we struck an excellent road adapted for wheeled traffic. This surprised me considerably, as in Marocco, there being no carts or carriages, such a thing as a road does not exist. Crossing the stream by a wooden bridge, we followed the right bank for some distance. As we proceeded lower down the valley we were dumbfounded at the extraordinary beauty and fertility of this Central African Paradise, in which we had so unexpectedly found ourselves. Every turn of the road disclosed some vista of enchanting loveliness. The lower out-works and buttresses of the mountain were cleft by wooded glens, down which rivulets of the clearest water flowed amid brakes of tamarisks and oleander, and clustering ferns and creepers. Nightingales were singing in the bushes, their notes blending melodiously with the soft coo of turtle-doves ; and the kingfisher flashed like a jewel from bough to bough. Looking up these miniature gorges the eye roved over verdant glades and forests of myrtle, ever-green oak, sycamore, and cypress, with the crags and snows of Atlas for a background. Each of these views made an exquisite picture in itself, such as an artist could easily include within the compass of a single frame. As we were anxious to arrive as soon as possible at the town, we resisted the temptation to linger over these lovely scenes, and pushed on amid meadows and gardens and orchards of pomegranate, fig, peach, apricot, and other fruit trees ; between hedges of tangled tamarind and cactus, festooned with clustering lilac, jasmine, and honeysuckle,—till we found ourselves approaching the city gates.

We saw several natives at work in the fields as we

passed. They were mostly tall, fine-looking men, and by no means of a wild or barbarous appearance. They wore the ordinary dress of the Moorish peasantry —jellabia, turban, and slippers, but we noticed that many of them were remarkably fair, with blue eyes, and sometimes with red hair, as though northern blood flowed in their veins. Urquhart suggested that they might be descendants of the Goths, or Vandals, who for over a century colonized North-West Africa ; but then, what could have brought them so far south ? They naturally regarded us with curious eyes, but greeted us courteously and, I was glad to hear, in the Arabic language. We should anyhow be able to make ourselves understood to our new friends. One thing I noticed particularly was that directly we had passed they returned to their work, from which I inferred that they were more industrious than the natives of Marocco. Their agriculture, moreover, was far less rude, and the ploughs and other implements were of more modern type than those in use among the Moors. Nor, like the latter, were the husbandmen armed to the teeth with sword and gun and pistol. In fact, there was a peaceable, civilized, and prosperous air about them all, and we saw no beggars or other indications of poverty. The very birds and beasts were as tame as possible, and certain animals, half rabbit, half hare, which were nibbling at the grass by the roadside, never budged an inch as we passed. Red-legged Barbary partridges ran whistling from under our feet as we walked through the fields, with the confidence born of long immunity from attack. A spirit of tranquillity and peace breathed over all Nature, animate and inanimate alike. Everywhere around was the glory of sunshine and the fragrance of flowers, the babbling of cool rills, the music of birds, and the hum of insect life ; and we felt, weary and way-worn as we were, that we could gladly rest and bask away the remainder of our lives in this heaven-favoured spot. Truly, a fitting abode for the mysterious Order to whom we were about to be introduced. What manner of men, we wondered, would the Brethren prove to be who lived in this lovely retreat? We could only trust that they would prove worthy of their environment.

The town, as I said before, was built in the usual Moorish style, but it was totally deficient in those essentially Oriental characteristics—dirt and decay. Nor was it encompassed by an outer wall, or, indeed, by fortifications of any description, which confirmed us in the opinion we had previously formed of the peaceable character of the Atlanteans. Ali, who had all along been in a fever of excitement at the prospect of meeting his gooroo, eagerly inquired of the porter, who sat in a small recess inside the gate, whether he knew of any one of the name of Singmya Songo living in the town, or, if not, could he say where he was to be found? The porter replied that, sure enough, he knew the person in question, who was the principal *Mallem* (master) in the place, and that he would bring him to us in the course of a few minutes. The tone of deference and respect in which the porter pronounced the euphonious surname of the Adept seemed to show that we were about to be introduced to a man of no small consequence in the Atlantean community, and our expectations were raised accordingly. As for Ali, he was fairly transported with delight at the welcome news, and even Urquhart's usually impassive face beamed with a satisfaction which was too genuine to be concealed. The matter-of-fact Gerald, on the contrary, exhibited little emotion. For myself, I must own that my heart beat high at the prospect of seeing in the flesh one of those remarkable and divinely gifted beings of whose doings I had heard such wonderful accounts. The privilege of shaking hands with a real live Mahatma is one which has been granted to but few people in the world.

I remembered reading the narrative[1] of one who committed to paper his impressions of a similar meeting, and I take the liberty of transcribing it here in order to show the feelings with which one ought to be animated on so momentous an occasion. The writer describes how, while he was reading in his room, he was "ordered by the audible voice of his blessed gooroo" to leave all and go in search of Madame Blavatsky. Finding himself near the borders of Thibet, he "determined come what might, to cross the frontier and find the Mahatmas, or—DIE." He had barely crossed over into Sikkim, when he suddenly saw a solitary horseman galloping towards him from the opposite direction, a tall majestic man, with a short black beard, and long black hair hanging down to his breast. Looking up, he recognized him instantly. "I was in the awful presence of Him, of the same Mahatma, my own revered gooroo, whom I had seen before in his astral body on the balcony of the Theosophical head-quarters. . . . The very same instant saw me prostrated on the ground at his

[1] "Proceedings of the Society for Psychical Research," Part IX.

feet. . . . The majesty of his countenance, which seemed to me to be the impersonation of power and thought, held me rapt in awe. . . . I see HIM before me in flesh and blood ; and he speaks to me in accents of kindness and gentleness. What more do I want? My excess of happiness made me dumb."

It may be imagined, therefore, that my curiosity was aroused to a high pitch, and I wondered if my first impressions of the Adept would resemble those of the Hindoo gentleman whose narrative I have just quoted, and also whether he would appear in the astral form or in his usual workaday, fleshly body. I had to exercise a little patience, however, as the Mahatma could not be found immediately, and we were left standing in the street outside his house until such time as he should make his appearance.

While waiting for the Adept I occupied myself in taking stock of the holy man's residence. The chief thing which struck me about it was the entire absence of architectural ornamentation, as far as the outside was concerned. The sole attempt at adornment consisted in numerous cabalistic signs painted in red upon the stucco over the doorway, all of them pregnant with hidden meanings known only to Initiates. For instance, what ordinary person would be aware that the double triangle, or Solomon's Seal, engraved at the corner of the lintel, "represents deity in its Supreme Essence, male and female, and contains the squaring of the Circles, the so-called Philosopher's Stone, the great problems of Life and Death, and the mystery of Good and Evil, etc., etc."[1] That seems a good deal for one simple device to contain, and it

[1] "The Mystery of the Ages," by the Countess of Caithness, p. 156.

makes one shudder to think what may be comprised in that "etc., etc." Hardly less authentic in their mystic significance are the two symbols opposite the triangles, I O, " the unit and cipher, the line of force and circle of comprehension," known to the ancient Magians as the emblems of Energy and Space, Will and Love, and other dual abstractions. These characters, by the way, are not unknown in the West, where, together with the incomplete circle—thus, I O U—they constitute the trine symbol of Indebtedness, coupled, not unfrequently, with Impecuniosity.

True to his promise, the porter returned in the course of a few minutes with the "blessed gooroo." Perhaps my expectations had been unduly raised, but I must confess to a feeling of disappointment when the Adept arrived. It was no majestic Mejnour or venerable Rosicrucian, such as fancy had painted him, that met my gaze. There was nothing ethereal or awe-inspiring in the very ordinary-looking, small, elderly gentleman, with an iron-grey beard, a bald head, and a slight stoop, who came forward and introduced himself to us as the Mahatma Singmya Songo. He was pleased to appear to us in his full *rupa*, or material body, as the occultists would say, over which he wore a shirt with embroidered borders, and a long white garment somewhat resembling a Roman toga. On his feet were sandals of a peculiar make attached by leather thongs, and his nails, both of fingers and toes, were nearly half an inch long and sharpened, like birds' claws, to a fine point. His countenance wore a benevolent and slightly foolish expression, which was heightened by an enormous pair of goggles that he wore to protect his eyes from the glare of the sun. The cheek-bones were high and prominent, and the features of a decidedly Mongolian, rather than Indian, type. His head had a number of extraordinary knobs and protuberances upon it, and I think it would have puzzled a phrenologist to explain what qualities they denoted.

"Salutations to the holy Mahatma!" exclaimed Embarek, prostrating himself. "The peace of Allah and the blessing of the Prophet be upon him and his."

Briefly returning the salutation, Mahatma Singmya Songo courteously greeted us all in turn with the conventional salaam alikum, and other Arabic forms of welcome, and then, recognizing Ali, he fell upon his neck and embraced him as a father would his long-lost son. It was a slightly ridiculous, if affecting, sight to see those two old men hugging each other in this fashion, and I felt that it would need a long course of initiation in the occult mysteries to instil into my mind a proper sense of respect for poor old Ali's "blessed gooroo." The Persian, however, was far from sharing my feelings in the matter, for he entertained for his old teacher a feeling of regard in which personal affection was blended with veneration for his Adeptship. In fact, it might be said that he loved him both as a man and a Brother, and his heart overflowed with gratitude for the happy destiny which had brought them together once more.

At a sign from Singmya Songo we all followed him into the house. We were at once struck with the taste and elegance of the internal decorations, which contrasted agreeably with the bareness of the exterior. A fountain, well stocked with gold-fish, was plashing gently in the centre of a miniature

Moorish court, paved with rich mosaics. The windows were covered with fine *mooshrabeea*, or carved lattice-work. A handsome dado of blue and yellow tiles adorned the walls under the portico whose carved pilasters supported a wooden gallery that ran completely round the court. This abode Singmya Songo shared with his friend and companion in his astral flittings, Mahatma Kikkuppa Row. The latter happened to be absent at the time we arrived, but we were not long in making his acquaintance, and we continued to enjoy the hospitality of the two Brethren for several days.

CHAPTER XV.

THE OASIS AND ITS INHABITANTS.

THE capital, and, indeed, the only town of the oasis, unless we were to dignify sundry villages with that appellation, was called simply El Medinah, or The Town. It was a place of no great size, containing on a rough estimate barely a thousand inhabitants, since the natives of the oasis, being engaged chiefly in pastoral and agricultural pursuits, lived for the most part in the country, or in the numerous hamlets which were scattered about the foot of the mountain. The streets were tolerably wide, well paved, and scrupulously clean. There were no buildings of conspicuous beauty or height, but, as we wandered about the side-alleys, we came across several quaint nooks and corners and "prout-bits," such as would have pleased an artist's eye. The town was divided into two sections by the river, which was spanned by three picturesque bridges, covered in by wooden roofs in order to protect passengers from the sun and rain. We noticed that all the women walked about unveiled, as in European cities, and that most of them were very good-looking. Oriental custom, in its infinite wisdom, veils the faces of its women, and the traveller from the West is, or should be, grateful to it for concealing features which are usually of more than doubtful charm. The Atlantean ladies, on the other hand, kindly exposed their pretty faces to the public view, and nobody accused them of being lacking in modesty. It seemed strange, too, to see no beggars or other signs of misery and squalor, such as everywhere meet the eye in most eastern cities ; and the same air of contentment and prosperity that prevailed outside seemed likewise to reign within the walls.

Our entertainers spared no pains to make our stay as enjoyable as possible, and they were most obliging in taking us round and explaining to us the various points of interest in connection with this happy community. Mahatma Singmya Songo said that a country-house, situated about half a mile from the town, was being fitted up for our reception, and he hoped that it would be ready for us in the course of the next fortnight. Meanwhile, our time was amply occupied in exploring the neighbourhood, and collecting information concerning the habits and customs of the natives. Of the results of our investigations I propose to give a short sketch here, beginning with the geographical features of the district.

The oasis appeared to be of no great size, though for a long while we had no opportunity of accurately measuring its extent. About ten miles below the town, the river, which, borrowing its name from the mountain, was called the Wad el Kebeer, entered a dense and almost impenetrable forest. Beyond the forest its waters flowed out into the desert, either to join the Niger, or, more probably, to be swallowed up like the Draa in the thirsty sands of the Sahara. The valley, including the cultivated and pasture land on the lower slopes of the mountains, was in places as much as four or five miles wide, and supported a population which, together with a few peasants who lived on the opposite, or western, side of the Djebel Kebeer, amounted in all to nearly two thousand souls.

Mount Atlas itself was a wedge-shaped mass, running nearly due north and south, and about thirty miles in length at the base. It had three principal snow-clad peaks, of which the northernmost, being the highest, had masked the two others from our view when we first caught sight of the mountain in the desert. We calculated that this peak must attain an elevation of 19,000 or 20,000 feet, which would make it the rival of Kilimandjaro for the honour of being the highest summit on the African continent. The exact height of the town above the sea-level, according to our aneroids, was 7558 feet, and the snow-level at the time of our arrival was about 3000 feet higher. Owing partly to its elevation, partly to the proximity of the immense snow-fields, the climate of the oasis was as temperate as could be desired, and the heat of the noon-day sun was almost always mitigated by a refreshing breeze from the glaciers. The nights were deliciously cool, while in winter frost was by no means uncommon.

As regards the inhabitants of the oasis, they appeared to be an offshoot of the old Arab, or possibly Berber, stock ; though, as I have already said, their fair complexions led us to suppose that they had an admixture of northern blood. Undoubtedly the place was populated centuries before the Mahatmas arrived. Concerning the date of the earliest immigrations into the oasis, we have the authority of Pliny and Herodotus for saying that it was inhabited, at any rate, more than 2000 years ago. The old Atlantes (Herodotus also alludes to them under the name of "Atarantes," and he locates them somewhere in the region of the Sahara now occupied by the Tuariks), seem to have been a primitive people who passed their time in uttering "direful imprecations" against the sun, whose rays they found unpleasantly scorching—a somewhat futile occupation, but one which seemed to afford them abundant amusement. All the natives of Marocco have a *penchant* for uttering "direful imprecations," as I have explained elsewhere ; but I cannot say that we found the inhabitants of Mount Atlas especially proficient in the art. These Atlantes seem to have been a rather remarkable people in other ways, as, according to the above-mentioned authorities, they ate the flesh of no living animal, and belonged to that order of men who see no visions in their sleep. Many of the modern Atlanteans, on the contrary, were continually "seeing things," such as spooks, astral bodies, elementals, etc., etc., having learned the art of second sight from their Mahatma instructors.

Quiet, God-fearing, inoffensive folk were these latter-day Atlantes, living through their simple, pastoral lives in peace and contentment. There were exceedingly wealthy men amongst them (for gold beyond the dreams of avarice lay about the banks of the lower reaches of the river), but riches were little thought of. In a region so highly favoured of

Heaven, where a genial soil was added to a temperate climate, and Nature lavished her best gifts with an unstinting hand, every man, by the exercise of moderate industry, could have enough for all his wants, and more he did not desire. Ambition and the ceaseless pushing and striving to better one's self, which pervades every section of European society, was entirely absent here. Everybody was content with his own lot in life, and never thought of trying to raise himself in the social scale. There were no "masses," nor, if we except the Mahatmas, any "classes" either. Mohammedan in creed, they were yet wholly devoid of the fierce bigotry which characterizes their co-religionists in the north, and they looked up to the Brethren as their spiritual guides with a reverence which was touching to contemplate. It may seem strange that the Mahatmas, who of course professed the Buddhist religion (in its esoteric form), should secure the respect and submission of a Moslem community ; but it must be remembered that the occult Adepts attach little importance to the exoteric aspects of any creed, but direct their attention solely to those inner truths which underlie the husks and shells of all the religions of the world. Mysticism is of no dogma ; it readily adapts itself to any doctrinal system. Hence, the Mahatmas interfered in no way with the practice of the Mohammedan religion by the natives of the oasis, who, in their turn, regarded the Brethren as superior beings gifted with abnormal wisdom and miraculous powers over the forces of Nature.

The government of the oasis was republican and theocratic, if I may use the term, the spiritual and temporal power being united in the same persons, as in Mohammedan countries. The legislative body consisted of a council of leading Adepts, of whom one was annually elected president. Singmya Songo occupied the post during our visit. This council, as a matter of fact, partook more of the character of a vestry than a Parliament, since, there being little or no need for fresh legislation, and no questions of imperial policy to discuss, the debates were mostly on such matters as the making of roads and bridges, and the keeping in repair of the embankments which protected the fields from the floods that descended with great force and suddenness during the melting of the snows in spring. There was no army, partly because the inhabitants were not of a warlike disposition, but also for the still more excellent reason that there was no one for them to fight against.

The judges and magistrates and other officers of the executive were also chosen from among the Adepts. Strange to say, these officials were not paid, being impelled to do the work solely by a strict sense of duty. Their labours, however, were light, for crime was almost unknown, and disputes were of comparatively rare occurrence. A considerable number of officials had to be kept on hand owing to the frequent absence of the Brethren from the scene of their duties. The marvellous power possessed by Adepts of projecting themselves to distant places in their *lingas shariras*, or astral bodies, is well known ; and the Mahatmas of Mount Atlas were always going about in this fashion, and landing up unexpectedly in various corners of the earth—now appearing to the Indian ryot at work in his rice-field ; now startling

some commonplace burgher in one of the centres
of European civilization ; anon, scaring the fur-clad
Eskimo in his hut, or the noble Redskin in his
wigwam. On these occasions, they always left their
rupas, or material bodies, asleep in their houses at
Mount Atlas, carefully locking the doors and closing
the windows to prevent them being stolen or mislaid
in their absence. It would obviously be highly
annoying to return from a trip in your *linga sharira*
and find your outer husk, or work-a-day bodily shell,
missing. I am informed, on the highest occult
authority, that the feelings of the bather who, emerging
from the water, finds that some one has walked off
with his clothes, are a perfect fool to the indignation
of a Mahatma in his astral body, when he finds that
his *rupa* has been made away with, and his return to
objective existence in the flesh for the time being
rendered impossible.

CHAPTER XVI.

CONCERNING THE MAHATMAS.

IT must not be supposed that the Mahatmas of Mount Atlas were few in number or difficult of access. In India, as is well known, an Adept is a *rara avis*, whom all men have heard of, but few have been privileged to see or hold converse with. Out here, on the contrary, the Mahatmas were so numerous as to be rather a drug in the market than otherwise. Their usual avocations were those of pedagogues, or instructors to the youth of the oasis, for which service they hired themselves out for a moderate stipend. Talented and highly respectable Mahatmas, of proved honesty and efficiency, could be engaged at the rate of about forty *botkis* (an Atlantean coin equivalent to about half a crown in our money) per month. Being anxious myself to become posted, as far as possible, in the esoteric mysteries, I lost no time in looking out for a reliable *gooroo*, or teacher, and before long I got suited with one in the person of a certain Mahatma Sucha Row, a cousin of Kikkuppa Row, the chosen associate and mess-mate of our amiable host Singmya Songo. From Mahatma Sucha Row

I learned many of the precious fragments of occult lore which I am enabled to lay before my readers in the following pages, together with much that I do not feel myself at liberty to disclose. Those of my readers who are students of occultism, will no doubt be struck with the remarkable similarity of the information I received to certain expositions of esoteric doctrine which have appeared from time to time in England. I am sure that it cannot fail to be a source of unspeakable comfort to the talented authors and authoresses of those works to find the truth of their writings confirmed by one who, for some time, enjoyed the privilege of daily intercourse with the Mahatmas. Occasional divergences, more in form than substance, however, will no doubt be detected by the initiated; but, as Mr. Sinnett very justly remarks, "at these loftier levels of spiritual exaltation a supreme knowledge of esoteric doctrine blends all original sectarian differences." In other words, the inner truths of theosophy are the same all the world over.

Before I proceed with my narrative, I ought perhaps to say a word about the band of hermits who, as has been mentioned in an earlier chapter, occupied Mount Atlas before the arrival of the Mahatmas. These hermits, we subsequently learned, belonged to the sect of *Sufites*, or Mohammedan mystics, whose tenets, largely tinged with Buddhist esotericism, were in many respects akin to those of the Mahatmas. Hence, the two sects became gradually fused through the adoption by the Sufites of the doctrine and religious practice of the Thibetan new-comers; and, together, they formed the occult hierarchy of the

Atlantean community. Many of the Sufites, indeed, attained to the highest grades among the priests and votaries of the theosophic cult, which accounted for the mixture of Arabic and Asiatic names we found among the Brethren. The Indian esoteric terminology was in general use amongst them, though Arabic remained the language of ordinary conversation. The Adepts, whose vast stores of knowledge "amount to a species of omniscience as regards earthly affairs," were of course perfectly acquainted with all languages, and spoke Arabic, Hindustani, French, and English with equal ease and fluency.

I had to wait more than a fortnight for my hireling Adept, Sucha Row, as at the time of our arrival he had a situation as pedagogue in the family of a rich merchant who lived lower down the valley. His late employer gave him an excellent character, and as he only asked for thirty-five *botkis* a month, I think you will agree with me that I got him pretty cheap. I wanted to put him on board wages, not feeling very certain how a Mahatma ought to be fed. It appeared however, that it was not the custom of the country, so he used to take his meals with us, and, to tell the truth, for a member of a fraternity who are supposed to practise abstinence, he played a pretty good knife and fork.[1] He wasn't very much to look at ; but, then, not many of the Mahatmas were, as they paid little attention to the adornment of their rupas, or outer

---

[1] In justice to my Mahatma I ought to explain that his diet was strictly vegetarian. The Brethren of Mount Atlas object on principle to the eating of flesh. Their *menus* often reminded me of those six-penny dinners at the Vegetarian Restaurants in London, pease-broth, boiled beans, and lentil pudding being the staple fare.

envelopes of flesh. He was a thin, wizened little man, about five feet five inches in height, with patches of light sandy hair sprouting irregularly from his poll. He had the same Mongol type of features as Singmya Songo, and he wore the long finger and toe nails, which seemed to be the distinguishing mark of an Adept. Like most of his kidney, he wore large blue goggles, which by no means added to the dignity of his appearance ; but, unlike Singmya Songo, whose garments were pure white, he wore a long brown robe of some rough material, which made him look like a Franciscan friar. In character he was amiability itself, and he exhibited a most touching meekness of disposition, approaching nearer than any man I ever met to that ideal of humility which we Christians profess so loudly in theory, but in practice so studiously ignore. He was always apologizing about something or other, and endeavouring to efface himself in every possible way. In fact, he seemed to be possessed of the idea that he had no business to be living at all. Like Plotinus, he was ashamed of existing in fleshly form, and delighted above measure in that " separation from the body for the purpose of philosophizing well," which Pythagoras regarded as the highest good of all. Fortunately, the mysterious faculty by which Adepts can divest themselves of their rupas as easily as you or I can take off our great-coats, enabled him temporarily to gratify his tastes in this direction ; but he longed for the time when his emancipation from the fetters of the flesh should be completed by death. Hence, in no way was his abnegation of self more conspicuous than in consenting to continue his physical existence on earth

at all. As one of his chelas told me, he was only
" living on to oblige " his friends.

His qualifications as gooroo were unexceptionable,
and he was possessed of a flow of language ("gift of
the gab," Gerald profanely called it) which was little
short of marvellous. He was, on the whole, singularly
open in his explanations, but readers of occult books
will have noticed that most of the Brethren are a
curious mixture of engaging frankness and unaccountable reticence, and Mahatma Sucha Row was no
exception to the rule. Often, just as he seemed to
be on the point of making some important disclosure,
he would draw in his horns and, leaving his auditors
on the tenterhooks of impatient expectation, " wrap
himself," as Ali put it, " in the shroud of obscurity
and take refuge behind the curtain of silence." If
we persisted in our inquiries, or on the rare occasions
when we cornered him in argument, he had a disagree-
able habit of projecting himself in his astral body to
Thibet, or elsewhere, thereby rendering all further
discussion perfectly hopeless. Obviously, an ordinary
mortal cannot be otherwise than at a great dis-
advantage when arguing with an opponent endowed
with these remarkable powers.

Talking of the powers of the Mahatmas reminds
me that I have said little or nothing on that subject.
The Brethren of Mount Atlas were invested with
the same supernatural faculties as are attributed to
the Thibetan Adepts, only, I believe, to a still more
remarkable degree. I use the word " supernatural,"
be it understood, in the popular sense. The occult
reader is of course aware that there is no such thing
as supernaturalism, the Initiates merely having com-

mand over forces of Nature unknown to the common herd of sceptics. In spiritual matters their knowledge is the result, not of laborious intellectual reasoning, but of the development of the Sixth Sense, the Intuition, that glorious faculty which Kant and other German Idealists groped blindly after, but which the Mahatmas have possessed for ages. On the physical plane it is derived from that power of "psychological telegraphy," which enables them to project their souls anywhere they please, and learn what is going on all over the world. "The clairvoyant faculties of the Adept," as Mr. Sinnett accurately informs us, "are so perfect and complete that they amount to a species of omniscience as regards mundane affairs." Old Sucha Row, for instance, often projected his soul into the midst of Cabinet Councils in Downing Street. He knew perfectly well what games Boulanger was playing, and the schemes of State policy hatching in the brains of Prince Bismarck and the Czar. He could by a word have rendered unnecessary the labours of the Parnell Commission. But he never "let on" concerning any of these things, and it may well be imagined that, to a mind occupied with the tremendous mysteries of the Great Arcanum, and endowed with perceptions ranging over other worlds and other states of existence than ours, such mundane trivialities could not appear otherwise than absolutely unimportant.

And here let me parenthetically apologize if my language should sometimes seem to sink below the level demanded by the dignity of my subject. After all, I am but a humble neophyte in occult matters, and a good esoteric style is not acquired in a day.

The chief secret of success lies in the use of as many big words as possible, and, above all things, in beginning them with capital letters. There is much virtue in a capital letter, as all good mystics know. For instance, if I write of "the universal," or "the absolute," your attention will not be arrested; while before "the Universal" and "the Absolute" you must perforce stand awestruck, as in the presence of a great and imposing mystery.

The physical wonders worked by the Adepts have been the theme of many writers. It is well known that they possess perfect command over that mysterious occult force known in the East under its Sanscrit name of *Akâsa*. It has a variety of other names among the Initiates, such as "Astral Light," "Water of Phtha," "Soul of the Universe," "Magnes," or "Milk of the Celestial Virgin."[1]   In fact, you may call it "pigeon's milk," if you like, or anything else you please; no one will object, I am sure. It is a force of infinite potency and subtlety. It was known to occult science ages and ages ago, while we poor Westerners are only now just beginning to muddle along with steam and electricity. Personally, I do not despair of seeing steam-engines and other machines driven, and telegraphic messages sent, by the agency of pigeon's milk—*Akâsa*, I mean. Its introduction on the Underground Railway would be a distinct boon to City gentlemen, and would doubtless cause a considerable rise in "Districts," of which I am unfortunately a shareholder.

By means of *Akâsa* the Mahatmas performed many magical feats which greatly astonished the

[1] "Isis Unveiled," by Madame Blavatsky, p. 58.

natives, and caused them to regard the Adepts with a veneration due rather to gods than men. They also employed it as the motive power for innumerable mechanical contrivances. Their clocks and watches went by *Akâsa*, and only wanted winding up once a year. Their vehicles were propelled by it, horses being seldom used for this purpose. Tricycles worked by *Akâsa* were the ordinary means of conveyance. I noticed in Singmya Songo's house certain machines for simplifying and shortening various domestic processes, some of which struck me as being particularly ingenious. There was one of them for cleaning boots and shoes, either Moorish or European, which especially took my fancy, and I tried hard to worm the secret of its manufacture out of the Mahatma. The boots were put into an aperture at one end ; a handle was turned, and they came out almost immediately with a most beautiful polish. I fancied I saw in this machine boundless possibilities in the way of a Limited Liability Company to be brought out on the London Stock Exchange. "The Mount Atlas Automatic Boot Polisher Company, Limited," in one pound shares, introduced by means of an attractive prospectus to the notice of a discriminating public, could not fail to be a success and to command a high premium. The Mahatma, however, resolutely refused to part with the secret, so that my cherished project of company-promoting fell to the ground.

This mysterious force was also largely used for medicinal purposes, *Akâsa* pills, potions, and baths, being largely prescribed by the resident faculty.

But the cure in which the Atlanteans reposed the greatest faith was hypnotism, which had been brought to a degree of perfection which would have astonished "Professor" Kennedy himself. The remedy, as a rule, was applied locally, the patient not being sent off into a trance, but the part affected being alone mesmerized.

Amongst the other occult sciences studied by the Mahatmas of Mount Atlas it was only to be expected that astrology should find a principal place. The movements of the heavenly bodies were carefully noted by persons specially delegated for the task, and the course of future events was accurately divined therefrom. Under the able tuition of the erudite Sucha Row I made considerable progress in this abstruse but fascinating science, and after a few months' study I could cast a horoscope, and practise other arts of divination along with the best of them. Among other things, I noticed that the Mahatmas regulated their political and, more especially, their financial affairs largely by astrological observation, and I feel confident that the connection and inter-dependence between the fluctuations of the stock markets and the movements of the heavenly bodies are not sufficiently considered in Europe.[1] I have little doubt but that an "operator" on the "cover" system, who had a knowledge of astrology, would have a great advantage over his rivals who were ignorant of such matters. To take an example, let us suppose the planet Mercury to be in conjunction with Ursa Major. In the absence of other indications, an occult speculator would then certainly be a "bear"

---

* An article in *Lucifer*, April, 1889, entitled, "Sun-Spots and Commercial Crises," touches only the fringe of this most important question.

of stocks. If, on the other hand, the same planet had, in hermetic parlance, "a trine aspect on the ascendant," it would mean that "things" were going up, and, especially if the sun happened at the same time to be entering Taurus, he would of course be on the "bull" tack. I intend to try this system myself some day, and look forward to retiring shortly on a modest little competence as the result, though Gerald, in his cynical way, considers the bankruptcy court or Colney Hatch to be more probably my destination. He suggests that I should bring Sucha Row back to England, and take him into partnership in the Stock Exchange, in order to keep me informed of what is going on in the world of finance.

"'Pon my honour, I think it would be worth your while," he remarked to me one day; "he would be sure to put you on to a good thing or two. Don't I just wish I had had a Mahatma with me in the Birdcage at Newmarket the other day, when that forty-to-one chance romped in for the Cambridgeshire."

But I anticipate too much. All these great and important discoveries were not made in a day. A severe preliminary course of occult instruction, the details of which I will not inflict upon the reader, had to be gone through by me, as by every novice in the mysteries of the Great Arcanum, before I arrived at any of the higher branches of theosophic science. Suffice it to say that in Sucha Row I found the most patient and amiable of teachers. His efforts to instil into me and my companions the rudiments of esoteric lore were ably seconded by Singmya Songo and two or three of his associates, and under their guidance we made rapid progress in our studies.

CHAPTER XVII.

LEILA.

FOR many weeks our life at Mount Atlas pursued its quiet and uneventful tenor. Our mornings were passed, as a rule, in occult study under the supervision of the Mahatmas. In the afternoons we took long walks in the neighbourhood, where fresh beauties disclosing themselves every day delighted our eyes and added zest to our labours. In the evenings we again enjoyed esoteric converse with the Brethren.

About a month after our arrival we were installed in our new country house, which we much preferred to living in the town. It lay in the midst of a veritable Hesperides-garden of orange trees on the further side of the carpet of meadow which crept, flower-patterned with iris and asphodel, up to the base of the mountain. Above the house, the woods and vineyards, clambering the hillside, rose in successive billows of light and dark green foliage. Proceeding down the valley, you passed out of the orange-grove into one of mingled myrtle and tamarisk, which in its turn gave place to a forest consisting chiefly of sycamore, cypress, and holm-oak. Sucha Row resided with us, and, our house being quite close to the town, we contrived to see a great deal of his brother Mahatmas. Singmya Songo paid us frequent visits, while, on the other hand, we spent many evenings beneath his hospitable roof in El Medinah.

Besides the attractions of the scenery, the study of the flora and fauna of the oasis was a source of never failing amusement and interest. The variety and exquisite hues of the wild flowers were something little short of marvellous, and Urquhart, who included among his numerous tastes a passion for botany, was not long in making a large collection of choice and rare exotics. To Gerald and myself, the birds and beasts with which the forest teemed were a source of greater interest. We regarded them perforce with the eye of the naturalist rather than the sportsman. Our guns, I need hardly say, were laid aside, as the wanton slaughter of dumb animals for mere amusement would have been in the highest degree repugnant to the Adepts of a creed which, beyond all others, enjoins merciful consideration towards the brute creation. A natural consequence of the security they enjoyed was the tameness of all the birds and animals, to which I have alluded already. In fact, the sparrows and linnets were unpleasantly familiar, flying in at the windows at all hours, and fearlessly perching on the chairs and tables as we sat at meals.

Many of the wild birds possessed plumage of the most brilliant colours. Orioles, woodpeckers, hoopoes, and bee-eaters were among the most common, while humming-birds of exquisite beauty abounded in the woods, their iridescent hues glinting in the sunbeams as they darted from twig to twig. Conspicuous among the larger varieties was a bright canary-coloured bird something like a golden pheasant, only two or three times as big. The natives of Mount Atlas called it *Aboo Dahab* ("the Father of Gold,") and legend asserted that it fed upon the grains of gold which it picked up from the sands of the river bed. Gerald was of opinion that the *Aboo Dahab* was the Arab prototype of the western "oof-bird," differing only from that fowl in its exceeding tameness and the ease with which it could be captured.

In the course of one of our rambles in the neighbourhood an event occurred which was destined to have an important influence upon the destinies of one member, at any rate, of our party. Accompanied by Ali, we had walked for about two hours down the main valley to the mouth of one of the numerous gorges which intersected the sides of the Djebel Kebeer. This particular ravine, however, was of greater size and length than most of the others, and from the river bank our eyes could follow its windings up into the heart of the mountain for a considerable distance. Struck by the romantic beauty of the lower part of the glen, we resolved to explore its higher recesses. A narrow path led us beside a brook, which babbled merrily over the stones, leaping here and there in tiny cascades into pools glassy clear, fringed with soft moss-beds and maiden-hair fern, and overshadowed by cypress and sycamore. The grassy glades in this sylvan solitude could have been seldom trodden by the foot of man, and the deer (of which we came across a considerable number), rabbits, squirrels, and other four-footed denizens of the forest, held undisputed possession. About midday we emerged from the wood into a meadow, which lay embosomed in a cup-like hollow, hemmed in by steep, bush-covered declivities. Here we rested an hour to dispose of the provisions we had brought with us. As soon as we had finished our meal, and smoked a couple of pipes, we prepared to resume our walk, when we noticed that the sky, which in the morning had been perfectly cloudless, was becoming rapidly overcast. It was evident that we were in for a heavy storm. A loud thunderclap right over our heads was the prelude to such a downpour as one only sees in the tropics, and in a few minutes we were soaked to the skin. The lightning played in a quick succession of vivid flashes, followed almost immediately by deafening peals of thunder. During lunch we had noticed a white house perched on a promontory of rock two or three hundred feet above the stream, and as this was the only human habitation in sight, we repaired thither for shelter. Entering by a small wicket gate, we found ourselves in a picturesque garden, though the rain descending in torrents gave us little opportunity of admiring its beauty. We knocked at the door of the house, which was promptly opened to us by a tall Moor clad in a russet-brown jellabia, whom we correctly supposed to be the master of the house. He was a man of about fifty, with finely cut features and a black beard streaked with grey, and an erect, commanding figure. Our draggled appearance rendered almost unnecessary the explanation and apology we offered him for thus invading his abode.

" The peace of Allah and His holy Prophet be upon you, O strangers," he said, in that tone of grave and dignified courtesy peculiar to the high-bred Oriental. "Ye are welcome. Enter, and be seated."

Going in, we found ourselves in a small but cosy apartment, sumptuously furnished in Eastern style. A low divan, lined with soft, embroidered cushions, ran round the walls, which were draped with rich stuffs and hangings. A fire of sycamore logs was soon crackling on the hearth, and, taking off our wet things, we arrayed ourselves in the Moorish raiment furnished to us by our host. I noticed that Urquhart looked exceedingly well in his new attire, and he wore his haik and soulham as if to the manner born. Gerald, on the contrary, seemed hardly at home in the ample folds of his jellabia ; while, as for myself, I feared my more diminutive person would get lost in mine—it was so excessively roomy.

"Behold ! Nazarenes," said our entertainer, " it is well-nigh the hour of *el assar*" (the afternoon prayer). "It yet rains, and the evening shadows will soon begin to fall, and the way back to El Medinah is long and ill to traverse in the dark. If, therefore, ye can be content with a modest hospitality cheerfully bestowed, abide here for this night. To-morrow, if the storm abates, and the sky be fair, we will speed you on your way."

Thus pressed, we yielded, by no means unwillingly, to the good man's solicitation, and prepared to take up our quarters for the night. As the daylight waned we sat and talked over the fire, our entertainer showing a not unnatural eagerness to know who we were, whence we came, and how we had arrived at Mount Atlas. We readily acceded to his wishes, and told him the whole story of our adventures. He was

much interested in Urquhart's account of our narrow
escape from death in the simoom, and told us that we
ought to render thanks to Allah for preserving
us from the manifold perils of the Great Desert.
Having satisfied his curiosity concerning ourselves,
we ventured to ask him a few questions about himself.

"Of a truth, O sons of the English, after the full
measure of information which ye have vouchsafed
to me concerning yourselves, it were only fitting I
reciprocated your frankness. My name is Seedy
Aissa Alarby Ben Absalam. I am a merchant of El
Medinah, though in sooth it is but little business that
I transact nowadays. I am a servant of the one God
(blessed for ever be His name), and a lay brother
of the occult fraternity of the Djebel Kebeer. I
live in this house alone with my niece, the maid
Leila, whose coming for the service of the evening
meal I have been awaiting for this hour past. Stay,
methinks even now I hear her footstep upon the
threshold."

As he spoke, the door opened, and Leila entered
the room. I had expected to see a damsel of the
conventional Moorish type, dark-eyed, brown-skinned,
unspiritual, unintellectual; and we were all fairly
amazed at the wondrously beautiful apparition which
presented herself to our eyes. Her figure, tall, slender,
supple as a palm-stem waving in the breeze, was
enveloped in a white flowing robe girt at the waist
by a crimson sash. Her feet, small almost to a fault,
were encased in sandals, which displayed the contours
of an instep arched to perfection. Her hair, of a
glossy raven black, was parted from the brow, and

braided simply with a small silver cord. The pale, clear, olive complexion contained just a suggestion of rose-tint in the centre of the oval cheek. Her delicately pencilled eyebrows, almost meeting over the nose, according to the eastern ideal of female beauty, formed arches for great lustrous eyes of a deep blue-black, fringed with long silken lashes. The irises were clear and liquid, with occasional violet-coloured emanations. Now and again, a smile tinged with thought and sadness played about the tender curves of the exquisitely formed mouth, and her teeth gleamed like two rows of pearls in their coral setting. The graceful pose and setting of the small head on the shapely neck gave a suggestion of high-breeding, which was accentuated by a certain stateliness of manner, as of one more accustomed to command than to obey. But what struck me even more than these charms of form and feature, dazzling as they were, was the expression of the girl's face. It was not melancholy, nor even pensive, but the eyes had habitually a strange, dreamy, abstracted look, as of some spiritualized animal, yet, withal, full of intellectuality. In appearance she was a maiden of two or three and twenty, but the bearing and manner were those of one who had long since reached womanhood.

On seeing us, she stopped surprised, and for a moment seemed somewhat disconcerted, blushing slightly; but, quickly recovering her self-possession, she made us a slight but graceful courtesy. As we rose from our seats on her entrance, she directed at each of us a brief but penetrating glance. Gerald's tall figure she scanned with evident admiration, and then, my humbler person and Ali's receiving but a passing scrutiny, her gaze fell upon Urquhart. For a moment I observed that she bent upon him a searching look, as though she would read his very soul, and then she gave a slight start, and the colour left her cheeks. Presently, her eyes were withdrawn from him and wandered upwards, when for a brief space they regained their strange, far-away look, as though her mind was occupied in things not of this earth. Urquhart, too, usually so impassive, seemed strangely moved. His colour came and went, and he moved uneasily. Gerald also noticed their embarrassment, and slily nudged me with his elbow. In a few moments, however, both had regained their composure, and Leila seated herself beside her uncle, who playfully chid her for coming in so late.

"How now, my child?" he said, playing with her thick masses of hair which had escaped from under their silver band. "Where have you been playing truant at a time when your presence is more than ever needful? These strangers here have honoured us by seeking shelter beneath our roof, and we have but little entertainment provided for them."

"I was in the forest, uncle," she replied in a voice of singular *timbre* and sweetness, "and the rain came on suddenly, and I was forced to take shelter in the hollow trunk of an ancient oak until the downpour ceased. But I will delay no longer, and if our friends here will but be content with such humble cheer as I can set before them, it shall be prepared as speedily as possible."

So saying, she rose and left the room, leaving us all marvelling at her wonderful beauty and charm of manner. But there was one thing which, for the time, occupied my thoughts to the exclusion of everything else, and that was the emotion mutually displayed by her and Urquhart at this their first meeting. Could it be a case of love at first sight? Had Urquhart, whose heart had resisted the onslaughts of so many fair charmers in the centres of civilization, surrendered the citadel without a blow to this beautiful African maiden? But then, how to account for the emotion shown by the latter? Urquhart, with his unpolished exterior and somewhat blunt manners, was not the sort of fellow a girl would fall in love with all at once, and I could hardly believe that he could have made so rapid and easy a conquest. Nevertheless, argue as we might, some bond of union evidently existed between them, and Gerald whispered to me, as we left the room to get ready for dinner, that it was "evidently 'a case' between David and Miss Leila."

But whatever momentary loss of self-possession the two had displayed when they first met, their subsequent demeanour towards each other during the rest of our sojourn under Seedy Aissa's roof afforded no further grounds for our suspicions. The evening passed quickly by in pleasant converse, and we retired early to rest.

In the morning we awoke to find a day of unclouded skies and glorious sunshine. From my bedroom I looked out of the casement, through the trellis-work overgrown with creepers, jasmine, and honeysuckle, upon a prospect of enchanting beauty. The site of the house had been selected with great skill, commanding a view of the glen throughout its length, down to the valley of the Wad Kebeer. Above and behind us towered the cliffs and peaks of Mount Atlas, and the white tongue of a hanging glacier descended far down the mountain side to seemingly within a few hours' walk of the house. At the back of the garden were green meadows and Alpine pastures alive with browsing flocks and herds. In the garden itself a tiny brooklet, appropriately named *Aboo Safee* or "The Father of Limpidity," trickled down a dell fringed with oleander and broad-leaved hemlock. Rose and tulip, lily and bright-hued geranium, blossoming shrubs of various kinds, grew in profuse, yet judiciously restricted, luxuriance. The walls were overgrown with peach and apricot ; and orange, lemon, and other fruit-trees were planted sparingly about the velvet lawns, where a couple of slender, lustrous-eyed gazelles gambolled gracefully, and a peacock strutted majestically across the grass, dragging after him his gorgeous, iridescent train. The air was loaded with perfume, and vocal with the music of innumerable birds, and as I stood and listened to their melodious notes, the hum and murmur of bees, the bleating of sheep, and the lowing of the cattle in the meadows, my senses were bathed in a profound calm and contentment, and I would fain have lingered a while longer in these new-found bowers of our African Eden.

Indeed, Seedy Aissa urged us to prolong our stay, and we were all, especially Urquhart, loth to leave, but we feared lest our Mahatma friends at El Medinah should be getting anxious on our account ; so, in the afternoon, promising to renew our visit at the earliest opportunity, we bade our courteous host farewell, and set our faces homewards. We spoke little as we walked through the forest, being each occupied with his own thoughts. Only old Ali, who could seldom be silent for many minutes together, chattered away with much volubility and Oriental hyperbole in praise of the beauty of Leila.

"Of a verity, O Father of Whiskers," he cried, "the maid Leila is a pearl among women. Ah welli! woe is me, she hath already made roast meat of my heart. Her form is the form of a gazelle; her face is like the moon. Paradise is in her eye, and the light therein is as the light of the stars. Her mouth is a ring; her lips are of coral; her bosom an enchantment; her cheeks are beds of pale roses; her breath sweet as odours wafted from the citron-groves of Atlas." ("How do you know that, you old dog?" asked Gerald *sotto voce*). "Oollah!" he added with a deep sigh, "by the beard of the Prophet, she would be a veritable houri were she only a little fatter."

Urquhart seemed to anything but appreciate our faithful retainer's encomiums, sincere though they undoubtedly were; yet he spoke never a word, but strode on with a preoccupied air, as though he were engaged in a walking race. And, indeed, we had need to hurry, if we would arrive home before night-fall, for the sun was setting as we descended into the valley, and the glow of evening bathed forest, field, and river in a flood of ruddy gold, ere the shadows sped swiftly across the meadows and commenced to climb the eastern hills.

On our arrival at El Medinah we found, as we had anticipated, Sucha Row and the other Brethren much concerned for our safety. They feared we had met with some accident while rambling on the mountainside, and were about to send out parties in search of us. We explained the cause of our absence, and questioned Singmya Songo concerning Seedy Aissa and his fascinating niece. He would not give us any answer at that time, but asked us to spend the evening with him, which we gladly consented to do. He was then good enough to fully satisfy our curiosity on the point, and I may say at once that our interest in the fair Leila was heightened rather than diminished by what he told us.

We had hitherto imagined the occult community of Mount Atlas to consist exclusively of the Mahatmas, their chelas, and certain lay members like our late host, Seedy Aissa. The idea had never entered our heads that it might include lady theosophists as well. Yet such, to our surprise, we now found to be the case. The female students were rigorously separated from the males, and devoted themselves exclusively to the learning and development of a special branch of occult science, which I shall presently endeavour to shadow forth. They lived a sort of conventual existence in a large seminary, or college, of young lady chelas, situated in a remote valley among the mountains. And the Lady Superior of this college was none other than Leila, whose intellect and deep knowledge of the esoteric doctrine marked her out to the leading Mahatmas as a fitting occupant of so high and responsible a post.

And here I shall be compelled to crave the reader's patience for a short space. In order to give a clear conception of the position which Leila occupied in the Atlantean community, and, more important still, to explain the nature of the intercourse which sprang up between her and Urquhart, it will be necessary for me to treat of certain occult topics which, owing to their involved and recondite nature, I should otherwise have preferred to leave untouched. I am now about to partially withdraw the veil which has hitherto shrouded an Arcanum of mighty import. Please, therefore, give me your best attention.

CHAPTER XVIII.

CONCERNING CERTAIN OF THE DEEPER OCCULT MYSTERIES.

THE reader must not infer from the foregoing remarks that I am about to reveal the half of what I could tell if I chose. Theosophical doctrines ought never, in my opinion, to be sprung upon an unbelieving world in their entirety. These spiritual Arcana should rather be ladled out in small doses, as in large quantities they are apt to disagree with some mental constitutions. Only when the times are ripe for a fuller exposition can the curtain of the Inner Shrine of the Temple of Wisdom be wholly drawn aside. And those days are as yet, I fear, far distant, hidden deep in the womb of ages to come, when the seed-germs of instruction now planted shall blossom forth and expand into a perfect tree of knowledge.

The mysterious doctrines—gleams of light flashed from the hidden radiance—of which I am now enabled to offer a brief sketch to the general public, are those of the Biune Existence and the Sympneumatic Consciousness. Some faint glimmerings of these hermetic truths have already been revealed to the world by an eminent English mystic,[1] whose expositions, after making allowances for certain minor errors of detail, inevitable in works dealing with such abstruse subjects, I found to be surprisingly accurate as far as they go. For the sake of convenience, I shall quote from these works whenever the matter they contain coincides with the information I gathered from my revered Mahatma teachers concerning this most difficult branch of the Hidden Wisdom.

It is not generally known that in the earliest stage of the development of the human race man was bisexual, or androgynous—that is to say, both male and female. Yet such, Singmya Songo assured us, was actually the fact. The differentiation into sex was a process of comparatively late date, which will be described presently. The original man, being thus dual, or biune, in nature, possessed an ethereal or fluid body, of which the complementary sex-parts could be interwoven or separated at will, as the atomic elements composing the female principle might chance to combine or disintegrate with those composing the male. Gradually, however, by a process difficult to explain, but resulting from man's wilfully opening his organism to debasing sex-influences from the outer world, the sex elements drew apart. As Mr. Laurence Oliphant quite correctly puts it, in language very similar to that employed to me by Singmya Songo, "the androgynous Ego suffered an atomic dislocation in his outer organism, which involved a divorce from his own feminine complement." This change from unity to

---

[1] Mr. Laurence Oliphant, in his two works, "Sympneumata," and "Scientific Religion."

dualism, occultists tell us, constituted the "Fall of Man," as mystically described in the Book of Genesis. A further result of the Fall, in addition to the separation of the sex elements, was that man lost his ethereal fluid nature, and drew upon himself fleshly accretions from the lower animal kingdom. His original delicate organism became overlaid with the coarse husk of a solid material body, so that, instead of remaining an ethereal creature, whereof the male principle intertwined with the female, the two parts forming one biune whole, he became divided into two halves, man and woman, each incapable of inter-penetrating with its particles the subsurface spaces of the other, owing to its heavy outer covering of flesh. The spiritual part of man, as it exists now, is the sole remnant of his old ethereal nature, overlaid by the animal excrescence which we term "body."

In order rightly to apprehend this profound mystery, we must regard each man or woman we see walking about as the separate and mutilated man-half or woman-half, as the case may be, of an original biune creature which, by reason of its disorderly conduct in its·earlier stages of development, has lost its fluid, bisexual nature, and become divided into two parts as described above.

"Externally two persons," our worthy Mahatma remarked to me, "the twin portions of the sundered Ego are in reality one, although they have lost the power they once possessed of mutually permeating their respective atoms. Nay, men are ignorant, as a rule, of the very existence of their 'sympneuma,' their spiritual perceptions being blinded so long as they are held in the thraldom of the flesh."

The "sympneuma," I may say at once, is none other than the complementary being, the "better half" of our earlier ethereal state, who formed an integral part of our original self. She is our spiritual co-partner, whose life-elements are in mesmeric rapport, and whose atomic structure is in a mysterious way interlocked with our own. The sympneuma, for aught we know, may be a lady of our acquaintance in this world, or an incorporeal being of the astral sphere. Mr. Laurence Oliphant speaks of the sympneuma as being necessarily of the spiritual world, whereas the Mahatmas assure me that many of us, if we only knew it, have our sympneumas on earth. In this latter case, if the sympneuma is a "sensitive," or medium, portions of her particles may interweave with our own, and we may hold converse with her inner personality, but this rarely happens. Mankind in general are, as the Mahatma said, unconscious of the existence of their sympneuma, though many of us have a vague longing and a shadowy hope that such a being may exist.

> "Somewhere beneath the sun—
> These quivering heart-strings prove it—
> Somewhere there must be one
> Made for this heart to move it;"

to quote once more the pretty lines from "Ionica." A natural result of this longing is that people are apt sometimes to jump to a premature conclusion that they have found their sympneuma, a mistake which is sometimes attended with inconvenient results. For instance, the young lady who, remarking, "You air my affinerty," wanted to embrace Artemus Ward in the railway carriage, was only desirous of giving a practical illustration of the sympneumatic doctrine as she understood it. Such people mistake, or pretend to mistake, mere physical affection for the higher sympneumatic magnetism. Gentlemen of theosophical proclivities who fall in love with their friends' wives often excuse themselves on the ground that they are bound by the higher law of occult affinities. If, as sometimes happens, they run away with them, they advance the plea that their twin Egos are only obeying the inexorable laws of their being. Hence it will be seen that the sympneumatic doctrine is liable sometimes to mischievous perversion by evil-disposed persons.

The descent of man from his high ethereal state to his present degraded, corporeal condition was not effected in a moment. It was a gradual process. Fortunately, however, it has now reached its climax, and mankind is already commencing its re-ascent to its lost ethereal condition. Stout people, in particular, will be glad to learn that "the semi-animal layer that encompasses man's form is now in process of slow extinction,"[1] and the fleshly deposit will gradually slough away till man regains once more his original fluid condition. Shakespeare, who, though he did not perhaps know it himself, was in reality an occultist of high grade, speaks with prophetical inspiration in Hamlet's soliloquy—

> "O that this too too solid flesh would melt,
> Thaw, and resolve itself into a dew."

Slowly but surely the process is going forward, and Mahatma Kikkuppa Row estimates that in about fifteen or twenty centuries our bodies will have

[1] "Sympneumata," p. 183.

attained the consistency of calves'-foot jelly. From the jelly stage we shall further disintegrate and dissolve until we reach the state of fluidity in which man existed before his descent into material form. With the loss of our animal husking, or overlay, we shall regain our dual biune nature, which even now exists in the deeper interiors of persons of higher spiritual development.

But what on earth, the reader impatiently asks, has all this got to do with Leila? The connection will appear more clearly when I come to speak of the relations of that fascinating lady Mahatma with Urquhart ; but I may state at once that it was the study and development of the two kindred doctrines of the Biune Existence and the Sympneumatic Consciousness, to which the sisters of the Occult College, presided over by Leila, directed their undivided efforts. It was hoped that by the use of a moderate diet, consisting chiefly of pease-pudding, broad beans, and lentil soup, and by a strict attention to the proprieties, they might some day revert to the desirable conditions I have sketched above, when, freed from their casings of clay, their spirits might wander forth to interweave themselves with the particles of the male complementary beings who they knew were waiting for them in some part of the universe. Whether their desires are destined to be gratified or not, time alone can show. I can only say that I saw no signs of their approaching fulfilment during my stay at Mount Atlas, for a healthier and more robust set of young women I never set eyes upon.

It may readily be imagined that we were not long in seeking to renew our acquaintance with Scedy

Aissa and his charming niece. On the occasion of our next visit we varied our route by taking a path which led over one of the spurs which ran down from the central mass of the Djebel Kebeer. As the way was said to be difficult to find we were accompanied by one of Singmya Songo's chelas, or pupils, an amiable young man about twenty-five years of age, with a pale face and a very ascetic air, who was said to be making rapid strides in esoteric science. By-the-by, there was a curious fact connected with this chela, which I think I ought to mention. He had died less than thirty years before the date of the events narrated in this history, but had been brought back to earth-life within five years of his decease through the instrumentality of Singmya Songo. This was an example of those "artificial incarnations accomplished by the direct intervention of the Mahatmas," alluded to by Mr. Sinnett,[1] "when a chela . . . is brought back into incarnation almost immediately after his previous physical death without having been suffered to float into the current of natural causes at all." As Mr. Sinnett very properly remarks, the Mahatmas are quite incapable of "acting capriciously in such a matter," so, no doubt, the virtues or intelligence of our youthful guide were deemed to render him a fitting recipient of so high and exceptional an honour.

In the valley next to the one where Seedy Aissa lived we passed a large, handsome building of red sandstone, the grounds whereof were surrounded by a high wall. This proved to be the Occult College for female chelas, and a little further on we were

---

[1] "Esoteric Buddhism," p. 150.

gratified by the sight of a procession of the charming novices, all clad in robes of purest white, filing two and two through a glade in the forest. It was the midday promenade of the theosophic young ladies— the " morning canter of the fillies in training for the Biune stakes," as Gerald called it in his sporting fashion. We looked to see if the fair Leila was among their number, but our search was unavailing, for, as we afterwards learned, she had stayed at home to await our arrival, of which her clairvoyant perceptions had given her due warning. The lady chelas of the Occult College struck me as being a remarkably pretty, fresh-looking lot of girls; and their plump figures, and cheeks ruddy with the glow of health, seemed to afford little prospect of a rapid disintegration into the fluid, incorporeal state for which they were supposed to be yearning. Gerald was very anxious to be introduced; but, as it was strictly against the rules, he contented himself with making them a polite bow; and I regret to say I noticed a good deal of blushing and suppressed giggling in their ranks as we passed.

Crossing the brow of the hill, we dropped right upon Seedy Aissa's house. There we found Leila walking in the garden, watering and tending the flowers and shrubs which were ever the object of her loving care. The mutual emotion evinced by her and Urquhart on the occasion of their first introduction was hardly less apparent at this their second meeting. There could be no doubt that some bond of union existed between them, whether it was of ordinary love or some other tie of a more mysterious nature. The idea, which at the time struck Gerald as fantastic, had gradually taken possession of my mind, that Urquhart had met his sympneuma, his counterpart, in these distant wilds of Africa. Before the Mahatma had made me acquainted with the mysterious sympneumatic doctrines, I had read of "affinities," of complementary beings whose souls are said to be in harmony, and whose life-currents blend with our own, even when their material bodies are far apart. I knew, moreover, that Urquhart was a firm believer in the theory, and it struck me that we might have here the explanation of the strange link of sympathy which seemed to be so instantaneously established between him and Leila. Another fanciful notion that entered my head, was that they might stand to each other in the relation of mesmerist and hypnotic subject, or it was possible that Leila might be a sensitive, or person endowed with mediumistic powers, and that Urquhart had come within the zone, or aura, of her magnetic attraction. There was something in Leila's weird and eerie personality, and her dreamy, abstracted look, which forbade us to believe that this was a case of ordinary love. For the present, however, all was pure conjecture, and it seemed little use to indulge in vague speculations concerning matters which time would doubtless make more clear. That an affinity of some sort existed between them, and that they found pleasure in each other's society, was sufficiently obvious ; and Gerald and I thought that the present was pre-eminently one of those occasions when two are company, and three, or more, are not. Accordingly, making the excuse that we wished to pay our respects to Seedy Aissa, we left them together, and entered the house.

When, after the lapse of rather more than an hour, we came out again, we found them walking together on one of the gravel-paths which wound in and out among the flowers and shrubs. There was no appearance of constraint or embarrassment in their manner, and nobody could have said that they behaved in any way like a pair of lovers of the ordinary type. Urquhart told us that he was coming back with us that evening to El Medinah, but that he had arranged to return the following day, and spend a few days with the merchant and his niece. Accordingly, as the afternoon was wearing on, we set our faces homewards, and reached the town just before sunset.

CHAPTER XIX.

OUR doubts and speculations concerning the nature of the relations subsisting between Urquhart and Leila were finally set at rest by Sucha Row, when, after our return to El Medinah, Urquhart had left us to take up his abode temporarily in Seedy Aissa's house. My Mahatma was not disposed at first to be at all communicative on the subject, until I asked him somewhat sternly what he supposed I had engaged him for at a liberal weekly wage, if not to keep me thoroughly posted in occult matters of every description. He at once apologized profusely, in his meek, submissive fashion, and stammered forth something about his being under vows of secrecy with respect to certain things appertaining to the Hidden Wisdom. At the same time, he proceeded to unburden himself of much highly interesting information, which I will endeavour to present to the reader as succinctly as possible. Besides Gerald and myself, there were present at the interview Ali, Embarek, and Mohammed. I ought perhaps to explain that the latter had never acquired a taste for occultism

In fact, he roundly declared it to be the quintessence of bosh, and its devotees the grandfathers of all folly, while his behaviour and bearing towards the Brethren was wholly wanting in respect.

According to Sucha Row, Leila was, as we had by this time almost grown to believe, Urquhart's sympneuma, his spiritual bride, the twin soul which, having once formed his feminine co-partner in their original biune state, had since been wandering about the spheres in search of its mate. Along with his brother Mahatmas, Kikkuppa Row and Singmya Songo, he had known that their planets were in conjunction, and that, being meant for each other, they were some day fated to come together. But the Brethren had done nothing to hasten the meeting. They had left it to *Kismet*, the destiny which marches with slow but unerring steps to its end, and which not even the marvellous powers of the Adepts can avert, or cause to deviate one hair's breadth from its course.

"Verily, my friends," exclaimed my Mahatma, in his mild, benevolent way, "the communion of the complementary parts of the divided Ego, which some call Soul-Affinity, is a mystery hard to fathom. There is a chemistry on the spiritual, as on the physical, plane ; and the laws of Nature are equally inexorable in either sphere of her action. As an atom flies to the substance with which it has the greatest affinity, so by the higher magnetism of love kindred souls must sooner or later wing their ways together. Like must conjoin with like—if not in this world, then in other and higher spheres—when sense will decay and finally disappear, and the divided monads of the life-impulses of the Universe will re-unite their component elements.   I beg your pardon."

"Pray, don't stop," I remarked, as he cast a timid, inquiring glance at Gerald and myself; "we are all attention."

"Unity is one thing, Dualism is another," he went on.   "Yet are they in certain aspects identical.   Of a truth, this is a mystery—one of the profound Arcana of Being.   It has been well said that 'the laws of Matter are the potential Mathematics of the Absolute,' and——"

"Moulai Idrees defend us!" broke in Mohammed, who had been listening with ill-concealed impatience to what he called the outrageous twaddle talked by the Mahatma.   "Moulai Idrees defend us! what words are these?   Strange filth, indeed, is this we are devouring.   Have a care, Mr. Mahatma; do not laugh at our beards, lest haply you eat the stripes of abasement, and chew the cud of mortification."

He went on to express his opinion that he had never heard so much bosh talked in the course of his whole life as by the Mahatmas; and that, taking one thing with another, he had eaten more dirt during the few weeks he had spent at Mount Atlas than he usually reckoned to consume in the course of an entire year.

"Nay, brother," purred Sucha Row in his mellifluous, deprecatory tones, "be not angry with me.   I was but about to remark that the ultimate destiny of the human Ego, entangled as it is on earth in the eccentricities of its own self-volition, is to free itself from the trammels of Matter, and to become united with the latent principle of Infinity."

"Staferallah!" growled our worthy "father of cooking-pots," "this is worse than ever. Go to! go to! you son of Jehannum. Don't make an ass of yourself. In the name of the Prophet, what is all this but bosh, humbug?"

"Allah akbar, God is most powerful!" interposed Embarek, who had been listening with a reverential air to Sucha Row's remarks; "do not interrupt the blessed Mahatma. *Ma andish ras*, you have no sense. You have eaten of the *ras ed dubbah*, the hyæna's head. The words of the Brother are the distillations of pure wisdom, sweeter than honey in the honey-pot; but you have not brains to understand them. May the condescension of the holy Mahatma never diminish, and may his footsteps prosper."

"Condescension, forsooth!" exclaimed our cook. "What nonsense is this you are talking? However, it is all one to me. Go on, therefore, Mr. Mahatma," he added sardonically; "in the name of Allah, go on. We have made such a plentiful meal of dirt already, that by all means let us devour some more."

Embarek was about to make a suitable reply, and a quarrel seemed to be imminent when Gerald, curtly ordering both of them to "shut up," requested Sucha Row to go on with his discourse.

"But please," he said, "let us have rather less about Egos and the potential laws of Mathematics, or whatever you call them, and more about David and Miss Leila."

Thus admonished, poor Sucha Row, after more prefatory circumlocution, proceeded to explain that Leila, though a lady, was an Initiate of a high order, versed in all the deeper mysteries of occultism.

Profoundly imbued, above all, with the doctrines of the Biune Existence and the Sympneumatic Consciousness, she had awaited, with the patience born of a sure conviction, the coming of her soul-mate, which, her intuition told her, could not be long delayed. The interval she spent in preparing to give him a fitting reception. The preparation consisted chiefly in the suppression, by means of a severe course of penitentiary discipline, of all earthly appetites. True sympneumatic intercourse is, as will be more fully explained hereafter, as different from ordinary love as chalk is from cheese. The physical affection which we denominate passion must be rigorously stamped out,[1] for it is only when shorn of all desires and inclinations on the plane of the senses that the sympneuma can hold that soul-communion with its mate which constitutes the true spiritual marriage. Hence the probationary training which Leila enforced on her pupils of the Occult College she pursued with tenfold rigour and scrupulousness herself. She ate next to nothing, and what little food she took was of the coarsest and plainest kind. In this way she had risen to the highest grades of theosophic perfection and knowledge.

The sources of her inspiration were various. Among them, I may mention that she frequently became absorbed in trance-states, during which many things visible only to the eye of the clairvoyant were revealed to her. Further, Sucha Row assured us, and we afterwards had his information confirmed from her

---

[1] I am inclined to think that Count Leo Tolstoi must have had some inkling of the sympneumatic doctrine when he penned his remarkable work, "Kreutzer Sonata."

own lips, Leila, like some other modern mystics, kept a tame Genius, or Familiar, on hand, from whom she received "illuminations,"[1] or revelations, concerning things appertaining to the astral sphere. Her Genius was of the male persuasion, and he wore sapphire wings and a green body—rather an inartistic combination, I thought ; but Genii appear to have a fancy for gaudy raiment.[2] My experience is that lady occultists usually have male Genii, and the gentlemen female ones, which is as it should be.

Another curious fact connected with Urquhart's occult sweetheart, and confided to us by Sucha Row under a strict promise not to divulge it to Urquhart, was her age. He asserted that, notwithstanding her youthful appearance, she was in reality nearly fifty years old. Owing, no doubt, to her profound knowledge of the medicinal properties of *Akâsa*, she had managed to preserve her complexion by means of some occult preparation, possibly, " The Milk of the Celestial Virgin," or some other similar astral cosmetic. We should never have learned from Leila herself the secret of her advanced age, as she was always studiously reticent on the subject. Indeed, my experience is that occult ladies are just as touchy about that delicate question as their uninitiated sisters.

---

[1] For information on this interesting subject, see " 'Clothed with the Sun,' being the Book of the Illuminations of Anna (Bonus) Kingsford ; " edited by Edward Maitland. I gathered many details myself about it from an exhaustive treatise, entitled, " Struck by the Moon ; or, Got 'em Again," which was written by a lay chela of the Atlantean brotherhood.

[2] Mrs. Kingsford's Genius was "always in red." He was "a male, and his colour was ruby." Mr. Edward Maitland's, on the other hand, "is a female, and sapphire." " Clothed with the Sun," p. 279.

For instance, Mr. Sinnett records[1] that Madame Blavatsky "has always had a dislike to telling her age with exactitude, which does not spring in her case from the vanity which operates with some ladies, but has to do with occult embarrassment. The age of the body in which a given human entity may reside, or function, is held by occult Initiates to be sometimes a very misleading fact, and chelas under strict rules are, I believe, forbidden to tell their ages. In Madame Blavatsky's case the problem was somewhat complicated by the fact that she had, within the few years previous to my first knowledge of her, grown to somewhat unwieldy proportions."

Now, whatever Leila's faults may have been, I am quite sure that vanity was not one of them. Nor, again, was "the problem complicated" in her case by her being of "unwieldy proportions," as her supple, lissom frame had withstood the ravages of time as successfully as the pale roses of her cheeks. I am therefore driven to the conclusion that her anxiety to conceal her age must have "had to do with occult embarrassment."

In the course of a conversation we had a few days later, I asked Sucha Row if a belief in the curious doctrines of Biunity, and their kindred theories, was universal among the Initiates of Mount Atlas. He replied in the affirmative, adding that celibacy was considered essential to the Higher Life, and that all the Adepts were single. I ventured to inquire how the world was to be populated if ever the occult ideal was arrived at, and nobody married.

"I admit," he replied, "that the problem of race-

---

[1] "Incidents in the Life of Madame Blavatsky," p. 227.

reproduction, which you have raised, is a matter of deep interest and importance. At the same time, as far as present needs go, there will always be plenty of people found among the ordinary ruck of humanity, into whose minds the deeper truths of Being have not yet penetrated, to secure us against any danger of the extinction of the human species. Besides, let me tell you this, that we are slowly but surely reverting to the new conditions, or rather to the conditions which prevailed in the infancy of the human race. You may not be aware that originally procreation was effected, not by ordinary physiological means, but by respiration,[1] or what hermetic science calls 'generative exhalation,' and I feel confident that when man has regained his biune, fluid state, the creative powers of the human breath will be found fully equal to the task."

I should have liked to pursue this interesting topic further, but our conversation was interrupted by the somewhat unexpected arrival of Leila, Seedy Aissa, and Urquhart. The latter, it appeared, had persuaded the merchant and his niece to leave their mountain retreat and spend a few days beneath our roof. They consented to come for a week, but in the event their stay was prolonged, and a fortnight later they

---

[1] Mr. Laurence Oliphant tells us that "up to this time physiological birth was unknown, the human race being, by means of the respiratory organs, propagated in pairs, the male with the female, who formed the complete being, though it was divided materially as to its surface substance." The human organisms in those days appeared "in a bisexual aromal form, filled with the breath of life, and acquired, by atomic condensation and combination, the structural conditions necessary to their growth and development." "Scientific Religion," pp. 254, 255.

were still with us and their departure seemed to be postponed indefinitely.

As may be imagined, a considerable portion of the time which Leila could spare from her duties at the Occult College was spent in Urquhart's society. Their courtship, however, if such it could be called, seemed to us to be of a most peculiar and unusual kind. To begin with, they manifested none of that desire for privacy and retirement to secluded places, which engaged couples usually display. On the contrary, they seemed rather to prefer that Gerald and myself and the Mahatmas should be present at their interviews. Urquhart, indeed, was careful to explain (which was, indeed, becoming sufficiently obvious) that their relations were not those of ordinary lovers. For instance, as my lady readers will doubtless have by this time observed, there was absolutely no kissing. You, dear Madam, who read diligently your three-volume novel, expect, I know, at least two kisses (burning ones, too) on the average per page, or you don't think you have got your money's worth. But you must not look for anything of the sort in this true tale of love on the super-physical plane. Sympneumatic lovers never kiss. It is not considered proper, and, moreover, by engendering the grosser animal magnetism it impedes the current of true spiritual intercourse. Urquhart once admitted to me that he and Leila sometimes found this rigorous suppression of the natural impulses a matter of some little difficulty, but it had to be done, though now and again, especially in the latter stages of their intimacy, a sigh or a tender glance from Leila reminded us that she was but a woman after all.

Hence, I rather think they preferred that other persons should be present at their interviews, for fear they should be tempted to relapse into forbidden indulgences.

It is a somewhat difficult task to convey to the ordinary mind an exact notion of this peculiar kind of love, which, for want of a better word, and out of respect for Mr. Oliphant, who first introduced these curious theories to the British public, we shall continue to call "sympneumatic." As already explained, earthly passion does not, or should not, enter into it. It is, or should be, simply a matter of soul-intercourse, resulting in the "mutual melting of fluid organisms into heart-union." For the ultimate aim of sympneumatic lovers is the reduction of their bodies to their original ethereal condition, when alone they will be able to mutually permeate their fluid organisms and, as Mr. Laurence Oliphant has it, to "flow interiorly through each other's subsurface spaces."

This is what constitutes the true spiritual love-making, and I am assured by those who have tried it, and so ought to know, that it is much more satisfactory than the ordinary kind. In its highest development, when the original fluid state has been attained, the sympneumatic lover "lives," once more to quote Mr. Oliphant, "in the expanding chambers of his own subsurfaces" at the same time that, in some mysterious way, not to be explained to the ordinary understanding, he pervades the "organic realms of the subsurfaces" of the lady. His nervous sensitiveness becomes abnormally developed, as "the dormant inner consciousnesses of his atomic centres" are awakened, and his "groping tentacles receive a thrill which transmits itself throughout all the atoms of his structure."

The above is a brief sketch of the principles on which Urquhart and Leila conducted their occult wooing. I do not recommend this kind of love-making to persons of the average type, as they would probably find it rather insipid. It is only after a long course of probationary training in occult science and practice that mankind can hope to rise to those loftier spiritual altitudes to which Count Tolstoi, Mr. Oliphant, and a few other very superior people, have presumably attained.

CHAPTER XX.

OF THE CAVE OF THE ELEMENTALS.

SEVERAL weeks passed before Seedy Aissa and Leila his niece returned to their own home. During their stay with us Leila never allowed her intercourse with Urquhart to interfere with her responsible duties as a female Mahatma and Lady Superior of the Occult College, and these naturally occupied a considerable portion of her time. But besides this, she often absented herself for two or three days on end without telling anybody where she was going to, or when we might expect her return. I noticed that her uncle never seemed to manifest the slightest anxiety on her account during these periods of absence, nor chid her when she came back. Our curiosity was naturally aroused by these strange proceedings, but it was some time before we could get any explanation. Urquhart himself was as much in the dark as the rest of us, and I am sure he felt keenly, though he never said anything, Leila's reticence on the matter. We asked Ali, who during our stay at Mount Atlas had begun to give himself most portentous airs, if he knew anything about it. He looked very wise and mysterious, and said he believed that she repaired to a cave high up on the side of Mount Atlas, to perform certain occult rites there.

"Cave, you old ass! what cave?" interposed Gerald. "It's my opinion that you're cramming us."

But the Persian persisted in asserting that such a cave existed, though where it was he could not say. All he knew at present was that it was called the "Cave of the Elementals," but he hoped to gain some further information from one of Singmya Songo's chelas, with whom he had struck up a close acquaintance, and from whom he had learned what little he knew already.

We were discussing the matter when Sucha Row joined us. Noticing that he looked exceedingly pale and ill, I asked him what was the matter. He told me that he was suffering from a bad stomach-ache, which he attributed to the exhalation of impure Western magnetism from the rupas of us three Europeans. It is not pleasant to be told that you are breeding a plague around you, but, as Mr. Sinnett quite rightly says, it is this Western magnetism which the Mahatmas find "so trying," that, to escape it, they have to retire to the fastnesses of Thibet. I must say, however, that I had never before heard of its affecting the Adepts in this particular way.

I immediately asked Sucha Row if our information concerning the cave was correct, and, if so, what he meant by withholding it from me. On my uttering the words, "Cave of the Elementals," my Mahatma appeared very much startled, and, as once before, stammered forth some incoherent excuses about his being compelled to keep the secrets of his Order from getting out among the uninitiated. For reply, I reminded him severely of his duties to me as his employer, and informed him that, unless he showed himself more frank in future, I should be compelled, however reluctantly, to seek the services of some other and more communicative Mahatma. This threat had the effect of causing him to throw a little light on the matter, though he assured me that if it ever got to the ears of the Council of Mahatmas that he had been guilty of divulging hermetic secrets, it would go hard with him. The Cave of the Elementals, it appeared, was a large cavern in a belt of precipitous rock far up on the higher slopes of the Djebel Kebeer.

"It derives its name," he said, "from its being the abode of the elemental spirits, or Dwellers of the Threshold, as your English Bulwer Lytton calls them, those 'semi-intelligent creatures of the astral light,' who belong to a wholly different kingdom of nature from ourselves. It is by command over the elementals that the Adepts perform some of their greatest physical feats, and that the most remarkable phenomena of spiritualistic *séances* are brought about. Within the recesses of the cave, also, dwell the larvæ, or evil spirits inimical to the race of man, kept in subjection only by the controlling and beneficent powers of the higher Adepts. There, too, are vast stores of akâsa, or vril, that subtle force, or essence, by whose mysterious agency we Mahatmas are enabled to do so many astonishing things."

"Yes, and there, too, I suppose," chimed in Gerald, "is the perennial fount of the mystic fluid, bo-vril, pure beef force, or bovine essence, served hot to all the leading Mahatmas."

Sucha Row shook his head sorrowfully at Gerald's incorrigible flippancy, and held his peace. We tried hard to get out of him where the cavern was situated, but on this point he maintained a stubborn silence, which neither our threats nor entreaties could induce him to break. He told us, however, that the cave was the resort of Adepts of the highest grade, who performed there certain mysterious rites and functions. As to who these Adepts were, and what was the nature of their functions, we were left wholly in ignorance, though I gathered that some severe initiatory ordeal had to be undergone by all such as aspired to enter thereon. Sucha Row himself was not of the number of Initiates thus favoured, from which I inferred that Leila, who had free access to the cave, occupied a higher rank in the hierarchy of Mount Atlas than my worthy Mahatma. Ali was of opinion that the occupation of the Adepts in the Cave of the Elementals related to the storing and bottling up of the akâsa, and conveying it down for use in the valley; but this was pure conjecture, and, as I thought, absolute nonsense. The Persian, however, was successful in worming some interesting information out of his friend the chela, which threw considerable light on the reasons of the Mahatmas for prohibiting access to the cave, and concealing its whereabouts. The atmosphere of the cavern, the chela said, was highly charged with odylic fluid (sublimated akâsa), the currents of which were so strong as to be very dangerous to life in the case of inexperienced persons. Indeed, a legend existed to the effect that once upon a time a peasant, wandering on the mountains in search of some goats which had strayed from the flock, had taken refuge

in the cave for the night, and that, like Sennacherib
and his Assyrians, when he woke up next morning
he was a dead man. Overcome by the odic current,
he went off in a species of trance, during which his
spirit was withdrawn from its fleshly envelope, and
absorbed into the Absolute in the twinkling of an
eye. And the danger would be trebled, it was said,
if any two persons united by any bond of sympathy
or affinity, either, or both, of whom were unversed in
occult science, chanced to meet in the cave. For,
since the conditions prevailing therein were highly
favourable to the establishment of organic *rapport,*
their magnetic attraction, mutually, though unconsciously, exercised with tenfold power owing to the
odic currents, might cause the spirit to be drawn out
of the body against the will of its owner ; in which
case, the latter being unable to recall it without the
intervention of an Adept, death would almost inevitably ensue. Hence, none but Mahatmas of the
highest grade could with safety enter the cavern, and
the secret of its situation was jealously guarded from
the uninitiated.

All this was not particularly lucid or satisfactory,
and it may be supposed that we were far from resting
content with such meagre explanations. We determined, if ever the opportunity offered itself, to probe
the mystery to the bottom, but our researches were
of no avail, and for a long time we were forced to
remain in ignorance. It is always the unexpected
which happens, and how the secret was eventually
discovered, and our curiosity satisfied, the reader who
perseveres to the end of this volume, will learn.

CHAPTER XXI.

As may readily be imagined, Gerald and I were left a good deal to our own devices during the period of Urquhart's occult courtship. We were not by any means idle, however, and our studies in esoteric science continued to make satisfactory progress. Our minds were gradually yielding to that mysterious fascination which occultism seldom fails to exercise over those who come within the sphere of its attraction. The passion for the marvellous and the inscrutable, the desire of mystery, is universal among mankind, and a craving after the supernatural, in one form or another, is deep-seated in the human heart. We chafe at the limited scope of our earthly vision, and long to lift if it be but a corner of the veil which shrouds from our ken the arcana of the unseen world. And many there be who, less fortunate than myself and my two companions, having failed to reach the sources of the Hidden Wisdom, yet think they have had communings with the Invisible. Even as our physical gaze, after long straining to distinguish distant objects, gives shape and form to the creations of fancy, so it often happens that the mind's eye, by long dwelling on what it desires to see and know, cherishes the fantasies and chimeras of visions, and what are termed "occult revelations," as though they were living realities. For, with grief and shame be it spoken, the occultism of the West has, at any rate until lately, been little more than a vulgar passion for so-called miracles, an unhealthy appetite, which grows with what it feeds on, for "spookical" phenomena. Hence it is that society from time to time falls a prey to the machinations of spiritualistic charlatans and manifestation-mongers. *Populus vult decipi; decipiatur.* People believe such and such a thing to be true because they wish it to be so; and when the public is on the feed for miracles and new religious sensations, the wildest neo-nonsense is readily devoured, if only it bear the hall-mark and label of occultism.

Not but what among the motley crew of charlatans and occult impostors of every sort there are to be found many sincere and ardent workers in the field of theosophic research. The difficulty is to distinguish the true from the false, the base from the sterling coin. To the hardened sceptic the investigator of hidden truths can be but one of two things —knave or dupe, arch impostor or transcendental Juggins. Yet are these far from necessary alternatives. Occultism in England has of late directed itself more to the philosophical and ethical aspect of the subject, and its devotees have become in a larger measure weaned from "phenomena," leaving these to the spiritualist and miracle-monger. Moreover, in the universal craving for new forms of religious belief, which is so characteristic a feature of our day, theosophy has attracted its full share of attention. Just now doctrinal dilettantism is rife among the upper classes of society. Ladies and gentlemen of superior mental calibre are growing dissatisfied with the old forms of belief, and are continually on the look-out for some new thing in matters dogmatic. Fashions nowadays change as rapidly in spiritual affairs as they do in matters of dress, and every person of "culture" is expected to be up in the latest novelties of agnosticism. Hence, amid the wholesale dispensing of doctrinal quackeries, and in spite of the existing plethora of religions, there is surely room for yet one more creed. In these pages the reader has been introduced to the outlines of a new system. It is not the system of Mr. Sinnett, or Madame Blavatsky, or Mr. Laurence Oliphant, nor yet of Zadkiel or Dr. Cummings, though it contains elements common to all five. Such as it is, I confidently recommend it to the notice of all who hanker after "new thoughts." Perhaps some tired and hungry searcher for fresh "isms," who has run through Positivism, Esoteric Buddhism, Robert Elsmerism, and the whole gamut of novel religio-philosophic fads, may find at last a haven of rest in my Atlantean Occultism. Should it bring balm to the soul, and satisfaction to the intellect, of but one such "earnest inquirer," my labours in the oasis of the Djebel Kebeer will not have been wholly in vain. Meanwhile, it is time I returned to my narrative.

Our life at Mount Atlas pursued its even tenor. Urquhart and Leila continued their intercourse, sometimes in our own house, sometimes in Seedy Aissa's charming cottage.   I was bound to admit that I could not regard the relations subsisting between them as entirely satisfactory, and Gerald said he thought it would be much better if they gave up the "sym-pneumatic business," and went in for good old-fashioned love-making.   I fancied, too, that both of them were beginning to find the forced suppression of their natural impulses and affections a severe trial. Leila looked pale and worried, and she sometimes showed a tendency to irritability, which was by no means natural to her; while Urquhart himself wore a harassed and careworn expression.

Nothing of note occurred for many weeks on end, so, to avoid unnecessary prolixity, I subjoin a few extracts from the journal which I kept regularly throughout our sojourn in the oasis.

March 13.—Things all going wrong to-day.   Leila in a very bad temper, because she makes no pro-gress towards attaining the Biune existence.   She finds her flesh "too, too solid"—it won't melt or resolve itself into a dew; in fact, as Gerald says, she "gets no forrarder."   Urquhart out of sorts, in sympathy with Leila.   My Mahatma, too, is getting exceedingly trying.   He has lately developed a bad habit of going off into trance-states, and remaining so for days on end.   He turned up very late this morning, presenting an exceedingly boozed appear-ance.   Asked him what he had been doing.   He said he had just emerged from a state of "ecstatic re-sumption into the universal," wherein he had had a radiant vision of EN SOPH, the All Wise (what on earth's that?)   Told him not to do it again.

15*th.*—Sucha Row more aggravating than ever.

He won't keep still a minute. Whenever he is wanted he projects himself on the astral current to some distant part of the earth—a most annoying practice. He has been three times to Thibet between breakfast and lunch to-day, which, you will admit, is a good deal too much even for an Adept. He is just like a very lively flea which, whenever you try and catch it, hops off goodness knows where. Am afraid I shall have to give my Mahatma the sack. He's eating his head off here, and does nothing for his victuals. (*Mem.* Next time I engage a Mahatma, shall let him find himself.) An Adept ought not to do himself too well, or he gets fat, which does not do for a person who has to project himself on astral currents and all that sort of thing. Besides, having to find his own beer and washing (though the last doesn't amount to much) exercises a distinctly sobering effect, and helps to keep him about the premises.

18*th.*—My Mahatma's bad example has to-day been the cause of a ludicrous incident, which, however, was rather nearly being attended with serious consequences. Old Ali, fired with a noble ambition, tried to attain *moksha* (spiritual progress) by getting out of his rupa and absorbing himself into the Absolute. The attempt was not a success, as the poor old man fell down in a fit and had to be carried out and dosed with akâsa pills. Mohammed thinks that it serves him quite right for making such an ass of himself, and says that the wind has inflated Ali's brain and that he carries his head much too high.

" Staferallah !" said our cook, " if he does not have a care he will become even as that father of all asses, Sucha Row himself. May the blessed Prophet and

R

his saints keep and defend me from all such tom-fooleries."

20th.—Have given Sucha Row a month's warning. He is never to be found when he is wanted, and persists in projecting himself on the astral current at all times and seasons. It is useless his pleading that he always leaves his rupa behind him when absent on these expeditions, as my experience shows that a rupa, apart from its linga sharira, is about as useful for all practical purposes as a cast-off cobra-skin would be to a snake-charmer.

21st.—Am about to advertise in the *Occult Gazette* of Mount Atlas for a new gooroo. The *Occult Gazette* is the leading "daily" of the oasis, and its circulation is much the largest of any paper in these parts. In form and appearance it somewhat resembles our English theosophical magazine, *Lucifer.* The editor, who is a chela of one of the leading Adepts, seems to have rather an easy time of it, if Singmya Songo is to be believed. He just thinks over what is to appear in his next issue, and then goes to sleep in his arm-chair. When he wakes up in the morning he finds his "copy" neatly written out by invisible hands,[1] and ready to go to press.

Running my eye down the advertising columns of

---

[1] Curiously enough, Mr. Sinnett records ("The Occult World," p. 159) similar experiences on the part of Madame Blavatsky when engaged on her great work, "Isis Unveiled." Sometimes when she got up of a morning the "dear old lady" (thus irreverently does Mr. Sinnett speak of our Western Sibyl) would find thirty slips added to the manuscript she had left on her table overnight. Hence it is that many good Christians are of opinion that "the old gentleman" must have had quite as large a share as the "old lady" in the composition of that remarkable work !

the *Occult Gazette*, I have just come across the following :—"An experienced Mahatma, sober, industrious, honest, and *truthful*" (he evidently makes a strong point of the "truthful," no doubt on account of its being so rare a quality), "seeks a situation as gooroo to a single gentleman or small family. Unexceptionable references. Six years with his last employer, who was finally absorbed into the Absolute. Wages not so much an object as a comfortable home." What on earth's the good of a comfortable home, I should like to know, to a fellow who is always flitting about in a disembodied state? However, it looks like business, and I shall communicate with him at once.

23rd.—Mahatma turned up to-day. Proved to be none other than an old acquaintance of the name of Ram Chutnee, whom we have met occasionally in Singmya Songo's house. Have engaged Ram Chutnee on the same terms as I did Sucha Row, but gave him strictly to understand that he is not to go gadding about in his linga sharira, but pay constant attention to his duties as gooroo.

CHAPTER XXII.

THE END OF SINGMYA SONGO.

I DON'T know whether it was to be accounted for, like the influenza, by the state of the atmosphere, but a regular epidemic of astral flittings, trance-absorptions, and other occult junkettings, set in among the Mahatmas about this time.   Quite the most important and remarkable of these was the passage of Singmya Songo's Ego-spirit to Nirvana, a feat which is only achieved by the very highest Adepts, and which frequently results, as I regret to say it did in this instance, in putting an abrupt end to their earthly career.   That Singmya Songo was such an Adept, as well by right of descent as by theosophic accomplishments, will be gathered from the following particulars, which I shall here take the opportunity of setting forth concerning him.

It transpired that our worthy friend and host was actually a reincarnation of the great Thibetan Mahatma, Ihava Songto Singo, who was himself, as occultists know, a material embodiment of the spirit of one " Nabang Lob Sang, the sixth incarnation of Tsong-kha-pa, himself an incarnation of Amithaba or

Buddha."[1] The records of all these incarnations, as Mr. Sinnett informs us, "are preserved in the Gon-pa (lamasery) of Tda-shi Hlum-po" in Thibet, and Sucha Row had seen them with his own eyes. It is well known that the Mahatmas have the power, when they reincarnate, of guiding their spiritual Egos and selecting the body into which they are about to enter; and it was often a source of considerable wonder to me how it was that Singmya Songo came to choose such a stunted, wizened, insignificant, little fleshly tenement as his own. No doubt he must have felt, like Mr. Sinnett's Adept in a similar case, much "cramped and embarrassed, and, as ordinary imagination might suggest, very uncomfortable and ill at ease;" and it is perfectly true that "re-incarnation of the kind described is not a privilege which Adepts avail themselves of with pleasure."

Singmya Songo was thoroughly aware of his numerous distinctions, and comported himself with the air of one who has to bear the burden of greatness, but would willingly lay it down. Indeed, his self-complacency was quite amusing at times, and he fully justified Mohammed's remark that "the wind had got into his brain."

The greatest pleasure in life is to be pleased with one's self. Conversely, the sharpest pangs are those of mortified vanity. Hence, Singmya Songo, being thoroughly satisfied with himself, and seldom or never having his pride ruffled, was perfectly happy. Still, the crowning achievement of his occult career had not, up to this time, been attained. I allude once more to the passage of his Ego-spirit into the

---

[1] "Esoteric Buddhism," p. 190.

ineffable condition of Nirvana. Now, Nirvana, as everybody knows, is the Buddhist Paradise, a sort of state of negative bliss—not annihilation [1] by any means, as some erroneously think, but yet a state in which all individuality is lost and merged in the Universal. Mr. Sinnett describes Nirvana as "a sublime state of conscious rest in omniscience." Not a very satisfactory definition, you will say, but I regret that, my own Ego-spirit not yet having made the passage in question, I am unable to improve upon it.

In Singmya Songo's case the thing happened in this wise. He had for several weeks been getting into a very sleepy, almost comatose, state. He was continually going off into trances which sometimes lasted several days, and from which his brother Mahatmas found it increasingly difficult to awake him. Finally, he became merged in so deep a state of trance-absorption, that the unremitting efforts of the Adepts to bring him round proved unavailing for an entire week. Kikkuppa Row, his chosen friend and associate, shook his head and expressed his opinion that matters were getting serious, but it was not till the eighth day that the truth dawned upon them that the Mahatma's Ego-spirit had left its fleshly tenement and gone off on a trip to Nirvana on its own account. Now, as Mr. Sinnett points out, on occasions like these "the resources of occult science are strained" in order to protect the physical body

---

[1] "If any say Nirvana is to cease,
    Say unto such they lie ;
    If any say Nirvana is to live,
    Say unto such they err."
            The Light of Asia.

from decay. It was exceedingly hot, and by no means good "keeping" weather, and it seemed to me about even betting that the Mahatma would be getting in a somewhat unsanitary state, to say the least of it, before his Ego-spirit turned up again.

Kikkuppa Row acted with commendable promptitude. He at once put himself in communication with his friend's Ego-spirit, by means of the system of astral telegraphy known to the Adepts, and sent him an imperative summons to come back immediately. But here again, as Mr. Sinnett explains, there is always a great risk that, when once Nirvana is attained, the Ego will be unwilling to return. In fact, it is pretty certain that he will not do so unless he happens to be a very self-sacrificing Ego, devotedly attached to the "idea of duty in its purest abstractions;" and I regret to say that Singmya Songo's Ego was not of this superior sort. In reply to Kikkuppa Row's summons he sent back a very flippant message to the effect that (I am quoting from memory) he was a jolly sight too comfortable where he was to think of leaving. "Behold!" he said, "I am luxuriating in the bliss of Non-Being! Let me tell you that living in 'a sublime state of conscious rest in omniscience' is the best fun in the world. Hope you're pretty well. Good-bye."

The heartless conduct of this unprincipled Ego cannot be too severely reprehended, and I regret to say that the consequences were all that we had feared. The "resources of occult science" utterly failed to preserve Singmya Songo's physical body from decay. Accordingly, at the end of a fortnight his sorrowing friends, fearing that if they delayed any longer they might incur a visit from the sanitary inspector of El Medinah, were forced to carry him out and bury him. If ever his Ego has a fancy to forego the ineffable, if somewhat indefinite, joys of Nirvana, and revisits this earth, he will find all that remains of his late abode in the flesh beneath the green sod which luxuriates in the shade of an umbrageous oak at the foot of Mount Atlas.

CHAPTER XXIII.

WE ASCEND MOUNT ATLAS.

WE had explored nearly all the environs of our African home ; but the greatest expedition of all, and the one upon which we had all set our hearts, yet remained unaccomplished. It was obviously impossible for three Englishmen of roving and more or less adventurous dispositions to live several months at the base of a lofty and unknown mountain without being seized with a burning desire to ascend it. We had, in fact, only delayed making a start until the season should be more favourable to the undertaking, and the summer sun should have melted the snow which, even in spring, descended far down the mountain-side. From time to time we had made careful surveys of the peak with our telescopes, and had fixed upon the outlines of a route which we hoped would prove feasible. The natives, of course, laughed to scorn our presumptuous idea of scaling the mighty horn, as natives always do laugh to scorn travellers from far-off countries who come to conquer the mountains they are incapable of climbing themselves. They told us that a Mahatma might possibly project himself to the summit in his *linga sharira*, but for ordinary mortals to attempt such a thing in their plain *rupas*, or objective bodies, was little short of sheer madness. None the less, we commenced to make our preparations, and instructed a *mallem*, or blacksmith, in the town to make us three ice-axes. When finished they were not precisely the sort of weapons which Alpine Clubmen are accustomed to use, but we had no doubt about their serving our purpose sufficiently well.

It was one fine morning in June when Gerald, who had long been chafing at our forced inaction, began to urge upon Urquhart the desirability of our attempting the ascent.

" Look here, old man," he said, " it's about time we began to think about making a start. The snow is almost melted now, and the weather's splendid. ' Il faut profiter du beau temps,' as Peter Taugwalder used to say to me at Zermatt ; so let's get under weigh before it takes a turn for the worse."

Urquhart, who had been equally eager for the expedition, was easily persuaded ; and we had made up our minds to set forth early the following week, when an unexpected obstacle arose. As soon as Leila heard of our intention she protested strenuously against Urquhart's embarking on so difficult and dangerous an enterprise.

" Surely ye are mad," she cried. " I will not have you go. Verily, the mountain is sacred, and disaster will surely befall him who would rashly dare to profane its virgin snows."

As she spoke, the look of piteous entreaty and terror upon her face was more eloquent than any words could have been. It was plain that Urquhart wavered in his purpose, and a look of irresolution, such as I have seldom seen his features wear, passed over his face. His eye wandered from the parted sweetness of Leila's coral lips up to those dazzling heights where the silver spear of Atlas pierced the azure vault of the sky. Doubt was upon him. On the one hand, there was his promise to Gerald, often repeated, that he would make the ascent with him; and, more potent influence still, there was the inborn love of the mountaineer for his peaks, and the reluctance to leave unattempted an ascent which would be the climax and the crowning achievement of our expedition. On the other hand, there was the restraining force of Leila's soft, pleading voice and her tearful face, which his growing love made it hard for him to resist.

Gerald, seeing his friend's indecision, and being himself in nowise disposed to give up the expedition upon which he had set his heart, suggested a way out of the difficulty.

"Look here, David," he said, "we don't want to lay you under any constraint in the matter. If you would rather not go, Jim and I will try Mount Atlas by ourselves. I dare say we shall get on all right, though of course we would much rather you came with us."

"Not for a thousand worlds!" cried Urquhart with unwonted animation. "You know how particular I am about there never being less than three people on one rope when crossing glaciers ; so don't imagine I shall ever allow you two to attempt a peak like the Djebel Kebeer alone."

In the end Gerald prevailed, and, in spite of Leila's

tears and protestations, it was arranged that we should all start together the next morning but one. The whole of the following day was spent in making those preparations for the ascent which are familiar to all Alpine climbers. An ample stock of provisions, both fresh and dried, was laid in, together with blankets, cooking utensils, and other camping requisites ; and two of the tents were subjected to a process of botching and mending, of which they stood in sore need. A couple of mules were likewise ordered to be in readiness for us, and we hired a whole *posse* of porters to carry our things up to the highest sleeping-place.

The sun had not yet topped the hills to the east of El Medinah when our cavalcade started from the town. Ali and two or three of our Mahatma friends came to see us off, as also did Leila and her uncle. Tears like big pearls coursed down her lovely cheeks as she bid us farewell, and I began to think that sympneumatic love could not be so very different from ordinary love, after all. Old Ali was likewise much moved, and, as usual, gave a minute description of the state of his liver and other internal organs in consequence of his emotion. He vowed that the lovely Leila had made roast meat of his heart, and joined his entreaties to her own in order to induce Urquhart to desist from the enterprise.

" Try not the mountain, O my master ! " he cried, and pointed to the northern *arête* of Atlas. " See ye not where yon crag beetles over the dizzy gulf ? Wherefore would ye plant the footsteps of trepidation upon the rocks of insecurity, and be hurled from the peak of terror into the abyss of destruction ? Verily, the Father of the Nose is a rash and headstrong youth, who will not hearken to the dictates of prudence and the promptings of ripe wisdom and experience. Full well I know that my speech is but as wind in your ears, and that ye will not be moved thereby from your determination, for the heart of obstinacy is hard and stubborn as the oak, and will not readily yield to persuasion. Yet will the hour come, yea, is now close at hand, when it shall repent you that ye heeded neither the counsels of age nor the entreaties of love. Of a truth, bitter are the teachings of adversity, but by them alone can the froward be guided along the paths of wisdom."

The old man's voice rose shrilly as he gave forth these prophetic utterances, but they fell on deaf ears, for our minds were made up. Gerald, mounting his mule, bade Ali abandon the speech of imbecility, lest he (Gerald) might be tempted to make black with the fist of pugnacity the optics of senile garrulity; and then, the baggage animals being loaded, we prepared to start. Leila turned away with a flood of tears, and a deathly pallor overspread Urquhart's sunburnt countenance. Seedy Aissa bade us farewell with an air of grave and dignified solicitude; the Mahatmas poured their blessings on our heads; the Moors belaboured their beasts, and we were off. Across the verdant meadows, up through the myrtle groves and forest glades, a long winding path led us by the cliffs to the upland pastures, where sheep and cattle innumerable browsed lazily, or else lay down exhausted by the heat. Two hours more, and we had passed for the first time the region of vegetation, and entered upon one of sterile and rocky grandeur.

The route we had selected, after a careful survey of

the mountain from below, lay along the ridge of a mighty spur which abutted on the north-eastern face of Atlas. This spur formed the northern side of a huge *corral*, or circular hollow, scooped out of the mountain like a Pyrenæan cirque, over two miles wide, and surrounded on its three sides by lofty precipices crowned with jagged peaks piled one above the other—Pelion on Ossa—the grim guardians of a peaceful valley which nestled at their base. Above these peaks, but masked partially by a screen of dark rock, the region of snow and ice commenced, and the water discharged therefrom leaped in a thousand cataracts, pearly-white, like threads of finest lace, down the cliffs of the corral. Here and there the trickling streamlets were dissipated in mid-air by the wind into spray, which, illumined by the sunbeams, fell in a rainbow shower of ruby, sapphire, and emerald hues.

Towards four o'clock the ground became too steep and rocky for the mules, so, putting our tents and other *impedimenta* on the backs of the porters, we sent the animals back to El Medinah. Continuing our climb upwards, we reached towards sundown a bit of tolerably flat ground, and determined to pitch the tents there for the night.

While the Moors busied themselves in preparing for our bivouac we strolled to the edge of the cliff and looked across the corral. Night was coming on, and the shadows ran swiftly up the forests and the grassy wolds, to where the sun shed his last roseate glow on the vast snow-fields of the upper ice-region. Heavens! what a glorious spectacle! What mountaineer could gaze thereon and remain unmoved? For "sunwards, lo you! how it towers sheer up, a world of mountains, the diadem and centre of the mountain region! A hundred and a hundred savage peaks, in the last light of day ; all glowing, of gold and amethyst, like giant spirits of the wilderness ; there in their silence, in their solitude, even as on the night when Noah's deluge first dried!"[1] Sunset among the mountains has never been described more beautifully ; and we read that Teufelsdröckh (though the Herr Professor was no mountaineer) "gazed over those stupendous masses with wonder, *almost* with longing desire ; never till this hour had he known Nature, that she was One, that she was his mother and divine. And as the ruddy glow was fading into clearness in the sky, and the sun had now departed, a murmur of eternity and immensity, of death and of life, stole through his soul ; and he felt as if death and life were one, as if the earth were not dead, as if the spirit of the earth had its throne in that splendour, and his own spirit were therewith holding communion."

To the true mountaineer such feelings are familiar, even though he lack the eloquence to express them in words. To him the peaks *are* a source, not only of wonder, but also of " longing desire," which cannot be satisfied until he has set his foot upon their snow-crowned heads, and seen their glory face to face.

For a moment longer the western peak of Atlas glowed like a volcano ; then, its fires suddenly extinguished, it stood solitarily forth in cold and grim majesty. At our feet the precipice dropped some thousands of feet into the corral, and far, far below we could hear the tinkling of the cowbells and the

----

[1] " Sartor Resartus," p. 106.

voices of shepherds calling to their flocks. The brief African twilight soon passed, and, as the life of day ebbed rapidly away and the air grew chill and frosty, we sought the shelter of our tent. Our aneroids gave the height at something over 12,000 feet, and we calculated that we had mounted nearly 5000 in the course of the day.

After supper and a pipe we prepared to turn in, but before doing so we went out and had a last look round. The starry hosts slowly mustered in their bright array, till they glittered like fire-flies in the unclouded heavens, and the waterfalls gleamed like sheeted ghosts in the pale moonbeams against the sombre grandeur of the cliffs of the corral, and high above all towered the silver glory of the horn of Atlas. We could have lingered longer over this sublime scene, but we had had a hard day's work, and a still harder one awaited us on the morrow. The torrents sang us a lullaby as we curled ourselves up under our blankets, and in a few moments a chorus of snores announced that, for the majority of the party at any rate, the fatigues of the day were being forgotten in slumber.

For myself, no doubt owing to the exciting influence of the rarefied atmosphere, I could get but little sleep. Urquhart, too, though as an old and practised mountaineer he was less affected by the air, passed a restless and perturbed night, turning over and over on his side and talking continually in his sleep. When we got up, which was in the small hours of the morning, and the Moors were preparing our cocoa, Gerald rallied him on the subject, and asked if he had been disturbed by nightmare.

"No," he said after a pause; "not nightmare—only a very strange dream. What its meaning or import may be I cannot say, though sure I am that it is a presage of some approaching event affecting Leila and myself. Methought I had wandered forth alone upon the side of a lofty mountain, and I stood in a vast cavern near its summit; and as I stood there a strange feeling came over me, and I was sure that I was dying, though wherefore I knew not. I felt no fear, and I even seemed to welcome the approach of death. As life was ebbing away and my vital faculties grew weaker, my psychic perceptions gained abnormal strength and clearness, and my vision strove to penetrate the veil which separates this phenomenal world from the infinite beyond. Already death seemed very near, and, standing thus at the very threshold, as it were, of the astral world, I became conscious of the presence of one whose being was in union, and whose life-pulses vibrated in harmony, with my own. I knew well that my soul's mate was at hand, but it was some time before my straining gaze was rewarded by the sight of the astral shape of her I love. For awhile she, my life's lode-star, my soul's beacon-light, stood afar off beckoning to me. A strange, appealing look of love and sweet sadness beamed in her eyes, and I struggled, but in vain, to reach her. The magnetism which subsists between kindred spirits drew me towards her, but the fetters of the flesh still held me in thrall. At last, as I struggled, something seemed to burst within my brain, the link which bound me to the material world snapped, and I was free to join her; and our twin souls were united and wafted far away through

S

the outer cycles of the revolving firmament, out into the furthest realms of infinite peace. And now in some mysterious way we seemed each to be having a double existence. In the invisible world our psychic personalities seemed indwelling one with another in closest communion, while on earth our material bodies continued to live and move and have their being as before. And I knew then for a certainty, what I had only dimly conceived before, that our earthly affections are gross and unsatisfying compared with the true love which shall be ours in the hereafter beyond the grave. All this, however, appeared to me but vague and shadowy, as in a dream, and I was striving to gain a clearer apprehension of my strangely altered condition, when you, Gerald, turning over on your side, gave me a violent kick, and I awoke."

"Humph!" remarked Gerald sententiously; "a very remarkable dream, and not at all of the order of those for which lobster or plum-pudding could be held accountable—even supposing we had had the chance of indulging in such luxuries. I am sorry my toe should have brought it to a premature conclusion, as the rest of it might have been more interesting still. But here's the cocoa ready, and we've no time to talk about dreams now."

It was two hours still before dawn, and our appetites were not greatly tempted by the frugal fare which was set before us. In less than half an hour the meal had been finished, and then, leaving the porters to carry our things back to El Medinah, we three shouldered the bag of provisions, the rope, and the other requisites for the final ascent of the peak, and started alone. We had an hour's wearisome tramp by lantern-light before a few faint arrows of light, the welcome harbingers of day, appeared over the desert behind us. The dull sapphire hue of night yet lingered in the western sky, while a pale saffron flush, which presently deepened into the orange light of dawn, overspread the east. The peaks and glaciers around us blushed at the first kiss of morning as the sun rose and wooed all Nature with his shower of golden beams. We would willingly have paused awhile to gaze upon this glorious scene, but time was precious, and we contented ourselves with once more glancing at those tremendous heights above us, which, a short time ago so cold and forbidding, but now resplendent in the rays of the newly risen sun, seemed to invite our footsteps upwards. With slow and regular paces we plodded steadily on. Suddenly a tiny white cloud, at first no greater than the puff of smoke from a cannon's mouth, issued from the opposing wall of the corral, and a long sullen roar, like some salvo of Alpine artillery, broke the stillness of the morning air and rolled reverberating round the precipices. The cloud augmented in volume till it shrouded half the mountain in a white veil of finely powdered snow. When it dispersed we saw that a huge avalanche of mingled ice and snow, detached by the sun's heat from its moorings at the summit of the cliff, had hurled itself some thousands of feet down to the bottom of the corral, where a pile of débris, heaped up against the rocks, gave us an idea of what vast masses must have fallen.

Quitting finally the last traces of vegetation, we crossed a desolate, rock-strewn plateau, and found ourselves approaching a large glacier. The ice at its lower end being much broken up, we took to the left-hand lateral moraine, and followed its crest for a considerable distance. The going was as bad as it usually is upon such places, the loose crumbling surface being studded with big boulders, which every now and then became dislodged, and crashed down the sides, threatening to carry us with them. Presently the moraine terminated, and we were forced, by no means unwillingly, on to the glacier, which for a short time presented no manner of difficulty. After a while, however, the surface of the vast frozen river grew more and more broken by *séracs*, or hummocks of ice, while higher up the ice-fall, which ran right across the glacier, threatened to prove a serious obstacle to our progress. At this point Urquhart called a halt, and we were all tied together by the rope. The order of our going was as follows :—Urquhart, as the oldest and most experienced climber, had the place of honour in the van; I, being a novice in Alpine craft, was placed in the middle; and Gerald brought up the rear.

Slowly and carefully we threaded our way upwards, scrambling over the summits of hoary hillocks of ice, or else traversing at their base, by means of steps cut with the axes, the rim of yawning crevasses. In these frozen valleys the outer world was shut out from our view, and we seemed lost in a species of equatorial polar region. All round was a wilderness of icy spires and turrets, some of them hundreds of feet in height; pillars of unimaginable forms, curved, straight, spiral; long, winding grottoes and caves, from whose recesses the running streams gave forth the most extraordinary sounds, as though some huge natural water-mill were working within; chasms of seemingly infinite depth, spanned by bridges festooned with gigantic icicles, all tinged with that lovely, indescribable glacial blue, which must be seen to be realized, and which no painter has ever yet succeeded in transferring to canvas.

After nearly two hours of this sort of work, during which we advanced only a few hundred yards, we emerged on to the upper plateau of glacier, and for a time all was plain sailing. Higher up, however, a second and more formidable ice-fall barred the way, and, remembering the time which we had expended on the lower séracs, we determined, if possible, to quit the glacier and take to the rocks. On our right the mountain rose in a series of precipices, some two thousand feet in height, up to the final ridge, which we trusted would lead us to the summit. After a careful survey, we—that is, Gerald and Urquhart, for I could lay claim to no mountaineering knowledge myself—came to the conclusion that at one point there was a feasible route up the face, and we determined to try it. But how were we to get off the glacier? Between us and the rocks ran a formidable *schrund*, or chasm, of immense depth and several yards in width. However, after following the schrund for a short distance we were fortunate in finding a natural bridge, formed by a huge boulder which had fallen from the cliff and become wedged in between the rocks and the ice. Here we rested half an hour for breakfast, though what with the fatigue and the rarefied air, it was very little that I could eat, and I was surprised to see even so old a campaigner as

Urquhart similarly affected.   On the other hand, Gerald's vigorous appetite, which rose superior to every trial, was in no way impaired.

Scrambling over the boulder which bridged the chasm, we tackled the rocks, and after some stiff climbing, which, however, presented fewer difficulties than we had anticipated, we found ourselves standing on the crest of the ridge—*arête*, I believe, is the more correct Alpine term.   A magnificent panorama here unfolded itself, and we had our first glimpse of the habitable country on the western slopes of the Djebel Kebeer, and the Great Desert beyond.   The mountain fell away less precipitously on this side, and we looked down on a region of minor mountain chains, intersected by numerous valleys branching out in different directions.   None of these valleys, however, appeared to rival in width or beauty that of the Wad el Kebeer, which had doubtless been selected by the Atlantean colonists on account of its superior size and fertility.

After a few minutes' breathing time we began to climb the arête.   It was most uncomfortably narrow, and broken in places by jagged teeth of rock, which at times were exceedingly difficult to surmount.   It struck me that this sort of thing was all very well for tight-rope dancers, but most unsuitable for respectable middle-aged gentlemen like Urquhart and myself. Here and there the ridge of snow was drifted up into a knife-like edge, on which we had to maintain a precarious balance.   On our left was the dizzy cliff which we had just ascended, on our right a frozen snow-slope of extraordinary steepness descended to a wide expanse of glacier over two thousand feet below.

I felt horribly giddy at some of these places, and my knees trembled so that at times I thought I must fall. The feeling, however, gradually wore off, and after a while I began to see that what I had imagined to be giddiness was in reality nothing more than the terror which is the natural result of inexperience.

Presently, our progress was barred by a rocky pinnacle, which reared its head above the summit of the cliff, like a turret from the battlement of a fortress. To scale it was obviously impossible, for its sides were smooth and almost completely vertical. On the other hand, in order to turn it we should have to traverse fully three yards of a perpendicular wall of rock which beetled over a hideous abyss, clinging, like flies to a window-pane, to such tiny foothold and handhold as we could find. There was a miniature ledge, about one and a half inches wide, running along the face of the rock, and one or two crevices gave our finger-tips something to hold on to, but it was a truly awful place to pass. How we ever accomplished it I don't know. I remember well, in the middle of it all, taking a look down between my legs into empty space, and catching a glimpse of the glacier which swam in the dizzy atmosphere some thousands of feet beneath us. I thought for a moment that that look would have finished me. My brain reeled, and every visible object seemed to dance before my eyes ; but I pulled myself together, and with a desperate effort, and a haul of the rope from Urquhart, who had planted himself securely on the rocks above, I at last found myself landed on the other side.

"A pretty nasty bit, that," Gerald sententiously observed, as soon as we were all safely across.

"Rather like the corner on the arête of the Zinal Rothhorn—eh, David?—only much worse."

I had never been up the Zinal Rothhorn, but I thought to myself that if it was anything like the place we had just crossed I would take care to give it a wide berth. And yet, as my fears subsided, I began now for the first time to feel the fascinations of mountain climbing. I was excited and exhilarated by the keen air, by the danger, by the sense of obstacles surmounted, of difficulties overcome. Those vast precipices, which but a short while since caused a sinking of the heart, now moved me rather to awe and admiration. Amid the splendours of the mountains the mind after a time is uplifted, and becomes attuned to the glorious Nature around you; the imagination is stimulated, the latent manhood within you is called forth, and, the first natural sensation of dread past, death itself seems to lose half its terrors. In the desert I feared exceedingly to die. During the simoom I contemplated the end which seemed to be approaching with absolute horror. Not so here among the mountains. If I slip, thought I, what a glorious sepulchre is mine! Yon silvery glacier for my eternal tomb, and the vast pyramid of Atlas for a headstone. It is curious, by the way, how reflections such as these serve to tranquillize the mind in the presence of danger. *Pompa mortis magis terret quam mors ipsa*—"rob him of his ugly trappings and circumstance, and you may regard death almost with equanimity."

Surely, in these irreverent and over-busy days it is something to dwell amid scenes where a sense of awe and contemplation and reverence may be engendered;

something to commune alone with Nature in those
sublimer aspects of hers, which, while they bring home
to us the utter insignificance and puniness of man,
engrave upon our hearts the majestic order and
beauty of the universe. The snow-fed cataract; the
avalanche crashing down the mountain-side; the
glacier creeping onwards with age-long, resistless
course; the ice-spires toppling into the frozen gulfs
at their base; the hurricane which sweeps around the
crags; the thunder-rattle leaping from cliff to cliff
athwart the storm; the lightning flash which threatens
to dash you from your dizzy eminence;—all these,
and much more besides, seem like a reflection of
Omnipotence—of that Power in whose hands man is
but as dust and nothingness. The peak, too, which
soars above our heads, is it not, in a way, symbolical
of our best hopes and aspirations, the goal that we
may never reach, but the struggle after whose attainment is at least elevating and ennobling?

I may be lacking in the power to give expression
to these thoughts, but those who are true mountaineers
—I do not speak of climbers of the "greased pole"
order, but of men who love the mountains for their
own sake—will know what I mean. For to see and
to feel all these things in their true significance,
one must climb. At the time I am now writing of
I was no mountaineer myself. Nevertheless, though
deeply imbued with a truly British reverence for
every form of athletic prowess, I have always reserved
my chiefest admiration for the men who have dis-
tinguished themselves by feats of skill and daring
among the peaks. And this, not only because
mountaineering calls forth the highest qualities, both

physical and mental, such as pluck, patience, nerve, endurance, mutual and self-reliance, but also because, almost alone among manly sports, it powerfully stimulates the imagination. Wherefore, having now been initiated into these Alpine mysteries, having communed, so to speak, with the spirit of the mountains, I say to each and all of my readers, "Go thou, and do likewise." Do you desire health and strength? You will find them on the mountains. Are you a man of lofty contemplation or desperate imaginings? The peaks will supply you alike with food for reflection and a field for adventure. Especially is this so among virgin snows and untrodden summits, where the explorer is continually finding himself in the presence of the unexpected and the unknown. Wherefore, once more I say, "Go and climb."

CHAPTER XXIV.

VICTORY !

IT was now getting on towards four o'clock, and we were still far from the point where the arête terminated in the final snow-slope which led up to the summit. It was becoming more and more evident that, whether we liked it or not, we were in for another night upon the mountain—a night, too, which would be spent under far less pleasant conditions than the previous one. Any doubts we may have had on the matter were speedily set at rest by the sudden appearance of a blue-black cloud, which gathered rapidly round the northernmost peak of Atlas. Soon the whole sky became overcast. The wind sprang up, and grew into a perfect hurricane from the N.W., while a driving scud of mingled sleet and hail smote our faces. A tremendous peal of thunder, followed almost instantaneously by a blinding flash, caused us to stop and see if any of our number had been struck. Happily we had all escaped, but the electric fluid could be distinctly felt playing about us, and causing our axes literally to hum, which showed how real had been our danger. We were evidently caught by one of those storms which come on with such terrible suddenness in tropical regions. Our position on the narrow arête, exposed as we were to the full force of the blast, and offering a conspicuous target to the lightning, was one of extreme peril. During the more violent gusts we were forced to lie down at full length and cling with might and main to the rock, else we should inevitably have been hurled over the precipice. Presently, Urquhart halted at a spot where a jutting pinnacle of crag afforded some shelter from the sweep and drift of the storm, and a narrow ledge at its base just gave the three of us room to stand together. As we took up our quarters on this dizzy perch, an eagle rose scared from his eyrie, and, with a rush and whirr of outstretched pinions, swept by us so close as to almost brush our faces with his wing-tips; then, screaming, sailed upwards to the crags on our right.

Dusk came on, and then night, but the storm showed no signs of abating. The air was literally aboil with driving mists and twisting, twirling snow-wreaths, which eddied and danced in mad frolic about our heads. The thunder roared and rattled, and the lightning licked the crags with forked tongues of flame, or else leaped in zigzag flashes athwart the sky. Some of the lightning effects were marvellously beautiful, and even the terrible nature of our situation could not prevent us from expressing our admiration. Now and again great rifts and chasms of fire would appear in some heavily-charged cloud, and the electric fluid slid down the centre in serpentine rivulets of blue, *eau-de-nil*, or rose-coloured flame. Time after time these wondrous natural pyrotechnic displays were repeated, and the chain, or ribbon, lightning presented itself in ever-varying form and effect.

All night long we hung quivering and clinging to the crag, drenched to the skin, and suffering torments from the cold. We kept rubbing each other all over, partly to keep up our circulation, partly as a means of resisting the insidious feeling of drowsiness which from time to time came over us. For from sleep under such circumstances there would be no awakening.

For four long hours the tempest lashed us in its fury, and, as we listened to the howling and moaning of the wind, it seemed as though the wailing Genii of the storm were issuing from their craggy caves bent upon wreaking vengeance upon the rash invaders of their mountain fastnesses.

Oh, the agony of that long night! I thought morning would never come. Towards midnight the storm suddenly ceased, but our miseries continued long after dawn had broken cold and grey on a world of damp fog and trailing mists. Presently, as the sun rose and gathered force, fragments of tremulous vapour parted under his rays, like golden threads unravelling ; and we looked down upon a billowy ocean of cloud, its waves tipped here and there with beams of golden light. Atlas, like a coy maiden, still veiled its head ; but about its sides the mists, broken up by the force of the gale, were tortured into strange forms by the wind-wizard ; or else, gathered in nebular masses, bank upon bank, they rolled slowly up the flanks of the mountain. The air was full of moisture, and the sun had not yet asserted his sovereignty. From the highest horn of Altas diaphanous streamers of vapour, lit up with a pale watery effulgence, floated away like pennons from a ship's masthead. But their gauzy filaments gradually parted asunder, and by eight o'clock all traces of the storm had disappeared ; the clouds were in full retreat, and the sun shone forth triumphant out of a clear sky. Nevertheless, we still ached in every joint, and our limbs were so stiff from long exposure to the cold that we could with difficulty crawl from our rocky shelf to a more comfortable resting-place on the arête. Here we sat and basked awhile in the sun, until our wearied bodies began to gain new strength and vitality from his rays. Fortunately, the " rücksacks " which contained our provisions had successfully resisted the wet, and none of the food was spoiled.

Continuing on our way, we found that the arête grew easier as we advanced, and presently it came to an end. We were now at the foot of the snow-slope which formed the northern face of the final cone of the mountain, whose slender, graceful outlines, like a silvery spike cleaving the turquoise sky, we had so often admired from below. At last we seemed to be within reach of the goal of our hopes and ambition. We calculated that the cone could not be more than fifteen hundred feet high, and, though it was exceedingly steep, we did not anticipate much difficulty in ascending it. But we had reckoned without the *schrund*, a huge rent or crack in the glacier running along the base of the cone, which came very near bringing our expedition to a premature end. A thin cornice of snow, which partially bridged the chasm, had concealed it from our view till we had arrived

almost upon the brink. It was five or six yards wide
at the narrowest part, and the upper lip was fully
three feet higher than the lower, so that, though an
active climber descending the mountain might perhaps
leap across, it was quite impossible to do so from the
lower side.

We searched diligently for some place narrow
enough to allow of our passing, but in vain, and we
were almost at our wits' end. True, the crevasse was
spanned in one or two places by white, treacherous-
looking snow-crusts, from which huge, jagged icicles
depended; but these natural bridges were so thin
and rotten that we hardly dared to trust them with
our weight. Not knowing what to do, we sat down
and had breakfast.

"Look here, boys," said Urquhart, "one of two
things has got to be done. Either we must turn tail
and make our way back to El Medinah as best we can,
or else we must see if any of these confounded bridges
will bear us. Which is it to be?"

"Well, I'm not going back, anyhow, without having
a try," replied Gerard. Are you game, Jim?"

I protested that, as I knew nothing about mountaineering, I could not offer an opinion, but that I
placed myself in their hands, and would do whatever
they thought fit.

"In that case," said Urquhart, "as I am lighter
than you, Gerald, I will go first. Meanwhile, undo
the rope, you two, and leave the end long enough to
allow me to get across. And mind you are ready to
hold me tight, or else, if I go through, I shall drag
both of you after me."

In obedience to his instructions, we planted ourselves firmly in the snow, and, giving the rope a turn round our wrists, stood prepared for all emergencies. Throwing himself flat on his stomach in the snow, Urquhart began to crawl slowly and cautiously over the bridge. Every moment I feared to hear the crack of breaking ice, and to see him disappear in the crevasse; but no, the bridge held, and in a few moments he had his axe planted in the snow on the other side, and was pulling himself up with it. My turn came next. I experienced a curious creepy sensation when I found myself over the centre of that horrible chasm, crawling like a serpent in the snow, with the rope tied tightly round my middle, and expecting each instant to find myself suspended thereby in mid-air. However, I was no less fortunate than Urquhart, and passed over in safety. We were more apprehensive about Gerald, on account of his greater weight, and our fears proved to be not without reason, for hardly had he got half-way across, when, with a dull, scrunching sound, the treacherous crust gave way, and he was dangling at the end of the rope in the crevasse. Happily, the jerk came upon Urquhart and myself simultaneously, though for a moment I feared lest our united efforts should be unequal to supporting his weight; but Gerald, who never once lost his presence of mind, managed to get his toe in a small crevice in the ice, and so lessened the strain and enabled us to haul him out.

Our troubles were now nearly over, so far as the ascent was concerned, as the final snow-slope, in spite of its steepness, was perfectly easy. The rarefaction of the atmosphere however, combined with the sun's heat, began to tell powerfully upon me. My heart went thump, thump, against my ribs, and I was forced to pause and take breath every few yards. But, as at length we neared the summit, exhausted as we were, we seemed to gather fresh strength at this supreme moment when our long and toilsome climb was about to be crowned with success. In the last hundred yards the slope grew less steep, and the sense of triumph lent wings to our worn-out bodies. All sense of fatigue was forgotten in the delicious consciousness that victory was within our grasp, and, quickening our steps almost into a run, we arrived breathless but exultant on the highest pinnacle of Mount Atlas.

The top, which from the valley seemed like the apex of a cone, proved on closer acquaintance to be a narrow knife-like ridge of snow over a hundred yards in length. The natural reaction from our great exertions came over us, and, throwing ourselves on the snow, we lay and basked in the sun, whose rays, even at this vast elevation, tempered only by a moderate breeze from the west, seemed to lose hardly any of their power. On consulting our aneroids we found that we were at a height of 18,950 feet. Our spirits were bathed in a sense of profound contentment, and, overcome by fatigue, we yielded awhile to the soft influences of the sky, and sought repose. But when the first feelings of lassitude had passed away we rose, and, as we looked forth on the indescribably glorious scene above, below, and around us, fresh and more powerful emotions asserted themselves. Our hearts were full to overflowing, and, now that the victory was gained, our pent-up feelings burst forth, and we shouted aloud in an ecstacy of triumph. The romance and poetry of the peaks flooded our souls, and a thousand thoughts and memories surged tumultuously through our over-wrought brains. All the various accidents and adventures which had befallen us on our journey, the scenes in desert, and mountain, and valley, passed in rapid review before me. But with my exultation there mingled a still deeper sense of gratitude that we should have been spared to see and to accomplish so much. For my own part, I had seldom aspired to conquer peaks of the most ordinary description, but to be among the first to stand on the virgin summit of a lofty and hitherto undiscovered mountain sur-passed my wildest dreams.

To describe the view from the summit is utterly beyond my poor powers. Surely, never did the eye of man gaze forth upon so glorious and wondrous a panorama. The first things that arrested our eyes were the two southern peaks of Mount Atlas, the middle one a massive pyramid of snow, the other triple-crested, with its eastern face falling sheer in a terrific precipice of rock and hanging ice-wall. The intervening space was filled by an immense glacier-filled valley, or depression, whose snow-fields, dazzling our eyes with their awful whiteness, and undefiled by the foot of man, seemed like emblems of absolute purity. We noted with delight the delicate curves of the wind-drifted snow, which diversified the glittering surface with faint and almost imperceptible shadows. Westwards, we looked down upon a world of purple mountains and forest-clad foothills, intersected by complex ramifications of shadowy valleys and gorges, fringed with shaggy wood, in whose depths the streamlets glanced and glittered in the sunshine, as they leaped merrily down to where the green meadows lay nestling at the foot of russet-brown cliffs. Turning to the east, our glance swept the crater-like hollow of the corral, and between two opposing walls of rock, which formed the portals of this vast natural amphitheatre, we had a glimpse, as of some miniature art-gem set in a dark, heavy frame, of a bit of our own valley, with the white houses of El Medinah plainly visible, and the Wad Kebeer winding like a silver thread amid the emerald pastures and the yellowing fields of corn. And beyond all this—beyond the gleaming glaciers and the tall, snow-clad peaks, beyond the rugged mountain ranges, and the pleasant woods and meadows lying at their base, beyond our lovely valley, and beyond El Medinah, with its learned Brethren and its happy peaceful peasantry—illimitable on every side, its vast expanses swimming in the heat-burdened atmosphere, lay the huge, yellow, African desert. Mount Atlas and our oasis stood forth like some tiny, solitary islet, sparkling in the midst of a shoreless ocean of sand, for in vain we strained our eyes to discover some break or gap in its tawny waves. Far beyond mortal ken they stretched away in never-ending undulations, their billowy outlines and shimmering golden hues growing fainter and fainter in dimly distant perspective, till they finally melted away in the soft, luminous haze which veiled the entire horizon.

CHAPTER XXV.

THE AVALANCHE.

IT was close upon mid-day, and though we were sorely tempted to linger on the summit, time was pressing, so we bethought ourselves of commencing the descent. We had almost made up our minds to take a new route down. In the first place, we dreaded the risk of re-crossing the schrund, especially now that the only possible bridge over it was broken. Secondly, the desire of further exploring this most interesting mountain was strong within us, and, though we did not know what obstacles and difficulties might lie below concealed from our view, we trusted to the chapter of accidents to extricate us from them. Fortune had always been on our side up till now, and we trusted to her befriending us to the end of the chapter.

Before starting, we made a careful survey of the mountain. We noticed that the snow-slope on the south-eastern face lay at a comparatively easy angle, and if only there were no lines of impassable cliff along the lower slopes, the descent on that side seemed likely to present fewer difficulties than those we had encountered on the way up.

Skirting the crest of the ridge of snow some little distance from the edge, so as to avoid breaking through the overhanging cornice, we passed on to the western extremity of the summit and commenced the descent. For some time all went smoothly enough. The snow, of which large quantities had fallen in the night, was exceedingly soft, and dissolved rapidly in the fierce noontide heat. We sank in over our knees in some places, while in others we were able to glissade rapidly down some hundreds of yards at a time. In this way we arrived in less than an hour at a small plateau, which had hitherto masked our view of the lower part of the mountain. Here we halted a few minutes to make a fresh survey of our route. The mountain appeared to be a good deal escarped in places, but not more so than we had expected, and we decided to make a detour to the right, in order, if possible, to turn some cliffs and rock-terraces which ran along the face. On the way we crossed a large couloir, or gully, half-filled with snow. We could not see where the snow in this couloir ended, but it evidently extended far beyond the normal snow-line, which was now only a short distance below us. The tempting prospect of a long and easy glissade, thereby resting our weary limbs and saving much valuable time, induced us to ignore the dangers which might be awaiting us at the lower end of the couloir, and to trust ourselves to the snow. It had been better for us had we decided otherwise. What befell I will set forth in as few words as possible.

We had not made many steps in the snow before we noticed that it was abnormally loose and soft, and that, withal, it kept up a continual hissing, while small fragments continually detached themselves from the main mass and rolled down the slope. This circumstance should have been enough in itself to act as a warning to us, had we been in a proper frame of mind to exercise caution. But we were all too much exhilarated by our successful ascent, too anxious to get down with all possible speed, to pay due heed to these premonitory signs of danger. Accordingly, planting ourselves in the centre of the couloir we made ready for a long glissade. Urquhart gave the word, and we all three shot away simultaneously like an arrow from the bow. We went at a rattling pace, and must have covered over a thousand feet in a very few minutes before we came to a stop. After a short breathing-space we were off again, but we had not gone far on our second venture before we saw that below us the couloir dipped suddenly at a steeper angle. The hissing of the snow grew louder and louder as we drew near the edge of the dip, and the weight of our bodies every now and then set large masses in motion. Urquhart, who was in front, saw our danger at a glance, and shouted loudly to warn us.

"Stop! for God's sake, stop! or we shall start an avalanche and all be killed!"

Digging the butts of our ice-axes into the snow, we put on the drag with all the force at our command. But it was too late, and our very efforts to check our headlong career precipitated the catastrophe we were endeavouring to avert. The pace was slackening, and we had well-nigh brought ourselves to a halt, when suddenly the hissing of the snow was momentarily drowned by an ominous, dull, grinding sound, and a large crack or fissure, extending from side to side of the couloir, appeared in the snow a few yards behind us. We were conscious of a curious undefinable sensation, and, to our unutterable horror, we found that the whole mass on which we stood *was moving slowly downwards.*

"Oh, my God! it's all over with us now," cried Urquhart. As he spoke, he made a desperate effort to pull himself up, but in vain, and, abandoning his axe, he threw himself at full length face downwards on the snow.

I can never forget that terrible moment. Overwhelmed with a sense of my utter helplessness, I made no attempt to stop myself, for I felt that I was being borne onwards by an irresistible power to certain destruction. There was a hissing sound as of ten thousand serpents in concert, which latterly, as the avalanche augmented in speed and volume, grew into a dull, confused roar. Twice I was buried and almost smothered by the falling masses; twice I rose to the crest of the snowy billow; and, as I peered through the cloud of powdery snow which, like wind-tossed spray from a cataract, filled the air, the rocky walls of the couloir appeared to be flying past us at lightning speed. Faster and faster we sped, and I performed one or two somersaults which I knew, if repeated much oftener, must inevitably result in my neck being broken. With a rush and a roar the snowy mass swept onwards, mingled with falling blocks of ice and stones. Once again I went under, and again rose to the surface; and then something struck me a tremendous blow on the back of the head, and I remembered no more.

When I came to I was lying on a bank of snow at the foot of an overhanging rock. I tried to collect my scattered senses, and to remember what had happened to me, but it was some time before I could gather any clear conception as to how I had come there. Consciousness returned but slowly. I remember feeling a draught of cold air, which acted as a cordial, and helped to bring my dazed faculties into play. Then I heard Gerald's voice, and I experienced an intense sensation of relief at the thought that my companions were alive likewise, and that I was not left alone upon the mountain.

"Oh, he'll soon be all right. The colour is coming back to his face already. What a knock he must have got! It must have been one of those falling stones that did it."

Then I remembered it all—our glissade down the couloir, the avalanche, and the blow upon my head which had caused me to swoon.

"Probably," replied Urquhart. "It's a wonder his skull wasn't fractured. But look! there are his eyes opening. Hullo, Jim, old man! how do you feel now?"

I replied faintly that I was all right, which was not the strict truth, as I felt exceedingly weak and dizzy, and my head pained me fearfully. I had received a deep cut behind the right temple, and must have lost a great deal of blood. However, by applying lumps of snow and ice to the wound they had managed to arrest the bleeding, and Urquhart bandaged it up very skilfully with a couple of handkerchiefs. A nip of brandy from his flask revived me considerably, and I sat up and looked round. We were at the bottom of a dark, narrow ravine, something like a Colorado cañon, which trended in a westerly direction right up into the heart of the mountain. Huge walls of cliff, many hundred feet in height, towered above us on either side, so sheer that in places they almost met overhead, leaving only a thin streak of blue sky visible between. The lower depths of the chasm were enveloped in the profoundest gloom. From the curious formation of the rocks we conjectured that the fissure must have been the result of some tremendous convulsion of Nature, by which the mountain mass had been rent asunder. Shattered and contorted columns of granite, jagged aiguilles riven and splintered into a thousand fantastic pinnacles, Titanic buttresses carved by frost and sun and rain into the most monstrous shapes, big boulders poised aloft, and seemingly tottering to their fall, were tossed in wild confusion about the sides of the ravine. To my fevered fancy they appeared like mountain fiends scowling at the rash intruders within their craggy solitudes, and their terrific forms, coupled with the intense gloom and the pain I suffered, caused a deep feeling of despondency to weigh upon my spirits. For a while I sat and brooded in silence, till I was roused from my reverie by the sound of Gerald's voice once more.

"Well, Jim, my boy, we've all had a pretty narrow squeak, but you are the only one of us who has suffered much damage. I hope you're feeling better."

"Oh, I shall be right enough in a minute," I said. "But tell me what happened. I remember our being carried down by the avalanche, but after that knock on the head everything was a blank to me."

"Well, I can't say I have a very clear idea of what occurred myself," replied Gerald. "All I know is that I seemed to be tumbling head over heels downhill like lightning, and that what with the snow and the rate at which we were going I was nearly suffocated. I never lost consciousness, but my senses were numbed so that I never felt afraid, and for a time seemed to be, as it were, in a dream. When I got to the bottom there was a tremendous weight of snow on my chest, and I thought that I should be crushed to death, but with a desperate effort I managed to get myself free, and then I began to look about for you and David. David's legs were sticking out of the snow in a most comical way, his body being covered up completely. I soon hauled him out, and as soon as he had got his wind back we started to find you, but not a trace of you could we see. However, after a few minutes' search David caught sight of your head appearing out of the snow right up at the top of the avalanche. We had a tough job to dig you out, you were so firmly embedded ; and I can tell you it was just a stroke of luck your landing head uppermost, or you would not be here talking to us now."

There could be little doubt that I had had a most providential escape, and I felt deeply thankful that my life had been spared. Urquhart himself was rather badly bruised in places, but none of his injuries were serious. As for Gerald, he had escaped almost scot-free. I have often noticed that if an Englishman, an Irishman, and a Scotchman get into a mess together, it is always the Irishman that comes out best. That delightfully happy-go-lucky way they have seems to stand them in better stead than the most deliberate care or prudence.

Looking up at the scene of our adventure, I saw that the lower end of the couloir down which we had been shot was a steep slope of smooth, water-worn rock, terminating in a drop of about ten or twelve feet. Happily, the front part of the avalanche had almost filled this up before we reached it, and the snow had made us a comparatively soft bed to fall upon; otherwise we must all have inevitably been killed. The couloir was one of many which descended into the gorge on either side. They had evidently been formed by the action of the water that flowed down from the snow-fields above, and their several rivulets united in a small stream, which trickled between the boulders that lay heaped one above the other at the bottom of the ravine.

It was a fortunate circumstance that Urquhart's rücksack containing the bulk of our provisions, which he kept firmly strapped on his back, had not been lost in the fall. There was a tolerable supply of food left, and for the present, at any rate, we were not haunted by the fear of starvation. After partaking of some of the contents of the sack, which had not been rendered more savoury by the time they had been kept there, we applied our minds to the problem of making our escape from the gloomy prison in which we were confined. Our first idea was to re-ascend the couloir and make our way over the shoulder of the mountain to the left of the ravine. With this view Urquhart and Gerald, leaving me to await their return, mounted the heap of snow and débris left by the avalanche, and reconnoitred the lower end of the couloir. In a few minutes they came back and reported the ascent to be utterly impracticable, owing to the smoothness and steepness of the rocks. There was nothing for it, therefore, but to descend the ravine and endeavour to find an exit lower down. I was still weak from loss of blood and the shock I had received, and the tramp over the loose blocks of jagged rock, which every now and then became dislodged and rolled thundering down the gorge, was very painful to me. We had to proceed very gingerly, and in the steeper places particularly we all walked abreast so as to avoid rolling stones on each other. It was necessary, moreover, to keep a sharp look-out for those which now and again fell of their own accord from above, and clattered by us in the most alarming fashion. At the first sound of these discharges of Alpine artillery we clung as closely as possible to the sides of the chasm ; but one stone which came leaping down and describing long parabolas in the air, passed with a strange whirring sound most unpleasantly close to my head.

We continued in this way for over an hour until we reached a place where the gorge seemed to come to an end, and far below we could hear the plashing of water on the rocks, which told us that we were on the brink of a cascade. We rolled a stone over the edge, and from the sound as it fell we judged the precipice to be perpendicular and of great height. And now what were we to do? It was folly even to think of trying to climb down the waterfall. The cliffs still rose sheer on either side of the ravine, and the nature of the rock in the lateral gullies which intersected them gave little promise of their affording us a means of escape. However, Urquhart and Gerald started to try two or three of the least formidable-looking ones. Being too faint and exhausted to accompany them, I remained where I was and awaited the result of their investigations. It was with pain and difficulty that I had dragged myself thus far, and I feared that, even supposing that they found a practicable couloir, a climb up a thousand or more feet of precipice would be utterly beyond my powers. In half an hour my companions returned, and a glance at their faces afforded me little hope or encouragement. They had the same tale as before to tell of precipitous rocks, worn glassy smooth by the age-long trickling of the melting of the snows, and affording no hold for hand or foot. And if strong and active climbers like Gerald and Urquhart had failed to scale them, what hope was there for me in my enfeebled state?

Gradually the horrible nature of our position dawned upon us. We were prisoners in this fearful natural dungeon, caught in a trap prepared of our own folly, and face to face with the worst and most lingering of deaths. We might, by dint of strictest economy, eke out our provisions over two or three days at the most, and then—the slow agonies of starvation. It would have been something could we have spent what brief span of life might yet be allotted us in the open air, our brows fanned by the breezes of heaven, and our last moments soothed by the glad sunshine; but the prospect of perishing by inches in this cold and gloomy gulf, where no ray of sunlight penetrated, added a new horror to our situation. We shouted aloud, in the faint hope of being heard by some shepherd wandering upon the mountain-side, but echo alone made jeering answer to our cries. The rocks appeared to be closing in, as it were, over our heads ; and their monstrous forms, like petrified djins of the mountain, yet seemingly instinct with life and expression, grinned down upon us as though in mockery of our misery.

Two days passed, and, our food having been consumed almost to the last crumb of stale and mouldy bread, we were beginning to experience the first sharp pangs of hunger. Poor Gerald, who, besides being much the youngest, was also gifted with the largest appetite, was becoming utterly prostrated. His face grew drawn and pinched, and great black hollows appeared under his eyes. Urquhart, who never for a moment gave way to despair, occupied himself daily in a hopeless search for some means of exit from the gorge, until sheer weakness compelled him to desist. My own case was even more serious than theirs owing to the injuries I had received, and I had already made up my mind, ere the worst came to the worst, to make a desperate effort to descend the cascade. Better a thousand times, thought I, to be dashed to pieces on those cruel rocks in the act of striving to get free, than to surrender without an effort to the slow harbinger of death.

On the morning of the third day, therefore, no sign of relief or possibility of escape appearing, I announced my intention of reaching, alive or dead, the foot of the cliff at the side of the waterfall. Gerald approved of the idea, and prepared to act upon it with me.

"Yes, Jim," he said, "you are right ; and I will go

with you. At least we can all die together. It is practically suicide, I know, but, situated as we are, there is nothing else left for us to do except to sit here and die by inches of starvation. Don't you think so, David?"

But Urquhart strenuously opposed our resolution.

"No," he cried,—"a thousand times no! There may be hope yet, and in any case I for one will not yield to despair, or seek in a self-inflicted death a coward's refuge from misfortune. If no means of succour presents itself, and if the moment arrives when the last ray of hope shall have disappeared, I will yet remain and meet, with such fortitude as I may, the fate it pleases Heaven to send me."

The strong, steadfast, God-fearing character of the man upheld him even in this hour of bitter trial. His deeply religious nature shrank from the deed we proposed, and his high courage and hopefulness impelled him to continue the struggle with the great vanquisher, Death, even to the end.

Gerald and I bowed our heads and held our peace, awed into submission by our friend's quiet air of authority and conviction. Yet in my heart I could not help echoing Hamlet's soliloquy—

> "Oh, that the Almighty had not fixed
> His canon 'gainst self-slaughter!"

It seemed hard, when no possible chance of escape presented itself, to be compelled to prolong our miserable existence in this living tomb, and to endure sufferings which a single step forward might put an end to.

And what those sufferings were can be more readily imagined than described. The bitterness of death itself is less terrible than the anticipation of a doom which the victim knows must be preceded by long, lingering hours of agony. All I hoped for was that the end might come as speedily as possible. At the most, life could endure but a few days longer; and then we should sink into the last long sleep, our miseries would be swallowed up in death, and our bones would whiten in this vast rocky sepulchre.

CHAPTER XXVI.

WITHIN THE CAVE OF THE ELEMENTALS.

IT was the evening of the third day. To add an additional misery to the dreadful gnawing pains which assailed our stomachs, a bitter cold wind sprang up from the east, and whistled and moaned through every nook and cranny of the gorge. In order to gain some shelter from the blast we crawled a few yards up a small gully in the right-hand wall of the ravine, and lay down on a smooth slab of rock. Night came on, and with it the most intense cold. My strength was rapidly giving out, for the wound in my head and the fatigues of our journey had left me ill fitted to endure the cravings of famine. I was seized all over my body with terrible cramps, and suffered the most fearful agony, which lasted some hours. Then, when worn-out nature could endure no more, a feeling of numbness supervened, and I almost lost consciousness. Indeed, I am certain that had it not been for the exertions of my companions, who, forgetting their own miserable plight, kept rubbing me and supplying me with small doses of brandy, I should never have lived to see the morning.

U

The night was dark, for there was no moon, and the starlight was not sufficiently brilliant to illuminate the recesses of the gorge. For hours on end we lay huddled together on the cold slab, wondering when the end would come, and longing for the time when death should release us from our sufferings. It must have been well past midnight, when Urquhart, who was also beginning to suffer from cramp, got up and began to walk to and fro in order to restore his failing circulation. Suddenly he stopped, and, looking up the gully, uttered a startled exclamation.

"What on earth is that? Quick, Gerald! Come here and look at that light."

Gerald with difficulty raised himself and joined Urquhart, and, stimulated by curiosity, with their aid I also managed to struggle to my feet. A strange sight met my eyes. A film of mist had overspread the sky, and it was almost pitch dark in the upper part of our gully, but from the centre of a mass of rock a few yards above us there issued a large irregular globe of light. It was very faint, of a pale blueish hue, and it shone fitfully, sometimes disappearing altogether for a minute or two, like some gigantic glow-worm or mountain will-o'-the-wisp. The effect was peculiarly weird and awesome, and we continued to regard this curious phenomenon, as long as it was visible, with wonder and astonishment.

"What the deuce can it be?" queried Gerald.

"What, indeed?" echoed Urquhart. "Probably some kind of *ignis fatuus*, though that sort of thing is generally seen only in marshy land; and, besides, this light is such a curious colour. Why it should appear in a place like this passes my comprehension;

but we'll go and have a look up there to-morrow. See, there it is again."

Once more for a moment the pale, mysterious light shone forth, then slowly died away, and we saw no more of it that night.

The morning was a great deal warmer, the cold wind having dropped, and we all felt much better, though still very weak. As soon as the circulation was fully restored to our half-frozen bodies we scrambled up the gully to the place whence the light had apparently issued. We had little expectation of solving the mystery of its origin, and were therefore not a little astonished at the discovery we made. About thirty feet above us the gully narrowed to a perpendicular chimney, or crack in the rock, and at the bottom of this chimney was a large circular hole nearly five feet in diameter. On closer examination the hole proved to be the mouth of a tunnel which had been bored horizontally into the mountain. It was evidently the work of human hands, and the sharp edges of the rock, unworn by the action of weather or time, seemed to point to its having been made comparatively recently.

"Well," exclaimed Urquhart, " I should just like to know what this can be. Somebody has been here before us, for I'll lay anything that that hole was not made by natural means. I vote we explore it."

"Yes. Why not?" I remarked in a somewhat moody way. "While we are about it, we may just as well die in a hole underground as down at the bottom of that confounded ravine. It seems more decent, anyhow."

"Come, cheer up, Jim, old man," Urquhart cheerily

responded. "That knock on your head seems to have depressed your spirits. For my part, I don't at all see why we should take such a gloomy view of the situation. That light came out of the hole. Something must have caused the light, and what that something is I mean to find out, if possible."

"Quite right, David," echoed Gerald, who, though but a short time ago he had been overwhelmed by despondency, now readily responded to his friend's more cheerful mood. "Quite right. Don't let's throw up the sponge yet. Who knows but what the tunnel may lead us out somewhere? Anyhow, I agree with you that we may as well go and see. Have you got the lantern?"

Happily, the lantern was still intact in its case, so, without further parleying, Urquhart lit it and led the way into the bore-hole. The floor sloped gently downwards, and by the light of the lantern we had no difficulty in making our way along. The shaft was bored straight into the rock, such windings as there were being scarcely perceptible. Here and there the roof was sufficiently high to enable us to walk upright, but in most places we had to stoop slightly. The walls were reeking with moisture, and an odour like that from some old disused charnel-house pervaded the heavy air. Our footsteps echoed mournfully down the long, natural corridor as we tramped slowly on, and bats innumerable, scared out of their sleeping-places in the rock-crevices, whizzed about and fluttered, like winged imps of darkness, in our faces. The further we advanced the more fearfully close and oppressive grew the atmosphere, so that we were forced to stop every few minutes and gasp for breath, while the perspiration ran from us in streams. Hardly could we drag our worn-out bodies along, to such a state of exhaustion had famine and fatigue reduced us; yet, knowing that in the tunnel lay our last and only hope of escape, we still struggled forward. Sooner would we perish of suffocation here in the heart of the mountain than retrace our steps back to a worse and more lingering death in the ravine. But the stifling heat grew greater and greater, my head throbbed almost to bursting, and my brain reeled, until at last, exhausted nature giving up the struggle, I sank almost fainting to the ground.

"Leave me, for God's sake, leave me," I gasped. "I can go no further. Do you two go on and endeavour to save yourselves, and let me die here."

But the noble fellows would not hear of it, and, each taking hold of one arm, they strove to place me on my feet again.

"Come, pull yourself together, Jim," said Urquhart in a hoarse whisper, for he could speak no louder. "Try and struggle on a little further."

Thus exhorted, I endeavoured to raise myself with their aid; but all the strength seemed to have left my limbs, and, my companions being unequal to supporting my weight, we all sank upon the floor of the shaft together.

How long we lay there I know not; but some minutes must have passed, and I verily believe we should never have risen again but for a lucky accident which I shall explain presently. My strength was ebbing fast; I could scarcely breathe, and it seemed as though death must be very near, when there fell on my ears a low rumbling sound, which seemed to

proceed from the very bowels of the earth. Almost
simultaneously, a puff of air *from the inside* smote
our faces, and, looking up, we saw issuing through an
aperture in front of us, which we took to be the
termination of the tunnel, a light similar to the one
which had attracted our notice during the night.
What lay beyond we could not make out distinctly,
nor could we see what it was that caused this strange
phenomenon. The air, however, revived us considerably, and, struggling to our feet, we made our way
with faltering steps to the place whence the light
came.

Here our eyes encountered a most extraordinary
spectacle. We were standing at the mouth of the
shaft, and on the threshold of a vast cavern, dim,
silent, mysterious, like some ancient heathen fane. As
our gaze grew accustomed to the strange light which
pervaded the cave, we were enabled to take in the
details of what at first appeared to us like some
blurred, indistinct, and confused vision. The sides
of the cavern had been artificially hollowed out at
intervals into a number of chambers, or recesses,
which recalled to mind the chapels along the aisles
of Roman Catholic cathedrals. From the vaulted
roof, some seventy or eighty feet over our heads, huge
pointed stalactites depended. On the floor, and here
and there upon the walls were traced cabalistic circles,
triangles interlaced, pentagrams, zodiacal signs, and
other mystic devices. Facing us at the opposite end
of the cave, was another tunnel or passage, much
wider and loftier than the one in which we stood,
leading out into the open air. The daylight entered
by this opening, but its rays failed to penetrate the

dark recesses of the cavern, which was dimly lighted by lamps of octagonal shape and quaint Oriental design, suspended by long brass chains from the roof. A fire was burning dimly in a small brazier in one of the chambers at the further end of the cave, and by the fitful glow of its embers we could distinguish four or five white-robed figures grouped round about it. Amidst their weird, unearthly surroundings they seemed more like gnomes or spirits of another world than mortal men, and for an instant or two we stood irresolute, not knowing whether to move forward or not. Urquhart, however, took the initiative on this, as on most other occasions, and advanced boldly into the middle of the cave. Hearing footsteps, the Mahatmas—for such they proved to be—turned round, and one of them, a tall, majestic personage clad in a long woollen garment of spotless white, and with a long grey beard sweeping to his waist, whom we rightly supposed to be the chief Adept, rose and came forward.

"Peace be with you," he said in deep, organ-like tones, pronouncing his words slowly and with great distinctness. "Who and whence are ye, and how come ye within the hallowed precincts of the Cave of the Elementals?"

There was no longer any doubt, therefore, that, as we had already guessed, we had found ourselves in the mysterious cavern concerning which we had heard vague rumours at El Medinah, and which had so greatly stimulated our curiosity. We had little dreamed that the mystery was destined to be solved so soon and in so extraordinary a manner.

"We are three travellers from a far-off country,"

replied Urquhart, "and we have resided for some time past in El Medinah. We lost our way upon the mountain and were well-nigh starved to death, when a happy chance conducted us here." And he briefly narrated to the Adept the story of our adventures.

The White Brother (to call him by his proper designation) listened attentively, and then, as soon as Urquhart had finished his tale, he called one of the subordinate Mahatmas and bade him attend to our wants. At his invitation we seated ourselves on couches of carved wood which stood in a corner of the recess, and presently they brought us some flat cakes of bread, and clear cold water in silver goblets.

Oh, the bliss of tasting that first mouthful of food! We could have devoured a dozen loaves apiece, but the Mahatmas, than whom no women could have shown themselves more kind and tender in their ministrations, would only allow us to have a few small morsels to begin with. One of them, noticing the wound in my head, bathed it carefully and applied some healing anodyne, which relieved the pain instantly. As soon as I had eaten sparingly of the bread I lay down on my couch, and, overcome by weariness, soon sank into a deep sleep, which lasted many hours.

It was night when I awoke. Near me were the recumbent forms of my companions and two or three of the Mahatmas, who, I noticed, snored as loudly as any ordinary mortals could have done, the White Brother in particular vying with Gerald in the hideousness of the sounds he gave forth. I had lost all sense of fatigue, and in its place an unaccountable feeling of restlessness came over me, which impelled me to get up from my couch. I did so as quietly as possible, in order to avoid waking my companions, and stole gently forth out of the recess, which was strewn with Oriental rugs covered with a soft thick pile, into the body of the cave. All the Mahatmas (they were seven in number) were asleep except one, a thin, wizened, wrinkled old man, who watched beside a large brazier of peculiar shape and workmanship, which, though it stood not far from the mouth of the shaft by which we had entered the cave, had hitherto escaped my notice. It was three-sided, each side being formed by a grinning demon's face beaten out in high relief, and it stood upon three curved legs terminating in feet moulded into the semblance of a lion's paws. A large circle intersected by two triangles had been traced in the rock floor, and the brazier stood exactly in the centre. In it there burned some substance which shed around a vapour-ous glow of a pale, ghastly, blueish tinge ; and every now and then, as the attendant Mahatma stirred it, the flame leaped up into sudden brilliancy, illuminating with its weird radiance the vast rock walls and roof of the cavern. The mystery of the light we had seen the previous evening was now explained, and I was enabled for the first time to take in the details of our new surroundings. The main entrance to the cave was covered over with a heavy curtain which swayed gently to and fro in the draught, and I now saw that the mouth of our shaft was partially closed by a massive sliding oaken panel let cunningly into the rock. It was the rolling back of this panel which had caused the rumbling sound we had heard in the tunnel, and admitted the draught of air which saved our lives. The shaft itself, as we afterwards learned, had been bored for the purpose of ventilating the cave, and the panel was kept open or shut according to the temperature inside. Happily for us, at the same moment that we were being almost suffocated in the tunnel, the Mahatmas in the cave were also getting uncomfortably hot, and so the panel was slid back to admit the air. The passage was also used by them sometimes in order to draw water from the stream which flowed down the gorge wherein we had been imprisoned.

What, thought I, are all these cabalistic signs and portents; of what nature these mystical rites performed by the Mahatmas? What strange alchemy lies hid in yon brazier with its mysterious fuel burning, like the fire in Vesta's temple, night and day? It was long before I was destined to become acquainted with the solution of these problems, and the extraordinary events which were soon about to be brought to pass effectually banished for awhile from my mind all curiosity on the subject.

The spasmodic flashes passed quickly away, leaving only a faint half-light remaining, and as the flame fell there rose from the brazier a thick vapour that diffused throughout the cave a faint subtle odour, which at first almost overpowered me with its fumes. I felt weak and dizzy, my knees tottered, and I thought that I should swoon. Meanwhile, the form of the aged Mahatma loomed dim and indistinct as he stood, like some mediæval alchemist or necromancer, beside his brazier. Denser and denser grew the fumes. The figure of the Mahatma was now scarcely visible. The mists curled and eddied slowly upwards, seeming to gather form and consistency by degrees, and finally, to my horror and astonishment, wreathing themselves into all manner of horrible shapes—phantoms of fiendish aspect, aerial monsters with leering diabolical faces, and eyes glaring with malignity and hate. Now one would melt away and its place would be immediately taken by some other and more grotesque spectre, which writhed and coiled awhile in the vapour, yet seemingly formed out of it, now growing, now diminishing in size, until it faded away like its predecessor. These were the visualized elementals, or larvæ, of the cave, immaterial and impalpable, yet clearly perceptible by my eyes, which the magnetic currents had in some measure rendered clairvoyant. I stood spell-bound gazing intently upon the apparitions. My heart grew cold with terror and the blood almost froze in my veins. I thought that my imagination was playing me a trick, until the old Adept, who likewise seemed aware of their presence, suddenly turned round and, with a wave of a wand he carried in his hand, caused the whole crew of shadowy ogres to vanish into the vapours whence they sprang.

Presently, as the phantoms did not reappear, my terror subsided, and, the former feeling of faintness and dizziness having entirely passed away, I became conscious of a new sensation of buoyancy and exhilaration such as I had never yet experienced. My vitality seemed higher and stronger than I ever remembered it to have been before. Strange thrills and prickings and tinglings, somewhat similar to those produced by galvanic currents, pervaded my whole organism, and my nerves were strung to their highest pitch. These symptoms were, no doubt, attributable to the odylic currents which permeated the cavern. The atmosphere was charged to an extraordinary degree with magnetism, which seemed to arouse faculties which had hitherto lain dormant within me. My brain was filled almost to bursting with thoughts and ideas utterly different from any that I had ever conceived before. My imagination overleaped the limits of the phenomenal world, and my mental vision seemed to rove over the boundless realms of the ideal. I almost felt inclined to emulate the feats of the Adepts, and to try an excursion into the unseen world in my astral body, and I verily believe that in the intoxication of the moment, if I had not called to mind the ridiculous figure cut by poor old Ali when he made a similar attempt, I should have endeavoured to absorb myself into the Infinite. Fortunately, however, the remembrance of what happened on that occasion had a distinctly sobering effect upon me, and no doubt saved me from making an idiot of myself. Anyhow, I gave up the idea and crept quietly back to bed, and once more slept soundly until long after dawn.

I got up feeling as fit and as fresh as possible, and, withal, most uncommonly hungry. My head had ceased entirely to pain me, and the wound appeared to be healing rapidly, doubtless owing to the magical properties of the balm which the Mahatma had applied to it. My companions seemed no less re-freshed by their long sleep, but Urquhart's face wore the grave, thoughtful expression which I had seen it assume on other occasions when anything had occurred to perplex or trouble him. He told me that he had had a repetition, in a slightly altered form, of the strange dream which had disturbed his slumbers on the night of our bivouac on the side of Mount Atlas.

"What this vision may portend," said he, "I know not. Yet I have in my inmost heart the same sure foreboding as before that it is a warning of some impending catastrophe or event that immediately concerns Leila and myself. What do you make of it, Jim?"

For reply, I could only disclaim all power or faculty of expounding visions, whether other people's or my own, and Gerald and I both did our best to reason away these gloomy notions from Urquhart's mind. As for Gerald, he simply laughed at the whole thing, and I think Urquhart was a little hurt by his levity about what he himself considered a very serious matter. In any case, nothing could shake his conviction that the vision had been sent to him for some purpose, and that it was the presage of some approaching disaster. At the time I am now writing about I was not a believer myself in dreams or dream-stories, but subsequent occurrences, with which the reader will shortly become acquainted, have gone far to modify my scepticism.

Nothing of note happened that day. The atmospheric conditions prevailing in the cave operated with no less force upon my companions than myself. They both experienced the same tingling, pricking sensations, and Gerald told me that he felt as though a galvanic battery was being continually turned upon him. Remembering the fate, as related by Ali, of the shepherd who had taken refuge in the cave, and had had the soul drawn out of his body, we were a little nervous lest we might be overtaken in sleep by a similar catastrophe.

"I vote we get out of this beastly cave as soon as we can," Gerald remarked to me. "There is something uncanny about it all, and I don't relish the society of these Adept magicians with their mystical rites, and that blue light from the brazier gives me the jumps. It may be all very well for an occult sort of chap like David, but it is no place for plain, commonplace folk such as you and I."

However, when we announced our intention of taking an airing outside, the Adepts interposed and prevented us leaving the cave. The secret of its situation, said they, could not be allowed to transpire, and for the present we must consider ourselves as prisoners within its walls. When the time for our departure arrived we should be blindfolded and led down to a place whence we could easily find the road to El Medinah. I must admit that our captivity was not of a particularly irksome nature, as the Mahatmas spared no pains to make us comfortable, and all our wants were strictly attended to.

The day passed and the shades of evening were beginning to fall. Gerald and I were standing together, thinking of nothing particular, when suddenly a shadow darkened the entrance to the cavern. Looking up, we saw a ghost-like figure in long, white, flowing raiment, crossing the threshold. It was impossible in the dim twilight to make out the features, but something in the gait and bearing of the newcomer, whom at first I took to be one of the Mahatmas, attracted my attention, and impelled me to go and see who it was.

Judge of my unutterable astonishment when I found myself face to face with Leila.

CHAPTER XXVII.

THE RE-UNION OF THE SYMPNEUMATA.

I SPOKE to her, but she heeded not my greeting, and
in fact seemed quite unconscious of my presence.
Her eyes were fixed and glassy, and she stared
straight in front of her like one who gazes and sees
nothing. Her face was very pale, and her features
were set rigidly and void of expression, and the dark,
violet-coloured hollows beneath her eyes seemed to
tell of great fatigue or mental anxiety. I thought
that her figure had lost somewhat of its old grace and
suppleness as she walked, or rather glided mechanically forward, towards a small group, composed of
Urquhart and Gerald and three of the Brethren.
Her movements and appearance were those of a
person entranced, and being drawn onwards by some
invisible power, or of one who, being hypnotized,
obeys unconsciously the mesmeric summons.

I shall endeavour to set forth the extraordinary
occurrences of this evening as shortly and as distinctly
as possible. Yet, when I try to recall all that
happened, my memory seems faint and blurred, like
that of a person who has received some severe shock

to his nervous system, and tries in vain to gather a definite impression of the cause. Even now, as I think over it, the whole thing seems like a dream, and if I had not the most absolute proof of the reality of what I saw I should certainly have supposed myself to be the victim of some strange hallucination.

On reaching the group in which Urquhart stood, Leila, uttering not a word, nor looking to right hand or left, gilded straight up to him, and, placing her hands upon his shoulders, gazed steadfastly into his face. She was evidently in one of those ecstatic trance-conditions in which she was often absorbed, and during which the secrets of the unseen world were revealed to her. I knew that to her physical senses her occult lover was all the time invisible, and that if she saw him at all it was with the eye of the clairvoyant. Yet to my fancy her love seemed to shine through the mesmeric veil, and, all unconscious as she was, there was something infinitely pathetic in her mute, wistful gaze, like that of some dumb animal that would speak could it but find the power of utterance, upon the man on whom her heart was fixed, and whose being was destined to form part of her own.

Gently removing her arms from his shoulders, Urquhart led her to the largest of the three couches which stood in the recess, and bade her lie down and rest. She obeyed automatically, and as she reclined upon the soft cushions Urquhart arranged the pillows beneath her head, and then stole gently away. I noticed that he was deadly pale, and a look almost of anguish came over his face.

"Be silent, all of you," murmured the White

Brother; "the maid Leila is entranced in the ecstatic
sleep which ye of the West call mesmeric. Albeit, ye
are ignorant of the true nature thereof. Let her be
now; it were well she rest awhile undisturbed. In
due time I will exercise my occult art upon her, and
recall the wandering spirit to its home. Verily we
are in the presence of a great mystery, whereof ye
shall learn more hereafter. What is to be, shall be,
and the issue, whatsoever befall, may not be averted."

Night set in, and the pendant lamps cast their soft
light upon Leila's recumbent form, revealing the
exquisitely chiselled features, now pale and still as in
death, and, through the clinging folds of her white
drapery, the delicately curving contours of her slender
figure. Her eyes remained open, and she lay perfectly
still, and, but for her heavy breathing, like one dead.
Meanwhile the flame leaped high in the mystic
brazier, and the spasmodic jets of blue fire shed their
ghastly glow around. The atmosphere literally
coruscated with the magnetic emanations, causing
our hearts to leap, our veins to swell, and our pulses
to beat high. I do not know how far it was owing to
the tension of our nerves resulting from the strange
things we had seen and experienced, but the odic
currents seemed to be playing upon us with tenfold
force, and the strange sensations of lightness and
buoyancy became more intense than ever.

For a long time—I should think it must have been
fully two hours—we sat without speaking a word.
Then the White Brother rose, and, going over to the
couch where Leila lay, proceeded to awaken her.
What he did I do not know, as his back was turned
to us, but I did not see him make any of the passes

which ordinary mesmerists make use of in order to bring their subjects out of the trance-state. In any case, the process, whatever it may have been, was effective and almost instantaneous in its result. Her eyelids moved, a faint flush of pink overspread her cheeks, a strong tremor convulsed her frame, and she awoke. For a moment she appeared dazed, and knit her brows, and covered her eyes with her hands, as though striving to collect her thoughts.

Urquhart had moved forward in the interval, and when she looked up he was standing over her. With a sudden cry, she raised herself to a sitting posture upon the couch, and, taking his hand in hers, she bent a glance full of unutterable love and yearning upon him.

"Oh, heart of my heart, and soul of my soul," she cried, "what is it brings thee hither? Is blind chance the cause, or is the destiny which hath linked our souls together now hastening to its accomplishment? Behold, six nights ago I saw thee in a vision, and thy spirit summoned mine to meet thee, and for two days I wandered forth upon the mountain seeking thee, but could not find thee. And yester even again I saw the same vision, and I knew that thou wert here, and lo! I have come to thee."

Her voice, which was pitched high when she began to speak, gradually died away in exquisitely musical cadence. A cloud of doubt and perplexity settled on her brow, and she once more buried her face in her hands. When she removed them we saw that she was deadly pale, though her features wore no expression of suffering. Her eyes had regained their rapt, ecstatic look, and, as with outstretched arms she gazed intently upwards, they seemed to pierce the material veil which limits our mortal vision, and to penetrate the arcana of the spiritual world. Never had she seemed so radiantly, so indescribably lovely as now. There was something in her face not of this earth, which recalled to mind those pictures of mediæval female saints and martyrs that one sees in the Italian galleries. When she spoke again it was in a faint, far-away tone, so low that we could scarcely hear what she said.

" Oh, David, David, hold me ; I feel faint and cold. Surely, some great change is come upon me. Slowly it steals over my being, and even now I seem to be on the threshold of another world, there to await the coming of my love. Night wraps me in her sable pinions, and soon I shall fall into the last, long sleep. Be it so. I am ready. Fare thee well."

It was evident that, overcome probably by the odylic currents of the cave, she was once more sinking into the mesmeric trance. For a moment her body grew rigid ; her pupils dilated, and there was a convulsive twitching of the eyelids. Then a violent trembling overcame her, her frame relaxed, and she sank back upon the pillows. As she did so, her jet-black hair escaped its encircling fillet, and, half veiling the shapely neck and throat, fell in a raven cloud about her shoulders, intensifying by contrast the marble pallor of her countenance.

Urquhart, seeing her on the point of swooning, was about to support her with his arms, when suddenly a great change came over him, and he was smitten by the same mysterious force which had overcome Leila. His body swayed and reeled. His face became ashen, and a spasm of agony, short but sharp, passed over it like a cloud, and he clutched convulsively the head of the couch to save himself from falling. For a moment he seemed to be resisting the spell with the full energy of his potent will, but all in vain. The mesmeric, or magnetic, influence, whatever its precise nature may have been, was being exerted upon him with a force which no human organism unfortified by a knowledge of the higher occult sciences could withstand. His knees gave way beneath him, his grip relaxed, and he fell forward prone on the edge of the couch.

Gerald, seeing his friend's plight, would have sprung forward to his assistance had not the Mahatmas restrained him. And indeed it was apparent that Urquhart was beyond all ordinary human aid. At a sign from the White Brother one of the Adepts placed his now almost inanimate body on the couch face upwards beside that of Leila.

And now a strange and awe-inspiring spectacle presented itself to our gaze. Side by side the lovers lay, perfectly motionless save for the heavy breathing with which their bosoms rose and fell in unison. Presently their respiration grew quicker and more difficult, and at length it almost ceased. In an agony of fear I cried out that they were dying, and, forgetting the injunctions of the Adepts, I was about to rush to their aid. But when I tried to move I found that some invisible force held my limbs in thrall, and, powerless to stir hand or foot, I stood rooted spellbound to the spot. For a few minutes I remained thus, struggling vainly with the irresistible force, and gazing intently at the sleepers, when lo! the breath

of their mouths seemed to gather shape and substance,
and hovered in mid-air above their recumbent bodies.
Was I dreaming? Did my senses deceive me, or
were those two shadowy figures, faint simulacra of
the human form, that I saw emanating from the
slumbering pair? I rubbed my eyes and looked
again. There could be no doubt about it. Two
mystic shapes, vague, shadowy, undefinable in outline,
yet plain to my vision, and clearly recognizable as
the ethereal duplicates of Urquhart's and Leila's
earthly bodies.

Once more the brazier shed its gruesome glow on
rocky wall and floor, on vaulted roof and hanging
stalactite, and illumined with its weird effulgence the
astral figures, making apparent their identity with
their material prototypes. Yet were they transfigured,
withal, into an aspect of supernatural beauty, which
was awesome to behold. Again the glow almost died
away, and for a brief space the two spirits lingered
lovingly over the sleepers, as though loth finally to
quit their earthly tenements; then, parting from
them, they slowly floated obliquely upwards towards
the further end of the cave. As they neared the
gloom which enshrouded the lofty roof the mystic
figures were wafted closer together, till to our straining eyes they almost seemed to blend, and at last,
marvellous to relate, they melted one into another.
Then did it seem as though, in Tennyson's words—

> " The mortal limits of the Self were loosed
> And passed into the Nameless, as a cloud
> Melts into heaven.

For fainter and fainter grew the mingled shapes, until
finally they faded away in the encircling darkness;

and thus floating through the gates of the visible world, these twin spirits of the astral ether, radiantly beautiful, their union now made complete, passed out into the infinite ocean of the Unseen.

*   *   *   *   *

For a moment I stood dazed and bewildered. I felt as though I had been in a swoon, or had received some severe mental shock. My faculties were stunned ; my mind was a blank, and I strove in vain to shape clearly in my mind what had occurred. A thousand wild, confused ideas were conjured up in my fevered brain. My temples throbbed almost to bursting, and I felt that unless something occurred to relieve the strain I must go mad. One burning desire, and one only, possessed me—namely, to get out of the cave as soon as possible, and I was utterly oblivious of what was going on around me. I was roused from my stupor by a sound of suppressed sobbing behind me. It was Gerald, who, burying his face in his hands, had burst into an uncontrollable fit of weeping. He had loved his friend with more than a brother's love, and the parting, which he feared was for ever, was more than he could bear.

Seeing his distress, the White Brother approached him, and, laying his hand gently upon his shoulder, spoke as follows :—

" Be comforted, my brother. Our friends are not dead ; they do but sleep for awhile. When their spirits shall have accomplished their appointed course in the astral spheres they will return to finish their earthly probation, and reinhabit their tenements of clay. The re-union of the twin souls whereof ye have been witnesses is but temporary, and needs must they be again dissevered in order to complete, in this ephemeral world of causes, what span of life may yet be allotted them. Behold, their hour is not yet come, nay, shall not come until Destiny, with whom Death himself cannot war, shall have marched with slow foot to its end. Till then the bodies cannot perish, but will await here the return of their quickening spirits."

So saying, he led Gerald gently by the arm, and bade him lie down upon his couch and repose awhile. Gerald obeyed like a child, and, indeed, it was apparent that, as he told me afterwards, he was stupefied like myself, and hardly knew what he was doing. I, too, prepared to seek the rest which I felt I sorely needed, but before doing so I turned to cast one last glance upon the entranced forms of Urquhart and Leila. There they lay, pale and still as the dead, yet was there nothing else death-like in their appearance. The bodies were not stiff, and Leila's in particular seemed to retain all its former pliancy and willowy grace. The look of suffering had vanished completely from Urquhart's face, and his rugged features, now calm and peaceful in the mesmeric slumber, appeared almost beautiful in their placid serenity. Leila's lips were parted, and the faint, sweet semblance of a smile yet lingered on their tender curves. The great lustrous eyes were now veiled beneath the drooping, satin lids. Her snow-white arms were half bare and crossed upon her bosom, and the dark masses of hair lay heaped in glossy waves about the pillow, forming a splendid setting for the pale, almost unearthly, beauty of her

upturned countenance.   I thought of the lines in
Shelley's fantasy — [1]

> "And there the bodies lay, age after age,
>   Mute, breathing, warm, and undecaying,
> Like one asleep in a green hermitage,
>   With gentle sleep about its eyelids playing,
> And living in its dreams beyond the rage
>   Of death or life."

And as I gazed upon them I tried to form in my
mind some coherent notion of what had happened,
and to find, if possible, some explanation of the marvellous phenomena we had witnessed. The severance
of soul from body I imagined to be due, in some
mysterious way, to the magnetic action of the currents
of odylic fluid. I remembered, too, that Ali's chela
friend had told him how the force of their emanations
would be augmented tenfold in the case of persons
united, like Urquhart and Leila, by strong ties of
soul-affinity. But the final melting of the two astral
shapes one into the other—what could have been the
true cause or import thereof? Was this the blending
of spirit with spirit—the consummation of the sympneumatic wedlock, as explained to us by the Brethren
of Mount Atlas, and foreshadowed in Urquhart's
dream? Had we beheld with our very eyes the
re-union of the complementary essences, the twin Egos
disjoined temporarily in earth-life, into the biune
man-woman of the earliest days of the human race?
It seemed useless to conjecture, and my wearied brain
was unequal to the task of following out the train of
thought which these mysterious occurrences suggested.
Accordingly, worn out by the fatigues and the

---

[1] "The Witch of Atlas."

harrowing experiences of the last few days, I stretched myself on my couch and sought to forget them in slumber.

It was early morning, and the soft grey light of dawn was creeping into the cave, when I was aroused by one of the Brethren, who bade Gerald and myself rise and come forth with him. I got up mechanically, my eyes filled with sleep, and hardly knowing what I was doing. Gerald was already up, and it was with intense relief that we learned that we were to be allowed to leave the cave and return to El Medinah. At the mouth of the cavern bandages were placed over our eyes, and we were led forth blindfold far down the mountain-side. After we had continued in this way for some hours we turned suddenly to the left, and then, our bandages being removed, we found ourselves on a path leading down a narrow glen, which, the Mahatma told us, would conduct us to the valley of the Wad Kebeer. Here we rested awhile; then, bidding our guide farewell, we proceeded on our way, and arrived late in the evening at El Medinah.

THE END.

PRINTED BY WILLIAM CLOWES AND SONS, LIMITED, LONDON AND BECCLES.

A CATALOGUE OF WORKS

IN

GENERAL LITERATURE

PUBLISHED BY

MESSRS. LONGMANS, GREEN, & CO.,

39 PATERNOSTER ROW, LONDON, E.C.

MESSRS. LONGMANS, GREEN, & CO.

Issue the undermentioned Lists of their Publications, which may be had post free on application :—

1. MONTHLY LIST OF NEW WORKS AND NEW EDITIONS.

2. QUARTERLY LIST OF ANNOUNCEMENTS AND NEW WORKS.

3. NOTES ON BOOKS; BEING AN ANALYSIS OF THE WORKS PUBLISHED DURING EACH QUARTER.

4. CATALOGUE OF SCIENTIFIC WORKS.

5. CATALOGUE OF MEDICAL AND SURGICAL WORKS.

6. CATALOGUE OF SCHOOL BOOKS AND EDUCATIONAL WORKS.

7. CATALOGUE OF BOOKS FOR ELEMENTARY SCHOOLS AND PUPIL TEACHERS.

8. CATALOGUE OF THEOLOGICAL WORKS BY DIVINES AND MEMBERS OF THE CHURCH OF ENGLAND.

9. CATALOGUE OF WORKS IN GENERAL LITERATURE.

ABBEY (Rev. C. J.) and OVERTON (Rev. J. H.).—THE ENGLISH CHURCH IN THE EIGHTEENTH CENTURY. Cr. 8vo. 7s. 6d.

ABBOTT (Evelyn).—A HISTORY OF GREECE. In Two Parts.

Part I.—From the Earliest Times to the Ionian Revolt. Cr. 8vo. 10s. 6d.
Part II. Vol. I.—500-445 B.C. [*In the Press.*] Vol. II.—[*In Preparation.*]

——— HELLENICA. A Collection of Essays on Greek Poetry, Philosophy, History, and Religion. Edited by EVELYN ABBOTT. 8vo. 16s.

ACLAND (A. H. Dyke) and RANSOME (Cyril).—A HANDBOOK IN OUTLINE OF THE POLITICAL HISTORY OF ENGLAND TO 1890. Chronologically Arranged. Crown 8vo. 6s.

ACTON (Eliza).—MODERN COOKERY. With 150 Woodcuts. Fcp. 8vo. 4s. 6d.

A. K. H. B.—THE ESSAYS AND CONTRIBUTIONS OF. Crown 8vo. 3*s.* 6*d.* each.

Autumn Holidays of a Country Parson.

Changed Aspects of Unchanged Truths.

Commonplace Philosopher.

Counsel and Comfort from a City Pulpit.

Critical Essays of a Country Parson.

East Coast Days and Memories.

Graver Thoughts of a Country Parson. Three Series.

Landscapes, Churches, and Moralities.

Leisure Hours in Town.

Lessons of Middle Age.

Our Little Life. Two Series.

Our Homely Comedy and Tragedy.

Present Day Thoughts.

Recreations of a Country Parson. Three Series.

Seaside Musings.

Sunday Afternoons in the Parish Church of a Scottish University City.

———— 'To Meet the Day' through the Christian Year; being a Text of Scripture, with an Original Meditation and a Short Selection in Verse for Every Day. Crown 8vo. 4*s.* 6*d.*

AMERICAN WHIST, Illustrated: containing the Laws and Principles of the Game, the Analysis of the New Play. By G. W. P. Fcp. 8vo. 6*s.* 6*d.*

AMOS (Sheldon).—A PRIMER OF THE ENGLISH CONSTITUTION AND GOVERNMENT. Crown 8vo. 6*s.*

ANNUAL REGISTER (The). A Review of Public Events at Home and Abroad, for the year 1890. 8vo. 18*s.*

₊ Volumes of the 'Annual Register' for the years 1863-1889 can still be had.

ANSTEY (F.).—THE BLACK POODLE, and other Stories. Crown 8vo. 2*s.* boards. ; 2*s.* 6*d.* cloth.

———— VOCES POPULI. Reprinted from *Punch*. First Series, with 20 Illustrations by J. BERNARD PARTRIDGE. Fcp. 4to. 5*s.*

ARISTOTLE—The Works of.

———— THE POLITICS, G. Bekker's Greek Text of Books I. III. IV. (VII.), with an English Translation by W. E. BOLLAND, and short Introductory Essays by ANDREW LANG. Crown 8vo. 7*s.* 6*d.*

———— THE POLITICS, Introductory Essays. By ANDREW LANG. (From Bolland and Lang's ' Politics '.) Crown 8vo. 2*s.* 6*d.*

———— THE ETHICS, Greek Text, illustrated with Essays and Notes. By Sir ALEXANDER GRANT, Bart. 2 vols. 8vo. 32*s.*

———— THE NICOMACHEAN ETHICS, newly translated into English. By ROBERT WILLIAMS. Crown 8vo. 7*s.* 6*d.*

ARMSTRONG (G. F. Savage-).—POEMS: Lyrical and Dramatic. Fcp. 8vo. 6*s.*

BY THE SAME AUTHOR. Fcp. 8vo.

King Saul. 5*s.*

King David. 5*s.*

King Solomon. 6*s.*

Ugone; a Tragedy. 6*s.*

A Garland from Greece. Poems. 9*s.*

Stories of Wicklow. Poems. 9*s.*

Mephistopheles in Broadcloth; a Satire. 4*s.*

The Life and Letters of Edmond J. Armstrong. 7*s.* 6*d.*

ARMSTRONG (E. J.).—POETICAL WORKS. Fcp. 8vo. 5*s.*

———— ESSAYS AND SKETCHES. Fcp. 8vo. 5*s.*

ARNOLD (Sir Edwin).—THE LIGHT OF THE WORLD, or the Great Consummation. A Poem. Crown 8vo. 7s. 6d. *net*.

ARNOLD (Dr. T.). INTRODUCTORY LECTURES ON MODERN HISTORY. 8vo. 7s. 6d.

———— SERMONS PREACHED MOSTLY IN THE CHAPEL OF RUGBY SCHOOL. 6 vols. crown 8vo. 30s., or separately, 5s. each.

———— MISCELLANEOUS WORKS. 8vo. 7s. 6d.

ASHLEY (J. W.).—ENGLISH ECONOMIC HISTORY AND THEORY. Part I.—The Middle Ages. Crown 8vo. 5s.

ATELIER (The) du Lys; or, An Art Student in the Reign of Terror. By the Author of 'Mademoiselle Mori'. Crown 8vo. 2s. 6d.

BY THE SAME AUTHOR. Crown 2s. 6d. each.

MADEMOISELLE MORI.	A CHILD OF THE REVOLU-
THAT CHILD.	TION.
UNDER A CLOUD.	HESTER'S VENTURE.
THE FIDDLER OF LUGAU.	IN THE OLDEN TIME.

BACON.—COMPLETE WORKS. Edited by R. L. ELLIS, J. SPEDDING, and D. D. HEATH. 7 vols. 8vo. £3 13s. 6d.

———— LETTERS AND LIFE, INCLUDING ALL HIS OCCASIONAL WORKS. Edited by J. SPEDDING. 7 vols. 8vo. £4 4s.

———— THE ESSAYS; with Annotations. By Archbishop WHATELY. 8vo. 10s. 6d.

———— THE ESSAYS; with Introduction, Notes, and Index. By E. A. ABBOTT. 2 vols. Fcp. 8vo. 6s. Text and Index only. Fcp. 8vo. 2s. 6d.

BADMINTON LIBRARY (The), edited by the DUKE OF BEAUFORT, assisted by ALFRED E. T. WATSON.

HUNTING. By the DUKE OF BEAUFORT, and MOWBRAY MORRIS. With 53 Illustrations. Crown 8vo. 10s. 6d.

FISHING. By H. CHOLMONDELEY-PENNELL.
    Vol. I. Salmon, Trout, and Grayling. 158 Illustrations. Crown 8vo. 10s. 6d.
    Vol. II. Pike and other Coarse Fish. 132 Illustrations. Crown 8vo. 10s. 6d.

RACING AND STEEPLECHASING. By the EARL OF SUFFOLK AND BERKSHIRE, W. G. CRAVEN, &c. 56 Illustrations. Crown 8vo. 10s. 6d.

SHOOTING. By LORD WALSINGHAM, and Sir RALPH PAYNE-GALLWEY, Bart.
    Vol. I. Field and Covert. With 105 Illustrations. Crown 8vo. 10s. 6d.
    Vol. II. Moor and Marsh. With 65 Illustrations. Crown 8vo. 10s. 6d.

CYCLING. By VISCOUNT BURY (Earl of Albemarle) and G. LACY HILLIER. With 89 Illustrations. Crown 8vo. 10s. 6d.

ATHLETICS AND FOOTBALL. By MONTAGUE SHEARMAN. With 41 Illustrations. Crown 8vo. 10s. 6d.

BOATING. By W. B. WOODGATE. With 49 Illustrations. Crown 8vo. 10s. 6d.

CRICKET. By A. G. STEEL and the Hon. R. H. LYTTELTON. With 63 Illustrations. Crown 8vo. 10s. 6d.

DRIVING. By the DUKE OF BEAUFORT. With 65 Illustrations. Crown 8vo. 10s. 6d.

BADMINTON LIBRARY (The)—*(continued)*.

FENCING, BOXING, AND WRESTLING. By WALTER H. POLLOCK, F. C. GROVE, C. PREVOST, E. B. MICHELL, and WALTER ARMSTRONG. With 42 Illustrations. Crown 8vo. 10s. 6d.

GOLF. By HORACE HUTCHINSON, the Rt. Hon. A. J. BALFOUR, M.P., ANDREW LANG, Sir W. G. SIMPSON, Bart., &c. With 88 Illustrations. Crown 8vo. 10s. 6d.

TENNIS, LAWN TENNIS, RACKETS, AND FIVES. By J. M. and C. G. HEATHCOTE, E. O. PLEYDELL-BOUVERIE, and A. C. AINGER. With 79 Illustrations. Crown 8vo. 10s. 6d.

RIDING AND POLO. By Captain ROBERT WEIR, Riding-Master, R.H.G., J. MORAY BROWN, &c. With 59 Illustrations. Cr. 8vo.

BAGEHOT (Walter).—BIOGRAPHICAL STUDIES. 8vo. 12s.

———— ECONOMIC STUDIES. 8vo. 10s. 6d.

———— LITERARY STUDIES. 2 vols. 8vo. 28s.

———— THE POSTULATES OF ENGLISH POLITICAL ECONOMY. Crown 8vo. 2s. 6d.

———— A PRACTICAL PLAN FOR ASSIMILATING THE ENGLISH AND AMERICAN MONEY AS A STEP TOWARDS A UNIVERSAL MONEY. Crown 8vo. 2s. 6d.

BAGWELL (Richard).—IRELAND UNDER THE TUDORS. (3 vols.) Vols. I. and II. From the first invasion of the Northmen to the year 1578. 8vo. 32s. Vol. III. 1578-1603. 8vo. 18s.

BAIN (Alex.).—MENTAL AND MORAL SCIENCE. Crown 8vo. 10s. 6d.

———— SENSES AND THE INTELLECT. 8vo. 15s.

———— EMOTIONS AND THE WILL. 8vo. 15s.

———— LOGIC, DEDUCTIVE AND INDUCTIVE. Part I. *Deduction*, 4s. Part II., *Induction*, 6s. 6d.

———— PRACTICAL ESSAYS. Crown 8vo. 2s.

BAKER (James).—BY THE WESTERN SEA: a Novel. Cr. 8vo. 3s. 6d.

BAKER.—EIGHT YEARS IN CEYLON. With 6 Illustrations. Crown 8vo. 3s. 6d.

———— THE RIFLE AND THE HOUND IN CEYLON. With 6 Illustrations. Crown 8vo. 3s. 6d.

BALL (The Rt. Hon. T. J.).—THE REFORMED CHURCH OF IRELAND (1537-1889). 8vo. 7s. 6d.

———— HISTORICAL REVIEW OF THE LEGISLATIVE SYSTEMS OPERATIVE IN IRELAND (1172-1800). 8vo. 6s.

BEACONSFIELD (The Earl of).—NOVELS AND TALES. The Hughenden Edition. With 2 Portraits and 11 Vignettes. 11 vols. Crown 8vo. 42s.

Endymion.	**Venetia.**	**Alroy, Ixion, &c.**
Lothair.	**Henrietta Temple.**	**The Young Duke, &c.**
Coningsby.	**Contarini Fleming, &c.**	**Vivian Grey.**
Tancred. Sybil.		

NOVELS AND TALES. Cheap Edition. 11 vols. Crown 8vo. 1s. each, boards; 1s. 6d. each, cloth.

BECKER (Professor).—GALLUS; or, Roman Scenes in the Time of Augustus.　Post 8vo. 7*s.* 6*d.*

———— CHARICLES; or, Illustrations of the Private Life of the Ancient Greeks.　Post 8vo. 7*s.* 6*d.*

BELL (Mrs. Hugh).—WILL O' THE WISP: a Story.　Crown 8vo. 3*s.* 6*d.*

———— CHAMBER COMEDIES.　Crown 8vo. 6*s.*

BLAKE (J.).—TABLES FOR THE CONVERSION OF 5 PER CENT. INTEREST FROM $\frac{1}{16}$ TO 7 PER CENT.　8vo. 12*s.* 6*d.*

BOOK (THE) OF WEDDING DAYS.　Arranged on the Plan of a Birthday Book.　With 96 Illustrated Borders, Frontispiece, and Title-page by Walter Crane; and Quotations for each Day.　Compiled and Arranged by K. E. J. REID, MAY ROSS, and MABEL BAMFIELD.　4to. 21*s.*

BRASSEY (Lady).—A VOYAGE IN THE 'SUNBEAM,' OUR HOME ON THE OCEAN FOR ELEVEN MONTHS.

Library Edition.　With 8 Maps and Charts, and 118 Illustrations, 8vo. 21*s.*
Cabinet Edition.　With Map and 66 Illustrations, Crown 8vo. 7*s.* 6*d.*
Cheap Edition.　With 66 Illustrations, Crown 8vo. 3*s.* 6*d.*
School Edition.　With 37 Illustrations, Fcp. 2*s.* cloth, or 3*s.* white parchment.
Popular Edition.　With 60 Illustrations, 4to. 6*d.* sewed, 1*s.* cloth.

———— SUNSHINE AND STORM IN THE EAST.

Library Edition.　With 2 Maps and 114 Illustrations, 8vo. 21*s.*
Cabinet Edition.　With 2 Maps and 114 Illustrations, Crown 8vo. 7*s.* 6*d.*
Popular Edition.　With 103 Illustrations, 4to. 6*d.* sewed, 1*s.* cloth.

———— IN THE TRADES, THE TROPICS, AND THE 'ROARING FORTIES'.

Cabinet Edition.　With Map and 220 Illustrations, Crown 8vo. 7*s.* 6*d.*
Popular Edition.　With 183 Illustrations, 4to. 6*d.* sewed, 1*s.* cloth.

———— THE LAST VOYAGE TO INDIA AND AUSTRALIA IN THE 'SUNBEAM'.　With Charts and Maps, and 40 Illustrations in Monotone (20 full-page), and nearly 200 Illustrations in the Text.　8vo. 21*s.*

———— THREE VOYAGES IN THE 'SUNBEAM'.　Popular Edition.　With 346 Illustrations, 4to. 2*s.* 6*d.*

BRAY (Charles).—THE PHILOSOPHY OF NECESSITY; or, Law in Mind as in Matter.　Crown 8vo. 5*s.*

BRIGHT (Rev. J. Franck).—A HISTORY OF ENGLAND.　4 vols. Cr. 8vo.
Period I.—Mediæval Monarchy: The Departure of the Romans to Richard III. From A.D. 449 to 1485.　4*s.* 6*d.*
Period II.—Personal Monarchy: Henry VII. to James II.　From 1485 to 1688.　5*s.*
Period III.—Constitutional Monarchy: William and Mary to William IV. From 1689 to 1837.　7*s.* 6*d.*
Period IV.—The Growth of Democracy: Victoria.　From 1837 to 1880.　6*s.*

BRYDEN (H. A.).—KLOOF AND KARROO: Sport, Legend, and Natural History in Cape Colony.　With 17 Illustrations.　8vo. 10*s.* 6*d.*

BUCKLE (Henry Thomas).—HISTORY OF CIVILISATION IN ENGLAND AND FRANCE, SPAIN AND SCOTLAND.　3 vols. Cr. 8vo. 24*s.*

BULL (Thomas).—HINTS TO MOTHERS ON THE MANAGEMENT OF THEIR HEALTH during the Period of Pregnancy. Fcp. 8vo. 1s. 6d.

———— THE MATERNAL MANAGEMENT OF CHILDREN IN HEALTH AND DISEASE. Fcp. 8vo. 1s. 6d.

BUTLER (Samuel).—EREWHON. Crown 8vo. 5s.

———— THE FAIR HAVEN. A Work in Defence of the Miraculous Element in our Lord's Ministry. Crown 8vo. 7s. 6d.

———— LIFE AND HABIT. An Essay after a Completer View of Evolution. Cr. 8vo. 7s. 6d.

———— EVOLUTION, OLD AND NEW. Crown 8vo. 10s. 6d.

———— UNCONSCIOUS MEMORY. Crown 8vo. 7s. 6d.

———— ALPS AND SANCTUARIES OF PIEDMONT AND THE CANTON TICINO. Illustrated. Pott 4to. 10s. 6d.

———— SELECTIONS FROM WORKS. Crown 8vo. 7s. 6d.

———— LUCK, OR CUNNING, AS THE MAIN MEANS OF ORGANIC MODIFICATION? Crown 8vo. 7s. 6d.

———— EX VOTO. An Account of the Sacro Monte or New Jerusalem at Varallo-Sesia. Crown 8vo. 10s. 6d.

———— HOLBEIN'S 'LA DANSE'. 3s.

CARLYLE (Thomas).—THOMAS CARLYLE: a History of his Life. By J. A. FROUDE. 1795-1835, 2 vols. Cr. 8vo. 7s. 1834-1881, 2 vols. Cr. 8vo. 7s.

CASE (Thomas).—PHYSICAL REALISM : being an Analytical Philosophy from the Physical Objects of Science to the Physical Data of Sense. 8vo. 15s.

CHETWYND (Sir George).—RACING REMINISCENCES AND EXPERIENCES OF THE TURF. 2 vols. 8vo. 21s.

CHILD (Gilbert W.).—CHURCH AND STATE UNDER THE TUDORS. 8vo. 15s.

CHISHOLM (G. G.).—HANDBOOK OF COMMERCIAL GEOGRAPHY. With 29 Maps. 8vo. 16s.

CHURCH (Sir Richard).—Commander-in-Chief of the Greeks in the War of Independence : a Memoir. By STANLEY LANE-POOLE. 8vo. 5s.

CLIVE (Mrs. Archer).—POEMS. Including the IX. Poems. Fcp. 8vo. 6s.

CLODD (Edward).—THE STORY OF CREATION : a Plain Account of Evolution. With 77 Illustrations. Crown 8vo. 3s. 6d.

CLUTTERBUCK (W. J.).—THE SKIPPER IN ARCTIC SEAS. With 39 Illustrations. Crown 8vo. 10s. 6d.

COLENSO (J. W.).—THE PENTATEUCH AND BOOK OF JOSHUA CRITICALLY EXAMINED. Crown 8vo. 6s.

COLMORE (G.).—A LIVING EPITAPH : a Novel. Crown 8vo. 6s.

COMYN (L. N.).—ATHERSTONE PRIORY : a Tale. Crown 8vo. 2s. 6d.

CONINGTON (John).—THE ÆNEID OF VIRGIL. Translated into English Verse. Crown 8vo. 6s.

———— THE POEMS OF VIRGIL. Translated into English Prose. Cr. 8vo. 6s.

COX (Rev. Sir G. W.).—A HISTORY OF GREECE, from the Earliest Period to the Death of Alexander the Great. With 11 Maps. Cr. 8vo. 7s. 6d.

CRAKE (Rev. A. D.).—HISTORICAL TALES. Cr. 8vo. 5 vols. 2s. 6d. each.

Edwy the Fair; or, The First Chronicle of Æscendune.

Alfgar the Dane; or, The Second Chronicle of Æscendune.

The Rival Heirs: being the Third and Last Chronicle of Æscendune.

The House of Walderne. A Tale of the Cloister and the Forest in the Days of the Barons' Wars.

Brain Fitz-Count. A Story of Wallingford Castle and Dorchester Abbey.

——— HISTORY OF THE CHURCH UNDER THE ROMAN EMPIRE, A.D. 30-476. Crown 8vo. 7s. 6d.

CREIGHTON (Mandell, D.D.)—HISTORY OF THE PAPACY DURING THE REFORMATION. 8vo. Vols. I. and II., 1378-1464, 32s. ; Vols. III. and IV., 1464-1518, 24s.

CRUMP (A.).—A SHORT ENQUIRY INTO THE FORMATION OF POLITICAL OPINION, from the Reign of the Great Families to the Advent of Democracy. 8vo. 7s. 6d.

——— AN INVESTIGATION INTO THE CAUSES OF THE GREAT FALL IN PRICES which took place coincidently with the Demonetisation of Silver by Germany. 8vo. 6s.

CURZON (Hon. George N.).—RUSSIA IN CENTRAL ASIA IN 1889 AND THE ANGLO-RUSSIAN QUESTION. 8vo. 21s.

DANTE.—LA COMMEDIA DI DANTE. A New Text, carefully Revised with the aid of the most recent Editions and Collations. Small 8vo. 6s.

DELAND (Mrs.).—JOHN WARD, PREACHER. Cr. 8vo. 2s. bds., 2s. 6d. cl.

——— SIDNEY: a Novel. Crown 8vo. 6s.

——— THE OLD GARDEN, and other Verses. Fcp. 8vo. 5s.

DE REDCLIFFE.—THE LIFE OF THE RIGHT HON. STRATFORD CANNING: VISCOUNT STRATFORD DE REDCLIFFE. By STANLEY LANE-POOLE. With 3 Portraits. Crown 8vo. 7s. 6d.

DE SALIS (Mrs.).—Works by :—

Savouries à la Mode. Fcp. 8vo. 1s. 6d.

Entrées à la Mode. Fcp. 8vo. 1s. 6d.

Soups and Dressed Fish à la Mode. Fcp. 8vo. 1s. 6d.

Oysters à la Mode. Fcp. 8vo. 1s. 6d.

Sweets and Supper Dishes à la Mode. Fcp. 8vo. 1s. 6d.

Dressed Vegetables à la Mode. Fcp. 8vo. 1s. 6d.

Dressed Game and Poultry à la Mode. Fcp. 8vo. 1s. 6d.

Puddings and Pastry à la Mode. Fcp. 8vo. 1s. 6d.

Cakes and Confections à la Mode. Fcp. 8vo. 1s. 6d.

Drinks à la Mode. Fcp. 8vo. 1s. 6d.

Tempting Dishes for Small Incomes. Fcp. 8vo. 1s. 6d.

Floral Decorations. Fcp. 8vo. 1s. 6d.

Wrinkles and Notions for every Household. Crown 8vo. 2s. 6d.

DE TOCQUEVILLE (Alexis).—DEMOCRACY IN AMERICA. Translated by HENRY REEVE, C.B. 2 vols. Crown 8vo. 16s.

DOWELL (Stephen).—A HISTORY OF TAXATION AND TAXES IN ENGLAND. 4 vols. 8vo. Vols. I and II., The History of Taxation, 21s. Vols. III. and IV., The History of Taxes, 21s.

DOYLE (A. Conan).—MICAH CLARKE: a Tale of Monmouth's Rebellion. With Frontispiece and Vignette. Crown 8vo. 3s. 6d.

——— THE CAPTAIN OF THE POLESTAR; and other Tales. Cr. 8vo. 6s.

DRANE (Augusta T.).—THE HISTORY OF ST. DOMINIC, FOUNDER OF THE FRIAR PREACHERS. With 32 Illustrations. 8vo. 15*s.*

DUBLIN UNIVERSITY PRESS SERIES (The): a Series of Works undertaken by the Provost and Senior Fellows of Trinity College, Dublin.

Abbot's (T. K.) Codex Rescriptus Dublinensis of St. Matthew. 4to. 21*s.*
—————— **Evangeliorum Versio Antehieronymiana ex Codice Usseriano (Dublinensi).** 2 vols. Cr. 8vo. 21*s.*
Allman's (G. J.) Greek Geometry from Thales to Euclid. 8vo. 10*s.* 6*d.*
Burnside (W. S.) and Panton's (A. W.) Theory of Equations. 8vo. 12*s.* 6*d.*
Casey's (John) Sequel to Euclid's Elements. Crown 8vo. 3*s.* 6*d.*
—————— **Analytical Geometry of the Conic Sections.** Crown 8vo. 7*s.* 6*d.*
Davies' (J. F.) Eumenides of Æschylus. With Metrical English Translation. 8vo. 7*s.*
Dublin Translations into Greek and Latin Verse. Edited by R. Y. Tyrrell. 8vo. 6*s.*
Graves' (R. P.) Life of Sir William Hamilton. 3 vols. 15*s.* each.
Griffin (R. W.) on Parabola, Ellipse, and Hyperbola. Crown 8vo. 6*s.*
Hobart's (W. K.) Medical Language of St. Luke. 8vo. 16*s.*
Leslie's (T. E. Cliffe) Essays in Political Economy. 8vo. 10*s.* 6*d.*
Macalister's (A.) Zoology and Morphology of Vertebrata. 8vo. 10*s.* 6*d.*
MacCullagh's (James) Mathematical and other Tracts. 8vo. 15*s.*

Maguire's (T.) Parmenides of Plato, Text with Introduction, Analysis, &c. 8vo. 7*s.* 6*d.*
Monck's (W. H. S.) Introduction to Logic. Crown 8vo. 5*s.*
Robert's (R. A.) Examples on the Analytic Geometry of Plane Conics. Crown 8vo. 5*s.*
Southey's (R.) Correspondence with Caroline Bowles. Edited by E. Dowden. 8vo. 14*s.*
Stubbs' (J. W.) History of the University of Dublin, from its Foundation to the End of the Eighteenth Century. 8vo. 12*s.* 6*d.*
Thornhill's (W. J.) The Æneid of Virgil, freely translated into English Blank Verse. Crown 8vo. 7*s.* 6*d.*
Tyrell's (R. Y.) Cicero's Correspondence. Vols. I., II. and III. 8vo. each 12*s.*
—————— **The Acharnians of Aristophanes,** translated into English Verse. Crown 8vo. 1*s.*
Webb's (T. E.) Goethe's Faust, Translation and Notes. 8vo. 12*s.* 6*d.*
—————— **The Veil of Isis;** a Series of Essays on Idealism. 8vo. 10*s.* 6*d.*
Wilkin's (G.) The Growth of the Homeric Poems. 8vo. 6*s.*

EWALD (Heinrich).—THE ANTIQUITIES OF ISRAEL. 8vo. 12*s.* 6*d.*

—————— THE HISTORY OF ISRAEL. 8vo. Vols. I. and II. 24*s.* Vols. III. and IV. 21*s.* Vol. V. 18*s.* Vol. VI. 16*s.* Vol. VII. 21*s.* Vol. VIII. 18*s.*

FARNELL (G. S.).—THE GREEK LYRIC POETS. 8vo. 16*s.*

FARRAR (F. W.).—LANGUAGE AND LANGUAGES. Crown 8vo. 6*s.*

FIRTH (J. C.).—NATION MAKING: a Story of New Zealand Savageism and Civilisation. Crown 8vo. 6*s.*

FITZWYGRAM (Major-General Sir F.).—HORSES AND STABLES. With 19 pages of Illustrations. 8vo. 5*s.*

FORD (Horace).—THE THEORY AND PRACTICE OF ARCHERY. New Edition, thoroughly Revised and Re-written by W. Butt. 8vo. 14*s.*

FOUARD (Abbé Constant).—THE CHRIST THE SON OF GOD. With Introduction by Cardinal Manning. 2 vols. Crown 8vo. 14*s.*

FOX (C. J.).—THE EARLY HISTORY OF CHARLES JAMES FOX. By the Right Hon. Sir. G. O. Trevelyan, Bart.
Library Edition. 8vo. 18s. | Cabinet Edition. Crown 8vo. 6s.

FRANCIS (Francis).—A BOOK ON ANGLING : including full Illustrated Lists of Salmon Flies. Post 8vo. 15s.

FREEMAN (E. A.).—THE HISTORICAL GEOGRAPHY OF EUROPE. With 65 Maps. 2 vols. 8vo. 31s. 6d.

FROUDE (James A.).—THE HISTORY OF ENGLAND, from the Fall of Wolsey to the Defeat of the Spanish Armada. 12 vols. Crown 8vo. £2 2s.

———— THE ENGLISH IN IRELAND IN THE EIGHTEENTH CENTURY. 3 vols. Crown 8vo. 18s.

———— SHORT STUDIES ON GREAT SUBJECTS.
Cabinet Edition. 4 vols. Cr. 8vo. 24s. | Cheap Edit. 4 vols. Cr. 8vo. 3s. 6d. ea.

———— CÆSAR : a Sketch. Crown 8vo. 3s. 6d.

———— OCEANA ; OR, ENGLAND AND HER COLONIES. With 9 Illustrations. Crown 8vo. 2s. boards, 2s. 6d. cloth.

———— THE ENGLISH IN THE WEST INDIES ; or, the Bow of Ulysses. With 9 Illustrations. Crown 8vo. 2s. boards, 2s. 6d. cloth.

———— THE TWO CHIEFS OF DUNBOY ; an Irish Romance of the Last Century. Crown 8vo. 3s. 6d.

———— THOMAS CARLYLE, a History of his Life. 1795 to 1835. 2 vols. Crown 8vo. 7s. 1834 to 1881. 2 vols. Crown 8vo. 7s.

GALLWEY (Sir Ralph Payne-).—LETTERS TO YOUNG SHOOTERS. (First Series.) On the Choice and Use of a Gun. Crown 8vo. 7s. 6d.

GARDINER (Samuel Rawson). —HISTORY OF ENGLAND, 1603-1642. 10 vols. Crown 8vo. price 6s. each.

———— A HISTORY OF THE GREAT CIVIL WAR, 1642-1649. (3 vols.) Vol. I. 1642-1644. With 24 Maps. 8vo. 21s. (*out of print*). Vol. II. 1644-1647. With 21 Maps. 8vo. 24s. Vol. III. 1647-1649. [*In the Press.*

———— THE STUDENT'S HISTORY OF ENGLAND. Vol. I. B.C. 55-A.D. 1509, with 173 Illustrations, Crown 8vo. 4s. Vol. II. 1509-1689. with 96 Illustrations. Crown 8vo. 4s. Vol. III. 1689-1885, with Illustrations. Crown 8vo. 4s. Complete in 1 vol. Crown 8vo.

GIBERNE (Agnes).—MISS DEVEREUX, SPINSTER. 2 vols. Crown 8vo. 17s.

———— RALPH HARDCASTLE'S WILL. With Frontispiece. Cr. 8vo. 5s.

———— NIGEL BROWNING. Crown 8vo. 5s.

GOETHE.—FAUST. A New Translation chiefly in Blank Verse ; with Introduction and Notes. By James Adey Birds. Crown 8vo. 6s.

———— FAUST. The Second Part. A New Translation in Verse. By James Adey Birds. Crown 8vo. 6s.

GREEN (T. H.)—THE WORKS OF THOMAS HILL GREEN. (3 Vols.) Vols. I. and II. 8vo. 16s. each. Vol. III. 8vo. 21s.

———— THE WITNESS OF GOD AND FAITH : Two Lay Sermons. Fcp. 8vo. 2s.

GREVILLE (C. C. F.).—A JOURNAL OF THE REIGNS OF KING GEORGE IV., KING WILLIAM IV., AND QUEEN VICTORIA. Edited by H. Reeve. 8 vols. Crown 8vo. 6s. each.

GWILT (Joseph).—AN ENCYCLOPÆDIA OF ARCHITECTURE. With more than 1700 Engravings on Wood. 8vo. 52*s*. 6*d*.

HAGGARD (Ella).—LIFE AND ITS AUTHOR: an Essay in Verse. With a Memoir by H. Rider Haggard, and Portrait. Fcp. 8vo. 3*s*. 6*d*.

HAGGARD (H. Rider).—SHE. With 32 Illustrations. Crown 8vo. 3*s*. 6*d*.
———— ALLAN QUATERMAIN. With 31 Illustrations. Crown 8vo. 3*s*. 6*d*.
———— MAIWA'S REVENGE. Crown 8vo. 2*s*. boards, 2*s*. 6*d*. cloth.
———— COLONEL QUARITCH, V.C. Crown 8vo. 3*s*. 6*d*.
———— CLEOPATRA: With 29 Illustrations. Crown 8vo. 3*s*. 6*d*.
———— BEATRICE. Crown 8vo. 6*s*.
———— ERIC BRIGHTEYES. With 51 Illustrations. Crown 8vo. 6*s*.

HAGGARD (H. Rider) and LANG (Andrew).—THE WORLD'S DESIRE. Crown 8vo. 6*s*.

HALLIWELL-PHILLIPPS (J. O.)—A CALENDAR OF THE HALLI-WELL-PHILLIPPS COLLECTION OF SHAKESPEAREAN RARITIES. Second Edition. Enlarged by Ernest E. Baker. 8vo. 10*s*. 6*d*.
———— OUTLINE OF THE LIFE OF SHAKESPEARE. 2 vols. Royal 8vo. 21*s*.

HARRISON (Jane E.).—MYTHS OF THE ODYSSEY IN ART AND LITERATURE. Illustrated with Outline Drawings. 8vo. 18*s*.

HARRISON (F. Bayford).—THE CONTEMPORARY HISTORY OF THE FRENCH REVOLUTION. Crown 8vo. 3*s*. 6*d*.

HARTE (Bret).—IN THE CARQUINEZ WOODS. Fcp. 8vo. 1*s*. bds., 1*s*. 6*d*. cloth.
———— BY SHORE AND SEDGE. 16mo. 1*s*.
———— ON THE FRONTIER. 16mo. 1*s*.

HARTWIG (Dr.).—THE SEA AND ITS LIVING WONDERS. With 12 Plates and 303 Woodcuts. 8vo. 10*s*. 6*d*.
THE TROPICAL WORLD. With 8 Plates and 172 Woodcuts. 8vo. 10*s*. 6*d*.
THE POLAR WORLD. With 3 Maps, 8 Plates and 85 Woodcuts. 8vo. 10*s*. 6*d*.
THE SUBTERRANEAN WORLD. With 3 Maps and 80 Woodcuts. 8vo. 10*s*. 6*d*.
THE AERIAL WORLD. With Map, 8 Plates and 60 Woodcuts. 8vo. 10*s*. 6*d*.

HAVELOCK.—MEMOIRS OF SIR HENRY HAVELOCK, K.C.B. By JOHN CLARK MARSHMAN. Crown 8vo. 3*s*. 6*d*.

HEARN (W. Edward).—THE GOVERNMENT OF ENGLAND: its Structure and its Development. 8vo. 16*s*.
———— THE ARYAN HOUSEHOLD: its Structure and ts Development. An Introduction to Comparative Jurisprudence. 8vo. 16*s*.

HISTORIC TOWNS. Edited by E. A. FREEMAN and Rev. WILLIAM HUNT. With Maps and Plans. Crown 8vo. 3*s*. 6*d*. each.

Bristol. By Rev. W. Hunt.	**Winchester.** By Rev. G. W. Kitchin.
Carlisle. By Dr. Mandell Creighton.	**New York.** By Theodore Roosevelt.
Cinque Ports. By Montagu Burrows.	**Boston (U.S.).** By Henry Cabot
Colchester. By Rev. E. L. Cutts.	Lodge.
Exeter. By E. A. Freeman.	**York.** By Rev. James Raine.
London. By Rev. W. J. Loftie.	[*In preparation.*
Oxford. By Rev. C. W. Boase.	

HODGSON (Shadworth H.).—TIME AND SPACE: a Metaphysical Essay. 8vo. 16s.

———— THE THEORY OF PRACTICE: an Ethical Enquiry. 2 vols. 8vo. 24s.

———— THE PHILOSOPHY OF REFLECTION. 2 vols. 8vo. 21s.

———— OUTCAST ESSAYS AND VERSE TRANSLATIONS. Crown 8vo. 8s. 6d.

HOWITT (William).—VISITS TO REMARKABLE PLACES. 80 Illustrations. Crown 8vo. 3s. 6d.

HULLAH (John).—COURSE OF LECTURES ON THE HISTORY OF MODERN MUSIC. 8vo. 8s. 6d.

———— COURSE OF LECTURES ON THE TRANSITION PERIOD OF MUSICAL HISTORY. 8vo. 10s. 6d.

HUME.—THE PHILOSOPHICAL WORKS OF DAVID HUME. Edited by T. H. GREEN and T. H. GROSE. 4 vols. 8vo. 56s.

HUTCHINSON (Horace).—CREATURES OF CIRCUMSTANCE: a Novel. 3 vols. Crown 8vo. 25s. 6d.

———— CRICKETING SAWS AND STORIES. With rectilinear Illustrations by the Author. 16mo. 1s.

———— FAMOUS GOLF LINKS. By HORACE G. HUTCHINSON, ANDREW LANG, H. S. C. EVERARD, T. RUTHERFORD CLARK, &c. With numerous Illustrations by F. P. Hopkins, T. Hodges, H. S. King, &c. Crown 8vo. 6s.

HUTH (Alfred H.).—THE MARRIAGE OF NEAR KIN. Royal 8vo. 21s.

INGELOW (Jean).—POETICAL WORKS. Vols. I. and II. Fcp. 8vo. 12s. Vol. III. Fcp. 8vo. 5s.

———— LYRICAL AND OTHER POEMS. Selected from the Writings of JEAN INGELOW. Fcp. 8vo. 2s. 6d. cloth plain, 3s. cloth gilt.

———— VERY YOUNG and QUITE ANOTHER STORY: Two Stories. Crown 8vo. 6s.

JAMESON (Mrs.).—SACRED AND LEGENDARY ART. With 19 Etchings and 187 Woodcuts. 2 vols. 8vo. 20s. net.

———— LEGENDS OF THE MADONNA, the Virgin Mary as represented in Sacred and Legendary Art. With 27 Etchings and 165 Woodcuts. 8vo. 10s. net.

———— LEGENDS OF THE MONASTIC ORDERS. With 11 Etchings and 88 Woodcuts. 8vo. 10s. net.

———— HISTORY OF OUR LORD. His Types and Precursors. Completed by LADY EASTLAKE. With 31 Etchings and 281 Woodcuts. 2 vols. 8vo. 20s. net.

JEFFERIES (Richard).—FIELD AND HEDGEROW. Last Essays. Crown 8vo. 3s. 6d.

———— THE STORY OF MY HEART: My Autobiography. Crown 8vo. 3s. 6d

JENNINGS (Rev. A. C.).—ECCLESIA ANGLICANA. A History of the Church of Christ in England. Crown 8vo. 7s. 6d.

JESSOP (G. H.).—JUDGE LYNCH: a Tale of the California Vineyards. Crown 8vo. 6s.

———— GERALD FFRENCH'S FRIENDS. Crown 8vo. 6s.

JOHNSON (J. & J. H.).—THE PATENTEE'S MANUAL; a Treatise on the Law and Practice of Letters Patent. 8vo. 10s. 6d.

JORDAN (William Leighton).—THE STANDARD OF VALUE. 8vo. 6s.

JUSTINIAN.—THE INSTITUTES OF JUSTINIAN; Latin Text, with English Introduction, &c. By Thomas C. Sandars. 8vo. 18s.

KALISCH (M. M.).—BIBLE STUDIES. Part I. The Prophecies of Balaam. 8vo. 10s. 6d. Part II. The Book of Jonah. 8vo. 10s. 6d.

KALISCH (M. M.).—COMMENTARY ON THE OLD TESTAMENT; with a New Translation. Vol. I. Genesis, 8vo. 18s., or adapted for the General Reader, 12s. Vol. II. Exodus, 15s., or adapted for the General Reader, 12s. Vol. III. Leviticus, Part I. 15s., or adapted for the General Reader, 8s. Vol. IV. Leviticus, Part II. 15s., or adapted for the General Reader, 8s.

KANT (Immanuel).—CRITIQUE OF PRACTICAL REASON, AND OTHER WORKS ON THE THEORY OF ETHICS. 8vo. 12s. 6d.

———— INTRODUCTION TO LOGIC. Translated by T. K. Abbott. Notes by S. T. Coleridge. 8vo. 6s.

KENDALL (May).—FROM A GARRET. Crown 8vo. 6s.

———— DREAMS TO SELL; Poems. Fcp. 8vo. 6s.

———— 'SUCH IS LIFE': a Novel. Crown 8vo. 6s.

KENNEDY (Arthur Clark).—PICTURES IN RHYME. With 4 Illustrations by Maurice Greiffenhagen. Crown 8vo. 6s.

KILLICK (Rev. A. H.).—HANDBOOK TO MILL'S SYSTEM OF LOGIC. Crown 8vo. 3s. 6d.

KNIGHT (E. F.).—THE CRUISE OF THE 'ALERTE'; the Narrative of a Search for Treasure on the Desert Island of Trinidad. With 2 Maps and 23 Illustrations. Crown 8vo. 10s. 6d.

———— SAVE ME FROM MY FRIENDS: a Novel. Crown 8vo. 6s.

LADD (George T.).—ELEMENTS OF PHYSIOLOGICAL PSYCHO-LOGY. 8vo. 21s.

———— OUTLINES OF PHYSIOLOGICAL PSYCHOLOGY. A Text-Book of Mental Science for Academies and Colleges. 8vo. 12s.

LANG (Andrew).—CUSTOM AND MYTH: Studies of Early Usage and Belief. With 15 Illustrations. Crown 8vo. 7s. 6d.

———— BOOKS AND BOOKMEN. With 2 Coloured Plates and 17 Illustrations. Crown 8vo. 6s. 6d.

———— GRASS OF PARNASSUS. A Volume of Selected Verses. Fcp. 8vo. 6s.

———— BALLADS OF BOOKS. Edited by Andrew Lang. Fcp. 8vo. 6s.

———— THE BLUE FAIRY BOOK. Edited by Andrew Lang. With 8 Plates and 130 Illustrations in the Text. Crown 8vo. 6s.

———— THE RED FAIRY BOOK. Edited by Andrew Lang. With 4 Plates and 96 Illustrations in the Text. Crown 8vo. 6s.

LAVIGERIE.—CARDINAL LAVIGERIE AND THE AFRICAN SLAVE TRADE. 8vo. 14*s.*

LAYARD (Nina F.).—POEMS. Crown 8vo. 6*s.*

LECKY (W. E. H.).—HISTORY OF ENGLAND IN THE EIGHTEENTH CENTURY. 8vo. Vols. I. and II. 1700-1760. 36*s.* Vols. III. and IV. 1760-1784. 36*s.* Vols. V. and VI. 1784-1793. 36*s.* Vols. VII. and VIII. 1793-1800. 36*s.*

———— THE HISTORY OF EUROPEAN MORALS FROM AUGUSTUS TO CHARLEMAGNE. 2 vols. Crown 8vo. 16*s.*

———— HISTORY OF THE RISE AND INFLUENCE OF THE SPIRIT OF RATIONALISM IN EUROPE. 2 vols. Crown 8vo. 16*s.*

LEES (J. A.) and CLUTTERBUCK (W. J.).—B.C. 1887, A RAMBLE IN BRITISH COLUMBIA. With Map and 75 Illustrations. Cr. 8vo. 6*s.*

LEGER (Louis).—A HISTORY OF AUSTRO-HUNGARY. From the Earliest Time to the year 1889. With Preface by E. A. Freeman. Cr. 8vo. 10*s.* 6*d.*

LEWES (George Henry).—THE HISTORY OF PHILOSOPHY, from Thales to Comte. 2 vols. 8vo. 32*s.*

LIDDELL (Colonel R. T.).—MEMOIRS OF THE TENTH ROYAL HUSSARS. With Numerous Illustrations. 2 vols. Imperial 8vo. 63*s.*

LONGMAN (Frederick W.).—CHESS OPENINGS. Fcp. 8vo. 2*s.* 6*d.*

———— FREDERICK THE GREAT AND THE SEVEN YEARS' WAR. Fcp. 8vo. 2*s.* 6*d.*

LOUDON (J. C.).—ENCYCLOPÆDIA OF GARDENING. With 1000 Woodcuts. 8vo. 21*s.*

———— ENCYCLOPÆDIA OF AGRICULTURE; the Laying-out, Improvement, and Management of Landed Property. With 1100 Woodcuts. 8vo. 21*s.*

———— ENCYCLOPÆDIA OF PLANTS; the Specific Character, &c., of all Plants found in Great Britain. With 12,000 Woodcuts. 8vo. 42*s.*

LUBBOCK (Sir J.).—THE ORIGIN OF CIVILISATION and the Primitive Condition of Man. With 5 Plates and 20 Illustrations in the Text. 8vo. 18*s.*

LYALL (Edna).—THE AUTOBIOGRAPHY OF A SLANDER. Fcp. 8vo. 1*s.* sewed.

LYDE (Lionel W.).—AN INTRODUCTION TO ANCIENT HISTORY. With 3 Coloured Maps. Crown 8vo. 3*s.*

MACAULAY (Lord).—COMPLETE WORKS OF LORD MACAULAY. Library Edition, 8 vols. 8vo. £5 5*s.* | Cabinet Edition, 16 vols. post 8vo. £4 16*s.*

———— HISTORY OF ENGLAND FROM THE ACCESSION OF JAMES THE SECOND.

Popular Edition, 2 vols. Crown 8vo. 5*s.* | People's Edition, 4 vols. Crown 8vo. 16*s.*
Student's Edition, 2 vols. Crown 8vo. 12*s.* | Cabinet Edition, 8 vols. Post 8vo. 48*s.*
| Library Edition, 5 vols. 8vo. £4.

———— CRITICAL AND HISTORICAL ESSAYS, WITH LAYS OF ANCIENT ROME, in 1 volume.

Popular Edition, Crown 8vo. 2*s.* 6*d.* | Authorised Edition, Crown 8vo. 2*s.* 6*d.*, or 3*s.* 6*d.* gilt edges.

MACAULAY (Lord).—ESSAYS (*continued*).

———— CRITICAL AND HISTORICAL ESSAYS.

Student's Edition. Crown 8vo. 6s.
People's Edition, 2 vols. Crown 8vo. 8s.

Trevelyan Edition, 2 vols. Crown 8vo. 9s.
Cabinet Edition, 4 vols. Post 8vo. 24s.
Library Edition, 3 vols. 8vo. 36s.

———— ESSAYS which may be had separately, price 6d. each sewed. 1s. each cloth.

Addison and Walpole.
Frederic the Great.
Croker's Boswell's Johnson.
Hallam's Constitutional History.
Warren Hastings (3d. sewed, 6d. cloth).
The Earl of Chatham (Two Essays).

Ranke and Gladstone.
Milton and Machiavelli.
Lord Bacon.
Lord Clive.
Lord Byron, and the Comic Dramatists of the Restoration.

The Essay on Warren Hastings, annotated by S. Hales. Fcp. 8vo. 1s. 6d.

The Essay on Lord Clive, annotated by H. Courthope Bowen. Fcp. 8vo. 2s. 6d.

———— SPEECHES. People's Edition, Crown 8vo. 3s. 6d.

———— LAYS OF ANCIENT ROME, &c. Illustrated by G. Scharf. Library Edition. Fcp. 4to. 10s. 6d.

Bijou Edition, 18mo. 2s. 6d. gilt top.

Popular Edition, Fcp. 4to. 6d. sewed, 1s. cloth.

———————————————— Illustrated by J. R. Weguelin. Crown 8vo. 3s. 6d. gilt edges.

———————————— Cabinet Edition, Post 8vo. 3s. 6d.

Annotated Edition, Fcp. 8vo. 1s. sewed, 1s. 6d. cloth.

———— MISCELLANEOUS WRITINGS.

People's Edition. Crown 8vo. 4s. 6d. | Library Edition, 2 vols. 8vo. 21s.

———— MISCELLANEOUS WRITINGS AND SPEECHES.

Popular Edition. Crown 8vo. 2s. 6d.
Student's Edition. Crown 8vo. 6s.

Cabinet Edition, Post 8vo. 24s.

———— SELECTIONS FROM THE WRITINGS OF LORD MACAULAY. Edited, with Notes, by the Right Hon. Sir G. O. TREVELYAN. Crown 8vo. 6s.

———— THE LIFE AND LETTERS OF LORD MACAULAY. By the Right Hon. Sir G. O. TREVELYAN.

Popular Edition. Crown. 8vo. 2s. 6d.
Student's Edition. Crown 8vo. 6s.

Cabinet Edition, 2 vols. Post 8vo. 12s.
Library Edition, 2 vols. 8vo. 36s.

MACDONALD (George).—UNSPOKEN SERMONS. Three Series. Crown 8vo. 3s. 6d. each.

———— THE MIRACLES OF OUR LORD. Crown 8vo. 3s. 6d.

———— A BOOK OF STRIFE, IN THE FORM OF THE DIARY OF AN OLD SOUL : Poems. 12mo. 6s.

MACFARREN (Sir G. A.).—LECTURES ON HARMONY. 8vo. 12s.

MACKAIL (J. W.).—SELECT EPIGRAMS FROM THE GREEK ANTHOLOGY. With a Revised Text, Introduction, Translation, &c. 8vo. 16s.

MACLEOD (Henry D.).—THE ELEMENTS OF BANKING. Crown 8vo. 3s. 6d.

———— THE THEORY AND PRACTICE OF BANKING. Vol. I. 8vo. 12s., Vol. II. 14s.

———— THE THEORY OF CREDIT. 8vo. Vol. I. [*New Edition in the Press*]; Vol. II. Part I. 4s. 6d. ; Vol. II. Part II. 10s. 6d.

McCULLOCH (J. R.).—THE DICTIONARY OF COMMERCE and Commercial Navigation. With 11 Maps and 30 Charts. 8vo. 63*s.*

MACVINE (John).—SIXTY-THREE YEARS' ANGLING, from the Mountain Streamlet to the Mighty Tay. Crown 8vo. 10*s.* 6*d.*

MALMESBURY (The Earl of).—MEMOIRS OF AN EX-MINISTER. Crown 8vo. 7*s.* 6*d.*

MANUALS OF CATHOLIC PHILOSOPHY (*Stonyhurst Series*).

Logic. By Richard F. Clarke. Crown 8vo. 5*s.*

First Principles of Knowledge. By John Rickaby. Crown 8vo. 5*s.*

Moral Philosophy (Ethics and Natural Law). By Joseph Rickaby. Crown 8vo. 5*s.*

General Metaphysics. By John Rickaby. Crown 8vo. 5*s.*

Psychology. By Michael Maher. Crown 8vo. 6*s.* 6*d.*

Natural Theology. By Bernard Boedder. Crown 8vo. 6*s.* 6*d.*

A Manual of Political Economy. By C. S. Devas. 6*s.* 6*d.*   [*In preparation.*

MARTINEAU (James).—HOURS OF THOUGHT ON SACRED THINGS. Two Volumes of Sermons. 2 vols. Crown 8vo. 7*s.* 6*d.* each.

——— ENDEAVOURS AFTER THE CHRISTIAN LIFE. Discourses. Crown 8vo. 7*s.* 6*d.*

——— THE SEAT OF AUTHORITY IN RELIGION. 8vo. 14*s.*

——— ESSAYS, REVIEWS, AND ADDRESSES. 4 vols. Crown 8vo. 7*s.* 6*d.* each.

I. Personal : Political.
II. Ecclesiastical : Historical.

III. Theological : Philosophical.
IV. Academical : Religious.

[*In course of publication.*

MASON (Agnes).—THE STEPS OF THE SUN : Daily Readings of Prose. 16mo. 3*s.* 6*d.*

MAUNDER'S TREASURIES. Fcp. 8vo. 6*s.* each volume.

Biographical Treasury.
Treasury of Natural History. With 900 Woodcuts.
Treasury of Geography. With 7 Maps and 16 Plates.
Scientific and Literary Treasury.
Historical Treasury.
Treasury of Knowledge.

The Treasury of Bible Knowledge. By the Rev. J. AYRE. With 5 Maps, 15 Plates, and 300 Woodcuts. Fcp. 8vo. 6*s.*
The Treasury of Botany. Edited by J. LINDLEY and T. MOORE. With 274 Woodcuts and 20 Steel Plates. 2 vols.

MATTHEWS (Brander).—A FAMILY TREE, and other Stories. Crown 8vo. 6*s.*

——— PEN AND INK—School Papers. Crown 8vo. 5*s.*

MAX MÜLLER (F.).—SELECTED ESSAYS ON LANGUAGE, MYTHOLOGY, AND RELIGION. 2 vols. Crown 8vo. 16*s.*

——— LECTURES ON THE SCIENCE OF LANGUAGE. 2 vols. Crown 8vo. 16*s.*

——— THREE LECTURES ON THE SCIENCE OF LANGUAGE. Cr. 8vo. 3*s.*

——— THE SCIENCE OF LANGUAGE, founded on Lectures delivered at the Royal Institution in 1861 and 1863. 2 vols. Crown 8vo. 21*s.*

——— HIBBERT LECTURES ON THE ORIGIN AND GROWTH OF RELIGION, as illustrated by the Religions of India. Crown 8vo. 7*s.* 6*d.*

MAX MÜLLER (F.)—INTRODUCTION TO THE SCIENCE OF RE-LIGION; Four Lectures delivered at the Royal Institution. Crown 8vo. 7s. 6d.

———— NATURAL RELIGION. The Gifford Lectures, delivered before the University of Glasgow in 1888. Crown 8vo. 10s. 6d.

———— PHYSICAL RELIGION. The Gifford Lectures, delivered before the University of Glasgow in 1890. Crown 8vo. 10s. 6d.

———— THE SCIENCE OF THOUGHT. 8vo. 21s.

———— THREE INTRODUCTORY LECTURES ON THE SCIENCE OF THOUGHT. 8vo. 2s. 6d.

———— BIOGRAPHIES OF WORDS, AND THE HOME OF THE ARYAS. Crown 8vo. 7s. 6d.

———— A SANSKRIT GRAMMAR FOR BEGINNERS. New and Abridged Edition. By A. A. MacDonell. Crown 8vo. 6s.

MAY (Sir Thomas Erskine).—THE CONSTITUTIONAL HISTORY OF ENGLAND since the Accession of George III. 3 vols. Crown 8vo. 18s.

MEADE (L. T.).—THE O'DONNELLS OF INCHFAWN. Crown 8vo. 6s.

———— DADDY'S BOY. With Illustrations. Crown 8vo. 5s.

———— DEB AND THE DUCHESS. Illustrated by M. E. Edwards. Cr. 8vo. 5s.

———— HOUSE OF SURPRISES. Illustrated by E. M. Scannell. Cr. 8vo. 3s. 6d.

———— THE BERESFORD PRIZE. Illustrated by M. E. Edwards. Cr. 8vo. 5s.

MEATH (The Earl of).—SOCIAL ARROWS: Reprinted Articles on various Social Subjects. Crown 8vo. 5s.

———— PROSPERITY OR PAUPERISM? Physical, Industrial, and Technical Training. Edited by the Earl of Meath. 8vo. 5s.

MELVILLE (G. J. Whyte).—Novels by. Crown 8vo. 1s. each, boards; 1s. 6d. each, cloth.

The Gladiators.	The Queen's Maries.	Digby Grand.
The Interpreter.	Holmby House.	General Bounce.
Good for Nothing.	Kate Coventry.	

MENDELSSOHN.—THE LETTERS OF FELIX MENDELSSOHN. Translated by Lady Wallace. 2 vols. Crown 8vo. 10s.

MERIVALE (Rev. Chas.).—HISTORY OF THE ROMANS UNDER THE EMPIRE. Cabinet Edition, 8 vols. Crown 8vo. 48s. Popular Edition, 8 vols. Crown 8vo. 3s. 6d. each.

———— THE FALL OF THE ROMAN REPUBLIC: a Short History of the Last Century of the Commonwealth. 12mo. 7s. 6d.

———— GENERAL HISTORY OF ROME FROM B.C. 753 TO A.D. 476. Cr. 8vo. 7s. 6d.

———— THE ROMAN TRIUMVIRATES. With Maps. Fcp. 8vo. 2s. 6d.

MILES (W. A.).—THE CORRESPONDENCE OF WILLIAM AUGUSTUS MILES ON THE FRENCH REVOLUTION, 1789-1817. 2 vols. 8vo. 32s.

MILL (James).—ANALYSIS OF THE PHENOMENA OF THE HUMAN MIND. 2 vols. 8vo. 28s.

MILL (John Stuart).—PRINCIPLES OF POLITICAL ECONOMY. Library Edition, 2 vols. 8vo. 30s. | People's Edition, 1 vol. Crown 8vo. 5s.

———— A SYSTEM OF LOGIC. Crown 8vo. 5s.

———— ON LIBERTY. Crown 8vo. 1s. 4d.

MILL (J. S.).—ON REPRESENTATIVE GOVERNMENT. Crown 8vo. 2s.

———— UTILITARIANISM. 8vo. 5s.

———— EXAMINATION OF SIR WILLIAM HAMILTON'S PHILO-
SOPHY. 8vo. 16s.

———— NATURE, THE UTILITY OF RELIGION AND THEISM. Three
Essays, 8vo. 5s.

MOLESWORTH (Mrs.).—MARRYING AND GIVING IN MARRIAGE :
a Novel. Fcp. 8vo. 2s. 6d.

———— SILVERTHORNS. With Illustrations by F. Noel Paton. Cr. 8vo. 5s.

———— THE PALACE IN THE GARDEN. With Illustrations. Cr. 8vo. 5s.

———— THE THIRD MISS ST. QUENTIN. Crown 8vo. 6s.

———— NEIGHBOURS. With Illustrations by M. Ellen Edwards. Cr. 8vo. 6s.

———— THE STORY OF A SPRING MORNING. With Illustrations. Cr. 8vo. 5s.

MOON (G. Washington).—THE KING'S ENGLISH. Fcp. 8vo. 3s. 6d.

MOORE (Edward).—DANTE AND HIS EARLY BIOGRAPHERS.
Crown 8vo. 4s. 6d.

MULHALL (Michael G.).—HISTORY OF PRICES SINCE THE YEAR
1850. Crown 8vo. 6s.

MURDOCK (Henry).—THE RECONSTRUCTION OF EUROPE : a
Sketch of the Diplomatic and Military History of Continental Europe, from
the Rise to the Fall of the Second French Empire. Crown 8vo. 9s.

MURRAY (David Christie and Henry).—A DANGEROUS CATS-
PAW : a Story. Crown 8vo. 2s. 6d.

MURRAY (Christie) and HERMAN (Henry).—WILD DARRIE :
a Story. Crown 8vo. 2s. boards ; 2s. 6d. cloth.

NANSEN (Dr. Fridtjof).—THE FIRST CROSSING OF GREENLAND.
With 5 Maps, 12 Plates, and 150 Illustrations in the Text. 2 vols. 8vo. 36s.

NAPIER.—THE LIFE OF SIR JOSEPH NAPIER, BART., EX-LORD
CHANCELLOR OF IRELAND. By ALEX. CHARLES EWALD. 8vo. 15s.

———— THE LECTURES, ESSAYS, AND LETTERS OF THE RIGHT
HON. SIR JOSEPH NAPIER, BART. 8vo. 12s. 6d

NESBIT (E.).—LEAVES OF LIFE : Verses. Crown 8vo. 5s.

NEWMAN.—THE LETTERS AND CORRESPONDENCE OF JOHN
HENRY NEWMAN during his Life in the English Church. With a brief
Autobiographical Memoir. Edited by Anne Mozley. With Portraits, 2 vols.
8vo. 30s. *net.*

NEWMAN (Cardinal).—Works by :—

Sermons to Mixed Congregations.
Crown 8vo. 6s.

Sermons on Various Occasions. Cr.
8vo. 6s.

**The Idea of a University defined and
illustrated.** Cabinet Edition, Cr. 8vo.
7s. Cheap Edition, Cr. 8vo. 3s. 6d.

Historical Sketches. Cabinet Edition,
3 vols. Crown 8vo. 6s. each. Cheap
Edition, 3 vols. Cr. 8vo. 3s. 6d. each.

The Arians of the Fourth Century.
Cabinet Edition, Crown 8vo. 6s.
Cheap Edition, Crown 8vo. 3s. 6d.

**Select Treatises of St. Athanasius in
Controversy with the Arians.** Freely
Translated. 2 vols. Cr. 8vo. 15s.

**Discussions and Arguments on Various
Subjects.** Cabinet Edition, Crown
8vo. 6s. Cheap Edition, Crown
8vo. 3s. 6d.

NEWMAN (Cardinal).—Works by :—(*continued*).

Apologia Pro Vitâ Sua. Cabinet Ed., Crown 8vo. 6s. Cheap Ed. 3s. 6d.

Development of Christian Doctrine. Cabinet Edition, Crown 8vo. 6s. Cheap Edition, Cr. 8vo. 3s. 6d.

Certain Difficulties felt by Anglicans in Catholic Teaching Considered. Cabinet Edition. Vol. I. Crown 8vo. 7s. 6d. ; Vol. II. Crown 8vo. 5s. 6d.

The Via Media of the Anglican Church, Illustrated in Lectures, &c. Cabinet Edition, 2 vols. Cr. 8vo. 6s. each. Cheap Edition, 2 vols. Crown 8vo. 3s. 6d.

Essays, Critical and Historical. Cabinet Edition, 2 vols. Crown 8vo. 12s. Cheap Edition, 2 vols. Cr. 8vo. 7s.

Biblical and Ecclesiastical Miracles. Cabinet Edition, Crown 8vo. 6s. Cheap Edition, Crown 8vo. 3s. 6d.

Present Position of Catholics in England. Crown 8vo. 7s. 6d.

Tracts. 1. Dissertatiunculæ. 2. On the Text of the Seven Epistles of St. Ignatius. 3. Doctrinal Causes of Arianism. 4. Apollinarianism. 5. St. Cyril's Formula. 6. Ordo de Tempore. 7. Douay Version of Scripture. Crown 8vo. 8s.

An Essay in Aid of a Grammar of Assent. Cabinet Edition, Crown 8vo. 7s. 6d. Cheap Edition, Crown 8vo. 3s. 6d.

Callista : a Tale of the Third Century. Cabinet Edition, Crown 8vo. 6s. Cheap Edition, Crown 8vo. 3s. 6d.

Loss and Gain : a Tale. Cabinet Edition, Crown 8vo. 6s. Cheap Edition, Crown 8vo. 3s. 6d.

The Dream of Gerontius. 16mo. 6d. sewed, 1s. cloth.

Verses on Various Occasions. Cabinet Edition, Crown 8vo. 6s. Cheap Edition, Crown 8vo. 3s. 6d.

*** *For Cardinal Newman's other Works see Messrs. Longmans & Co.'s Catalogue of Theological Works.*

NORRIS (W. E.).—MRS. FENTON : a Sketch. Crown 8vo. 6s.

NORTON (Charles L.).—POLITICAL AMERICANISMS : a Glossary of Terms and Phrases Current in American Politics. Crown 8vo. 2s. 6d.

———— A HANDBOOK OF FLORIDA. 49 Maps and Plans. Fcp. 8vo. 5s.

NORTHCOTE (W. H.).—LATHES AND TURNING, Simple, Mechanical, and Ornamental. With 338 Illustrations. 8vo. 18s.

O'BRIEN (William.)—WHEN WE WERE BOYS : a Novel. Crown 8vo. 2s. 6d.

OLIPHANT (Mrs.).—MADAM. Crown 8vo. 1s. boards ; 1s. 6d. cloth.

———— IN TRUST. Crown 8vo. 1s. boards ; 1s. 6d. cloth.

———— LADY CAR : the Sequel of a Life. Crown 8vo. 2s. 6d.

OMAN (C. W. C.).—A HISTORY OF GREECE FROM THE EARLIEST TIMES TO THE MACEDONIAN CONQUEST. With Maps. Cr. 8vo. 4s. 6d.

O'REILLY (Mrs.).—HURSTLEIGH DENE : a Tale. Crown 8vo. 5s.

PAUL (Hermann).—PRINCIPLES OF THE HISTORY OF LANGUAGE. Translated by H. A. Strong. 8vo. 10s. 6d.

PAYN (James).—THE LUCK OF THE DARRELLS. Cr. 8vo. 1s. bds. ; 1s. 6d. cl.

———— THICKER THAN WATER. Crown 8vo. 1s. boards ; 1s. 6d. cloth.

PERRING (Sir Philip).—HARD KNOTS IN SHAKESPEARE. 8vo. 7s. 6d.

———— THE 'WORKS AND DAYS' OF MOSES. Crown 8vo. 3s. 6d.

PHILLIPPS-WOLLEY (C.).—SNAP: a Legend of the Lone Mountain. With 13 Illustrations by H. G. Willink. Crown 8vo. 6s.

POLE (W.).—THE THEORY OF THE MODERN SCIENTIFIC GAME OF WHIST. Fcp. 8vo. 2s. 6d.

POLLOCK (W. H. and Lady).—THE SEAL OF FATE. Cr. 8vo. 6s.

POOLE (W. H. and Mrs.).—COOKERY FOR THE DIABETIC. Fcp. 8vo. 2s. 6d.

PRENDERGAST (John P.).—IRELAND, FROM THE RESTORATION TO THE REVOLUTION, 1660-1690. 8vo. 5s.

PROCTOR (R.A.).—Works by:—

Old and New Astronomy. 12 Parts, 2s. 6d. each. Supplementary Section, 1s. Complete in 1 vol. 4to. 36s. [*In course of publication.*

The Orbs Around Us. Crown 8vo. 5s.

Other Worlds than Ours. With 14 Illustrations. Crown 8vo. 5s.

The Moon. Crown 8vo. 5s.

Universe of Stars. 8vo. 10s. 6d.

Larger Star Atlas for the Library, in 12 Circular Maps, with Introduction and 2 Index Pages. Folio, 15s. or Maps only, 12s. 6d.

The Student's Atlas. In 12 Circular Maps. 8vo. 5s.

New Star Atlas. In 12 Circular Maps. Crown 8vo. 5s.

Light Science for Leisure Hours. 3 vols. Crown 8vo. 5s. each.

Chance and Luck. Crown 8vo. 2s. boards; 2s. 6d. cloth.

Pleasant Ways in Science. Cr. 8vo. 5s.

How to Play Whist: with the Laws and Etiquette of Whist. Crown 8vo. 3s. 6d.

Home Whist: an Easy Guide to Correct Play. 16mo. 1s.

Studies of Venus-Transits. With 7 Diagrams and 10 Plates. 8vo. 5s.

The Stars in their Season. 12 Maps. Royal 8vo. 5s.

Star Primer. Showing the Starry Sky Week by Week, in 24 Hourly Maps. Crown 4to. 2s. 6d.

The Seasons Pictured in 48 Sun-Views of the Earth, and 24 Zodiacal Maps, &c. Demy 4to. 5s.

Strength and Happiness. With 9 Illustrations. Crown 8vo. 5s.

Strength: How to get Strong and keep Strong. Crown 8vo. 2s.

Rough Ways Made Smooth. Essays on Scientific Subjects. Crown 8vo. 5s.

Our Place among Infinities. Cr. 8vo. 5s.

The Expanse of Heaven. Cr. 8vo. 5s.

The Great Pyramid. Crown 8vo. 5s.

Myths and Marvels of Astronomy. Crown 8vo. 5s.

Nature Studies. By Grant Allen, A. Wilson, T. Foster, E. Clodd, and R. A. Proctor. Crown 8vo. 5s.

Leisure Readings. By E. Clodd, A. Wilson, T. Foster, A. C. Ranyard, and R. A. Proctor. Crown 8vo. 5s.

PRYCE (John).—THE ANCIENT BRITISH CHURCH: an Historical Essay. Crown 8vo. 6s.

RANSOME (Cyril).—THE RISE OF CONSTITUTIONAL GOVERNMENT IN ENGLAND: being a Series of Twenty Lectures. Crown 8vo. 6s.

RAWLINSON (Canon G.).—THE HISTORY OF PHŒNICIA. 8vo. 24s.

RENDLE (William) and NORMAN (Philip).—THE INNS OF OLD SOUTHWARK, and their Associations. With Illustrations. Royal 8vo. 28s.

RIBOT (Th.).—THE PSYCHOLOGY OF ATTENTION. Crown 8vo. 3s.

RICH (A.).—A DICTIONARY OF ROMAN AND GREEK ANTIQUITIES. With 2000 Woodcuts. Crown 8vo. 7s. 6d.

RICHARDSON (Dr. B. W.).—NATIONAL HEALTH. A Review of the Works of Sir Edwin Chadwick, K.C.B. Crown 4s. 6d.

RILEY (Athelstan).—ATHOS; or, The Mountain of the Monks. With Map and 29 Illustrations. 8vo. 21s.

ROBERTS (Alexander).—GREEK THE LANGUAGE OF CHRIST AND HIS APOSTLES. 8vo. 18s.

ROGET (John Lewis).—A HISTORY OF THE 'OLD WATER COLOUR' SOCIETY. 2 vols. Royal 8vo. 42s.

ROGET (Peter M.).—THESAURUS OF ENGLISH WORDS AND PHRASES. Crown 8vo. 10s. 6d.

RONALDS (Alfred).—THE FLY-FISHER'S ETYMOLOGY. With 20 Coloured Plates. 8vo. 14s.

ROSSETTI (Maria Francesca).—A SHADOW OF DANTE: being an Essay towards studying Himself, his World, and his Pilgrimage. Cr. 8vo. 10s. 6d.

RUSSELL.—A LIFE OF LORD JOHN RUSSELL. By SPENCER WALPOLE. 2 vols. 8vo. 36s. Cabinet Edition, 2 vols. Crown 8vo. 12s.

SEEBOHM (Frederick).—THE OXFORD REFORMERS—JOHN COLET, ERASMUS, AND THOMAS MORE. 8vo. 14s.

——— THE ENGLISH VILLAGE COMMUNITY Examined in its Relations to the Manorial and Tribal Systems, &c. 13 Maps and Plates. 8vo. 16s.

——— THE ERA OF THE PROTESTANT REVOLUTION. With Map. Fcp. 8vo. 2s. 6d.

SEWELL (Elizabeth M.).—STORIES AND TALES. Crown 8vo. 1s. 6d. each, cloth plain; 2s. 6d. each, cloth extra, gilt edges :—

Amy Herbert.	Katharine Ashton.	Gertrude.
The Earl's Daughter.	Margaret Percival.	Ivors.
The Experience of Life.	Laneton Parsonage.	Home Life.
A Glimpse of the World.	Ursula.	After Life.
Cleve Hall.		

SHAKESPEARE.—BOWDLER'S FAMILY SHAKESPEARE. 1 vol. 8vo. With 36 Woodcuts, 14s., or in 6 vols. Fcp. 8vo. 21s.

——— OUTLINE OF THE LIFE OF SHAKESPEARE. By J. O. HALLIWELL-PHILLIPPS. 2 vols. Royal 8vo. £1 1s.

——— SHAKESPEARE'S TRUE LIFE. By JAMES WALTER. With 500 Illustrations. Imp. 8vo. 21s.

——— THE SHAKESPEARE BIRTHDAY BOOK. By MARY F. DUNBAR. 32mo. 1s. 6d. cloth. With Photographs, 32mo. 5s. Drawing Room Edition, with Photographs, Fcp. 8vo. 10s. 6d.

SHORT (T. V.).—SKETCH OF THE HISTORY OF THE CHURCH OF ENGLAND to the Revolution of 1688. Crown 8vo. 7s. 6d.

SILVER LIBRARY, The.—Crown 8vo. price 3s. 6d. each volume.

She: A History of Adventure. By H. Rider Haggard. 32 Illustrations.

Allan Quatermain. By H. Rider Haggard. With 20 Illustrations.

Colonel Quaritch, V.C.: a Tale of Country Life. By H. Rider Haggard.

Cleopatra. By H. Rider Haggard. With 29 Full-page Illustrations.

Micah Clarke. A Tale of Monmouth's Rebellion. By A. Conan Doyle.

Petland Revisited. By the Rev. J. G. Wood. With 33 Illustrations.

Strange Dwellings: a Description of the Habitations of Animals. By the Rev. J. G. Wood. With 60 Illustrations.

Out of Doors. Original Articles on Practical Natural History. By the Rev. J. G. Wood. 11 Illustrations.

Familiar History of Birds. By Edward Stanley, D.D. 160 Illustrations.

Eight Years in Ceylon. By Sir S. W. Baker. With 6 Illustrations.

Rifle and Hound in Ceylon. By Sir S. W. Baker. With 6 Illustrations.

Story of Creation: a Plain Account of Evolution. By Edward Clodd. With 77 Illustrations.

Life of the Duke of Wellington. By the Rev. G. R. Gleig. With Portrait.

History of the Romans under the Empire. By the Very Rev. Charles Merivale. 8 vols.

Memoirs of Major-General Sir Henry Havelock. By J. Clark Marshman.

Short Studies on Great Subjects. By James A. Froude. 4 vols.

Cæsar: a Sketch. By James A. Froude.

Thomas Carlyle: a History of his Life. By J. A. Froude. 1795-1835. 2 vols. 1834-1881. 2 vols.

The Two Chiefs of Dunboy: an Irish Romance of the Last Century. By James A. Froude.

Visits to Remarkable Places. By William Howitt. 80 Illustrations.

Field and Hedgerow. Last Essays of Richard Jefferies. With Portrait.

The Story of My Heart; My Autobiography. By Richard Jefferies.

Apologia Pro Vita Sua. By Cardinal Newman.

Callista: a Tale of the Third Century. By Cardinal Newman.

Loss and Gain: a Tale. By Cardinal Newman.

Essays, Critical and Historical. By Cardinal Newman. 2 vols.

An Essay on the Development of Christian Doctrine. By Cardinal Newman.

The Arians of the Fourth Century. By Cardinal Newman.

Verses on Various Occasions. By Cardinal Newman.

Parochial and Plain Sermons. By Cardinal Newman. 8 vols.

Selection, adapted to the Seasons of the Ecclesiastical Year, from the 'Parochial and Plain Sermons'. By Cardinal Newman.

Certain Difficulties felt by Anglicans in Catholic Teaching Considered. By Cardinal Newman. 2 vols.

The Idea of a University defined and Illustrated. By Cardinal Newman.

Essays on Biblical and Ecclesiastical Miracles. By Cardinal Newman.

Discussions and Arguments on Various Subjects. By Cardinal Newman.

An Essay in Aid of a Grammar of Assent. By Cardinal Newman.

The Elements of Banking. By Henry D. Macleod.

A Voyage in the 'Sunbeam'. With 66 Illustrations. By Lady Brassey.

SMITH (R. Bosworth).—CARTHAGE AND THE CARTHAGINIANS. Maps, Plans, &c. Crown 8vo. 6s.

SOPHOCLES. Translated into English Verse. By ROBERT WHITELAW. Crown 8vo. 8s. 6d.

STANLEY (E.).—A FAMILIAR HISTORY OF BIRDS. With 160 Woodcuts. Crown 8vo. 3s. 6d.

STEEL (J. H.).—A TREATISE ON THE DISEASES OF THE DOG; being a Manual of Canine Pathology. 88 Illustrations. 8vo. 10s. 6d.

———— A TREATISE ON THE DISEASES OF THE OX; being a Manual of Bovine Pathology. 2 Plates and 117 Woodcuts. 8vo. 15s.

———— A TREATISE ON THE DISEASES OF THE SHEEP; being a Manual of Ovine Pathology. With Coloured Plate and 99 Woodcuts. 8vo. 12s.

STEPHEN (Sir James).— ESSAYS IN ECCLESIASTICAL BIOGRAPHY. Crown 8vo. 7s. 6d.

STEPHENS (H. Morse).—A HISTORY OF THE FRENCH REVOLUTION. 3 vols. 8vo. Vol. I. 18s. *Ready.*   [*Vol. II. in the press.*

STEVENSON (Robt. Louis).—A CHILD'S GARDEN OF VERSES. Small Fcp. 8vo. 5s.

———— THE DYNAMITER. Fcp. 8vo. 1s. sewed, 1s. 6d. cloth.

———— STRANGE CASE OF DR. JEKYLL AND MR. HYDE. Fcp. 8vo. 1s. sewed, 1s. 6d. cloth.

STEVENSON (Robert Louis) and OSBOURNE (Lloyd).—THE WRONG BOX. Crown 8vo. 5s.

STOCK (St. George). --DEDUCTIVE LOGIC. Fcp. 8vo. 3s. 6d.

'STONEHENGE.'—THE DOG IN HEALTH AND DISEASE. With 84 Wood Engravings. Square Crown 8vo. 7s. 6d.

STRONG (Herbert A.), LOGEMAN (Willem S.) and WHEELER (B. I.).—INTRODUCTION TO THE STUDY OF THE HISTORY OF LANGUAGE. 8vo. 10s. 6d.

SUPERNATURAL RELIGION; an Inquiry into the Reality of Divine Revelation. 3 vols. 8vo. 36s.

REPLY (A) TO DR. LIGHTFOOT'S ESSAYS. By the Author of 'Supernatural Religion'. 8vo. 6s.

SYMES (J. E.).—PRELUDE TO MODERN HISTORY: being a Brief Sketch of the World's History from the Third to the Ninth Century. With 5 Maps. Crown 8vo. 2s. 6d.

TAYLOR (Colonel Meadows).—A STUDENT'S MANUAL OF THE HISTORY OF INDIA, from the Earliest Period to the Present Time. Crown 8vo. 7s. 6d.

THOMPSON (D. Greenleaf).—THE PROBLEM OF EVIL: an Introduction to the Practical Sciences. 8vo. 10s. 6d.

———— A SYSTEM OF PSYCHOLOGY. 2 vols. 8vo. 36s.

———— THE RELIGIOUS SENTIMENTS OF THE HUMAN MIND. 8vo. 7s. 6d.

———— SOCIAL PROGRESS: an Essay. 8vo. 7s. 6d.

———— THE PHILOSOPHY OF FICTION IN LITERATURE: an Essay. Crown 8vo. 6s.

THREE IN NORWAY. By Two of THEM. With a Map and 59 Illustrations. Crown 8vo. 2s. boards ; 2s. 6d. cloth.

TOYNBEE (Arnold).—LECTURES ON THE INDUSTRIAL REVOLUTION OF THE 18th CENTURY IN ENGLAND. 8vo. 10s. 6d.

TREVELYAN (Sir G. O., Bart.).—THE LIFE AND LETTERS OF LORD MACAULAY.

Popular Edition. Crown 8vo. 2s. 6d. | Cabinet Edition, 2 vols. Cr. 8vo. 12s.
Student's Edition. Crown 8vo. 6s. | Library Edition, 2 vols. 8vo. 36s.

———— THE EARLY HISTORY OF CHARLES JAMES FOX. Library Edition, 8vo. 18s. Cabinet Edition, Crown 8vo. 6s.

TROLLOPE (Anthony).—THE WARDEN. Cr. 8vo. 1s. bds., 1s. 6d. cl.
———— BARCHESTER TOWERS. Crown 8vo. 1s. boards, 1s. 6d. cloth.

VIRGIL.—PUBLI VERGILI MARONIS BUCOLICA, GEORGICA, ÆNEIS; the Works of VIRGIL, Latin Text, with English Commentary and Index. By B. H. KENNEDY. Crown 8vo. 10s. 6d.

———— THE ÆNEID OF VIRGIL. Translated into English Verse. By John Conington. Crown 8vo. 6s.

———— THE POEMS OF VIRGIL. Translated into English Prose. By John Conington. Crown 8vo. 6s.

———— THE ECLOGUES AND GEORGICS OF VIRGIL. Translated from the Latin by J. W. Mackail. Printed on Dutch Hand-made Paper. 16mo. 5s.

WAKEMAN (H. O.) and HASSALL (A.).—ESSAYS INTRODUCTORY TO THE STUDY OF ENGLISH CONSTITUTIONAL HISTORY. By Resident Members of the University of Oxford. Edited by H. O. WAKEMAN and A. HASSALL. Crown 8vo. 6s.

WALKER (A. Campbell-).—THE CORRECT CARD; or, How to Play at Whist ; a Whist Catechism. Fcp. 8vo. 2s. 6d.

WALPOLE (Spencer).—HISTORY OF ENGLAND FROM THE CONCLUSION OF THE GREAT WAR IN 1815 to 1858. Library Edition. 5 vols. 8vo. £4 10s. Cabinet Edition. 6 vols. Crown 8vo. 6s. each.

WELLINGTON.—LIFE OF THE DUKE OF WELLINGTON. By the Rev. G. R. GLEIG. Crown 8vo. 3s. 6d.

WELLS (David A.).—RECENT ECONOMIC CHANGES and their Effect on the Production and Distribution of Wealth and the Well-being of Society. Crown 8vo. 10s. 6d.

WENDT (Ernest Emil).—PAPERS ON MARITIME LEGISLATION, with a Translation of the German Mercantile Laws relating to Maritime Commerce. Royal 8vo. £1 11s. 6d.

WEYMAN (Stanley J.).—THE HOUSE OF THE WOLF : a Romance. Crown 8vo. 6s.

WHATELY (E. Jane).—ENGLISH SYNONYMS. Edited by Archbishop WHATELY. Fcp. 8vo. 3s.

———— LIFE AND CORRESPONDENCE OF ARCHBISHOP WHATELY. With Portrait. Crown 8vo. 10s. 6d.

WHATELY (Archbishop).—ELEMENTS OF LOGIC. Cr. 8vo. 4s. 6d.
———— ELEMENTS OF RHETORIC. Crown 8vo. 4s. 6d.
———— LESSONS ON REASONING. Fcp. 8vo. 1s. 6d.
———— BACON'S ESSAYS, with Annotations. 8vo. 10s. 6d.

WILCOCKS (J. C.).—THE SEA FISHERMAN. Comprising the Chief Methods of Hook and Line Fishing in the British and other Seas, and Remarks on Nets, Boats, and Boating. Profusely Illustrated. Crown 8vo. 6s.

WILLICH (Charles M.).—POPULAR TABLES for giving Information for ascertaining the value of Lifehold, Leasehold, and Church Property, the Public Funds, &c. Edited by H. BENCE JONES. Crown 8vo. 10s. 6d.

WILLOUGHBY (Captain Sir John C.).—EAST AFRICA AND ITS BIG GAME. The Narrative of a Sporting Trip from Zanzibar to the Borders of the Masai. Illustrated by G. D. Giles and Mrs. Gordon Hake. Royal 8vo. 21s.

WITT (Prof.)—Works by. Translated by Frances Younghusband.

———— THE TROJAN WAR. Crown 8vo. 2s.

———— MYTHS OF HELLAS; or, Greek Tales. Crown 8vo. 3s. 6d.

———— THE WANDERINGS OF ULYSSES. Crown 8vo. 3s. 6d.

———— THE RETREAT OF THE TEN THOUSAND; being the Story of Xenophon's 'Anabasis'. With Illustrations.

WOLFF (Henry W.).—RAMBLES IN THE BLACK FOREST. Crown 8vo. 7s. 6d.

———— THE WATERING PLACES OF THE VOSGES. With Map. Crown 8vo. 4s. 6d.

WOOD (Rev. J. G.).—HOMES WITHOUT HANDS; a Description of the Habitations of Animals, classed according to the Principle of Construction. With 140 Illustrations. 8vo. 10s. 6d.

———— INSECTS AT HOME; a Popular Account of British Insects, their Structure, Habits, and Transformations. With 700 Illustrations. 8vo. 10s. 6d.

———— INSECTS ABROAD; a Popular Account of Foreign Insects, their Structure, Habits, and Transformations. With 600 Illustrations. 8vo. 10s. 6d.

———— BIBLE ANIMALS; a Description of every Living Creature mentioned in the Scriptures. With 112 Illustrations. 8vo. 10s. 6d.

———— STRANGE DWELLINGS; abridged from 'Homes without Hands'. With 60 Illustrations. Crown 8vo. 3s. 6d.

———— OUT OF DOORS; a Selection of Original Articles on Practical Natural History. With 11 Illustrations. Crown 8vo. 3s. 6d.

———— PETLAND REVISITED. With 33 Illustrations. Crown 8vo. 3s. 6d.

YOUATT (William).—THE HORSE. With numerous Woodcuts. 8vo. 7s. 6d.

———— THE DOG. With numerous Woodcuts. 8vo. 6s.

ZELLER (Dr. E.).—HISTORY OF ECLECTICISM IN GREEK PHILO-SOPHY. Translated by Sarah F. Alleyne. Crown 8vo. 10s. 6d.

———— THE STOICS, EPICUREANS, AND SCEPTICS. Translated by the Rev. O. J. Reichel. Crown 8vo. 15s.

———— SOCRATES AND THE SOCRATIC SCHOOLS. Translated by the Rev. O. J. Reichel. Crown 8vo. 10s. 6d.

———— PLATO AND THE OLDER ACADEMY. Translated by Sarah F. Alleyne and Alfred Goodwin. Crown 8vo. 18s.

———— THE PRE-SOCRATIC SCHOOLS: a History of Greek Philosophy from the Earliest Period to the time of Socrates. Translated by Sarah F. Alleyne. 2 vols. Crown 8vo. 30s.

———— OUTLINES OF THE HISTORY OF GREEK PHILOSOPHY. Translated by Sarah F. Alleyne and Evelyn Abbott. Crown 8vo. 10s. 6d.

50,000—7/91.   ABERDEEN UNIVERSITY PRESS.

www.ingramcontent.com/pod-product-compliance
Lightning Source LLC
Chambersburg PA
CBHW031137120726
47905CB00006B/1716